Resounding praise for **JO NESBØ** and
THE REDBREAST

"A hugely impr... ...cope
and skilled in e... ...cores,
though, is in it... ...right
to the end. . . . ...t."

Los Angeles Times

"Reading *The Redbreast* is like watching a hit movie.
Author Jo Nesbø's scenes are so vivid that you can
imagine them playing across the big screen. The pacing
is swift. The plot is precise and intricate. The characters
are intriguing. And the novel combines two of the best
cinematic genres: war sagas and crime thrillers. . . .
Nesbø has won European literary awards but is essentially
unknown to Americans. That should change. . . . Like
Harry, *The Redbreast* is surprisingly witty at times
and often grim. But it's always smart."

USA Today

"Ranks with the best . . . *The Redbreast* is an admirable
meditation on how, generation after generation,
the ugliest human instincts manifest themselves in a
criminality that calls itself politics."

Seattle Times

"Utterly delicious . . . [Nesbø's] sense of pace is unerring,
and the way he builds up suspense in parallel montages
will incite Pavlovian page-turning. By the end, events
happen so quickly that you barely have time to realize that
one of the most sinister characters has managed to evade
scrutiny. Is a sequel in the air? It can't come fast enough."

Time Out New York

"Nesbø has been one of Norway's leading crime-fiction authors for ten years, and his American debut shows why. Moving from World War Two to the last days of 1999 and into the new century, the novel unfurls a complex plot in which the wounds of history continue to bleed into the present. . . . Nesbø has a terrific feel for character, and Hole, while sharing characteristics with so many similarly melancholic modern cops (including, of course, Mankell's Kurt Wallander), carves a place of distinction for himself in a crowded field."
Booklist (*Starred Review*)

"Imagine the very best of Michael Connelly and Ian Rankin combined; he's that good. . . . The action keeps going like a juggernaut. Nesbø uses history and his parents' war memories as a charred background to jumpstart political events as real as today's headlines."
Madison County Herald

"Flawlessly paced, it's a page-turner you won't want to put down, with fascinating characters to boot."
Time Out London

"Required reading . . . For many of us, the only thing familiar about Oslo is that it's where the Nobel Prizes come from. Nesbø changes that with his book, dubbed the 'best Norwegian crime novel ever.'"
New York Post

"Fans of Henning Mankell and Karin Fossum will have a seriously difficult time putting *The Redbreast* down."
BookPage

By Jo Nesbø

THE DEVIL'S STAR
NEMESIS
THE REDBREAST

JO NESBØ

The Redbreast

A HARRY HOLE NOVEL

**Translated from the Norwegian
by Don Bartlett**

HARPER

An Imprint of HarperCollinsPublishers

First published in Norway as *Redstrupe* by Aschehoug & Co. (W. Nygaard), Oslo.

Published in Great Britain in 2006 by Harvill Secker, an Imprint of Random House.

HARPER

An Imprint of HarperCollins*Publishers*
10 East 53rd Street
New York, New York 10022-5299

Copyright © 2000 by Jo Nesbø; English translation copyright © 2006 by Don Bartlett
Excerpt from *The Devil's Star* copyright © 2003 by Jo Nesbø; English-language translation copyright © 2005 by Don Bartlett
ISBN 978-0-06-206842-2

First Harper mass market printing: September 2011
First Harper paperback printing: January 2009
First Harper hardcover printing: December 2007

But little by little he gained courage, flew close to him, and drew with his little bill a thorn that had become embedded in the brow of the Crucified One. And as he did this there fell on his breast a drop of blood from the face of the Crucified One – it spread quickly and floated out and coloured all the little fine breast feathers.

Then the Crucified One opened his lips and whispered to the bird: 'Because of thy compassion, thou hast won all that thy kind have been striving after, ever since the world was created.'

Selma Lagerlöf, Robin Redbreast,
Christ Legends

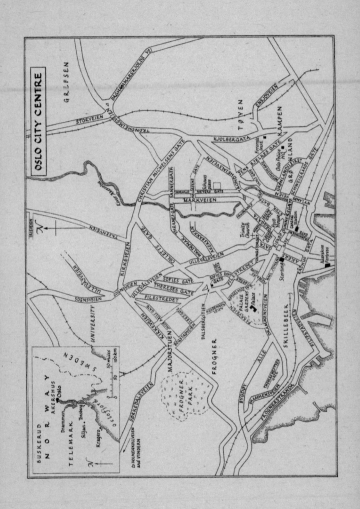

Part One

EARTH TO EARTH

1

Toll Barrier at Alnabru. 1 November 1999.

A GREY BIRD GLIDED IN AND OUT OF HARRY'S field of vision. He drummed his fingers on the steering wheel. Slow time. Somebody had been talking about 'slow time' on TV yesterday. This was slow time. Like on Christmas Eve before Father Christmas came. Or sitting in the electric chair before the current was turned on.

He drummed harder.

They were parked in the open area behind the ticket booths at the toll gate. Ellen turned up the radio a notch. The commentator spoke with reverence and solemnity.

'The plane landed fifty minutes ago, and at exactly 6.38 a.m. the President set foot on Norwegian soil. He was welcomed by the Mayor of Ullensaker. It is a wonderful autumn day here in Oslo: a splendid Norwegian backdrop to this summit meeting. Let us hear again what the President said at the press conference half an hour ago.'

It was the third time. Again Harry saw the screaming press corps thronging against the barrier. The men in grey suits on the other side, who made only a half-hearted attempt not to look like Secret Service agents, hunched their shoulders and then relaxed them as they scanned the crowd, checked

for the twelfth time that their earpieces were correctly positioned, scanned the crowd, dwelled for a few seconds on a
photographer whose telephoto lens was a little too long, continued scanning, checked for the thirteenth time that their
earpieces were in position. Someone welcomed the President
in English, everything went quiet. Then a scratching noise in
a microphone.

'First, let me say I'm delighted to be here . . .' the President
said for the fourth time in husky, broad American-English.

'I read that a well-known American psychologist thinks
the President has an MPD,' Ellen said.

'MPD?'

'Multiple Personality Disorder. Dr Jekyll and Mr Hyde.
The psychologist thought his normal personality was not
aware that the other one, the sex beast, was having relations
with all these women. And that was why a Court of Impeach-
ment couldn't accuse him of having lied under oath about it.'

'Jesus,' Harry said, looking up at the helicopter hovering
high above them.

On the radio, someone speaking with a Norwegian accent asked, 'Mr President, this is the fourth visit to Norway
by a sitting US President. How does it feel?'

Pause.

'It's really nice to be back here. And I see it as even more
important that the leaders of the state of Israel and of the
Palestinian people can meet here. The key to —'

'Can you remember anything from your previous visit to
Norway, Mr President?'

'Yes, of course. In today's talks I hope that we can —'

'What significance have Oslo and Norway had for world
peace, Mr President?'

'Norway has played an important role.'

A voice without a Norwegian accent: 'What concrete results does the President consider to be realistic?'

The recording was cut and someone from the studio took
over.

'We heard there the President saying that Norway has had a crucial role in . . . er, the Middle Eastern peace process. Right now the President is on his way to —'

Harry groaned and switched off the radio. 'What is it with this country, Ellen?'

She shrugged her shoulders.

'Passed Post 27,' the walkie-talkie on the dashboard crackled.

He looked at her.

'Everyone ready at their posts?' he asked. She nodded.

'Here we go,' he said. She rolled her eyes. It was the fifth time he had said that since the procession set off from Gardemoen Airport. From where they were parked they could see the empty motorway stretch out from the toll barrier up towards Trosterud and Furuset. The blue light on the roof rotated sluggishly. Harry rolled down the car window to stick out his hand and remove a withered yellow leaf caught under the windscreen wiper.

'A robin redbreast,' Ellen said, pointing. 'Rare to see one so late in autumn.'

'Where?'

'There. On the roof of the toll booth.'

Harry lowered his head and peered through the windscreen.

'Oh yes. So that's a robin redbreast?'

'Yep. But you probably can't tell the difference between that and a redwing, I imagine?'

'Right.' Harry shaded his eyes. Was he becoming shortsighted?

'It's a rare bird, the redbreast,' Ellen said, screwing the top back on the thermos.

'Is that a fact?' Harry said.

'Ninety per cent of them migrate south. A few take the risk, as it were, and stay here.'

'*As it were?*'

Another crackle on the radio: 'Post 62 to HQ. There's an

unmarked car parked by the road two hundred metres before the turn-off for Lørenskog.'

A deep voice with a Bergen accent answered from HQ: 'One moment, 62. We'll look into it.'

Silence.

'Did you check the toilets?' Harry asked, nodding towards the Esso station.

'Yes, the petrol station has been cleared of all customers and employees. Everyone except the boss. We've locked him in his office.'

'Toll booths as well?'

'Done. Relax, Harry, all the checks have been done. Yes, the ones that stay do so in the hope that it will be a mild winter, right? That may be OK, but if they're wrong, they die. So why not head south, just in case, you might be wondering. Are they just lazy, the birds that stay?'

Harry looked in the mirror and saw the guards on either side of the railway bridge. Dressed in black with helmets and MP5 machine guns hanging around their necks. Even from where he was he could see the tension in their body language.

'The point is that if it's a mild winter, they can choose the best nesting places before the others return,' Ellen said, while trying to stuff the thermos into the already full glove compartment. 'It's a calculated risk, you see. You're either laughing all over your face or you're in deep, deep shit. Whether to take the risk or not. If you take the gamble, you may fall off the twig frozen stiff one night and not thaw out till spring. Bottle it and you might not have anywhere to nest when you return. These are, as it were, the eternal dilemmas you're confronted with.'

'You've got body armour on, haven't you?' Harry twisted round to check. 'Have you or haven't you?'

She tapped her chest with her knuckles by way of reply.

'Lightweight?'

She nodded.

'For fuck's sake, Ellen! I gave the order for ballistic vests to be worn. Not those Mickey Mouse vests.'

'Do you know what the Secret Service guys use?'

'Let me guess. Lightweight vests?'

'That's right.'

'Do you know what I don't give a shit about?'

'Let me guess. The Secret Service?'

'That's right.'

She laughed. Harry managed a smile too. There was a crackle from the radio.

'HQ to post 62. The Secret Service say it's their car parked on the turn-off to Lørenskog.'

'Post 62. Message received.'

'You see,' Harry said, banging the steering wheel in irritation, 'no communication. The Secret Service people do their own thing. What's that car doing up there without our knowledge? Eh?'

'Checking that we're doing our job,' Ellen said.

'According to the instructions *they* gave us.'

'You'll be allowed to make *some* decisions, so stop grumbling,' she said. 'And stop that drumming on the wheel.'

Harry's hands obediently leapt into his lap. She smiled. He let out one long stream of air: 'Yeah, yeah, yeah.'

His fingers found the butt of his service revolver, a .38 calibre Smith & Wesson, six shots. In his belt he had two additional magazines, each holding six shots. He patted the revolver, knowing that, strictly speaking, he wasn't actually authorised to carry a weapon. Perhaps he really was becoming short-sighted; after the forty-hour course last winter he had failed the shooting test. Although that was not so unusual, it was the first time it had happened to Harry and he didn't like it at all. All he had to do was take the test again – many had to take it four or five times – but for one reason or another Harry continued to put it off.

More crackling noises: 'Passed point 28.'

'One more point to go in the Romerike police district,' Harry said. 'The next one is Karihaugen and then it's us.'

'Why can't they do it how we used to? Just say where the motorcade is instead of all these stupid numbers,' Ellen asked in a grumbling tone.

'Guess.'

They answered in unison: 'The Secret Service!' And laughed.

'Passed point 29.'

He looked at his watch.

'OK, they'll be here in three minutes. I'll change the frequency on the walkie-talkie to Oslo police district. Run the final checks.'

Ellen closed her eyes to concentrate on the positive checks that came back one after the other. She put the microphone back into position. 'Everything in place and ready.'

'Thanks. Put your helmet on.'

'Eh? Honestly, Harry.'

'You heard what I said.'

'Put your helmet on yourself!'

'Mine's too small.'

A new voice. 'Passed point 1.'

'Oh shit, sometimes you're just so . . . unprofessional.' Ellen pulled the helmet over her head, fastened the chin strap and made faces in the driving mirror.

'Love you too,' said Harry, studying the road in front of them through binoculars. 'I can see them.'

At the top of the incline leading to Karihaugen the sun glinted off metal. For the moment Harry could only see the first car in the motorcade, but he knew the order: six motorcycles from the Norwegian police escort department, two Norwegian police escort cars, a Secret Service car, then two identical Cadillac Fleetwoods (special Secret Service cars flown in from the US) and the President sitting in one of them. Which one was kept secret. Or perhaps he was sitting in both, Harry thought. One for Jekyll and one for Hyde.

Then came the bigger vehicles: ambulance, communications car and several Secret Service cars.

'Everything seems quiet enough,' Harry said. His binoculars moved slowly from right to left. The air quivered above the tarmac even though it was a cool November morning.

Ellen could see the outline of the first car. In thirty seconds they would have passed the toll gates and half the job would be over. And in two days' time, when the same cars had passed the toll going in the opposite direction, she and Harry could go back to their usual work. She preferred dealing with dead people in the Serious Crime Unit to getting up at three in the morning to sit in a cold Volvo with an irritable Harry, who was clearly burdened by the responsibility he had been given.

Apart from Harry's regular breathing, there was total quiet in the car. She checked that the light indicators on both radios were green. The motorcade was almost at the bottom of the hill. She decided she would go to Tørst and get drunk after the job. There was a guy there she had exchanged looks with; he had black curls and brown, slightly dangerous eyes. Lean. Looked a bit bohemian, intellectual. Perhaps . . .

'What the —'

Harry had already grabbed the microphone. 'There's someone in the third booth from the left. Can anyone identify this individual?'

The radio answered with a crackling silence as Ellen's gaze raced from one booth to the next in the row. There! She saw a man's back behind the brown glass of the box – only forty or fifty metres away. The silhouette of the figure was clear in the light from behind, as was the short barrel with the sights protruding over his shoulder.

'Weapon!' she shouted. 'He's got a machine gun.'

'Fuck!' Harry kicked open the car door, took hold of the frame and swung out. Ellen stared at the motorcade. It couldn't be more than a few hundred metres off. Harry stuck his head inside the car.

'He's not one of ours, but he could be Secret Service,' he said. 'Call HQ.' He already had the revolver in his hand.

'Harry . . .'

'Now! And give a blast on the horn if HQ say it's one of theirs.'

Harry started to run towards the toll booth and the back of the man dressed in a suit. From the barrel, Harry guessed the gun was an Uzi. The raw early morning air smarted in his lungs.

'Police!' he shouted in Norwegian, then in English.

No reaction. The thick glass of the box was manufactured to deaden the traffic noise outside. The man had turned his head towards the motorcade now and Harry could see his dark Ray-Bans. Secret Service. Or someone who wanted to give that impression.

Twenty metres now.

How did he get inside a locked booth if he wasn't one of theirs? Damn! Harry could already hear the motorcycles. He wouldn't make it to the box.

He released the safety catch and took aim, praying that the car horn would shatter the stillness of this strange morning on a closed motorway he had never wanted at any time to be anywhere near. The instructions were clear, but he was unable to shut out his thoughts: *Thin vest. No communication. Shoot, it is not your fault. Has he got a family?*

The motorcade was coming from directly behind the toll booth, and it was coming fast. In a couple of seconds the Cadillacs would be level with the booths. From the corner of his left eye he noticed a movement, a little bird taking off from the roof.

Whether to take the risk or not . . . the eternal dilemma.

He thought about the low neck on the vest, lowered the revolver half an inch. The roar of the motorcycles was deafening.

2

Oslo. 5 October 1999.

'THAT'S THE GREAT BETRAYAL,' THE SHAVEN-headed man said, looking down at his manuscript. The head, the eyebrows, the bulging forearms, even the huge hands gripping the lectern, everything was clean-shaven and neat. He leaned over to the microphone.

'Since 1945, National Socialism's enemies have been masters of the land; they have developed and put into practice their democratic and economic principles. Consequently, not on one single day has the sun gone down on a world without war. Even here in Europe we have experienced war and genocide. In the Third World millions starve to death – and Europe is threatened by mass immigration and the resultant chaos, deprivation and struggle for survival.'

He paused to gaze around him. There was a stony silence in the room; only one person in the audience, on the benches behind him, clapped tentatively. When he continued, fired up now, the red light under the microphone lit up ominously, indicating that the recording signal was distorted.

'There is little to separate even us from oblivious affluence and the day we have to rely on ourselves and the community around us. A war, an economic or ecological disaster, and the entire network of laws and rules which turns us all too quickly into passive social clients is suddenly no longer there. The previous great betrayal took place on 9 April 1940, when our so-called national leaders fled from the enemy to save their own skins, and took the gold reserves with them to finance a life of luxury in London. Now the enemy is here again. And those who are supposed to protect our interests have let us down once more. They let the enemy build mosques in our midst, let them rob our old folk and mingle blood with our women. It is no more than our duty as Norwegians to protect our race and to eliminate those who fail us.'

He turned the page, but a cough from the podium in front of him made him stop and look up.

'Thank you, I think we've heard enough,' the judge said, peering over his glasses. 'Has the prosecution counsel any more questions for the accused?'

The sun shone across courtroom 17 in Oslo Crown Court, giving the hairless man an illusory halo. He was wearing a white shirt and a slim tie, presumably on advice from his defending counsel, Johan Krohn Jr., who right now was leaning backwards in his chair, flicking a pen between middle and forefinger. Krohn disliked most things about this situation. He disliked the direction the prosecutor's questions had taken, the way his client, Sverre Olsen, had openly declared his programme, and the fact that Olsen had deemed it appropriate to roll up his shirtsleeves to display to the judge and colleagues on the panel the spider-web tattoos on both elbows and the row of swastikas on his left forearm. On his right forearm was tattooed a chain of Norse symbols and VALKYRIA, a neo-Nazi gang, in black gothic letters.

But there was something else about the whole procedure that rankled with him. He just couldn't put his finger on what.

The Public Prosecutor, a little man by the name of Herman Groth, pushed the microphone away with his little finger, which was decorated with a ring bearing the symbol of the lawyers' union.

'Just a couple of questions to finish, Your Honour.' The voice was gentle and subdued. The light under the microphone showed green.

'So when, at nine o' clock on 3 January, you went into Dennis Kebab in Dronningens gate, it was with the clear intention of performing the duty of protecting our race which you were just talking about?'

Johan Krohn launched himself at the microphone.

'My client has already answered that a row developed between himself and the Vietnamese owner.' Red light. 'He was provoked,' Krohn said. 'There's absolutely no reason to suggest premeditation.'

Groth closed his eyes.

'If what your defending counsel says is correct, herr Olsen, it was therefore quite by chance that you were carrying a baseball bat at the time?'

'For self-defence,' Krohn interrupted and threw his arms up in despair. 'Your Honour, my client has already answered these questions.'

The judge rubbed his chin as he surveyed the counsel for the defence. Everyone knew that Johan Krohn Jr. was a defence constellation in the ascendancy – particularly Johan Krohn himself – and that was presumably what finally made the judge accede with some irritation: 'I agree with the defending counsel. Unless the prosecutor has anything new to add, may I suggest we move on?'

Groth opened his eyes so that a narrow white stripe could be seen above and beneath the iris. He inclined his head. With a fatigued movement, he raised a newspaper aloft.

'This is *Dagbladet* from 25 January. In an interview on page eight one of the accused's co-idealogues —'

'I object . . .' Krohn began.

Groth sighed. 'Let me change that to a man who expresses racist views.'

The judge nodded, but sent Krohn an admonitory glare at the same time. Groth continued.

'This man, commenting on the attack at Dennis Kebab, says we need more racists like Sverre Olsen to regain control of Norway. In the interview the word "racist" is used as a term of respect. Does the accused consider himself a "racist"?'

'Yes, I am a racist,' said Olsen before Krohn managed to interpose. 'In the sense that I use the word.'

'And what might that be?' Groth smiled.

Krohn clenched his fists under the table and looked up at the podium, at the two associate judges flanking the judge. These three would decide the fate of his client for the next few years, and his own status in the Tostrupkjeller bar for the next few months. Two ordinary citizens representing the people, representing common-sense justice. They used to call them 'lay judges', but perhaps they had realised that it was too reminiscent of 'play judges'. To the right of the judge was a young man wearing a cheap, sensible suit, who hardly dared raise his eyes. The young, slightly plump woman to the left seemed to be pretending to follow the proceedings, while extending her neck so that the incipient double chin could not be seen from the floor. Average Norwegians. What did they know about people like Sverre Olsen? What did they want to know?

Eight witnesses had seen Sverre Olsen go into the burger bar with a baseball bat under his arm and, after a brief exchange of expletives, hit the owner, Ho Dai – a forty-year-old Vietnamese, who came to Norway with the boat people in 1978 – on the head. So hard that Ho Dai would never be able to walk again. When Olsen started to speak, Johan Krohn Jr. was already mentally shaping the appeal he would lodge with the High Court.

'Rac-ism,' Olsen read, having found the definition in his papers, 'is an eternal struggle against hereditary illness, degeneration and annihilation, as well as a dream of and a desire for a healthier society with a better quality of life. Racial mixture is a kind of bilateral genocide. In a world where there are plans to establish gene banks to preserve the smallest beetle, it is generally accepted that you can mix and destroy human races that have taken millennia to develop. In an article in the respected journal *American Psychologist* in 1972, fifty American and European scientists warned about the dangers of suppressing inheritance theory arguments.'

Olsen stopped, encompassed courtroom 17 in one sweeping glare and raised his right index finger. He had turned towards the prosecutor and Krohn could see the pale *Sieg Heil* tattoo on the shaven roll of fat between the back of his head and his neck – a mute shriek and a strangely grotesque contrast to the cool rhetoric of the court. In the ensuing silence Krohn could hear from the noise in the corridor that courtroom 18 had adjourned for lunch. Seconds passed. Krohn remembered something he had read about Adolf Hitler: that at mass rallies he would pause for effect for up to three minutes. When Olsen continued he beat the rhythm with his finger, as if to drum every word and sentence into the listeners' brains.

'Those of you who are trying to pretend that there is not a racial struggle going on here are either blind or traitors.'

He drank water from the glass the court usher had placed in front of him.

The prosecutor broke in: 'And in this racial struggle you and your supporters, of whom there are a number in this court today, are the only ones who have the right to attack?'

Boos from the skinheads in the public gallery.

'We don't attack, we defend ourselves,' Olsen said. 'It's the right and duty of every race.'

A shout from the benches, which Olsen caught and passed on with a smile: 'In fact, even among people from other races there is race-conscious National Socialism.'

Laughter and scattered applause from the gallery. The judge asked for silence before looking enquiringly at the prosecutor.

'That was all,' Groth said.

'Does the defence counsel have any more questions?'

Krohn shook his head.

'Then I would like the first witness for the prosecution to be brought in.'

The prosecutor nodded to the usher, who opened the door at the back of the room. There was a scraping of chairs outside, the door opened wide and a large man strolled in. Krohn noted that the man was wearing a suit jacket which was slightly too small, black jeans and large Dr Martens boots. The close-shaven head and the slim athletic body suggested an age somewhere around the early thirties – although the bloodshot eyes with bags underneath and the pale complexion with thin capillaries bursting sporadically into small red deltas pointed more in the region of fifty.

'Police Officer Harry Hole?' the judge asked when the man had taken a seat in the witness box.

'Yes.'

'No home address given, I see?'

'Private.' Hole pointed with his thumb over his shoulder. 'They tried to break into my place.'

More boos.

'Have you ever made an affirmation, Police Officer Hole? Taken the oath, in other words?'

'Yes.'

Krohn's head wobbled like the nodding dogs some motorists like to keep on their parcel shelf. He began feverishly to flick through the documents.

'You investigate murders for Crime Squad, don't you?' Groth said. 'Why were you given this case?'

'Because we wrongly assessed the case.'

'Oh?'

'We didn't think that Ho Dai would survive. You usually

don't with a smashed skull and parts of the insides on the outside.'

Krohn saw the faces of the associate judges wince involuntarily. But it didn't matter now. He had found the document with their names. And there it was: the mistake.

3

Karl Johans Gate. 5 October 1999.

YOU'RE GOING TO DIE, OLD CHAP.

The words were still ringing in the old man's ears when he walked down the steps to leave and stood still, blinded by the fierce autumn sun. As his pupils slowly shrank, he held on tight to the handrail and breathed in, slow and deep. He listened to the cacophony of cars, trams, the beeping sounds telling pedestrians they could cross. And voices – the excited, happy voices which hastened by to the accompaniment of the clatter of shoes. And music. Had he ever heard so much music? Nothing managed to drown the sound of the words though: *You're going to die, old chap.*

How many times had he stood here on the steps outside Dr Buer's surgery? Twice a year for forty years, that would make eighty times. Eighty normal days just like today, but never, not before today, had he noticed how much life there was in the streets, how much exhilaration, what voracious lust for life. It was October, but it felt like a day in May. The day peace broke out. Was he exaggerating? He could hear her voice, see her silhouette come running out of the sun, the outline of a face disappearing in a halo of white light.

You're going to die, old chap.

The whiteness took on colour and became Karl Johans gate. He arrived at the bottom step, stopped, looked to the right and then to the left as if he couldn't make up his mind which direction to take, and fell into a reverie. He gave a start as if someone had woken him and began to walk towards the Palace. His gait was hesitant, his eyes downcast and his gaunt figure stooped in the slightly oversized woollen coat.

'The cancer has spread,' Dr Buer had said.

'Right,' he had answered, looking at the doctor and wondering if that was something they learned at medical school, to take off their glasses when serious issues had to be talked about, or if it was something shortsighted doctors did to avoid looking patients in the eye. Dr Konrad Buer had begun to resemble his father as his hairline receded, and the bags under his eyes gave him a little of his father's aura of concern.

'In a nutshell?' the old man had asked in the voice of someone he had not heard in more than fifty years. They had been the hollow, rough, guttural sounds of a man with mortal dread quivering in his vocal cords.

'Yes, there is in fact a question about —'

'Please, doctor. I've looked death in the eye before.'

He had raised his voice, chosen words which forced it to stay firm, the way he wanted Dr Buer to hear them. The way he himself wanted to hear them.

The doctor's gaze had flitted across the table top, across the worn parquet floor and out of the dirty window. It had taken refuge out there for a while before returning and meeting his own. His hands had found a cloth to clean his glasses again and again.

'I know how you —'

'You know nothing, doctor.' The old man had heard himself utter a short, dry laugh. 'Don't take offence, Dr Buer, but I can guarantee you one thing: you know nothing.'

He had observed the doctor's discomfort and at the same time heard the tap dripping into the sink at the far end of the room. It was a new sound, and all of a sudden and incomprehensibly he seemed to have the hearing of a twenty-year-old.

Then Dr Buer had put his glasses back on, lifted a piece of paper as though the words he was going to say were written on it, cleared his throat and said: 'You're going to die, old chap.'

The old man would have preferred a little less familiarity.

He stopped by a gathering of people, where he heard a guitar being strummed and a voice singing a song that must have sounded old to everyone except him. He had heard it before, probably a quarter of a century ago, but to him it could have been yesterday. Everything was like that now – the further back in time it was, the closer and the clearer it seemed. He could remember things he hadn't thought of for years. Now he could close his eyes and see things projected on his retina that he had previously read about in his war diaries.

'You should have a year left, at any rate.'

One spring and one summer. He would be able to see every single yellowing leaf on the deciduous trees in Studenterlunden as if he were wearing new, stronger glasses. The same trees had stood there in 1945, or had they? They hadn't been very clear on that day, nothing had. The smiling faces, the furious faces, the shouts he barely heard, the car door being slammed shut and he might have had tears in his eyes because when he recalled the flags people were waving as they ran along the pavements, they were red and blurred. Their shouts: *The Crown Prince is back!*

He walked up the hill to the Palace where several people had collected to watch the changing of the guard. The echo of orders and the smack of rifle stock and boot heels reverberated against the pale yellow brick façade. There was the whirr of video cameras and he caught some German words. A young Japanese couple stood with their arms around each other, happily watching the show. He closed his eyes, tried to detect the smell of uniforms and gun oil. It was nonsense, of course; there was nothing here that smelled of his war.

He opened his eyes again. What did they know, these black-clad boy soldiers who were the social monarchy's parade-ground figures, performing symbolic actions they were too innocent to understand and too young to feel anything about. He thought about that day again, of the young Norwegians dressed as soldiers, or 'Swedish soldiers' as they had called them. In his eyes they had been tin soldiers; they hadn't known how to wear a uniform, even less how to treat a prisoner of war. They had been frightened and brutal; with cigarettes in their mouths and their uniform caps at a rakish slant, they had clung to their newly acquired weapons and tried to overcome their fear by smacking their rifle stocks into the prisoners' backs.

'Nazi swine,' they had said as they hit them, to receive instant forgiveness for their sins.

He breathed in and savoured the warm autumn day, but at that moment the pain came. He staggered backwards. Water in his lungs. In twelve months' time, maybe less, the inflammation and the pus would produce water, which would collect in his lungs. That was said to be the worst.

You're going to die, old chap.

Then came the cough. It was so violent that those standing closest to him moved away involuntarily.

4

Ministry of Foreign Affairs, Viktoria Terrasse. 5 October 1999.

THE UNDER SECRETARY FOR FOREIGN AFFAIRS, Bernt Brandhaug, strode down the corridor. He had left his office thirty seconds ago; in another forty-five he would be in the meeting room. He stretched his shoulders inside his jacket, felt that they more than filled it out, felt his back muscles strain against the material. *Latissimus dorsi* – the upper back muscles. He was sixty years old, but didn't look a day over fifty. Not that he was preoccupied with his appearance. He was well aware that he was an attractive man to look at, without needing to do very much more than the training that he loved anyway, as well as putting in a couple of sessions in the solarium in the winter and regularly plucking the grey hairs from what had become bushy eyebrows.

'Hi Lise!' he shouted as he passed the photocopier, and the young Foreign Office probationer jumped, managing only a wan smile before Brandhaug was round the next corner. Lise was a newly fledged lawyer and the daughter of a friend from university days. She had started only three weeks ago. And from that moment she had been aware that the Under Secretary, the highest civil servant in the building, knew who she

was. Would he be able to have her? Probably. Not that it
would happen. Necessarily.

He could already hear the buzz of voices before he
opened the door. He looked at his watch. Seventy-five seconds. Then he was inside, casting a fleeting glimpse around
the room to confirm that all the authorities summoned were
represented.

'Well, well, so you're Bjarne Møller?' he shouted with a
broad smile as he offered his hand across the table to a tall
thin man sitting beside Anne Størksen, the Chief Constable.

'You're the PAS, aren't you? I hear you're running the
roller-coaster leg of the Holmenkollen relay?'

This was one of Brandhaug's tricks. Coming by a little
piece of information about people he met for the first time.
Something that wasn't in their CV. It made them insecure.
Using the acronym PAS – the internal abbreviation for *Po-
litiavdelingssjef*, the head of Crime Squad – particularly
pleased him. Brandhaug sat down, winked at his old friend
Kurt Meirik, the head of *Politiets overvåkningstjeneste*, or
POT, the Security Service, and studied the others sitting
round the table.

As yet, no one knew who would take charge of the meeting as the representatives were equally high ranking, theoretically at least, coming from the Prime Minister's Office, Oslo
police district, Norwegian Security Service, Crime Squad
and Brandhaug's own Ministry of Foreign Affairs. The Prime
Minister's Office had called the meeting, but there was no
doubt that Oslo police district, in the guise of Anne Størksen,
and POT, in the shape of Kurt Meirik, wanted the operational
responsibility when procedures were that far advanced. The
Under Secretary of State from the Prime Minister's Office
looked as if he envisaged taking charge.

Brandhaug closed his eyes and listened.

The nice-to-see-you conversations stopped, the buzz of
voices slowly subsided and a table leg scraped on the floor.

Not yet. There was the rustling of papers, the clicking of pens – at important meetings like these most heads of department had their personal note-takers with them in case at a later point they began to blame each other for things that had happened. Someone coughed, but it came from the wrong end of the room and apart from that it wasn't the kind of cough that preceded speaking. Sharp intake of breath. Someone spoke.

'Let's begin then,' Bernt Brandhaug said, opening his eyes.

Heads turned towards him. It was the same every time. A half-open mouth, the Under Secretary of State's; a wry smile from Anne Størksen showing that she understood what had taken place – but otherwise, blank faces looking at him without a hint of recognition that the battle was already over.

'Welcome to the first co-ordination meeting. Our task is to get four of the world's most important men in and out of Norway more or less in one piece.'

Polite chuckles from around the table.

'On Monday, 1 November, we will receive a visit from the PLO leader Yasser Arafat, the Israeli PM Ehud Barak, the Russian PM Vladimir Putin and, last but not least, the cherry on the cake: at 6.15 a.m., in exactly twenty-seven days' time, Air Force One, with the American President on board, will be landing at Gardemoen Airport, Oslo.'

Brandhaug's gaze moved from face to face down the table. It stopped at the new one, Bjarne Møller's.

'If it isn't foggy, that is,' he said, earning himself a laugh and noticing with satisfaction that Møller forgot his nervousness for a moment and laughed along with the others. Brandhaug responded with a smile, revealing his strong teeth which had become even whiter since his last cosmetic treatment at the dentist's.

'We still don't know exactly how many people are coming,' Brandhaug said. 'The President had an entourage of 2,000 in Australia and 1,700 in Copenhagen.'

Mumbles around the table.

'However, in my experience, a guesstimate of around 700 is probably more realistic.'

Brandhaug was quietly confident his 'guesstimate' would soon be confirmed as he had received a fax an hour before with a list of the 712 people coming.

'Some of you are probably wondering why the President needs so many people for a two-day summit meeting. The answer is simple. What we are talking about here is the good old-fashioned rhetoric of power. Seven hundred, if my assessment is correct, is precisely the number of people Kaiser Friedrich III had with him when he entered Rome in 1468 to show the Pope who the most powerful man in the world was.'

More laughter round the table. Brandhaug winked at Anne Størksen. He had found the reference in *Aftenposten*. He brought his two palms together.

'I don't need to tell you how short a time one month is, but it means that we're going to need daily co-ordination meetings at ten in this room. Until these four men are off our hands you'll just have to drop everything else. There's a bar on holidays and time off. And sick leave. Any questions before we go on?'

'Well, we think —' the Under Secretary of State began.

'That includes depressions,' Brandhaug interrupted, and Bjarne Møller couldn't help laughing out loud.

'Well, we —' the Under Secretary began again.

'Over to you, Meirik,' Brandhaug called.

'What?'

The Head of the Security Service (POT) raised his shiny pate and looked at Brandhaug.

'You wanted to say something about POT's threat assessment?' Brandhaug said.

'Oh that,' Meirik said. 'We've brought copies with us.'

Meirik was from Tromsø and spoke a strangely haphazard mixture of Tromsø dialect and standard Norwegian. He nodded to a woman sitting beside him. Brandhaug's eyes lingered on her. OK, she wasn't wearing make-up, and her short brown hair was cut in a bob and held in an unbecoming hairslide. And her suit, a blue woollen job, was downright dull. But even though she had made herself look exaggeratedly sober, in the way that professional women who were afraid of not being taken seriously often did, he liked what he saw. Brown, gentle eyes and high cheekbones gave her an aristocratic, almost un-Norwegian appearance. He had seen her before, but the haircut was new. What was her name again – it was something biblical – Rakel? Perhaps she was recently divorced. That might explain the new haircut. She leaned over the attaché case between her and Meirik, and Brandhaug's eyes automatically sought the neckline on her blouse, but it was buttoned too high to show him anything of interest. Did she have children of school age? Would she have any objections to renting a room in one of the city centre hotels during the day? Was she turned on by power?

Brandhaug: 'Just give us a short resumé, Meirik.'

'Fine.'

'I would like to say one thing first . . .' the Under Secretary of State said.

'Shall we let Meirik finish first? Then you can say as much as you like afterwards, Bjørn.'

That was the first time Brandhaug had used the Under Secretary's Christian name.

'POT considers there to be a risk of an attack or the infliction of other damage,' Meirik said.

Brandhaug smiled. Out of the corner of his eye he saw the Chief Constable do the same. Smart girl, law degree and flawless administrative record. Perhaps he ought to invite her and her husband to a trout supper one evening. Brandhaug and his wife lived in a spacious timber house in the green belt in Nordberg. In winter you had only to put on your skis outside the garage and you were off. Brandhaug loved the house. His wife had thought it was too black. She said that all the dark wood made her afraid, and she didn't like the forest being around them, either. Yes, an invitation to supper. Solid timber, and fresh trout he'd caught himself. They were the right signals to give.

'I may remind you that four American presidents have died as a result of assassinations. Abraham Lincoln in 1865, James Garfield in 1881, John F. Kennedy in 1963 and . . .'

He turned to the woman with the high cheekbones who mouthed the name.

'Oh, yes, William McKinley. In . . .'

'1901,' Brandhaug said with a warm smile and a glance at his watch.

'Exactly. But there have been a great many more attempts over the years. Harry Truman, Gerald Ford and Ronald Reagan were all targets of serious attacks while they were in office.'

Brandhaug cleared his throat: 'You're forgetting that the present incumbent was shot at a few years ago. Or at least his house was.'

'That's true. But we don't include that type of incident as there would be too many. I doubt that any American president over the last twenty years has completed his term of office without at least ten attempts on his life being uncovered and the perpetrator arrested. The media were none the wiser.'

'Why not?'

Crime Squad chief Bjarne Møller imagined he had only thought the question and was as surprised as the others when he heard his own voice. He swallowed when he noticed the heads turning and tried to keep his eyes on Meirik, but couldn't help them wandering in Brandhaug's direction. The Under Secretary for Foreign Affairs winked reassuringly.

'Well, as you know, it's usual to keep attempted assassinations under wraps,' Meirik said, taking off his glasses.

They looked like the glasses which go darker as you go into the sun, worn by Horst Tappert in the Oberinspektor Derrick role, very popular with German mail-order catalogues.

'Attempted assassinations have proved to be at least as contagious as suicides. And besides, we in the field don't want to reveal our working practices.'

'What plans have been made regarding surveillance?' the Under Secretary of State asked.

The woman with the cheekbones passed Meirik a sheet and he put on his glasses again and read it.

'Eight men from the Secret Service are coming on Thursday. We will then start going through the hotels and the route, vet all those who will come into contact with the President and train the Norwegian police officers we're going to deploy. We'll need to call in units from Romerike, Asker and Bærum.'

'And they will be used to what end?' Brandhaug asked.

'Mainly observation duties. Around the American embassy, the hotel where the entourage will be staying, the car park —'

'In short, all the places where the President isn't.'

'POT will take care of that. With the American Secret Service.'

'I thought you didn't like doing surveillance jobs, Kurt?' Brandhaug said with a smirk.

The memory caused Kurt Meirik to grimace. During the Mining Conference in Oslo in 1998, POT had refused to offer surveillance on the basis of their own threat assessment. They concluded it was 'medium to low security risk'. On the second day of the conference the Norwegian Directorate of Immigration drew the conference's attention to the fact that one of the Norwegian drivers POT had cleared for the Croat delegation was a Bosnian Muslim. He had come to Norway in the 1970s and had Norwegian citizenship for many years. But in 1993 both his parents and four members of his family had been butchered by Croats at Mostar, in

Bosnia Herzegovina. When the man's flat was searched they had found two hand-grenades and a suicide letter. Of course, the press had never got a sniff of it, but the repercussions reached government level, and Kurt Meirik's career had hung in the balance until Bernt Brandhaug himself had intervened. The matter had been hushed up after the police inspector in charge of the security clearances had resigned. Brandhaug couldn't remember the man's name, but ever since then his working relations with Meirik had been excellent.

'Bjørn!' Brandhaug exclaimed, clapping his hands together. 'Now we're all keen to hear what it was you wanted to tell us. Come on!'

Brandhaug scanned the room, swiftly moving past Meirik's assistant, but not so swiftly that he didn't notice her looking at him. That is, she was looking in his direction, but her eyes were expressionless, blank. He considered whether to return her look, to see what expression would emerge when she realised what he was doing, but he dropped the idea. What was her name? Rakel, wasn't it?

5

Palace Gardens. 5 October 1999.

'ARE YOU DEAD?'

The old man opened his eyes and saw the outline of a head standing over him, but the face merged into a corona of white light. Was it her? Had she come to collect him already?

'Are you dead?' the bright voice repeated.

He didn't answer because he didn't know whether his eyes were open or he was simply dreaming. Or, as the voice asked him, if he was dead.

'What's your name?'

The head moved and he saw the tips of trees and blue sky. He *had* been dreaming. Something in a poem. *German bombers are overhead.* Nordahl Grieg. The King fleeing to England. His pupils began to adjust to the light again and he remembered he had sat down on the grass in the Palace Gardens to rest. He must have fallen asleep. A little boy crouched beside him and a pair of brown eyes looked at him from under a black fringe.

'My name's Ali,' the boy said.

A Pakistani boy? He had a strange, turned-up nose.

'Ali means God,' the boy said. 'What does your name mean?'

'My name's Daniel,' the old man said with a smile. 'It's a name from the Bible. It means "God is my judge".'

The boy looked at him.

'So, you're Daniel?'

'Yes,' the man said.

The boy didn't take his eyes off him and the old man felt disconcerted. Perhaps the young boy thought he was homeless as he was lying there fully clothed, using his woollen coat as a rug in the hot sun.

'Where's your mother?' he asked, to avoid the boy's probing stare.

'Over there.' The boy turned and pointed.

Two robust, dark-skinned women were sitting on the grass some distance away. Four children were frolicking around them, laughing.

'Then I'm the judge of you, I am,' the boy said.

'What?'

'Ali is God, isn't he? And God is the judge of Daniel. And my name's Ali and you're —'

The old man had stuck out his hand and tweaked Ali's nose. The boy squealed with delight. He saw the heads of the two women turn; one was getting to her feet so he let go.

'Your mother, Ali,' he said, motioning with his head in the direction of the approaching woman.

'Mummy!' the boy shouted. 'Look, I'm the judge of that man.'

The woman shouted to the boy in Urdu. The old man smiled, but the woman shunned him and looked sternly at her son, who finally obeyed and padded over to her. When they turned, her gaze swept across and past him as if he were invisible. He wanted to explain to her that he was not a bum, to tell her he'd had a hand in shaping society. He had invested in it, in spades, given everything he had until there was no more to give, apart from giving way, giving in, giving up. But he was unable to do that, he was tired and simply wanted to go home. Rest, then he would see. It was time some others paid.

He didn't hear the little boy shouting after him as he was leaving.

6

Police HQ, Grønland. 9 October 1999.

ELLEN GJELTEN LOOKED UP AT THE MAN WHO burst through the door.

'Good morning, Harry.'

'Fuck!'

Harry kicked the waste-paper basket beside his desk and it smashed into the wall next to Ellen's chair and rolled across the linoleum floor, spreading its contents everywhere: discarded attempts at reports (the Ekeberg killing); an empty pack of twenty cigarettes (Camel, tax free sticker); a green *Go'morn* yoghurt pot; *Dagsavisen*; a used cinema ticket (*Filmteateret: Fear & Loathing in Las Vegas*); a used pools coupon; a music magazine (*MOJO*, no. 69, February 1999, with a picture of Queen on the cover); a bottle of Coke (plastic, half-litre); and a yellow Post-it with a phone number he had considered ringing for a while.

Ellen looked up from her PC and studied the contents of the bin on the floor.

'Are you chucking the *MOJO* out, Harry?' she asked.

'Fuck!' Harry repeated. He wrestled off his tight suit jacket and threw it across the twenty metre square office he and Ellen Gjelten shared. The jacket hit the coat stand, but slid down to the floor.

'What's up?' Ellen asked, reaching out a hand to stop the swaying coat stand from falling.

'I found this in my pigeon-hole.'

Harry waved a document in the air.

'Looks like a court sentence.'

'Yep.'

'Dennis Kebab case?'

'Right.'

'And?'

'They gave Sverre Olsen the full whack. Three and a half years.'

'Jesus. You ought to be in a stupendous mood.'

'I was, for about a minute. Until I read this.'

Harry held up a fax.

'Well?'

'When Krohn got his copy of the sentence this morning, he responded by sending us a warning that he was going to pursue a claim of procedural error.'

Ellen made a face as if she had something nasty in her mouth.

'Ugh.'

'He wants the whole sentence quashed. You won't fucking believe it, but that slippery Krohn guy has screwed us on the oath.' Harry stood in front of the window. 'The associate judges only have to take the oath the first time they act as judges, but it must take place in the courtroom before the case begins. Krohn noticed that one associate judge was new. And that she didn't take her oath in the courtroom.'

'It's called affirmation.'

'Right. Now it turns out that according to the certificate of sentence the judge had attended to the affirmation of the associate judge in his office, just before the case started. He blames lack of time and new rules.'

Harry crumpled up the fax and threw it in a wide arc, missing Ellen's waste-paper basket by half a metre.

'And the result?' Ellen asked, kicking the fax to Harry's half of the office.

'The conviction will be deemed invalid and Sverre Olsen will be a free man for at least eighteen months until the case comes up again. And the rule of thumb is that the sentence will be a great deal milder because of the strain which the waiting period inflicts on the accused blah, blah, blah. With eight months already served in custody, it's more than bloody likely that Sverre Olsen is already a free man.'

Harry wasn't speaking to Ellen; she knew all the ins and outs of the case. He was speaking to his own reflection in the window, articulating the words to hear if they made any sense. He drew both hands across a sweaty skull, where until recently close-cropped blond hair had bristled. There was a simple reason for him having had the rest shaved off: last week he had been recognised again. A young guy, in a black woollen hat, Nikes and such large baggy trousers that the crotch hung between his knees, had come over to him while his pals sniggered in the background and asked if Harry was 'that Bruce Willis type guy in Australia'. It was three – three! – years ago since his face had decorated the front pages of newspapers and he had made a fool of himself on TV shows talking about the serial killer he had shot in Sydney. Harry had immediately gone and shaved off his hair. Ellen had suggested a beard.

'The worst thing is that I could swear that lawyer bastard had a draft appeal ready before the sentence was passed. He could have said something and the affirmation could have been taken there and then, but he sat there, rubbing his hands and waiting.'

Ellen shrugged her shoulders.

'That sort of thing happens. Good work by the defence counsel. Something has to be sacrificed on the altar of law and order. Pull yourself together, Harry.'

She said it with a mixture of sarcasm and sober statement of fact.

Harry rested his forehead against the cooling glass. Another one of those unexpectedly warm October days. He wondered where Ellen, the fresh, young policewoman with the pale, doll-like, sweet face, the little mouth and eyes as round as a ball, had developed such a tough exterior. She was a girl from a middle-class home, in her own words, an only child and spoiled rotten, who had even gone to a girl's boarding school in Switzerland. Who knows? Perhaps that *was* a tough enough upbringing.

Harry laid back his head and exhaled. Then he undid one of his shirt buttons.

'More, more,' Ellen whispered as she clapped encouragement.

'In neo-Nazi circles they call him Batman.'

'Got it. *Baseball* bat.'

'Not the Nazi – the lawyer.'

'Right. Interesting. Does that mean he's good-looking, rich, barking mad and has a six-pack and a cool car?'

Harry laughed. 'You should have your own TV show, Ellen. It's because Batman always wins. Besides, he's married.'

'Is that the only minus?'

'That . . . and him making monkeys of us every time,' Harry said, pouring himself a cup of the home-blended coffee Ellen had brought with her when she moved into the office two years ago. The snag was that Harry's palate could no longer tolerate the usual slop.

'Supreme Court judge?' she asked.

'Before he's forty.'

'Thousand kroner he isn't.'

'Done.'

They laughed and toasted with their cardboard cups.

'Can I have that *MOJO* magazine then?' she asked.

'There are pictures of Freddie Mercury's ten worst centre-

fold poses. Bare chest, arms akimbo and buck teeth sticking
out. The full whammy. There you are.'

'I like Freddie Mercury, I do. Liked.'

'I didn't say I didn't like him.'

The blue, punctured office chair, which had long been set
at the lowest notch, screamed in protest as Harry leaned
back, lost in thought. He picked up a yellow Post-it with
Ellen's writing on from the telephone in front of him.

'What's this?'

'You can read, can't you? Møller wants you.'

Harry trotted down the corridor, imagining as he went
the pursed mouth and the two deep furrows the boss would
get when he heard that Sverre Olsen had walked yet again.

By the photocopier a young, rosy-cheeked girl instantly
raised her eyes and smiled as Harry passed. He didn't manage a return smile. Presumably one of the office girls. Her
perfume was sweet and heavy, and simply irritated him. He
looked at the second hand on his watch.

So perfume had started irritating him now. What had got
into him? Ellen had said he lacked natural buoyancy, or whatever it was that meant most people could struggle to the
surface again. After his return from Bangkok he had been
down for so long that he had considered giving up ever returning to the surface. Everything had been cold and dark,
and all his impressions were somehow dulled. As if he were
deeply immersed in water. It had been so wonderfully quiet.
When people talked to him the words had been like bubbles
of air coming out of their mouths, hurrying upwards and
away. So that was what it was like to drown, he had thought,
and waited. But nothing happened. It was only a vacuum.
That was fine, though. He had survived.

Thanks to Ellen.

She had stepped in for him in those first weeks after his
return when he'd had to throw in the towel and go home. And
she had made sure that he didn't go to bars, ordered him to
breathe out when he was late for work, after which she

declared him fit or unfit accordingly. Had sent him home a couple of times and then kept quiet about it. It had taken time, but Harry had nothing particular to do. And Ellen had nodded with satisfaction on the first Friday they could confirm that he had turned up sober for work on five consecutive days.

In the end he had asked her straight out. Why, with police college and a law degree behind her and her whole life in front of her, had she voluntarily put this millstone around her neck? Didn't she realise that it wouldn't do her career any good? Did she have a problem finding normal, successful friends?

She had looked at him with a serious expression and answered that she only did it to soak up his experience. He was the best detective they had in Crime Squad. Rubbish, of course, but he had nonetheless felt flattered that she would bother to say so. Besides, Ellen was such an enthusiastic, ambitious detective that it was impossible not to be infected. For the last six months Harry had even begun to do good work again. Some of it even excellent. Such as on the Sverre Olsen case.

Ahead of him was Møller's door. Harry nodded in passing to a uniformed officer who pretended not to see him.

If he had been a contestant on Swedish TV's *The Robinson Expedition*, Harry thought, it would have taken them no more than a day to notice his bad karma and send him home. Send him home? My God, he was beginning to think in the same terminology as the shit TV3 programmes. That's what happened when you spent five hours every night in front of the TV. The idea was that if he was locked up in front of the goggle box in Sofies gate, at least he wouldn't be sitting in Schrøder's café.

He knocked twice immediately beneath the sign on the door: Bjarne Møller, PAS.

'Come in!'

Harry looked at his watch. Seventy-five seconds.

7

INSPECTOR BJARNE MØLLER WAS LYING RATHER than sitting in the chair, and a pair of long limbs stuck out between the desk legs. He had his hands folded behind his head – a beautiful specimen of what early race researchers called 'long skulls' – and a telephone gripped between ear and shoulder. His hair was cut in a kind of close crop, which Hole had recently compared with Kevin Costner's hairstyle in *The Bodyguard*. Møller hadn't seen *The Bodyguard*. He hadn't been to the cinema in fifteen years as fate had furnished him with an oversized sense of responsibility, too few hours, two children and a wife who only partly understood him.

'Let's go for that then,' Møller said, putting down the phone and looking at Harry across a desk weighed down with documents, overflowing ashtrays and paper cups. On the desktop a photograph of two boys dressed as Red Indians marked a kind of logical centre amid the chaos.

'There you are, Harry.'

'Here I am, boss.'

'I've been to a meeting at the Ministry of Foreign Affairs in connection with the summit in November here in Oslo.

The US President is coming . . . well, you read papers, don't you. Coffee, Harry?'

Møller had stood up and a couple of seven-league strides had already taken him to a filing cabinet on which, balanced atop a pile of papers, a coffee machine was coughing up a viscous substance.

'Thanks boss, but I —'

It was too late and Harry took the steaming cup.

'I'm especially looking forward to a visit from the Secret Service, with whom I'm sure we will have a cordial relationship as we get to know each other better.'

Møller had never quite learned to handle irony. That was just one of the things Harry appreciated about his boss.

Møller drew in his knees until they supported the bottom of the table. Harry leaned back to get the crumpled pack of Camels from his trouser pocket and raised an enquiring eyebrow at Møller, who quickly took the hint and pushed the brimming ashtray towards him.

'I'll be responsible for security along the roads to and from Gardemoen. As well as the President, there will be Barak —'

'Barak?'

'Ehud Barak. Prime Minister of Israel.'

'Jeez, so there's another fantastic Oslo agreement on the way, then?'

Møller stared despondently at the blue column of smoke rising to the ceiling.

'Don't tell me you haven't heard about it, Harry. Or I'll be even more worried about you than I already am. It was on all the front pages last week.'

Harry shrugged.

'Unreliable paper boy. Inflicting serious gaps in my general knowledge. A grave handicap to my social life.' He took another cautious sip of coffee, but then gave up and pushed it away. 'And my love life.'

'Really?' Møller eyed Harry with an expression suggesting he didn't know whether to relish or dread what was coming next.

'Of course. Who would find a man in his mid-thirties, who knows all the details about the lives of the people on *The Robinson Expedition* but can hardly name any head of state, or the Israeli President, sexy?'

'Prime Minister.'

'There you are. Now you know what I mean.'

Møller stifled a laugh. He had a tendency to laugh too easily. And a soft spot for the somewhat anguished officer with big ears that stuck out from the close-cropped cranium like two colourful butterfly wings. Even though Harry had caused Møller more trouble than was good for him. As a newly promoted PAS he had learned that the first commandment for a civil servant with career plans was to guard your back. When Møller cleared his throat to put the worrying questions he had made up his mind to ask, and dreaded asking, he first of all knitted his eyebrows to show Harry that his concern was of a professional and not an amicable nature.

'I hear you're still spending your time sitting in Schrøder's, Harry.'

'Less than ever, boss. There's so much good stuff on TV.'

'But you're still sitting and drinking?'

'They don't like you to stand.'

'Cut it out. Are you drinking again?'

'Minimally.'

'How minimally?'

'They'll throw me out if I drink any less.'

This time Møller couldn't hold back his laughter. 'I need three liaison officers to secure the road,' he said. 'Each will have ten men at their disposal from various police districts in Akershus, plus a couple of cadets from the final year at police college. I thought Tom Waaler . . .'

Waaler. Racist bastard and directly in line for the soon-to-be-announced inspector's job. Harry had heard enough about

Waaler's professional activities to know that they confirmed all the prejudices the public might have about the police. Apart from one: unfortunately Waaler was not stupid. His successes as a detective were so impressive that even Harry had to concede he deserved the inevitable promotion.

'And Weber . . .'

'The old sourpuss?'

'. . . and you, Harry.'

'Say that again?'

'You heard me.'

Harry pulled a face.

'Have you any objections?' Møller asked.

'Of course I have.'

'Why? This is an honourable mission, Harry. A feather in your cap.'

'Is it?' Harry stabbed out his cigarette furiously in the ashtray. 'Or is it the next stage in the rehabilitation process?'

'What do you mean?' Bjarne Møller looked wounded.

'I know that you defied good advice and had a run-in with a few people when you took me back into the fold after Bangkok. And I'm eternally grateful to you for that. But what is this? *Liaison Officer*? Sounds like an attempt to prove to the doubters that you were right, and they were wrong. That Hole is on his way up, that he can be given responsibility and all that.'

'Well?' Bjarne Møller had put his hands behind the long skull again.

'Well?' Harry aped. 'Is that what's behind it? Am I just a pawn again?'

Møller gave a sigh of despair.

'We're all pawns, Harry. There's always a hidden agenda. This is no worse than anything else. Do a good job and it'll be good for both of us. Is that so damned difficult?'

Harry sniffed, started to say something, caught himself, took a fresh run-up, then abandoned the idea. He flicked a new cigarette out of the pack.

'It's just that I feel like a bloody horse people bet on. And I loathe responsibility.'

Harry let the cigarette hang loosely from his lips without lighting it.

He owed Møller this favour, but what if he screwed up? Had Møller thought about that? *Liaison Officer.* He had been on the wagon for a while now, but he still had to be careful, take one day at a time. Hell, wasn't that one of the reasons he became a detective? To avoid having people underneath him, and to have as few as possible above him? Harry bit into the cigarette filter.

They heard voices out in the corridor by the coffee machine. It sounded like Waaler. Then peals of laughter. The new office girl perhaps. He still had the smell of her perfume in his nostrils.

'Fuck,' Harry said. *Fu-uck.* With two syllables, which made his cigarette jump twice in his mouth.

Møller had closed his eyes during Harry's moment of reflection and now he half-opened them. 'Can I take that as a yes?'

Harry stood up and walked out without saying a word.

8

Toll Barrier at Alnabru. 1 November 1999.

THE GREY BIRD GLIDED INTO HARRY'S FIELD OF vision and was on its way out again. He increased the pressure on the trigger of his .38 calibre Smith & Wesson while staring over the edge of his gun sights at the stationary back behind the glass. Someone had been talking about slow time on TV yesterday.

The car horn, Ellen. Press the damn horn. He has to be a Secret Service agent.

Slow time, like on Christmas Eve before Father Christmas comes.

The first motorcycle was level with the toll booth, and the robin was still a black dot on the outer margin of his vision. The time in the electric chair before the current . . .

Harry squeezed the trigger. One, two, three times.

And then time accelerated explosively. The coloured glass went white, spraying shards over the tarmac, and he caught sight of an arm disappearing under the line of the booth before the whisper of expensive American tyres was there – and gone.

He stared towards the booth. A couple of the yellow leaves swirled up by the motorcade were still floating through the air before settling on a dirty grey grass verge. He stared towards the booth. It was silent again, and for a moment all he could think was that he was standing at an ordinary Norwegian toll barrier on an ordinary Norwegian autumn day, with an ordinary Esso petrol station in the background. It even smelled of ordinary cold morning air: rotting leaves and car exhaust. And it struck him: perhaps none of this has really happened.

He was still staring towards the booth when the relentless lament of the Volvo car horn behind him sawed the day in two.

Part Two

GENESIS

9

1942.

THE FLARES LIT UP THE GREY NIGHT SKY, MAK-
ing it resemble a filthy top canvas cast over the drab, bare
landscape surrounding them on all sides. Perhaps the Russians had launched an offensive, perhaps it was a bluff; you
never really knew until it was over. Gudbrand was lying on
the edge of the trench with both legs drawn up beneath him,
holding his gun with both hands and listening to the distant
hollow booms as he watched the flares go down. He knew he
shouldn't watch the flares. You would become night-blind
and unable to see the Russian snipers wriggling out in the
snow in no man's land. But he couldn't see them anyway, had
never seen a single one; he just shot on command. As he was
doing now.

'There he is!'

It was Daniel Gudeson, the only town boy in the unit.
The others came from places with names ending in -dal.
Some of the dales were broad and some were deep, deserted
and dark, such as Gudbrand's home ground. But not Daniel.
Not Daniel of the pure, high forehead, the sparkling blue
eyes and the white smile. He was like a recruitment-poster
cut-out. He came from somewhere with horizons.

'Two o'clock, left of the scrub,' Daniel said.

Scrub? There can't be any scrub in the shell-crater land-scape here. Yes, there was because the others were shooting. Crack, bang, swish. Every fifth bullet went off in a parabola, like a firefly. Tracer fire. The bullet tore off into the dark, but it seemed suddenly to tire because its velocity decreased and then it sank somewhere out there. That was what it looked like at any rate. Gudbrand thought it impossible for such a slow bullet to kill anyone.

'He's getting away!' yelled an embittered, hate-filled voice. It was Sindre Fauke. His face almost merged with his camou-flage uniform and the small, close-set eyes stared out into the dark. He came from a remote farm high up in the Gudbrands-dalen region, probably some narrow enclave where the sun didn't shine since he was so pale. Gudbrand didn't know why Sindre had volunteered to fight on the Eastern Front, but he had heard that his parents and both brothers had joined the fascist *Nasjonal Samling* Party, and that they went around wearing bands on their arms and reporting fellow villagers they suspected of being partisans. Daniel said that one day the informers and all those who exploited the war for their own advantage would get a taste of the whip.

'No, he's not,' Daniel said in a low voice, his chin against his gun. 'No bloody Bolshevik gets away.'

'He knows we've seen him,' Sindre said. 'He'll get into that hollow down there.'

'No, he won't,' Daniel said and took aim.

Gudbrand stared out into the grey-white dark. White snow, white camouflage uniforms, white fire. The skies are lit up again. All sorts of shadows flit across the crust of the snow. Gudbrand stared up again. Yellow and red flashes on the ho-rizon, followed by several distant rumbles. It was as unreal as being at the cinema, except that it was thirty degrees be-low and there was no one to put your arm around. Perhaps it really was an offensive this time?

'You're too slow, Gudeson. He's gone.' Sindre spat in the snow.

'No, he hasn't,' Daniel said even quieter and took aim, and then again. Almost no frost smoke was coming out of his mouth any longer.

Then, a high-pitched, screaming whistle, a warning scream, and Gudbrand threw himself into the ice-covered bottom of the trench, with both hands over his head. The ground shook. It rained frozen brown clumps of earth; one hit Gudbrand's helmet and he watched it slide off in front of him. He waited until he was sure there was no more to come, then shoved his helmet back on. It had gone quiet and a fine white veil of snow particles stuck to his face. They say you never hear the shell that hits you, but Gudbrand had seen the result of enough whistling shells to know this wasn't true. A flare lit up the trench; he saw the others' white faces and their shadows as they scrambled towards him, keeping to the side of the trench and their heads well down, as the light gradually faded. But where was Daniel? Daniel!

'Daniel!'

'Got 'im,' Daniel said, still lying on the edge of the trench. Gudbrand couldn't believe his own ears.

'What did you say?'

Daniel slid down into the trench and shook off the snow and earth. He had a broad grin on his face.

'No Russian arsehole will be able to shoot at our watch tonight. Tormod is avenged.' He dug his heels into the edge of the trench so he didn't slip on the ice.

'Is he fuck!' That was Sindre. 'You didn't fucking hit him, Gudeson. I saw the Russian disappear down into the hollow.'

His small eyes jumped from one man to the next, as if to ask whether any of them believed Daniel's boast.

'Correct,' Daniel said. 'But it'll be light in two hours and he knew he'd have to be out before then.'

'That's right, and so he tried it a bit too soon,' Gudbrand

added smartly. 'He popped up on the other side. Isn't that right, Daniel?'

'Too soon or not,' Daniel smiled, 'I would have got him anyway.'

Sindre hissed: 'Just shut that big gob of yours, Gudeson.'

Daniel shrugged, checked the chamber and cocked his gun. Then he turned, hung the gun over his shoulder, kicked a boot into the frozen side of the trench and swung himself up over the top.

'Give me your spade, will you, Gudbrand.'

Daniel took the spade and straightened up to his full height. In his white winter uniform he was outlined against the black sky and the flare, which hung like an aura of light over his head.

He looks like an angel, Gudbrand thought.

'What the fuck are you doing, man!' That was Edvard Mosken, the leader of their section, shouting. The calm soldier from Mjøndøl seldom raised his voice with veterans like Daniel, Sindre and Gudbrand in the unit. It was usually the new arrivals who received a bawling out when they made mistakes. The earful they got saved many of their lives. Now Edvard Mosken was staring up at Daniel with the one wide-open eye that he never closed. Not even when he slept. Gudbrand had seen that for himself.

'Get under cover, Gudeson,' the section leader said.

But Daniel simply smiled and the next moment he was gone; the frost smoke from his mouth was left hanging over them for a tiny second. Then the flare behind the horizon sank and it was dark again.

'Gudeson!' Edvard shouted, clambering out of the trench. 'For fuck's sake!'

'Can you see him?' Gudbrand asked.

'Vanished.'

'What did the nutter want with the spade?' Sindre asked, looking at Gudbrand.

'Don't know,' Gudbrand said. 'To shift barbed wire maybe?'

'Why would he want to shift barbed wire?'

'Don't know.' Gudbrand didn't like Sindre's wild eyes. They reminded him of another country boy who had been there. He had gone crazy in the end, pissed in his shoes one night before going on duty and all his toes had had to be amputated afterwards. But he was back home in Norway now, so maybe he hadn't been so crazy after all. At any rate, he'd had the same wild eyes.

'Perhaps he's going for a walk in no man's land,' Gudbrand said.

'I know what's on the other side of the barbed wire. I wonder what he's doing there.'

'Perhaps the shell hit him on the head,' Hallgrim Dale said. 'Perhaps he's gone ga-ga.'

Hallgrim was the youngest in the section, only eighteen years old. No one really knew why he had enlisted. Adventure, Gudbrand thought. Dale maintained that he admired Hitler, but he knew nothing about politics. Daniel thought that he had left a girl in the family way.

'If the Russian is still alive, Gudeson will be shot before he gets fifty metres,' Edvard Mosken said.

'Daniel got him,' Gudbrand whispered.

'In that case one of the others will shoot Gudeson,' Edvard said, sticking his hand inside his camouflage jacket and pulling out a thin cigarette from his breast pocket. 'It's crawling with them out there tonight.'

He held the match in a cupped hand as he struck it hard against the crude matchbox. The sulphur ignited at second attempt and Edvard lit his cigarette, took a drag and passed it round without saying a word. All the men inhaled slowly and passed the cigarette on to their neighbour. No one said a word; they all seemed to have sunk into their own thoughts. But Gudbrand knew that, like him, they were listening.

Ten minutes passed without a sound.

'They say planes are going to bomb Lake Ladoga,' Hallgrim Dale said.

They had all heard the rumours about the Russians fleeing from Leningrad across the frozen lake. What was worse, though, was that the ice also meant that General Tsjukov could get supplies into the besieged town.

'They're supposed to be fainting in the streets from hunger over there,' Dale said, indicating the east.

But Gudbrand had been hearing that ever since he had been sent there, almost a year ago, and still they were out there shooting at you as soon as you stuck your head out of the trench. Last winter the Russian deserters – who'd had enough and chose to change sides for a little food and warmth – had come over to the trenches with their hands behind their heads. But the deserters were few and far between now, and the two hollow-eyed soldiers Gudbrand had seen coming over last week had looked at them in disbelief when they saw that the Norwegians were just as skinny as they were.

'Twenty minutes. He's not coming back,' Sindre said. 'He's had it. A goner.'

'Shut it!' Gudbrand took a step towards Sindre, who immediately stood up. Even though Sindre was a good head taller, it was obvious that he had no stomach for a fight. He probably remembered the Russian Gudbrand had killed some months ago. Who would have thought that nice, gentle Gudbrand had such ferocity in him? The Russian had sneaked unseen into their trench between two listening posts and had slaughtered all those sleeping in the two nearest bunkers, one full of Dutch soldiers and the other Australians, before he had got into their bunker. The lice had saved them.

They had lice everywhere, but particularly in warm places, such as under the arms, under the belt, around the crotch and ankles. Gudbrand, who lay nearest to the door, hadn't been able to sleep because of what they called louse sores on his legs – open sores which could be the size of a small coin, the edges of which were thick with lice feeding. Gudbrand had taken out his bayonet in a futile attempt to scrape them away when the Russian stood in the doorway to let loose with his gun. Gudbrand had only seen his silhouette, but knew instantly it was an enemy when he saw the outline of a Mosin–Nagant rifle being raised. With just the blunt bayonet Gudbrand had sliced the Russian's neck so expertly that he was drained of blood when they carried him out into the snow afterwards.

'Calm down, boys,' Edvard said, pulling Gudbrand to one side. 'You should go and get some sleep, Gudbrand. You were relieved an hour ago.'

'I'll go out and look for him,' Gudbrand said.

'No, you won't,' Edvard said.

'Yes, I will, I —'

'That's an order!' Edvard shook his shoulder. Gudbrand tried to break free, but the section leader held him in a tight grip.

Gudbrand's voice went higher and quivered with desperation; 'Perhaps he's wounded! Perhaps he's caught on the barbed wire!'

Edvard patted him on the shoulder. 'It'll soon be light,' he said. 'Then we can find out what happened.'

He shot a quick glance at the others, who had followed the scene in silence. They began to stamp their feet in the snow and mutter to each other. Gudbrand saw Edvard go over to Hallgrim Dale and whisper a few words in his ear. Dale listened and glowered at Gudbrand. Gudbrand knew very well what it meant. It was an order to keep an eye on him. A while ago now, someone had spread a rumour that he and Daniel were more than simply good friends. And that they couldn't be trusted. Mosken had asked straight out if they were planning to desert together. Of course they had denied this, but Mosken probably thought now that Daniel had used the opportunity to make a run for it. And that Gudbrand would 'look for' his comrade as part of the plan to go over to the other side together. It made Gudbrand laugh. True enough, dreaming about the wonderful promise of food, warmth and women the Russian loudspeakers spewed out over the barren battlefield in ingratiating German was attractive, but to *believe* it?

'Shall we take a bet on whether he comes back?' That was Sindre. 'Three food rations. What do you say?'

Gudbrand put his arms down by his sides and could feel the bayonet hanging from the belt inside his camouflage uniform.

'Nicht schießen, bitte!'

Gudbrand spun round and there, right above his head, he saw a ruddy face beneath a Russian cap smiling down at him from the edge of the trench. Then the man swung down over the edge and performed a soft Telemark landing on the ice.

'Daniel!' Gudbrand shouted.

'Da da da dum!' Daniel sang, doffing the Russian cap. *'Dobry vyecher.'*

The men stood rooted to the spot, staring at him.

'Hey, Edvard,' Daniel shouted. 'You'd better tighten things up with our Dutch friends. They've got at least fifty metres between the listening posts over there.'

Edvard was as silent and stunned as the others.

'Did you bury the Russian, Daniel?' Gudbrand's face was shiny with excitement.

'Bury him?' Daniel said. 'I even read the Lord's Prayer and sang to him. Are you hard of hearing or something? I'm sure they heard it on the other side.'

Then he jumped up on to the top edge of the trench, sat with his arms raised in the air and began to sing in a deep, warm voice: 'A mighty fortress is our God . . .'

The men cheered and Gudbrand laughed so much he had tears in his eyes.

'You devil, Daniel!' Dale exclaimed.

'Not Daniel . . . Call me . . .' Daniel took off the Russian cap and read the name on the inside of the lining. 'Uriah. He could bloody write as well. Well, well, but he was still a Bol-shevik.'

He jumped down from the edge and looked around him. 'No one has any objections to a common Jewish name, I hope?'

Total silence followed for a moment before the outburst of laughter came. Then the first of the men went over to slap him on the back.

10

Leningrad. 31 December 1942.

IT WAS COLD IN THE MACHINE-GUN POST. GUD-brand was wearing all the clothes he possessed. Nevertheless, his teeth were still chattering and he had lost the sensation in his fingers and toes. The worst was his legs. He had bound new rags around his feet, but that didn't help much.

He stared out into the dark. They hadn't heard much from the Ivans that evening. Perhaps they were celebrating New Year's Eve. Perhaps they were eating well. Lamb stew. Or ribs of lamb. Gudbrand knew, of course, that the Russians didn't have any meat, but he couldn't stop thinking about food nevertheless. As for themselves, they hadn't had much more than the usual lentil soup and bread. The bread had a green sheen to it, but they had become accustomed to that. And if it became so mouldy that it crumbled, they just boiled the soup with the bread in it.

'At least we got a sausage on Christmas Eve,' Gudbrand said.

'Shh,' Daniel said.

'There's no one out there this evening, Daniel. They're sitting eating medallions of venison. With a thick, light brown game sauce and bilberries. And almond potatoes.'

'Don't start talking about food again. Be quiet and see if you can spot anything.'

'I can't see a thing, Daniel. Nothing.'

They huddled together, keeping their heads down. Daniel was wearing the Russian cap. The steel helmet with the Waffen SS badge lay beside him. Gudbrand knew why. There was something about the shape of the helmet which caused the eternally ice-cold snow to pass under the rim and create a continual, nerve-grinding whistling sound inside the helmet, which was particularly unfortunate if you were on duty at the listening post.

'What's wrong with your eyes?' Daniel asked.

'Nothing. I just have quite bad night vision.'

'Is that all?'

'And then I'm a little colour blind.'

'A *little* colour blind?'

'Red and green. I can't tell the difference. The colours seem the same. I never saw any berries, for example, when we went into the forest to pick cranberries for the Sunday joint . . .'

'No more talk about food, I said!'

They were quiet. In the distance a machine gun chattered. The thermometer showed minus twenty-five. Last winter they'd had minus forty-five several nights in a row. Gudbrand consoled himself with the thought that the lice were less active in this cold. He wouldn't start itching until he went off duty and crept under the woollen blanket in his bunk. But they tolerated the cold better than he did, the beasts. Once he had carried out an experiment: he had left his vest out in the snow in the biting cold for three consecutive days. When he took the vest into the bunker again, it was a sheet of ice. But when he thawed it out in front of the stove, a teeming, crawling mass came to life and he threw it into the flames out of sheer disgust.

Daniel cleared his throat.

'How did you go about eating your Sunday joint then?'

Gudbrand needed no second bidding.

'First of all, Dad carved the joint, solemnly, like a priest, while we boys sat completely still, watching. Then Mum put two slices on each plate and poured on gravy, which was so thick that she had to take care she stirred it enough so that it didn't set. And there were loads of fresh, crisp Brussels sprouts. You should put your helmet on Daniel. What if you got shrapnel in your cap?'

'Imagine if a shell hit my cap. Carry on.'

Gudbrand closed his eyes and a smile played around his mouth.

'For dessert we had stewed prunes. Or brownies. That wasn't such usual fare. Mum had brought that tradition from Brooklyn.'

Daniel spat in the snow. As a rule, watch was an hour during the winter, but both Sindre Fauke and Hallgrim Dale were in bed with temperatures, so Edvard Mosken had decided to increase it to two hours until the section was back to full strength.

Daniel put a hand on Gudbrand's shoulder.

'You miss her, don't you? Your mother.'

Gudbrand laughed, spat in the same place in the snow as Daniel and gazed up at the frozen stars in the sky. There was a rustling sound in the snow and Daniel raised his head.

'Fox,' he said.

It was unbelievable, but even here, where every square metre had been bombed and mines were closer than the cobblestones in Karl Johans gate, there was animal life. Not much, but they had both seen hares and foxes. And the odd polecat. Obviously they tried to shoot whatever they saw. Everything was welcome in the pot. But after one of the Germans had been shot while he was out catching a hare, the top brass had got it into their heads that the Russians were releasing hares in front of the trenches to tempt men out into no man's land. As if the Russians would voluntarily give away a hare!

Gudbrand fingered his sore lips and looked at his watch. One hour left to the next watch. He suspected that Sindre had been shoving tobacco up his rectum to give himself a temperature; he was the sort who would do that.

'Why did you move home from the US?' Daniel asked.

'Wall Street Crash. My father lost his job at the shipyard.'

'There you are,' Daniel said. 'That's capitalism for you. The small guys slog away while the rich get fatter whether it's boom time or a slump.'

'Well, that's the way it is.'

'That's how it's been so far, but there'll be changes now. When we win the war, Hitler's got a little surprise up his sleeve for the people. And your father won't need to worry any more about being unemployed. You should join the *Nasjonal Samling*.'

'Do you really believe in all that?'

'Don't you?'

Gudbrand didn't like to contradict Daniel so he answered with a shrug of his shoulders, but Daniel repeated the question.

'Of course I believe in it,' Gudbrand said. 'But most of all I think about Norway. About not having to have Bolsheviks in the country. If they come, we'll definitely go back to America.'

'To a capitalist country?' Daniel's voice had become a little sharper now. 'A democracy in the hands of the wealthy, left to chance and corrupt leaders?'

'I'd rather that than communism.'

'Democracies have outlived their use, Gudbrand. Just look at Europe. England and France, they were going to the dogs long before the war began: unemployment, exploitation. There are only two people strong enough to stop Europe's nosedive into chaos now: Hitler and Stalin. That's the choice we have. A sister nation or barbarians. There's almost no one at home who seems to have understood what good luck it was for us that the Germans came first and not Stalin's butchers.'

Gudbrand nodded. It wasn't only what Daniel said, it was the way he said it. With such conviction.

All of a sudden all hell broke loose and the sky in front of them was white with flares, the ground shook and yellow flashes were followed by brown earth and snow which seemed to launch themselves into the air where the shells fell.

Gudbrand already lay at the bottom of the trench with his hands over his head, but the whole thing was over as quickly as it had begun. He looked up and there, back behind the trench, behind the machine gun, Daniel was roaring with laughter.

'What are you doing?' Gudbrand shouted. 'Use the siren! Get everyone up!'

But Daniel paid no attention. 'My dear old friend,' he shouted with tears of laughter in his eyes. 'Happy New Year!'

Daniel pointed to his watch and then it dawned on Gudbrand. Daniel had obviously been waiting for the Russians' New Year salute, because now he stuck his hand down in the snow which had been piled up against the sentry post to hide the machine gun.

'Brandy,' he shouted, triumphantly raising into the air a bottle containing a heel of brown liquid. 'I've saved this for more than three months. Help yourself.'

Gudbrand had crawled up on to his knees and smiled at Daniel.

'You first,' Gudbrand shouted.

'Sure?'

'Absolutely sure, old friend. You saved it up. But don't drink it all!'

Daniel hit the side of the cork until it came out and raised the bottle.

'To Leningrad. In spring we'll be toasting each other in the Winter Palace,' he proclaimed and took off his Russian cap. 'And by summer we'll be home, hailed as heroes in our beloved Norway.'

He put the bottle to his lips and threw back his head. The brown liquid gurgled and danced in the neck of the bottle. It twinkled as the glass reflected the light from the sinking flares, and in the years to come Gudbrand would ponder whether it was that the Russian sniper saw: the gleam from the bottle. The next moment Gudbrand heard a high-pitched popping noise and saw the bottle explode in Daniel's hands. There was a shower of glass and brandy and Gudbrand closed his eyes. He could feel his face was wet; it ran down his cheeks and instinctively he stuck out his tongue to catch a couple of drops. It tasted of almost nothing, just alcohol and something else – something sweet and metallic. The consistency was thick, probably because of the cold, Gudbrand thought, and he opened his eyes again. He couldn't see Daniel from the trench. He must have dived behind the machine gun when he knew that he had been seen, Gudbrand guessed, but he could feel his heart racing.

'Daniel?'

No answer.

'Daniel?'

Gudbrand got to his feet and crawled out of the trench. Daniel was on his back with his cartridge belt under his head and the Russian cap over his face. The snow was spattered with brandy and blood. Gudbrand took the cap in his hand. Daniel was staring with wide eyes up at the starry sky. He had a large, black, gaping hole in the middle of his forehead. Gudbrand still had the sweet metallic taste in his mouth and felt nauseous.

'Daniel.'

It was barely a whisper between his dry lips. Gudbrand thought Daniel looked like a little boy who wanted to draw angels in the snow but had fallen asleep. With a sob he lurched towards the siren and pulled the crank handle. As the flares sank into their hiding places, the piercing wail of the siren rose towards the heavens.

'That wasn't how it was supposed to be,' was all Gudbrand managed to say.

ooooooooo-OOOOOOOO . . . !

Edvard and the others had come out and stood behind

him. Someone shouted Gudbrand's name, but he didn't hear. He just wound the handle round and round. In the end Edvard went over and held the handle. Gudbrand let go, but didn't turn round; he remained where he was, staring at the trench and the sky as the tears froze solid on his cheeks. The lament of the siren subsided.

'That wasn't how it was supposed to be,' he whispered.

11

Leningrad. 1 January 1943.

DANIEL ALREADY HAD ICE CRYSTALS UNDER HIS nose and in the corners of his eyes and mouth when they carried him away. Often they used to leave them until they went stiff so they would be easier to carry, but Daniel was in the way of the machine gun. So two men had dragged him to a branch off the main trench where they laid him on two ammunition boxes kept for burning. Hallgrim Dale had tied sacking around his head so they didn't have to see the death mask with its ugly grin. Edvard had rung the mass grave in the Northern Sector and explained where Daniel was. They had promised to send two corpse-bearers at some point during the night. Then Mosken had ordered Sindre out of his sick bed to take the rest of the watch with Gudbrand. The first thing they had to do was clean the spattered machine gun.

'They've bombed Cologne to smithereens,' Sindre said.

They lay side by side on the edge of the trench, in the narrow hollow where they had a view over no man's land. Gudbrand didn't like being so close to Sindre.

'And Stalingrad is going down the drain.'

Gudbrand couldn't feel the cold; it was as if his head and body were filled with cotton and nothing bothered him any longer. All he felt was the ice-cold metal burning against his skin and the numb fingers which would not obey. He tried again. The stock and the trigger mechanism already lay on the woollen rug beside him in the snow, but it was harder undoing the final piece. In Sennheim they had been trained to dismantle and reassemble a machine gun blindfold. Sennheim, in beautiful, warm, German Elsass. It was different when you couldn't feel what your fingers were doing.

'Haven't you heard?' Sindre said. 'The Russians will get us. Just as they got Gudeson.'

Gudbrand remembered the German Wehrmacht captain who had been so amused when Sindre said he came from a farm on the outskirts of a place called Toten.

'Toten. Wie im Totenreich?' the captain had laughed.

He lost his grip on the bolt.

'Fuck it!' Gudbrand's voice quivered. 'It's all the blood sticking the parts together.'

He placed the top of the little tube of gun oil against the bolt and squeezed. The cold had made the yellowish liquid thick and sluggish; he knew that oil dissolved blood. He had used gun oil when his ear had been inflamed.

Sindre leaned over and fiddled with one of the cartridges.

'Jesus Christ,' he said. He looked up and grinned, showing the brown stains between his teeth. His pale, unshaven face was so close that Gudbrand could smell the foul breath they all had here after a while. Sindre held up a finger.

'Who'd have thought Daniel had so much brain, eh?'

Gudbrand turned away.

Sindre studied the tip of his finger. 'But he didn't use it much. Otherwise he wouldn't have come back from no man's land that night. I heard you talking about going over. Well, you were certainly . . . good friends, you two, weren't you?'

Gudbrand didn't hear at first; the words were too distant. Then the echo of them reached him, and he felt the warmth surge back into his body.

'The Germans are never going to let us retreat,' Sindre

said. 'We're going to die here, every man jack of them. You should have hopped it. The Bolsheviks aren't supposed to be as brutal as Hitler to people like you and Daniel. Such good friends, I mean.'

Gudbrand didn't answer. He could feel the heat in his fingertips now.

'We thought of nipping over there tonight,' Sindre said. 'Hallgrim Dale and I. Before it was too late.'

He twisted in the snow and eyed Gudbrand.

'Don't look so shocked, Johansen,' he grinned. 'Why do you think we said we were ill?'

Gudbrand curled his toes in his boots. He could feel them now. They felt warm and good. There was something else too.

'Do you want to join us, Johansen?' Sindre asked.

The lice! He was warm, but he couldn't feel the lice. Even the whistling sound under his helmet had stopped.

'So it was you who spread the rumours,' Gudbrand said.

'Which rumours?'

'Daniel and I talked about going to America, not over to the Russians. And not now, but *after* the war.'

Sindre shrugged, looked at his watch and got on to his knees.

'I'll shoot you if you try,' Gudbrand said.

'With what?' Sindre asked, gesturing towards the gun parts on the rug. Their rifles were in the bunker and they both knew that Gudbrand wouldn't be able to get there and back before Sindre had gone.

'Stay here and die if you want, Johansen. All the best to Dale, and tell him to follow.'

Gudbrand reached inside his uniform and pulled out his bayonet. The moonlight shone on the matt steel blade. Sindre shook his head.

'People like you and Gudeson are dreamers. Put the blade away and join me. The Russians are getting new provisions across Lake Ladoga now. Fresh meat.'

'I'm no traitor,' Gudbrand said.

Sindre stood up.

'If you try to kill me with that bayonet, the Dutch listening post will hear us and sound the alarm. Use your head. Who do you think they'll believe was trying to desert? You, with all the rumours there already are about your plans to do a runner, or me, a party member?'

'Sit down, Sindre Fauke.'

Sindre laughed.

'You're no killer, Gudbrand. I'm off now. Give me fifty metres before you sound the alarm, so that you're in the clear.'

They eyed each other. Small, feather-light snowflakes had begun to fall between them. Sindre smiled: 'Moonlight and snow at the same time. That's a rare sight, isn't it?'

12

Leningrad. 2 January 1943.

THE TRENCH THE FOUR MEN WERE STANDING IN was two kilometres north of their own section of the front, at the point where the trench doubled back, almost forming a loop. The captain stood in front of Gudbrand and was stamping his feet. It was snowing and there was already a thin layer of fine snow on the top of the captain's cap. Edvard Mosken stood next to the captain and observed Gudbrand with one eye wide open, the other almost closed.

'*So,*' the captain said. '*Er ist hinüber zu den Russen geflohen?* He's gone over to the Russians, has he?'

'*Ja,*' Gudbrand said.

'*Warum?*'

'*Das weiß ich nicht.*'

The captain gazed into the distance, sucked his teeth and stamped his feet. Then he nodded to Edvard, mumbled a few words to his *Rottenführer*, the German corporal accompanying him, then they saluted. The snow crunched as they left.

'That was that,' Edvard said. He was still watching Gudbrand.

'Yes,' Gudbrand said.

'Not much of an investigation.'

'No.'

'Who would have thought it?' The one wide-open eye stared lifelessly at Gudbrand.

'Men desert all the time here,' Gudbrand said. 'They can't investigate all of —'

'I mean, who would have thought it of Sindre? Who would have thought he would do something like that?'

'Yes, you could say that,' Gudbrand said.

'On the spur of the moment. Just got up and made a run for it.'

'Right.'

'Shame about the machine gun.' Edvard's voice was cold with sarcasm.

'Yes.'

'And you couldn't call the Dutch guards, either?'

'I shouted, but it was too late. It was dark.'

'The moon was shining.'

They squared up to each other.

'Do you know what I think?' Edvard said.

'No.'

'Yes, you do. I can see it in your face. Why, Gudbrand?'

'I didn't kill him.' Gudbrand's gaze was firmly fixed on Edvard's cyclops eye. 'I tried to talk to him. He didn't want to listen to me. Then he just ran off. What could I have done?'

Both of them were breathing heavily, hunched in the wind which tore at the vapour from their mouths.

'I remember the last time you had the same expression, Gudbrand. That was the night you killed the Russian in the bunker.'

Gudbrand shrugged. Edvard laid an icy mitten on Gudbrand's arm.

'Listen. Sindre was not a good soldier, perhaps he wasn't even a good person, but we're moral individuals and we have to try to maintain a certain standard and dignity in all this. Do you understand?'

'Can I go now?'

Edvard looked at Gudbrand. The rumours about Hitler no longer triumphing on all fronts had begun to reach them now. Nevertheless, the stream of Norwegian volunteers kept growing, and Daniel and Sindre had already been replaced by two boys from Tynset. New young faces the whole time. Some you remembered, some you forgot as soon as they were gone. Daniel was one that Edvard would remember, he knew that. Just as he knew that, before long, Sindre's face would be erased from his memory. Rubbed away. Edvard Junior would be two in a few days. He didn't proceed with this line of thought.

'Yes, go,' he said. 'And keep your head down.'

'Yes, of course,' Gudbrand said. 'I'll be sure to keep my head down.'

'Do you remember what Daniel said?' Edvard asked with a sort of smile. 'He said we walked so much of the time with a stoop that we would be hunchbacks by the time we returned home.'

A machine gun cackled in the distance.

13

Leningrad. 3 January 1943.

GUDBRAND AWOKE WITH A START. HE BLINKED A couple of times and saw only the outline of the row of planks in the bunk above him. There was a smell of sour wood and earth. Had he screamed? The other men insisted they were no longer kept awake by his screams. He lay there, feeling his pulse slowly calm down. He scratched his side – the lice never slept.

It was the same dream as always that woke him. He could still feel the paws on his chest, see the yellow eyes in the dark, the white predator's teeth with the stench of blood on them and the saliva that ran and ran. And hear the terrified heaving for breath. Was it his or the predator's? The dream was like that: he was asleep and awake at the same time, but he couldn't move. The animal's jaws were about to close around his throat when the chatter of a machine gun over by the door woke him, and he saw the animal being lifted off the blanket and flung against the earthen wall of the bunker as it was torn to pieces by the bullets. Then it was quiet, and on the floor lay a blood-strewn, amorphous mass of fur. A polecat. And then the man in the doorway stepped out of the dark and into the narrow strip of moonlight, so narrow that it only lit up half of his face. But something in the dream that night had been different. The muzzle of the gun smoked as it should and the man smiled as always, but he had a large black crater in his forehead. Gudbrand could see the moon through the hole in his skull when he turned to face him.

Gudbrand felt the cold draught of air from the open door, turned his head and froze when he saw the dark figure filling the doorway. Was he still dreaming? The figure strode into the room, but it was too dark for Gudbrand to see who it was.

The figure stopped abruptly.

'Are you awake, Gudbrand?' The voice was loud and clear. It was Edvard Mosken. A displeased mumble came from the other bunks. Edvard came right up to Gudbrand's bunk.

'You've got to get up,' he said.

Gudbrand groaned. 'You haven't read the list properly. I've just come off watch. It's Dale's —'

'He's back.'

'What do you mean?'

'Dale just came and woke me. Daniel's back.'

'What are you talking about?'

In the dark, Gudbrand saw only Edvard's white breath. Then he swung his legs off the bunk and took his boots out from under the blanket. He usually kept them there when he was asleep so the damp soles wouldn't freeze. He put on his coat, which had been lying on top of the thin woollen blanket, and followed Edvard outside. The stars twinkled above them, but the night sky was growing paler in the east. Somewhere he could hear terrible sobbing. Otherwise it was strangely still.

'New Dutch recruits,' Edvard said. 'They arrived yesterday and are just back from their first trip to no man's land.'

Dale stood in the middle of the trench in an odd pose, his head tilted to one side and his arms away from his body. He had tied his scarf round his chin and his emaciated face with closed eyes in deep sockets made him look like a beggar.

'Dale!' came the sharp command from Edvard. Dale woke up.

'Show us.'

Dale led the way. Gudbrand could feel his heart pumping faster. The cold bit into his cheeks; he still hadn't managed to freeze out the warm, dreamlike feeling he had brought with him from his bunk. The trench was so narrow that they had to walk in single file, and he could feel Edvard's eyes in his back.

'Here,' Dale said, pointing.

The wind whistled a hoarse tune under the rim of the helmet. On the ammunition boxes was a body with its limbs splayed stiffly out to the sides. The snow which had drifted into the trench had left a thin layer on top of the uniform. Sacking was tied round the head of the corpse.

'Fucking hell,' Dale said. He shook his head and stamped his feet.

Edvard didn't say a word. Gudbrand reckoned he was waiting for him.

'Why haven't the corpse-bearers collected him?' Gudbrand asked finally.

'They *did* collect him,' Edvard said. 'They were here yesterday afternoon.'

'So why did they bring him back?' Gudbrand noticed that Edvard was eyeing him.

'No one on the general staff knows of any orders to bring him back.'

'A misunderstanding?' Gudbrand said.

'Maybe.' Edvard flicked a thin, half-smoked cigarette out of a packet, turned away from the wind and lit it with a cupped match. He passed it on after a couple of drags.

'The men who took him maintain he was put in one of the mass graves in the Northern Sector.'

'If that's true, shouldn't he be buried?'

Edvard shook his head.

'They aren't buried until they've been burned. And they

only burn during the day so that the Russians can't take advantage of the light. And at night the new mass graves are open and unguarded. Someone must have taken Daniel from there.'

'Fucking hell,' Dale said again, taking the cigarette and inhaling greedily.

'So it's really true that they burn the bodies,' Gudbrand said. 'What for? In this cold?'

'I know that,' Dale said. 'It's because the ground is frozen. When the temperature rises in springtime, the earth pushes bodies upwards.' He reluctantly passed on the cigarette. 'Last winter we buried Vorpenes a long way behind our lines. In the spring we stumbled across him again. Well, what the foxes had left of him at any rate.'

'The question is,' Edvard said. 'How did Daniel end up here?'

Gudbrand shrugged.

'You had the last watch, Gudbrand.' Edvard had screwed up one eye and turned the cyclops eye on him. Gudbrand took his time with the cigarette. Dale coughed.

'I walked past here four times,' Gudbrand said, sending on the cigarette. 'He wasn't here then.'

'You could have gone up to the Northern Sector during your watch. And there are sledge tracks over here in the snow.'

'Could have been left by the corpse-bearers,' Gudbrand said.

'The tracks are over the last boot prints. And you say you walked past here four times.'

'Hell, Edvard, I can see it's Daniel over there too!' Gudbrand exploded. 'Of course someone put him there, and probably using a sledge. But if you're listening to what I'm saying you must be able to see that someone brought him here *after* I passed for the last time.'

Edvard didn't answer; instead, visibly annoyed, he ripped the final couple of centimetres of the cigarette out of Dale's pursed mouth and stared disapprovingly at the wet marks on the cigarette paper. Dale picked the shreds of tobacco off his tongue and scowled.

'Why in God's name would I bother with something like this?' Gudbrand asked. 'And how could I possibly drag a body from the Northern Sector over here without being stopped by patrols?'

'You could have gone through no man's land.'

Gudbrand shook his head in disbelief. 'Do you think I've gone mad, Edvard? What would I want with Daniel's body?'

Edvard took the last two drags of the cigarette, dropped the end in the snow and trod it in with his boot. He always did that, he didn't know why, but he couldn't stand the sight of smoking cigarette ends. The snow gave with a groan as he twisted his heel.

'No, I don't think you dragged Daniel here,' Edvard said. 'Because I don't think it's Daniel.'

Dale and Gudbrand recoiled.

'Of course it's Daniel,' Gudbrand said.

'Or someone with the same build,' Edvard said. 'And the same unit insignia on the uniform.'

'The sacking . . .'

'So you can see a difference in the sacking, can you?' Edvard jeered, but it was Gudbrand he was watching.

'It's Daniel,' Gudbrand said with a swallow. 'I recognise the boots.'

'So you think we should just call the corpse-bearers and ask them to take him away again, do you?' Edvard asked. 'Without taking a closer look. That was what you were counting on, wasn't it?'

'Go to hell, Edvard!'

'I'm not so sure it's my turn this time, Gudbrand. Take off the sacking, Dale.'

Dale gaped at the other two, who were glowering at each other like two rampant bulls.

'Do you hear me?' Edvard shouted. 'Cut away the sacking!'

'I'd prefer not to —'

'It's an order. This minute!'

Dale continued to hesitate. He looked from one to the other and at the rigid corpse on the ammunition chests. Then he shrugged his shoulders, unbuttoned his jacket and put his hand inside.

'Wait!' Edvard shouted. 'Ask if you can borrow Gudbrand's bayonet.'

Now Dale really was at sea. He looked quizzically at Gudbrand, who was shaking his head.

'What do you mean?' Edvard asked, still face to face with Gudbrand. 'Your standing orders are that you must always carry a bayonet, and you don't have one on you?'

Gudbrand didn't answer.

'You, the ultimate killing machine with a bayonet, Gudbrand. You haven't simply lost it, have you?'

Gudbrand still didn't answer.

'In that case, yes, you'll have to use your own, Dale.'

Gudbrand felt an irrepressible urge to tear the large staring eye out of the section leader's head. *Rottenführer*, that's what he was! Or rather a 'Rat-führer'. A rat with a rat's eyes and a rat's brain. Didn't he understand anything?

They heard a ripping noise behind them as the bayonet cut through the sacking, then a gasp from Dale. Both men whirled round. There, in the red light of the dawning day, a white face with a hideous grin stared up at them with a third black gaping eye in the forehead. It was Daniel alright, no question about it.

14

Ministry of Foreign Affairs.
4 November 1999.

BERNT BRANDHAUG LOOKED AT HIS WATCH AND
frowned. Eighty-two seconds, seven more than usual. Then
he strode over the threshold to the meeting room, sang out
his hearty 'Good morning' and smiled his famous white smile
to the four faces turned towards him.

Kurt Meirik, POT, sat on one side of the table with Rakel
(complete with unbecoming hairslide, power suit and severe
expression). It struck him that the suit seemed a little too
expensive for a secretary. He still held to his intuition that
she was divorced, but perhaps she had married well. Or did
she have wealthy parents? The fact that she was here again,
at a meeting that Brandhaug had signalled should take
place in total privacy, suggested she was higher up in POT
than he had at first assumed. He determined to find out
more about her.

Anne Størksen sat on the other side of the table with the
tall, thin Crime Squad boss, what was his name? First of all
it took him more than eighty seconds to get to the meeting
room, and now he couldn't remember a name — was he getting old?

He hadn't even thought this through to the end when the

previous night's events came back into his mind. He had invited Lise, the young Foreign Office probationer, out to what he called a little working lunch. Afterwards he offered her a drink at the Continental Hotel where, under the auspices of the Foreign Office, he had a permanent room at his disposal for meetings which required a little more discretion. Lise had not been difficult to ask out, she was an ambitious girl. But it had gone badly. A one-off, a drink too many perhaps, but surely he wasn't getting too old. Brandhaug shoved the idea to the back of his mind and sat down.

'Thank you for being able to come at such short notice,' he began. 'The confidential nature of this meeting does not need to be emphasised, of course, but I will do so anyway since not everyone has had so much experience of the business in hand.'

He cast a swift glance at everyone except Rakel, making it clear that the message was intended for her. Then he turned towards Anne Størksen.

'By the way, how is your man?'

The Chief Constable looked at him in some confusion.

'Your *police* man?' Brandhaug hastened to say. 'Hole, isn't that what he's called?'

She nodded to Møller, who had to clear his throat twice before he got going.

'Fine, under the circumstances. He's shaken of course. But . . . OK.' He shrugged to show that there wasn't a lot more to say.

Brandhaug raised a recently plucked eyebrow.

'Not so shaken that there might be the risk of a leak, I trust?'

'Erm,' Møller said. He saw the Chief Constable quickly turn towards him with a sidelong glance. 'I don't believe so. He's aware of the delicate nature of the matter. And of course he has been sworn to secrecy about what happened.'

'The same is true for the other police officers involved at the scene,' Anne Størksen added with alacrity.

'Let's hope this is under control then,' Brandhaug said. 'I'll just give you a brief update on the situation. I have just had a long conversation with the American ambassador and I believe I may say that we have agreed on the most important points in this tragic matter.'

He looked at each of them in turn. They gazed at him in an atmosphere of tense expectation. Waited for what he, Bernt Brandhaug, could tell them. The despondency he had felt a few seconds before seemed to have been erased.

'The ambassador was able to tell me that the Secret Service agent whom your man', – he motioned towards Møller and the Chief Constable – 'shot at the toll barrier is in a stable condition and he is off the danger list. His dorsal vertebrae are damaged and there is internal haemorrhaging, but the bulletproof vest saved him. I regret that we were unable to discover this information earlier, but for understandable reasons we have attempted to keep all communication about this affair to a minimum. Only the most essential details have been exchanged between a small number of involved parties.'

'Where is he?' Møller asked.

'Strictly speaking, you don't need to know that, Inspector Møller.'

He looked at Møller, whose face had assumed a strange expression. There was an oppressive silence in the room for a second. It was always a little embarrassing when someone had to be reminded that they were not allowed to know more than they needed for their job. Brandhaug smiled and spread his hands in regret as if to say: *I can well understand you asking, but that's the way it is.* Møller nodded and looked down at the table.

'OK,' Brandhaug said. 'I can tell you this much – after the operation he was flown to a military hospital in Germany.'

'Right.' Møller scratched the back of his neck. 'Erm . . .'

Brandhaug waited.

'I assume it's fine to let Hole know this? That the SS

agent is recovering, I mean. It will make the situation . . .
um . . . easier for him.'

Brandhaug looked at Møller. He had difficulty working
out the head of Crime Squad.

'That's fine.'

'What was it that you and the ambassador agreed on?' It
was Rakel.

'I'm coming to that,' Brandhaug said gently. Actually it
was his next point, but he disliked being interrupted in
this way. 'First of all, I would like to commend Møller and
the Oslo police on their quick appraisal at the scene. If the
reports are correct, it took a mere twelve minutes for the
agent to receive professional medical attention.'

'Hole and his colleague, Ellen Gjelten, drove him to Aker
Hospital,' Anne Størksen said.

'Admirably quick reactions,' Brandhaug said. 'And that is
a view which is shared by the American ambassador.'

Møller and the Chief Constable exchanged glances.

'Furthermore, the ambassador has spoken to the Secret
Service and there is no question of instituting proceedings
from the American side. Naturally.'

'Naturally,' Meirik chimed in.

'We also agreed that the error resided in the main with
the Americans. The agent in the toll booth should never have
been there. That is, it was permitted, but the Norwegian liaison officer at the scene should have been notified. The Norwegian policeman who was at the post at which the agent came
into the zone, and who should have – sorry, *could* have –
informed the liaison officer, reacted only to the ID the agent
showed him. The standing orders were that Secret Service
agents had access to all secure areas, and the policeman
therefore saw no reason to report it further. In retrospect, we
may say that he *ought* to have done.'

He looked at Anne Størksen, who gave no indication that
she would protest.

'The good news is that at this juncture it does not appear that anything has come out. I have not, however, called this meeting to discuss what we should do as a best-case scenario, which is precious little more than sit tight. I presume we do not need to consider such a thing. It would be absurdly naive to believe that this shooting incident will not leak out sooner or later.'

Bernt Brandhaug cupped his palms up and down as if to bundle the sentences into suitable sound bites.

'In addition to the twenty-odd people from POT, the FO and the co-ordination group who know about this matter, there were approximately fifteen police witnesses at the toll barrier. I do not wish to say a bad word about any of them. I am sure they will, on the whole, observe the customary pledges of secrecy. Nevertheless, they are ordinary police officers without any experience of the degree of secrecy which is necessary in these circumstances. There are, furthermore, employees at the Rikshospital, the airline, the toll company Fjellinje AS and the Plaza Hotel, who all, to a greater or lesser degree, have reason to be suspicious about what happened. There is no guarantee either that the motorcade was not being followed through binoculars from one of the surrounding buildings. One word from anyone who had anything to do with this and . . .' He blew out his cheeks to represent an explosion.

It went quiet around the table until Møller cleared his throat.

'And why is it so . . . um . . . dangerous if it comes out?'

Brandhaug nodded to demonstrate that this was not the most stupid question he had heard, which immediately gave Møller the intended sense that this was exactly what it was.

'The United States of America is more than just an ally,' Brandhaug began with an imperceptible smile. He said it with the same intonation that you use to explain to a non-Norwegian that Norway has a king and that the capital is Oslo.

'In 1920 Norway was one of Europe's poorest countries and probably still would be, had it not been for America's help. Forget politicians' rhetoric. Emigration, Marshall Aid, Elvis and the financing of the oil adventure have turned Norway into probably one of the most pro-American countries in the world. Those of us sitting here have worked for years to attain the positions we have in our careers today. But should it come to the ears of our politicians that anyone in this room is responsible for endangering the life of the President . . .'

Brandhaug left the rest of the sentence hanging in the air as he cast his eyes around the table.

'Fortunately for us,' he said, 'the Americans would rather concede a glitch with one of their Secret Service agents than concede a fundamental lack of co-operation with one of their closest allies.'

'That means', said Rakel without glancing up from the pad in front of her, '. . . that we do not need a Norwegian scapegoat.' Then she raised her eyes and looked directly at Bernt Brandhaug. 'Quite the contrary. We need a Norwegian hero, don't we?'

Brandhaug rested his gaze on her with a mixture of surprise and interest. Surprise because she had known so quickly where he was heading, and interest because he had realised she was definitely someone to be reckoned with.

'That's correct. The day it leaks out that a Norwegian policeman has shot a Secret Service agent, we have to have our version of events straight,' he said. 'And our version must be that nothing untoward happened on our side. Our liaison officer at the scene acted according to instructions and the blame lies solely with the Secret Service agent. This is a version both we and the Americans can live with. The challenge is getting the media to buy it. And that is why —'

'— we need a hero,' the Chief Constable added.

'Excuse me,' Møller said. 'Am I the only person here who doesn't get the nub of this?' He made a relatively unsuccessful attempt to add a brief chuckle.

'The officer showed presence of mind in what was a potentially threatening situation for the President,' Brandhaug said. 'If the person in the booth had been an assassin, which he was obliged to assume, in line with instructions laid down for this particular scenario, he would have saved the President's life. The fact that the individual turned out not to be an assassin doesn't change anything.'

'That's right,' Anne Størksen said. 'In such situations instructions take precedence over personal assessment.'

Meirik didn't say anything, but nodded in assent.

'Good,' Brandhaug said. 'The "nub", as you call it, Bjarne, is to convince the press, our superiors and everyone who has had any dealings with this case that we have had not a second's doubt that our liaison officer acted correctly. The "nub" is that we must behave as if to all practical intents and purposes he performed an heroic deed.'

Brandhaug could see Møller's consternation.

'Were we not to reward the officer, we would already have half-admitted that he made an error of judgment in shooting the agent, and, accordingly, that the security arrangements during the President's visit were wanting.'

Nods of assent around the table.

'Ergo . . .' Brandhaug said. He loved the word. It was a word clothed in armour, almost invincible because it called upon the authority of logic. *From this it follows that.*

'Ergo, we give him a medal?' It was Rakel again.

Brandhaug felt a twinge of irritation. The way she said 'medal'. As if they were writing the manuscript of a comedy in which all sorts of amusing suggestions were pounced on with enthusiasm. That his presentation was a comedy.

'No,' he said slowly, with emphasis. 'Not a medal. Medals and distinctions do not have the gravitas. Nor do they give us the credibility we are after.' He leaned back in the chair, his hands behind his head. 'Let's promote the guy. Let's make him an inspector.'

A long silence ensued.

'Inspector?' Bjarne Møller stared at Brandhaug in disbelief. 'For shooting a Secret Service agent?'

'It may sound a little macabre, but give it some thought.'

'It's . . .' Møller blinked and seemed to be on the point of saying a great deal, but he chose to keep his mouth shut.

'He does not have to perform the same duties that usually pertain to the rank of inspector,' Brandhaug heard the Chief Constable say. The words came with some hesitation. As if threading cotton through the eye of a needle.

'We have given this a little thought too, Anne,' he answered with gentle emphasis on her name. It was the first time he had used her Christian name. One of her eyebrows gave a slight jerk, but otherwise he didn't see anything to suggest that she objected. He continued: 'The problem is that if all the colleagues of this trigger-happy liaison officer of yours consider the promotion conspicuous and start to think of the title as window-dressing, then we haven't got very far. That is, we haven't got anywhere at all. If they suspect a cover-up, rumours will immediately begin to fly, and we will give the impression that we have consciously tried to hide the fact that we, you, this policeman, committed a blunder. In other words, we have to give him a post where it seems reasonable that no one can keep too close an eye on what he is actually doing. Put another way, a promotion combined with a move to a screened operation.'

'A screened operation. A free hand.' Rakel gave a wry smile. 'Sounds like you're thinking of sending him over to us.'

'What do you think, Kurt?' Brandhaug said.

Kurt Meirik scratched behind his ear while chuckling quietly.

'Yes,' he said. 'We can always find a home for an inspector, I reckon.'

Brandhaug bowed. 'That would be a great help.'

'Yes, we have to help each other when we can.'

'Terrific,' Brandhaug said with a broad smile and a glance at the clock on the wall to indicate that the meeting was over. Chairs scraped.

15

Sanksthanshaugen. 4 November 1999.

OVER THE SPEAKERS, PRINCE WAS PARTYING LIKE
it was 1999.

Ellen looked over at Tom Waaler, who had just that minute shoved a cassette into the machine and turned up the
volume so loud that the bass was making the dashboard vi-
brate. Prince's shrill falsetto pierced her eardrums.

'Groovy or what?' Tom shouted above the music. Ellen
didn't really want to offend him, so she simply shook her
head. Not that she had any preconceptions that Tom Waaler
was easy to offend, but she had decided not to go against the
grain for as long as it was possible. She hoped until the pairing of Tom Waaler with Ellen Gjelten came to an end. Bjarne
Møller, the head of their section, had definitely said that the
pairing was only provisional. Everyone knew that Tom would
get the new inspector's post in the spring.

'Black poof,' Tom shouted. '*Too* much.'

Ellen didn't answer. It was raining so hard that, even with
the wipers on full speed, the water lay like a soft filter on the
windscreen and made the buildings in Ullevålsveien look
like soft toy houses undulating to and fro. Møller had sent

them off this morning to find Harry. They had already rung his flat in Sofies gate and established that he was not at home. Or he didn't want to open up. Or he wasn't *capable* of opening up. Ellen feared the worst. She watched people hurrying along the pavement. They had distorted, bizarre features too, like in crazy mirrors at the fair.

'Turn left here and pull over outside Schrøder's,' she said. 'You can wait in the car and I'll go in.'

'Fine with me,' Waaler said. 'Drunks are the worst.'

She glanced at him from the side, but his expression didn't betray whether he meant Schrøder's morning clientele in general or Harry in particular. He pulled into the bus stop outside and as Ellen got out she saw that a Kaffebrenneri had opened on the other side of the street. Or perhaps it had been there for ages and she simply hadn't noticed it. On the bar stools along the windows young people in roll-necked sweaters sat reading foreign newspapers or staring out into the rain, holding large white coffee cups between their hands, presumably wondering if they had chosen the right subject at university, the right designer sofa, the right partner, the right football club or the right European town.

In the doorway to Schrøder's she almost bumped into a man wearing an Icelandic sweater. The alcohol had washed nearly all the blue from his irises; his hands were as big as frying pans and black with dirt. Ellen caught the sweet smell of sweat and stale alcohol as he sailed past. Inside, there was a slow morning atmosphere. Only four of the tables were occupied. Ellen had been there before, a long time ago, and as far as she could determine nothing had changed. Large pictures of Oslo in centuries past hung on the walls, and the brown paintwork and the faux glass ceiling in the middle gave it a little of the feel of an English pub. *Very* little, if you were absolutely honest. The plastic tables and benches made it look more like the smokers' saloon bar on a ferry along the Møre coast. At the back of the room a waitress wearing an apron was leaning against a counter and smoking while keeping half an eye on Ellen. Harry was sitting right in the corner near the window with his head down over the table. A half-empty beer glass in front of him.

'Hi,' Ellen said, taking a seat opposite him.

Harry looked up and nodded. As if he had been waiting exclusively for her. His head slipped down again.

'We've been trying to get hold of you. We rang your flat.'

'Was I at home?' he said in a flat tone, no smile.

'I don't know. Are you at home, Harry?' She indicated the glass.

He shrugged.

'He's going to live,' she said.

'I heard. Møller left a message on my answerphone.' His diction was surprisingly clear. 'He didn't say how badly injured he was. Plenty of nerves and stuff in the back, aren't there?'

He cocked his head, but Ellen didn't answer.

'Perhaps he'll only be paralysed?' Harry said, tapping his now-empty glass. '*Skål*.'

'Your sick leave runs out tomorrow,' she said. 'Then we'll be expecting to see you back on the job.'

He raised his head. 'Am I on sick leave?'

Ellen pushed a little plastic folder across the table. The back of a pink piece of paper could be seen inside.

'I've been talking to Møller. And Dr Aune. Take this copy of the sick leave form. Møller said it was normal to have a few days off to recover after a shooting incident in the line of duty. Come in tomorrow.'

His gaze shifted to the window with its coloured, uneven glass. Presumably for reasons of discretion, so that people inside could not be seen from the outside. The exact opposite of Kaffebrenneri, Ellen thought.

'Well? Are you coming?'

'Well,' he looked at her with the same glazed eyes she remembered from the mornings after he returned from Bangkok, 'I wouldn't bet on it.'

'Come anyway. There are a couple of amusing surprises waiting for you.'

'Surprises?' Harry laughed softly. 'I wonder what that could be? Early retirement? Honourable dismissal? Will the President give me the Purple Heart?'

He raised his head enough for Ellen to see his bloodshot eyes. She sighed and turned towards the window. Behind the rough glass, shapeless cars slid by, as in a psychedelic film.

'Why do you do this to yourself, Harry? You know, I know, *everyone* knows it wasn't your fault! Even the Secret Service admits it was their fault we weren't informed. And that we – you – acted properly.'

Harry spoke in a low voice without looking at her: 'Do you think his family will see it like that when he comes home in a wheelchair?'

'My God, Harry!' Ellen had raised her voice and saw that the woman at the counter was watching them with increasing interest. She could probably smell a juicy quarrel brewing.

'There are always some unlucky ones, some who don't make it, Harry. That's the way it is. It's no one's fault. Did you know that every year 60 per cent of all hedge sparrows die? 60 per cent! If we were to down tools and ponder the meaning of it, before we knew what was going on, we would end up among the 60 per cent ourselves, Harry.'

Harry didn't answer. He sat bobbing his head up and down over the checked tablecloth with black cigarette burns.

'I'm going to hate myself for saying this, Harry, but I would regard it as a personal favour if you would come tomorrow. Just turn up. I won't talk to you and you don't breathe on me, OK?'

Harry put his little finger through one of the holes in the cloth. Then he moved his glass so it covered one of the other holes. Ellen waited.

'Is that Waaler waiting in the car outside?' Harry asked.

Ellen nodded. She knew exactly how badly the two of them got on. She had an idea, wavered, then took the risk:

'He's got two hundred kroner on you not making an appearance.'

Harry laughed his soft laugh again. Then he supported his head on his hands and looked at her.

'You're a really bad liar, Ellen. But thank you for trying.'

'Fuck you.'

She drew in breath, was going to say something but changed her mind and observed Harry for a while. Then she breathed in again.

'OK, it's actually Møller who should tell you this, but now I'll tell you: they're going to make you an inspector in POT.'

Harry's laughter purred like the engine of a Cadillac Fleetwood. 'Alright, with a little practice, perhaps you won't be such a bad liar after all.'

'It's true!'

'It's impossible.' His gaze wandered out of the window again.

'Why? You're one of our best detectives. You've just proved you're a damned good policeman. You read law. You —'

'It's impossible, I'm telling you. Even if someone has come up with the crazy idea.'

'But why?'

'For a very simple reason. Wasn't it 60 per cent of those birds, you said?'

He pulled the tablecloth and the glass across the table.

'They're called hedge sparrows.'

'Right. And what do they die of?'

'What do you mean?'

'They don't just lie down and die, do they?'

'Of hunger. Predators. Cold. Exhaustion. Flying into windows perhaps. Anything and everything.'

'OK. I bet none of them is shot in the back by a Norwegian policeman without a firearms permit because he didn't pass the shooting test. A policeman who, as soon as this is discovered, will be prosecuted and probably sentenced to between

one and three years in prison. A pretty dodgy basis for promotion to inspector, don't you think?'

He lifted his glass and slammed it down on the plastic
folder.

'Which shooting test?' she asked.

He gave her a sharp look. She met his eyes with an expression of confidence.

'What do you mean?' he asked.

'I've no idea what you're talking about, Harry.'

'You know bloody well that —'

'As far as I'm aware, you passed the shooting test this
year. And Møller is of the same opinion. He even took a walk
to the gun-licensing office this morning to check with the
shooting instructor. They went through the files and, as far
as they could see, you had scored more than enough points
to pass. They don't make POT inspectors out of people who
shoot at Secret Service agents without proper accreditation,
you know.'

She flashed a broad smile to Harry, who now seemed more
bewildered than drunk.

'But I haven't got a gun licence!'

'Yes, you have. You just lost it. You'll find it, Harry,
you'll find it.'

'Now listen. I . . .'

He paused and stared down at the plastic folder in front
of him on the table. Ellen stood up.

'See you at nine, Inspector.'

All Harry could manage was a mute nod.

16

Radisson SAS, Holbergs Plass.
5 November 1999.

BETTY ANDRESEN HAD SUCH BLONDE, CURLY,
Dolly Parton hair it looked like a wig. It was not a wig, however, and all similarities with Dolly Parton finished with the
hair. Betty Andresen was tall and thin, and when she smiled,
as she was doing now, the crack in her mouth was small and
barely revealed her teeth. This smile was directed at the old
man on the other side of the desk in the reception area of the
Radisson SAS Hotel in Holbergs plass. It wasn't a reception
desk in the general understanding of the term, but one of several multi-functional 'islands' with computer monitors, which
allowed them to serve a number of guests at the same time.

'Good morning,' Betty Andresen said. That was something she had picked up at the hotel management school in
Stavanger, to distinguish between different times of the day
when she greeted people. Thus in six hours' time she would
say, 'Good afternoon,' and two hours later, 'Good evening.'
Then she would go home to her two-room apartment in Tor-
shov and wish there were someone to whom she could say,
'Good night.'

'I'd like to see a room as high up as possible.'

Betty Andresen stared at the dripping wet shoulders of

the old man's coat. It was pouring outside. A quivering rain-drop clung to the brim of his hat.

'You want to *see* a room?'

Betty Andresen's smile didn't flinch. She had been trained according to the principle, which she observed religiously, that everyone was to be treated as a guest until the opposite was proven irrefutably. But she knew equally well that what she had in front of her was an example of the genus: old-man-visiting-the-capital-who-would-like-to-see-the-view-from-the-SAS-hotel-without-paying. They were still coming here, particularly in the summer. And it wasn't only to see the view. Once a woman had asked to see the Palace Suite on the twenty-first floor so that she could describe it to her friends and tell them that she had stayed there. She had even offered Betty fifty kroner if she would enter her name in the guest book so that she could use it as proof.

'Single room or double?' Betty asked. 'Smoker or non-smoker?' Most started to falter at that point.

'Doesn't make any difference,' the old man said. 'The most important thing is the view. I'd like to see one facing south-west.'

'Yes, you'll be able to see the whole town from there.'

'Quite so. What is the best room you have?'

'The best is obviously the Palace Suite, but wait a moment. Shall I check if we have a standard room available?'

She clattered away on the keyboard and waited to see if he would take the bait. It didn't take long.

'I'd like to see the suite.'

Of course you would, she thought. She cast her eye over the old man. Betty was not an unreasonable woman. If an old man's greatest wish was to see the view from the SAS hotel, she wouldn't stand in his way.

'Let's go and have a look,' she said, flashing her most radiant smile, which was usually reserved for regular guests.

'Are you visiting someone here in Oslo?' she asked out of politeness in the lift.

'No,' the old man said. He had white bushy eyebrows like her father.

Betty pressed the lift button, the doors slid to and the lift was set in motion. She never got used to it – it was like being sucked up to heaven. The doors slid open and, as always, she half expected she would come out into a new and different world, more or less like the girl in *The Wizard of Oz*. But it was always the same old world. They walked through the corridors with matching wallpaper and carpets and expensive art on the walls. She put the key card in the lock of the suite, then said, 'After you,' and held the door open for the man, who slipped by with what she interpreted as an air of expectation.

'The Palace Suite measures 105 square metres,' Betty said. 'The suite has two bedrooms, each with their own king-size bed, and two bathrooms, each with Jacuzzi and telephone.'

She went into the room where the old man had taken up a position by the window.

'The furniture was designed by Poul Henriksen, a Danish designer,' she said, stroking her hand over the paper-thin glass top on the coffee table. 'Perhaps you would like to see the bathrooms?'

The old man didn't answer. He had kept his soaking-wet hat on, and in the silence that followed Betty heard a drip land on the cherrywood parquet floor. She stood beside him. From here they could see everything that was worth seeing: the Town Hall, the National Theatre, the Palace, the Norwegian Parliament – the Storting – and Akershus Fortress. Beneath them lay the Palace Gardens, where the trees pointed up towards a leaden grey sky with black splayed witches' fingers.

'You ought to come here on a fine spring day,' Betty said.

The old man turned and sent her an uncomprehending look, and Betty realised what she had just said. She might as well have added: *Since you have only come here to take in the view.*

She passed it off with a smile as well as she could. 'When the grass is green and the leaves are on the trees in the Palace Gardens. It's absolutely beautiful then.'

He studied her face, but his thoughts appeared to be elsewhere.

'You're right,' he said at last. 'Trees have leaves. I didn't think about that.'

He pointed to the window. 'Does this open?'

'A little,' Betty said, relieved at the change of topic. 'You twist the handle there.'

'Why only a little?'

'In case someone should get any silly ideas.'

'Silly ideas?'

She shot him a quick glance. Was the old man going a bit senile?

'Take a hike,' she said. 'Commit suicide, I mean. There are a lot of unhappy people who . . .' She made a gesture with her hand which was intended to illustrate what unhappy people do.

'So that's a silly idea, is it?' The old man rubbed his chin. Did she detect the hint of a smile among the wrinkles? 'Even if you're unhappy?'

'Yes,' Betty said resolutely. 'At least, in this hotel while I'm on duty.'

'While I'm on duty.' The old man chuckled. 'That was a good one, Betty Andresen.'

The mention of her name made her jump. Of course, he had read it on her name tag. There was nothing wrong with his eyesight then; the letters forming her name were as small as the letters of RECEPTIONIST were large. She pretended to take a discreet peek at the clock.

'Yes,' he said. 'You've probably got other more important things to do.'

'I suppose I have,' she said.

'I'll take it,' the old man said.

'I beg your pardon?'

'I'll take the room. Not for tonight, but —'

'You're taking the room?'

'Yes. It is available for booking, isn't it?'

'Mm, yes it is, but . . . it's terribly expensive.'

'I prefer to pay in advance.'

The old man pulled out a wallet from his inside pocket and removed a wad of notes.

'No, no, I didn't mean it like that, but 7,000 for one night. You wouldn't rather see —?'

'I like this room,' the old man said. 'Please count it, just in case.'

Betty stared at the thousand-kroner notes he wafted in front of her.

'We can sort out the payment when you come,' she said. 'Mm, when would you like to . . . ?'

'As you recommended, Betty. One day in the spring.'

'Right. Any particular day?'

'Of course.'

17

Police HQ. 5 November 1999.

BJARNE MØLLER SIGHED AND GAZED OUT OF THE window. His thoughts wandered freely as they had tended to do of late. The rain had held off, although the leaden grey sky still hung low over police HQ in Grønland. A dog trotted over the brown, lifeless lawn outside. There was a Crime Squad post vacant in Bergen. The deadline for applications was next week. He had heard from a colleague over there that it only rained twice every autumn in Bergen: from September to November, and from November to New Year. They always exaggerated, folk from Bergen did. He'd been there and he liked the town. It was a long way from the politicians in Oslo and it was small. He liked small.

'What?' Møller turned and met Harry's resigned expression.

'You were in the process of explaining to me that a move would do me good.'

'Oh?'

'Your words, boss.'

'Oh yes. Yes, that's right. We have to make sure we don't get stuck in a rut, with old habits and routines. We have to move on and develop. We have to get away.'

'There's getting away and getting away. POT is only three floors up.'

'Get away from everything, I mean. The head of the Security Service, Meirik, thinks you'll fit superbly into the post he has for you up there.'

'Don't jobs like that have to be advertised?'

'Don't worry about it, Harry.'

'No? But can I be allowed to wonder why on earth you want me in surveillance work. Do I look like undercover material?'

'No, no.'

'No?'

'I mean yes. Not *yes* exactly, but well . . . why not?'

'Why not?'

Møller scratched the back of his head furiously. His face had turned fiery red.

'For fuck's sake, Harry. We're offering you a job as an inspector, five notches up the pay scale, no more night shifts and a bit more respect from the bloody rookies. That's good going, Harry.'

'I like night shifts.'

'No one likes night shifts.'

'Why don't you give me the vacant inspector's post here?'

'Harry! Do me a favour and just say yes.'

Harry fidgeted with his paper cup. 'Boss,' he said. 'How long have we known each other?'

Møller raised an admonitory finger. 'Don't try that one on me. Not the we've-been-through-thick-and-thin-together number . . .'

'Seven years. And for seven years I've interviewed people in this city who are probably the most stupid beings to walk on two legs, and still I haven't met anyone who is a worse liar than you. Perhaps I'm stupid, but I still have a couple of brain cells left doing the best they can, and they're telling me that it can't exactly be my record that's earned me this post. Nor that, to my astonishment, I can suddenly have one of the best scores in the department at the annual shooting test. They're telling me that my plugging a Secret Service agent might have something to do with it. And you don't need to say a thing, boss.'

Møller opened his mouth, closed it again and instead demonstratively crossed his arms.

Harry continued: 'I know you're not responsible for putting on this show. And even if I can't see the whole picture, I have some imagination and I can guess the rest. If I'm right, it means that my own wishes regarding other options for my career in the police are of minor importance. So just answer me this. Have I any choice?'

Møller blinked, and kept blinking. He was thinking about Bergen again. Of snow-free winters. Of Sunday outings with his wife and boys on Mount Fløyen. Somewhere decent to grow up. A few good-natured pranks, a bit of hash, no criminal gangs and no fourteen-year-olds taking overdoses. Bergen police station. Yeah, well.

'No,' he said.

'Right,' Harry said. 'I didn't think so.' He crumpled the paper cup and took aim at the waste-paper basket. 'Up five pay grades, did you say?'

'And your own office.'

'Nicely partitioned off from the others, I would imagine.' He threw with a slow, deliberate arm movement. 'Overtime?'

'Not at that grade.'

'Then I'll have to hurry home at four.' The paper cup landed on the floor half a metre from the bin.

'I'm sure that's fine,' Møller said with a suggestion of a smile.

18

Palace Gardens. 10 November 1999.

IT WAS A COLD, CLEAR EVENING. THE FIRST
thing that struck the old man as he came out of the Metro
station was how many people were still in the street. He had
imagined that the centre would be almost deserted, but the
taxis in Karl Johans gate were shooting back and forth under the neon lights, and crowds of people were drifting up
and down the pavements. He stood at a pedestrian crossing
with a gang of swarthy youths jabbering away in another language and waited for the green man. He guessed they were
Pakistani. Or Arab perhaps. His thoughts were interrupted
by the changing lights and he stepped purposefully across
the road and up the hill towards the illuminated façade of the
Palace. Even here there were people, most of them young,
on their way to and from God-only-knew what. On the hill
he stopped for a breather, in front of the statue of Karl Johan
astride his horse, staring dreamily down towards the Storting and the power he had tried to have moved to the Palace
behind him.

It hadn't rained for over a week and the dried leaves
rustled as the old man turned right between the trees in the
gardens. He leaned back and studied the bare branches

outlined against the starry sky above. A verse from a poem
occurred to him:

> *Elm and poplar, birch and oak,*
> *Deathly pale, blackened cloak.*

*It would have been better if there hadn't been a moon this
evening,* he thought. On the other hand, it made it easier to
find what he was looking for: the huge oak tree he had rested
his head against the day he learned his life was approaching
its end. He followed the trunk with his eyes up to the crown
of the tree. How old could it be? Two hundred years? Three
hundred? The tree might already have been fully grown when
Karl Johan was proclaimed King of Norway. Nevertheless,
all life comes to an end. His own, the tree's, yes, even kings'
lives. He stood behind the tree so that he could not be seen
from the path and eased off his rucksack. Then he crouched
down, opened the rucksack and laid out the contents: three
bottles of a glyphosate solution, which the sales assistant in
a hardware shop in Kirkeveien had called Round-Up, and a
horse syringe with a strong steel point, which he bought at a
chemist's. He had said he was going to use the syringe for
cooking, to inject fat into meat, but that had been unnecessary because the assistant had just given him a bored look
and had probably forgotten him before he was out of the
door.

The old man looked quickly around before sticking the
long steel point through the cork on one of the bottles and
slowly withdrawing the plunger so that the shiny liquid filled
the syringe. He probed with his fingers until he found an
opening in the bark and stuck the syringe in. Things didn't
go as easily as he had imagined. He had to press hard for the
syringe to penetrate the tough wood. It wouldn't have any
effect if he injected the outer layer; he had to reach the cam-
bium, the tree's inner, life-giving organs. He applied more
pressure to the syringe. The needle shook. Damn! He mustn't

break it, he only had the one. The tip slid in, but after a few centimetres it came to a complete stop. Despite the chilly temperature, sweat was pouring off him. He gripped the syringe tight and was about to push again when he heard leaves rustling over by the path. He let go of the syringe. The sound came nearer. He closed his eyes and held his breath. The steps passed close by. When he opened his eyes again he glimpsed two figures disappearing behind the bushes, by the lookout point over Frederiks gate. He breathed out and turned his attention to the syringe again. He resolved to go for broke and pushed with all his might. And just as he was expecting to hear the sound of the needle snapping, it slid into the trunk. The old man mopped his brow. The rest was easy.

After ten minutes he had injected two bottles of the mixture and was well down the third when he heard voices approaching. Two figures came round the bushes at the lookout point and he assumed they were the same people he had seen before.

'Hello!' It was a man's voice.

The old man reacted instinctively. He straightened up and stood in front of the tree so that the tails of his coat obscured the syringe, which was still in the tree trunk. The next moment, he was blinded by light. He placed his hands in front of his face.

'Take the light away, Tom.' A woman.

The glare was gone and he saw a cone of light dancing between the trees in the gardens.

The pair came over to him and one, a woman in her early thirties with attractive though unexceptional features, held a card so close to his face that even in the meagre moonlight he could see her photograph, obviously taken when she was a bit younger, wearing a serious expression. Plus a name. Ellen something or other.

'Police,' she said. 'My apologies if we frightened you.'

'What are you doing here in the middle of the night, grandad?' the man asked. They were both wearing plain clothes, and under the man's black woollen hat he saw a good-looking young man with cold blue eyes staring back at him.

'I was only out walking,' the old man said, hoping that the tremble in his voice wouldn't be obvious.

'Is that so?' the one called Tom said. 'Behind a tree in the park, wearing a long coat. Do you know what we call that?'

'Stop it, Tom! Again, my apologies,' the woman said, turning to the old man. 'There was an attack here in the gardens some hours ago. A young boy was beaten up. Have you seen or heard anything?'

'I've only just got here,' the old man said, concentrating on the woman to avoid meeting the man's searching eyes. 'I haven't seen anything. Only Ursa Major and Ursa Minor.' He pointed to the sky. 'I'm sorry to hear that. Was he badly hurt?'

'Quite badly. Please excuse the disturbance,' she smiled. 'Have a nice evening.'

They went off and the old man closed his eyes and fell back against the tree trunk. The next moment he was pulled up by his lapels and felt hot breath in his ear. Then the young man's voice.

'If I ever catch you at it, I'll cut it off. Do you hear? I hate people like you.'

The hands let go of his lapels and were gone.

The old man collapsed and felt the cold moisture from the ground soak through his clothes. Inside his head, a voice hummed the same verse again and again.

Elm and poplar, birch and oak,
Deathly pale, blackened cloak.

19

Herbert's Pizza, Youngstorget.
12 November 1999.

SVERRE OLSEN WALKED IN, NODDED TO THE BOYS
at the corner table, bought a beer at the bar and took it over.
Not to the corner table, but to his own. It had been his table
for more than a year now, ever since he beat up the slit-eye at
Dennis Kebab. He was early and for the moment no one else
was sitting there, but soon the little pizzeria on the corner of
Torggata and Youngstorget would be full. It was benefit day.
He cast a glance at the boys in the corner. Three of the hard
core were sitting there, but he wasn't talking to them at the
moment. They belonged to the new party – *Nasjonalalliansen*
– and there had been ideological differences of opinion between them, one might say. He knew them from his time in
the youth section of the *Fedrelandspartiet*; they were patriotic enough, but now they were about to join the ranks of the
breakaway group. Roy Kvinset, irreproachably shaven-
headed, was, as always, dressed in tight faded jeans, boots
and a white T-shirt with the *Nasjonalalliansen* logo in red,
white and blue. Halle was new. He had dyed his hair black
and used hair oil to get it to lie flat. The moustache, was obviously what provoked people most – a neatly trimmed black
toothbrush moustache, an exact copy of the Führer's. He had

stopped sporting the riding breeches and boots; instead he wore green combat fatigues. Gregersen was the only one who looked like a normal youth: bomber jacket, goatee and sunglasses on his head. He was undoubtedly the most intelligent of the three.

Sverre's gaze panned around the room. A girl and boy were tucking into a pizza. He hadn't seen them before, but they didn't look like undercover police. Nor like journalists. Were they from the anti-fascist newspaper *Monitor* perhaps? He had exposed a *Monitor* bozo last winter, a man with scared eyes who had been in here a couple of times too many, who had acted drunk and started conversations with some of the regulars. Sverre had sniffed treachery in the air and they had taken him outside and torn off his sweater. He'd been wearing a wire. He had confessed that he was from *Monitor* before they even laid a hand on him. Scared stiff. Bunch of twats, these *Monitor* types. Thought this boys' game, this voluntary surveillance of fascist elements, was extremely important and dangerous, that they were secret agents whose lives were in constant danger. Yeah, well, as far as that was concerned, perhaps they weren't so different from a few in his own ranks, he had to admit. Anyway, the bozo had been sure they would kill him and was so frightened that he pissed himself. Quite literally. Sverre had spotted the dark stripe meandering down his trouser leg and across the tarmac. That was what he remembered best from that evening. The little stream of urine glittered dimly as it sought the lowest point in the sparsely lit back alley.

Sverre Olsen decided that the couple was just two hungry youngsters who happened to be passing by. The speed they were eating suggested that now they had become aware of the clientele and just wanted to get out as quickly as possible. By the window sat an old man in hat and coat. Perhaps a dipso, although his clothes sent a different message. But then again, they often looked like that for the first few days after the Salvation Army had dressed them – in nice second-hand

quality coats and suits which were a little out of fashion. As
he observed him, the old man suddenly looked up and met
his eye. He wasn't a dipso. The man had sparkling blue eyes
and Sverre automatically looked away. How the old bastard
stared!

Sverre concentrated on his mug of beer. It was time to
earn a bit of cash. Let his hair grow over the tattoo on his
neck, put on a long-sleeved shirt and get out there. There
was enough work. Shit work. The blacks had all the nice,
well-paid jobs. Poofs, heathens and blacks.

'May I sit down?'

Sverre raised his eyes. It was the old man; he stood above
him. Sverre hadn't even noticed him walk over.

'This is my table,' Sverre rebuffed.

'I only want a little chat.' The old man laid a newspaper on
the table between them and sat in the chair opposite. Sverre
watched him warily.

'Relax, I'm one of you,' he said.

'One of *who*?'

'One of the people who come here. National Socialists.'

'Oh yeah?'

Sverre moistened his lips and put the glass to his mouth.
The old man sat there, motionless, watching him. Calmly, as
if he had all the time in the world. And he probably did have,
he looked about seventy. At least. Could he be one of the old
extremists from *Zorn 88*? One of the shy financial backers
Sverre had heard about but never seen?

'I need a favour.' The old man spoke in a low voice.

'Oh yeah?' Sverre said. But he had toned down the overtly
condescending attitude a notch. You never knew, after all.

'Gun,' the old man said.

'What about a gun?'

'I need one. Can you help me?'

'Why should I?'

'Open the paper. Page twenty-eight.'

Sverre pulled the paper over and kept an eye on the old

man as he flicked through. On page twenty-eight there was
an article about neo-Nazis in Spain. By that bloody Resistance man, Even Juul. Thanks a lot. The big black and white
picture of a young man holding up a painting of Generalis-
simo Franco was partially obscured by a thousand-kroner
note.

'If you can help me . . .' the old man said.

Sverre shrugged.

'. . . there'll be nine thousand more on the way.'

'Oh yeah?' Sverre took another gulp. Looked around the
room. The young couple had gone, but Halle, Gregersen and
Kvinset were still sitting in the corner. And soon the others
would be coming and it would be impossible to have a discreet conversation. Ten thousand kroner.

'What kind of gun?'

'A rifle.'

'Should be able to manage that.'

The old man shook his head.

'A Märklin rifle.'

'Märklin? As in model trains?' Sverre asked.

A crack opened in the wrinkled face beneath the hat. The
old codger must have smiled.

'If you can't help me, tell me now. You can keep the thousand and we won't talk any more about it. I'll leave and we'll
never see each other again.'

Sverre experienced a brief rush of adrenaline. This was
not the everyday chat about axes, hunting rifles or the odd
stick of dynamite. This was the real McCoy. This guy was
for real.

The door opened. Sverre glanced over his shoulder at
the old man coming in. Not one of the boys, just the alkie in
the red Icelandic sweater. He could be a pain when he was
scrounging booze, but otherwise he was harmless enough.

'I'll see what I can do,' Sverre said, grabbing the thousand
kroner note.

Sverre didn't see what happened next. The old-man's

hand smacked down on his like an eagle's claw and fastened it to the table.

'That wasn't what I asked.' The voice was cold and crisp, like a sheet of ice.

Sverre tried to jerk his hand away, but couldn't. Couldn't release his hand from the grip of a senile old man!

'I asked if you could help me, and I want an answer. Yes or no. Understand?'

Sverre could feel his fury, his old friend and foe, mounting. For the time being, however, it had not repressed the other thought: ten thousand kroner. There was one man who could help him, a very special man. It wouldn't be cheap, but he had a feeling the old codger wouldn't haggle over the price.

'I . . . I can help you.'

'When?'

'Three days. Here. Same time.'

'Rubbish! You won't get hold of a rifle like that in three days.' The old man let go of his hand. 'But you run off to the man who can help you, and ask him to run over to the man who can help him, and then you meet me here in three days so that we can arrange the time and place for delivery.'

Sverre could lift 120 kilos on a bench press. How could this scrawny old . . . ?

'You tell me if the rifle has to be paid cash on delivery. You'll get the rest of your money in three days.'

'Yeah? What if I just take the money?'

'Then I'll come back and kill you.'

Sverre rubbed his wrists. He didn't ask for any further details.

An icy cold wind swept across the pavement outside the telephone booth by Torggata Baths as Sverre Olsen tapped in the numbers with trembling fingers. It was so fucking cold! He had holes in the toecaps of both boots too. The receiver was lifted at the other end.

'Yes?'

Sverre Olsen swallowed. Why was it the voice always made him feel so damned uneasy?

'It's me. Olsen.'

'Speak.'

'Someone needs a gun. A Märklin.'

No response.

'As in model trains,' Sverre added.

'I know what a Märklin is, Olsen.' The voice at the other end was flat, neutral; Sverre could feel the disdain. He didn't react because, though he hated the man at the other end, his terror of him was greater – he wasn't ashamed to admit that. This man had the reputation of being dangerous. Few people had heard of him, even in Sverre's circle, and Sverre didn't know his real name. But he had saved Sverre and his pals from a sticky situation more than once. All for the Cause, of course, not because he had any special liking for Sverre Olsen. Had Sverre known anyone else he thought could provide what he was after, he would have got in touch with them.

The voice: 'Who's asking and what do they want it for?'

'Some old guy. I've never seen him before. Said he was one of us. And I didn't exactly ask him who he was going to blow away, let's put it like that. No one perhaps. Perhaps he just wants it to —'

'Shut up, Olsen. Did he look as if he had money?'

'He was well dressed. And he gave me a thousand just to tell him whether I could help him or not.'

'He gave you a thousand to keep your mouth shut, not to answer any questions.'

'Right.'

'Interesting.'

'I'm meeting him again in three days. He wants to know then if we can get it.'

'*We?*'

'Yes, well . . .'

'If *I* can get it, you mean.'

'Of course, but . . .'

'What's he paying you for the job?'

Sverre paused. 'Ten big ones.'

'I'll match it. Ten. If the deal works out. Got it?'

'Got it.'

'So what are the ten for?'

'To keep my mouth shut.'

There was no feeling in Sverre's toes when he put down the phone. He needed new boots. He stood still, studying an inert crisp packet which the wind had hurled into the air and which was now being blown between cars in the direction of Storgata.

20

Herbert's Pizza. 15 November 1999.

THE OLD MAN LET THE GLASS DOOR TO HER-
bert's Pizza close behind him. He stood on the pavement
and waited. A Pakistani woman with a pram and her head
wrapped in a shawl passed by. Cars whizzed by in front of
him and he could see his flickering reflection in their windows and in the large glass panes of the pizzeria behind him.
To the left of the entrance the window had a large white cross
taped over it; it looked as if someone had tried to kick it in.
The pattern of white cracks in the glass was like a spider's
web. Behind, he could see Sverre Olsen, still sitting at the
table where they had agreed the details. Five weeks. The
container port. Pier 4. Two a.m. Password: Voice of an Angel. Probably the name of a pop song. He'd never heard of it,
but the title was appropriate. Unfortunately, the price had
been rather less appropriate: 750,000 Norwegian kroner.
But he wasn't going to discuss it. The question now was only
whether they would keep their end of the bargain or whether
they would rob him at the container port. He had appealed
to the young neo-Nazi's sense of loyalty by divulging that he
had fought at the Eastern Front, but he wasn't sure if he had
believed him. Or if it made any difference. He had even in-

vented a story about where he had served in case the young man started asking questions. But he hadn't.

Several more cars passed. Sverre Olsen had stayed put in the pizzeria, but someone else had stood up and was staggering towards the door at this moment. The old man remembered him; he had been there the last time too. And today he had kept his eyes on them the whole time. The door opened. He waited. There was a break in the traffic and he could hear that the man had come to a halt behind him. Then it came.

'Well now, is that him?'

The voice had that very special rasping quality which only many years of heavy alcohol abuse, smoking and insufficient sleep can produce.

'Do I know you?' the old man asked without turning.

'I reckon so, yes.'

The old man twisted his head round, studied him for a brief moment and turned away again.

'Can't say that I recognise you.'

'Jesus! You don't recognise an old war comrade?'

'Which war?'

'We fought for the same cause, you and I did.'

'If you say so. What do you want?'

'Eh?' the drunk asked, with one hand behind his ear.

'I asked what you wanted,' the old man repeated, louder this time.

'Ah, there's wanting and *wanting*. Nothing unusual about having a chat with old acquaintances, is there? Especially acquaintances you haven't seen for a long time. And especially people you thought were dead.'

The old man turned round.

'Do I look dead?'

The man in the red Icelandic sweater stared at him with eyes so bright blue they looked like turquoise marbles. It would be impossible to guess his age. Forty or eighty. But the old man knew exactly how old the drunk was. If he concentrated, he might even be able to remember his birth-day. During the war they had been very particular about cele-brating birthdays.

The drunk came a step closer. 'No, you don't look dead. Sick, yes, but not dead.'

He stretched out an enormous, grimy hand and the old man recognised the sweet stench of sweat, urine and vomit.

'What's up? Don't you want to shake an old comrade's hand?' His voice sounded like a death rattle.

The old man pressed the outstretched hand fleetingly with his own gloved hand.

'That's it,' he said. 'Now we've shaken hands. If there's nothing else you were wondering about, I'll be on my way.'

'Ah, wondering, yes.' The drunk rocked to and fro as he tried to focus on the old man. 'I was wondering what a man like you was doing in a hole like this. It's not so strange won-dering about that, is it? *He's just got lost*, I thought, the last time I saw you here. But you sat talking to that nasty piece of work who goes round beating people up with baseball bats. And you were sitting there today too . . .'

'Yes?'

'I was thinking I would have to ask one of the journalists who occasionally come here, you know. If they know what a respectable man like you is doing in such company. They know everything, you know. And what they don't know, they find out. For example, how it can be that a man everyone thought died during the war is alive again. They get their in-formation quick as fuck. Like that.'

He made a vain attempt at flicking his fingers.

'And then it's in the papers, you know.'

The old man sighed. 'Is there perhaps something I can help you with?'

'Do I look like I need anything?' The drunk spread his arms and flashed a toothless grin.

'I see,' said the old man, taking stock around him. 'Let's walk a little. I don't like spectators.'

'Eh?'

'I don't like spectators.'

'No, what do we want with them?'

The old man laid a hand lightly on the drunk's shoulder.

'Let's go in here.'

'*Show me the way to go*, comrade,' the drunk hummed hoarsely with a laugh.

They went through the archway next to Herbert's Pizza, where a row of large, grey, plastic wheelie bins overflowing with rubbish blocked the view from the street.

'You haven't already mentioned to anyone you've seen me, have you?'

'Are you mad? I thought I was seeing things at first. A ghost in broad daylight. At Herbert's!' He burst into a peal of laughter, but it quickly developed into a wet, gurgling cough. He bent forward and supported himself on the wall until the cough subsided. Then he stood up and dried the slime from the corners of his mouth. 'No, fortunately, otherwise they would have locked me up.'

'What do you think would be a fitting price for your silence?'

'Ah, a fitting price, hm, yes. I saw the ape take a thousand from your newspaper . . .'

'Yes?'

'A few of them would do a bit of good, that's for sure.'

'How many?'

'Well, how many have you got?'

The old man sighed, looked around once more to ensure there were no witnesses. Then he unbuttoned his coat and reached inside.

Sverre Olsen crossed Youngstorget with large strides, swinging a green plastic bag. Twenty minutes ago he had been sitting flat broke, with holes in his boots, at Herbert's and now he was walking in a shiny new pair of combat boots, high-laced, twelve eyelets on each side, bought from Top Secret in Henrik Ibsens gate. Plus he had an envelope which still contained eight shiny new big ones. And ten more in the offing. It was strange how things could change from one minute to the next. This autumn he had been on his way to three years in the clink when his lawyer had realised that the fat lady associate judge had taken her oath in the wrong place.

Sverre was in such a good mood that he reckoned he ought to invite Halle, Gregersen and Kvinset over to his table. Buy them a round. See how they reacted. Yes, he bloody would!

He crossed Pløens gate in front of a Paki woman with a pram and smiled at her out of pure devilry. On his way to the door of Herbert's he thought to himself that there wasn't much point in carrying around a plastic bag containing discarded boots. He went through the archway, flicked up the lid of one of the wheelie bins and threw in the plastic bag. On his way out again his attention was caught by two legs sticking out between two of the bins further to the back. He looked around. No one in the street. No one in the alley. What was it? A dipso? A junkie? He went closer. Where the legs protruded the bins had been shoved together. He could feel his pulse racing. Junkies became very upset if you disturbed them. Sverre stepped back and kicked one of the containers to the side.

'Ooh, fuck.'

It was odd that Sverre Olsen, who had almost killed a man himself, should never have seen a dead person before. And equally odd that it almost made his legs give way. The man sitting against the wall with one eye staring in each direction was as dead as it was possible to be. The cause of death was obvious. The smiling red wound in the neck showed where his throat had been cut. Even though the blood was only trickling now, it had clearly pumped out at first because the man's red Icelandic sweater was soaked and sticky. The stench of refuse and urine was overwhelming, and Sverre caught the taste of bile before two beers and a pizza came up. Afterwards, he stood leaning against the bins, spitting on to the tarmac. The toes of his new boots were yellow with vomit, but he didn't notice. He only had eyes for the little red stream glistening in the dark as it sought the lowest point in the back alley.

21

Leningrad. 17 January 1944.

A RUSSIAN YAK 1 FIGHTER PLANE THUNDERED over Edvard Mosken's head as he ran along the trench, bent double.

Generally speaking, the fighter planes didn't do a lot of damage. The Russians seemed to have run out of bombs. The latest thing he had heard was that they had equipped pilots with hand-grenades, which they were trying to lob into the trenches as they flew over.

Edvard had been in the Northern Sector to collect letters for the men and to catch up on the news. The whole autumn had been one long series of depressing reports of losses and retreats all along the Eastern Front. The Russians had recaptured Kiev in November, and in October the German army had narrowly avoided becoming surrounded north of the Black Sea. The situation was not made any easier by Hitler redirecting forces to the Western Front, but the most worrying thing was what Edvard had heard today. Two days ago Lieutenant General Gusev had launched a fierce offensive from Oranienbaum on the southern side of the Finnish Bay. Edvard remembered Oranienbaum because it was a small bridgehead they had passed on the march to Leningrad. They had let the

Russians keep it because it had no strategic importance. Now the Ivans had managed to assemble a whole army around the Kronstadt fort in secret, and according to reports Katusha cannons were tirelessly bombarding German positions. The once dense spruce forests had been reduced to firewood. It was true they had heard the music from Stalin's artillery in the distance for several nights now, but no one had guessed that things were so bad.

Edvard had taken the opportunity during the trip to go to the field hospital to visit one of his men who had lost a foot on a landmine in no man's land, but the nurse, a tiny Estonian woman with pained eyes in such dark blue sockets that she seemed to be wearing a mask, had only shaken her head and said the German word she had presumably practised most: *'Tot.'*

Edvard must have looked very sorry for himself, because she had tried to cheer him up by pointing to a bed where apparently there was another Norwegian.

'Leben,' she had said with a smile. But her eyes were still pained.

Edvard didn't know the man sleeping in the bed, but when he caught sight of the shiny white leather jacket hanging over the chair, he knew who it was: it was the company commander, Lindvig himself, from *Regiment Norge*. A legend. And now here he was. He decided he would spare the men this item of news.

Another fighter plane roared over their heads. Where were all these planes suddenly coming from? Last year the Ivans didn't appear to have any left.

He rounded a corner and saw a stooped Hallgrim Dale standing with his back to him.

'Dale!'

Dale didn't move. After a shell had knocked him unconscious last November, Dale didn't hear so well any more. He didn't talk much either, and he had the glazed, introverted eyes that men with shell-shock often had. Dale had complained of headaches at first, but the medical orderly who had attended to him said there wasn't a great deal they could do; they could only wait and see if he recovered. The shortage of fighting men was bad enough without sending healthy ones to the field hospital, he had said.

Edvard put an arm round Dale's shoulder. Dale swivelled round so suddenly and with such force that Edvard lost his footing on the ice which had become wet and slippery in the sun. *At least it's a mild winter*, Edvard thought, and he had to laugh as he lay there on his back, but the laughter died as he looked up into the barrel of Dale's rifle.

'Passwort!' Dale shouted. Over the rifle sights Edvard saw one wide-open eye.

'Hey, it's me, Dale.'

'Passwort!'

'Move that gun away! It's me, Edvard, for Christ's sake!'

'Passwort!'

'Gluthaufen.'

Edvard felt panic rising as he saw Dale's finger curling around the trigger. Couldn't he hear?

'Gluthaufen!' he shouted with all the power in his lungs. 'For Christ's sake, *Gluthaufen.*'

'Falsch! Ich schieße!'

My God, the man was insane! In a flash Edvard realised they had changed the password that morning. After he had gone to the Northern Sector. Dale's finger applied pressure to the trigger, but it wouldn't go any further. He had a strange wrinkle above his eye. Then he released the safety catch and cocked the gun again. Was this how it was going to end? After all he had survived, was he going to die from a bullet fired by a shell-shocked compatriot. Edvard stared into the black muzzle and waited for the jet of flame. Would he actually see it? Jesus Christ. He shifted his gaze past the rifle, into the blue sky above them where a black cross was outlined against the sky, a Russian fighter plane. It was too high up for them to hear. Then he closed his eyes.

'*Engelstimme!*' someone close at hand shouted.

Edvard opened his eyes and saw Dale blink twice behind the sights.

It was Gudbrand. He held his head beside Dale's and yelled in his ear.

'*Engelstimme!*'

Dale lowered the rifle. Then he grinned at Edvard and nodded. '*Engelstimme,*' he repeated.

Edvard closed his eyes again and breathed out.

'Are there any letters?' Gudbrand asked.

Edvard struggled to his feet and handed Gudbrand the pile. Dale still had the grin on his lips, but also the same vacant eyes. Edvard grabbed hold of Dale's gun barrel and stood his face.

'Is there anyone at home, Dale?'

He had meant to say it in his normal voice, but all that came out was a rough, husky whisper.

'He can't hear,' Gudbrand said, flicking through the letters.

'I wasn't aware he was so ill,' Edvard said, waving a hand in front of Dale's face.

'He shouldn't be here. Here's a letter from his family. Show it to him, and then you'll see what I mean.'

Edvard took the letter and held it up in front of Dale's face, but it evoked no reaction beyond a fleeting smile. Then he resumed his gaping into eternity, or whatever it was his gaze had been attracted by out there.

'You're right,' he said. 'He's had it.'

Gudbrand passed a letter to Edvard. 'How are things at home?' he asked.

'Oh, you know . . .' Edvard said, staring at the letter.

Gudbrand didn't know, because he and Edvard hadn't spoken much since last winter. It was odd, but even here, under these conditions, two people could easily manage to avoid each other if they wanted to enough. Not that Gudbrand disliked Edvard; on the contrary, he respected the Mjøndal man whom he considered a clever person, a brave soldier and supportive to the new, young men in the section. In the autumn they had promoted Edvard to *Scharführer*, which corresponded to the rank of sergeant in the Norwegian army, but his responsibilities had remained the same. Edvard joked that he had been promoted because all the others were dead, so they had a lot of sergeants' caps left over.

Gudbrand had often thought that in different circumstances the two of them might have been good friends. However, events the previous winter – Sindre's desertion and the mysterious reappearance of Daniel's corpse – had remained an issue between them.

The dull thud of a distant explosion broke the silence, followed by the chatter of machine guns.

'Opposition's stiffening,' Gudbrand said, more as a question than a statement.

'Yes,' Edvard said. 'It's this damned mild weather. Our supplies lorries are getting stuck in the mud.'

'Will we have to retreat?'

Edvard hunched his shoulders. 'A few kilometres perhaps. But we'll be back.'

Gudbrand shielded his eyes with his hand and looked towards the south. He had no desire to come back. He wanted to return home and see if there was still a life for him there.

'Have you seen the Norwegian road sign at the crossing outside the field hospital, the one with the sun cross?' he asked. 'With one arm pointing down the road to the east, showing: Leningrad five kilometres?'

Edvard nodded.

'Do you remember what's on the arm pointing west?'

'Oslo,' Edvard said. '2,611 kilometres.'

'It's a long way.'

'Yes, it is a long way.'

Dale had allowed Edvard to keep the rifle and sat on the

ground with his hands buried in the snow in front of him. His head hung like a snapped dandelion between his narrow shoulders. They heard another explosion, closer this time.

'Thank you very much for —'

'Not at all,' Gudbrand said quickly.

'I saw Olaf Lindvig in the hospital,' Edvard said. He didn't know why he had said that. Maybe because Gudbrand was the only person in the section, apart from Dale, who had been there as long as he had.

'Was he . . . ?'

'Just a minor wound, I believe. I saw his white uniform.'

'He's a good man, I hear.'

'Yes, we have many good men.'

They stood facing each other in silence.

Edvard coughed and thrust a hand in his pocket.

'I got a couple of Russian cigarettes from the Northern Sector. If you've got a light . . .'

Gudbrand nodded, unbuttoned his camouflage jacket, found his matches and struck one against the sandpaper. When he looked up, the first thing he saw was Edvard's enlarged cyclops eye. It was staring over his shoulder. Then he heard the whine.

'Down!' Edvard shrieked.

The next moment they were lying on the ice and the sky burst above them with a tearing sound. Gudbrand caught a glimpse of the rudder of a Russian fighter plane flying so low over the trenches that snow whirled up from the ground beneath. Then they were gone and it was quiet again.

'Well, I'm . . .' Gudbrand whispered.

'Jesus Christ,' Edvard groaned, turning on to his side and smiling at Gudbrand.

'I could see the pilot. He pulled back the glass and leaned out of the cockpit. The Ivans have gone mad.' He was panting with laughter. 'This is turning into a right old day, this is.'

Gudbrand stared at the broken match he still held in his hand. Then he began to laugh too.

'Ha, ha,' Dale went, looking at the other two from where he sat in the snow at the side of the trench. 'Hee, hee.'

Gudbrand caught Edvard's eye and they both began to roar with laughter. They laughed so much they were gasping for breath and at first they didn't hear the peculiar sound, coming ever closer.

Clink . . . clink . . .

It sounded like someone patiently hitting the ice with a hoe.

Clink . . .

Then came a sound of metal against metal and Gudbrand and Edvard turned to see Dale slowly keel over in the snow.

'What the hell —' Gudbrand started to say.

'Grenade!' screamed Edvard.

Gudbrand reacted instinctively to Edvard's scream and curled into a ball, but as he lay there he caught sight of the pin which was spinning round and round a metre away from him. A lump of metal was attached to one end. He felt his body freezing into the ice as he realised what was about to happen.

'Move away!' Edvard screamed behind him.

It was true, the Russian pilots really were throwing hand-grenades from aeroplanes. Gudbrand was on his back and tried to move away, but his arms and legs slipped on the wet ice.

'Gudbrand!'

The peculiar sound had been the hand-grenade bouncing across the ice into the bottom of the trench. It must have hit Dale right on the helmet!

'Gudbrand!'

The grenade spun round and round, bounced and danced again, and Gudbrand couldn't take his eyes off it. Four seconds from defusing to detonation, wasn't that what they had learned at Sennheim? The Russians' grenades might be different. Perhaps it was six? Or eight? Round and round the grenade whirled, like one of the big red spinning-tops his father had made him in Brooklyn. Gudbrand would spin it, and Sonny and his little brother stood watching and counting how long it kept going. 'Twenty-one, twenty-two . . .' Mummy called from the window on the second floor to say dinner was ready. He was to go in; Daddy would be coming home any minute. 'Just a minute,' he shouted up to her, 'the top's spinning!' But she didn't hear; she had already closed the window. Edvard wasn't shrieking any more, and all of a sudden it was quiet.

22

Doctor Buer's Surgery. 22 December 1999.

THE OLD MAN LOOKED AT HIS WATCH. HE HAD been sitting in the waiting room for a quarter of an hour now. He'd never had to wait in Konrad Buer's day. Konrad hadn't taken on more patients than he could manage in his schedule.

A man was sitting at the other end of the room. Dark-skinned, African. He was flicking through a weekly magazine, and the old man established that even at this distance he could read every letter on the front page. Something about the royal family. Was that what this African was sitting reading? An article about the Norwegian royal family? The idea was absurd.

The African turned the page. He had the type of moustache that went down at the ends, just like the courier the old man had met the previous night. It had been a brief meeting. The courier had arrived at the container port in a Volvo, probably a rented car. He had pulled up, the window had gone down with a hum and he had said the password: Voice of an Angel. He had had exactly the same kind of moustache. And sorrowful eyes. He had immediately said he didn't have the gun with him in the car for security reasons, but that they would drive to a place to get it. The old man had hesitated. Then he thought that if they had wanted to rob him, they would have done so at the container port. So he had got in and they had driven to the Radisson SAS hotel, of all places, in Holbergs plass. He had seen Betty Andresen behind the counter as they went through reception, but she had not looked in their direction.

The courier had counted the money in the suitcase while mumbling numbers in German. Then the old man had asked him. The courier had said that his parents came from some place in Elsass, to which the old man said, on a whim, that he had been there, to Sennheim. An impulse.

After he had read so much about the Märklin rifle on the Internet at the University Library, the weapon itself had been something of an anticlimax. It looked like a standard hunting rifle, only a little bigger. The courier had shown him how to assemble it and strip it; he called him 'Herr Uriah'. Then the old man put the dismantled rifle into a large shoulder-bag and took the lift down to reception. For a brief moment he had considered going over to Betty Andresen and asking her to order a taxi for him. Another impulse.

'Hello!'

The old man looked up.

'I think we'll have to give you a hearing test as well.'

Dr Buer stood in the doorway and made an attempt at a jovial smile. He led him into the surgery. The bags under the doctor's eyes had become even bigger.

'I called your name three times.'

I forget my name, the old man reflected. *I forget all my names.*

The old man deduced from the doctor's helping hand that he had bad news.

'Well, I've got the results of the samples we took,' he said, quickly, before he had settled into his chair. To get the bad news over and done with as fast as possible. 'And I'm afraid it has spread.'

'Of course it's spread,' the old man said. 'Isn't that what cancer cells do? Spread?'

'Ha, ha. Yes, it is.' Dr Buer brushed an invisible speck of dust off the desk.

'Cancer is like us,' the old man said. 'It just does what it has to do.'

'Yes,' Dr Buer said. He looked relaxed in a forced way, in his slumped sitting position.

'Like you, doctor. You just do what you have to do.'

'You're so right, so right.' Dr Buer smiled and put on his glasses. 'We're still considering chemotherapy. It would weaken you, but it could prolong . . . um . . .'

'My life?'

'Yes.'

'How long have I got left without chemo?'

Buer's Adam's apple bobbed up and down. 'A little less than we had first assumed.'

'Meaning?'

'Meaning that the cancer has spread from the liver via the blood stream to —'

'For Christ's sake, will you just tell me how long.'

Dr Buer gaped blankly.

'You hate this job, don't you?' the old man said.

'I beg your pardon?'

'Nothing. A date, please.'

'It's impossible to —'

Dr Buer jumped in his chair as the old man's fist hit the desktop so hard that the telephone receiver leapt off the cradle. He opened his mouth to say something, but stopped when he saw the old man's quivering forefinger. Then he sighed, took off his glasses and ran a tired hand over his face.

'This summer. June, perhaps earlier. August at the latest.'

'Great,' the old man said. 'That'll do fine. Pain?'

'Can come at any time. You'll be given medicine.'

'Will I be able to function?'

'Hard to say. Depends on the pain.'

'I must have medicine that enables me to function. It's important. Do you understand?'

'All painkillers —'

'I can take a lot of pain. I simply need something to keep me conscious so that I can think and act rationally.'

Happy Christmas. That was the last thing Dr Buer had said. The old man stood on the steps. At first he hadn't understood why the city was so full of people, but once he had been reminded of the imminent religious festival he saw the panic in the eyes of people dashing along the pavements in search of last-minute Christmas presents. Some shoppers had gathered round a pop group playing in Egerstorget. A man wearing a Salvation Army uniform was going round with a collection box. A junkie stamped his feet in the snow, his eyes flickering like stearin candles about to go out. Two teenage girls, arm in arm, passed him, rosy-cheeked and bursting with stories to tell about boys and expectations of their lives to come. And the candles. There were candles in every damned window. He raised his face to the Oslo sky; a warm, golden dome of reflected light from the city. My God, how he longed for her. Next Christmas, he thought. Next Christmas we will celebrate together, my darling.

Part Three

URIAH

23

Rudolf II Hospital, Vienna. 7 June 1944.

HELENA LANG WALKED WITH QUICK STEPS AS she pushed a trolley towards Ward 4. The windows were open and she breathed in, filling her lungs and head with the fresh smell of newly mown grass. No smell of death and destruction today. It was a year since Vienna had been bombed for the first time. In recent weeks, when the weather had been clear, they had been bombed every single night. Even though the Rudolf II Hospital was several kilometres away from the centre, raised aloft from the war in the green Viennese woods, the stench of smoke from the fires in the city had smothered the scents of summer.

Helena swung round a corner and smiled at Dr Brockhard, who appeared to want to stop and talk, then hurried on. Brockhard, with those rigid staring eyes of his behind glasses, always made her nervous and uncomfortable when they came face to face. Now and then she had the impression that these meetings in the corridor were not accidental. Her mother would probably have had respiratory problems if she had seen the way in which Helena avoided the promising young doctor, especially as Brockhard came from a particularly distinguished Viennese family. However, Helena liked

neither Brockhard nor his family, nor her mother's attempts
to use her as a ticket back into the upper echelons of society.
Her mother blamed the war for what had happened. It was to
blame for Helena's father, Henrik Lang, losing his Jewish
lenders so abruptly and thus not being able to pay his credi-
tors as arranged. The financial crisis had resulted in him having to improvise and he had made his Jewish bankers transfer
their bond holdings, which the Austrian state had confiscated, to Lang. And now Henrik Lang was in prison for having conspired with Jewish enemies of the state.

Unlike her mother, Helena missed her father more than
she missed the social status her family had enjoyed. She did
not miss, for example, the banquets, the adolescent, superficial conversations and the continual attempts to marry her
off to one of the spoiled rich boys.

She looked at her wristwatch and scurried along. A small
bird had obviously flown in through one of the open windows and now it was calmly sitting on one of the globe
lamps hanging from the high ceiling and singing. Some
days Helena found it incomprehensible that a war was raging outside. Perhaps it was because the forest, the tight rows
of spruce trees, closed out all the things they didn't want to
see. If you went into the wards, however, you soon knew
that the peace was illusory. The wounded soldiers with their
mutilated bodies and their battered psyches brought the war
home to them. To begin with, she had listened to their stories, practically convinced that with her strength of mind
and her faith she could help to lead them out of their misery.
Yet they all seemed to tell more of the same nightmare story
about how much man can and has to endure on earth, and
about the degradation involved in simply wanting to live.
Only the dead escape unscathed. So Helena stopped listening.
She pretended she was listening as she changed bandages,
checked temperatures and gave them medicine or food. And
when they were asleep she tried not to look at them, as even

then their faces continued to tell their stories. She could read suffering in the pale, boyish faces, brutality in the hardened, closed faces and a longing for death in the pain-contorted features of one man who had just found out that his foot would have to be amputated.

Nevertheless, she walked in today with quick, light steps. Perhaps it was because it was summer, perhaps it was because a doctor had told her how beautiful she was this morning, or perhaps it was because of the Norwegian patient in Ward 4 who would soon say *'Guten Morgen'* in his funny German. Then he would eat breakfast while giving her lingering looks as she went from bed to bed, serving the other patients, saying a few encouraging words to each one. For every fifth or sixth bed she attended to she cast a glance back at him and, if he smiled at her, she would quickly return the smile and continue as if nothing had happened. Nothing. And yet it was everything. It was the thought of these small moments that got her through the days now; that allowed her to laugh when the badly burned Kapitän Hadler in the bed by the door jokingly asked if they would soon send him his genitals back from the Eastern Front.

She pushed open the door to Ward 4. The sunlight flooding into the room made everything white – the walls, the ceiling, the sheets – shine. *That's what it must be like when you enter paradise*, she thought.

'Guten Morgen, Helena.'

She smiled at him. He was sitting in a chair beside the bed and reading a book.

'Did you sleep well, Uriah?' she asked him cheerfully.

'Like a bear,' he said.

'Bear?'

'Yes. In . . . what do you call it in German when they sleep all winter?'

'Ah, hibernation.'

'Yes, hibernation.'

They both laughed. Helena knew that the other patients were watching them. She mustn't spend more time with him than the others.

'And your head? It's getting a little better every day now, isn't it?'

'Yes indeed, it's getting better and better. One day I'll be just as good-looking as I used to be, you'll see.'

She remembered when they brought him in. It seemed to contravene the laws of nature that anyone could survive the hole he had in his forehead. She caught his teacup with the pot and it almost toppled over.

'Whoa!' he laughed. 'Were you out dancing until the wee small hours last night?'

She looked up. He winked at her.

'Mmm,' she said, and became flustered because she was lying about such a silly thing.

'What do you dance here in Vienna?'

'I mean, no, I wasn't dancing. I just went to bed late.'

'You probably dance waltzes, don't you? Viennese waltzes and so on.'

'Yes, I suppose we do,' she said, concentrating on the thermometer.

'Like this,' he said and stood up. Then he began to sing. The others looked up from their beds. The song was in an unfamiliar language, but he had such a warm, beautiful voice. The healthiest patients cheered and laughed as he pivoted round with small, careful waltz steps and the loose dressing gown cords swung with him.

'Come back here, Uriah, or I'll send you right back to the Eastern Front,' she shouted sternly.

He went back obediently and sat down. His name was not Uriah, but it was the name he had insisted they use.

'Do you know the Rhineland Polka?' he asked.

'Rhineland Polka?'

'It's a dance we've borrowed from the Rhineland. Shall I show you?'

'You sit there nice and still until you're well again.'

'And then I'll take you out in Vienna and teach you the Rhineland Polka.'

The hours he had spent in the summer sun on the veranda over the past days had given him a healthy complexion, and now his white teeth sparkled against his happy face.

'I think you sound well enough to be sent back already,' she countered, but was unable to stop the blush which had shot into her cheeks. She was standing ready to continue her round when she felt his hand against hers.

'Say yes,' he whispered.

She waved him away with a bright laugh and went on to the next bed with her heart singing like a little bird in her bosom.

'Well?' Dr Brockhard said, peering up from his papers when she came into his office, and as usual she didn't know if this 'well?' was a question, an introduction to a longer question or simply his way of speaking. So she just stood by the door.

'You asked to see me, Doctor?'

'Why do you insist on being so formal with me, Helena?' Brockhard sighed with a smile. 'My goodness, we've known each other since we were children, haven't we?'

'What was it you wanted from me?'

'I've decided to report the Norwegian in Ward 4 fit for duty.'

'I see.'

She didn't turn a hair. Why should she? Patients came here to become well again, then they left. The alternative was dying. That was life in a hospital.

'I passed on the report to the Wehrmacht five days ago. We have already received his new posting.'

'That was quick.' Her voice was firm and calm.

'Yes, they desperately need more men. We're fighting a war, as you know.'

'Yes,' she said. But didn't say what she was thinking: *We're fighting a war and you're sitting here hundreds of kilometres from the front, twenty-two years old, doing the job a seventy-year-old could have done. Thanks to Herr Brockhard Senior.*

'I thought I would ask you to give him his orders since the two of you seem to get on so well.'

She could feel him scrutinising her reaction.

'By the way, what is it that you like so much about him particularly, Helena? What distinguishes him from the four hundred other soldiers we have here at the hospital?'

She was about to protest, but he pre-empted her.

'Sorry, Helena, this is none of my business of course. It's just my curious nature. I . . .' He picked up a pen in front of him between the tips of his two index fingers, turned and looked out of the window. '. . . simply wonder what you can see in a foreign fortune-hunter who betrays his own country in order to curry favour with the conquering army. If you understand what I mean. How's your mother by the way?'

Helena swallowed before answering.

'You don't need to worry about my mother, Doctor. If you give me the orders, I'll pass them on.'

Brockhard turned to face her. He picked up a letter from the desk.

'He's being sent to the 3rd Panzer Division in Hungary. You know what that means, I take it?'

She frowned. 'The 3rd Panzer Division? He volunteered for the Waffen SS. Why should he be enlisted in the regular Wehrmacht?'

Brockhard shrugged his shoulders.

'In these times we have to accomplish what we can and perform the tasks we are set to do. Or don't you agree, Helena?'

'What do you mean?'

'He's in the infantry, isn't he? In other words, he has to run behind combat vehicles, not sit in them. A friend of mine who was in the Ukraine tells me that every single day they shoot Russians until their machine guns run hot and the bodies are piled high, but they keep pouring in as if there were no end to them.'

She only just managed to restrain herself from snatching the letter off Brockhard and ripping it to pieces.

'Perhaps a young woman like you should be a little realistic and not develop too strong an attachment to a man who, in all probability, you will never see again. Incidentally, that shawl really suits you, Helena. Is it a family heirloom?'

'I am surprised and happy to hear your considerate words, Doctor, but I can assure you they are completely redundant. I have no special feelings for this patient. Meals have to be served now, so if you would excuse me, Doctor . . .'

'Helena, Helena . . .' Brockhard shook his head and smiled. 'Do you really believe I am blind? Do you think I can watch the pain this is causing you with a light heart? The close friendship between our families makes me feel there are bonds which tie us together, Helena. Otherwise I would not talk to you in this confidential manner. Please forgive me, but you must have noticed that I bear warm feelings of affection for you, and —'

'Stop!'

'What?'

Helena had closed the door behind her and now she raised her voice.

'I'm a volunteer here, Brockhard. I'm not one of your nurses whom you can play with as you will. Give me that letter and say what you have to. Otherwise, I'll be on my way immediately.'

'My dear Helena,' Brockhard wore an expression of concern, 'don't you understand that this is up to you?'

'Up to me?'

'A full bill of health is an extremely subjective thing. Especially with regard to a head injury of that kind.'

'I see.'

'I could provide him with a medical certificate for another three months, and who knows if there will be any Eastern Front in three months' time?'

She looked at Brockhard, puzzled.

'You're a keen reader of the Bible, Helena. You know the story of King David, don't you? Who desires Bathsheba even though she is married to one of his soldiers? So he orders his generals to send the husband to the front line so that he will be killed. Then King David can woo Bathsheba unhindered.'

'What's that got to do with this?'

'Nothing. Nothing, Helena. I wouldn't dream of sending your heart's desire to the front if he was not fit enough. Or anyone else for that matter. That's exactly what I mean. And since you know this patient's state of health at least as well as I, I thought I might consult you before I make a final decision. If you consider him not to be fit enough, I ought perhaps to send a further medical certificate to the Wehrmacht.'

Slowly the nature of the situation began to sink in.

'Or what, Helena?'

She could hardly believe her ears: he wanted to use Uriah to force his way into her bed. How long had he spent working this one out? Had he been waiting for weeks for just the right moment? And how did he actually want her? As a wife or a lover?

'Well?' Brockhard asked.

Her head was racing as she tried to find a way out of the labyrinth. But all the exits were closed. Naturally. Brockhard wasn't a stupid man. As long as he had a certificate for Uriah, as a favour to her, she would have to obey his every whim. The posting would be deferred, but only when Uriah was gone would Brockhard cease to have any power over her. Power? Goodness, she hardly knew the Norwegian man. And she had no idea how he felt about her.

'I . . .' she began.

'Yes?'

He had leaned forward in his eagerness. She wanted to continue, wanted to say what she knew she had to say to break free, but something stopped her. It took her a second to understand what it was. It was the lies. It was a lie that she wanted to be free, a lie that she didn't know what Uriah felt for her, a lie that we always had to submit and to degrade ourselves to survive, it was all lies. She bit her lower lip as she felt it begin to tremble.

24

Bislett. New Year's Eve 1999.

IT WAS MIDDAY WHEN HARRY HOLE GOT OFF THE
tram at the Radisson SAS hotel in Holbergs gate and saw the
low morning sun reflecting briefly on the residential block
windows of the Rikshospital before disappearing back behind the clouds. He had been in his office for the last time.
To clear up, to make sure he had collected everything, he
had told himself. But the little that constituted his personal
effects found enough room in the supermarket carrier bag
he had taken from Kiwi the day before. Those who weren't
on duty were at home, preparing for the last party of the millennium. A paper streamer lay across the back of his chair
as a reminder of yesterday's little leaving party, under the
direction of Ellen, of course. Bjarne Møller's sober words of
farewell hadn't really been in keeping with her blue balloons
and sponge cake decorated with candles, but the little speech
had been nice enough anyway. Presumably the head of Crime
Squad knew that Harry would never have forgiven him had
he been verbose or sentimental. And Harry had to admit he
had felt a tinge of pride when Møller congratulated him on
being made an inspector and wished him luck in POT. Not
even Tom Waaler's sardonic smile and light shake of the head

from the spectators' ranks by the door at the back had destroyed the occasion.

The intention of the trip to the office had been to sit there one last time, in the creaking, broken office chair, in the room where he had spent almost seven years. Harry shivered. All this sentimentality, he wondered, wasn't that another sign he was getting on?

Harry walked up Holbergs gate and turned left into Sofies gate. Most of the properties in this narrow street were workers' flats dating back to the turn of the century and not in the best condition. But after the prices of flats had risen and young middle-class people who couldn't afford to live in Majorstuen had moved in, the area had received something of a face-lift. Now there was only one property which had not had its façade done up recently: number 8, Harry's. It didn't bother Harry in the least.

He let himself in and opened the postbox in the hallway. An offer on pizzas and an envelope from Oslo City Treasurer which he immediately assumed contained a reminder to pay his parking fine from last month. He swore as he went up the stairs. He had bought a fifteen-year-old Ford Escort at a bargain price from an uncle whom, strictly speaking, he didn't know. It was a bit rusty and the clutch was worn, it was true, but there was a neat sun roof. So far, however, there had been more parking fines and garage bills than hairs on your head. On top of that, the shit heap wouldn't start, so he had to remember to park at the top of a hill to push-start it.

He unlocked his front door. It was a spartanly equipped two-room flat. Clean and tidy, no carpets on the polished wooden floor. The only decorations on the walls were a photograph of his mother and Sis, and a poster of *The Godfather* he had pinched from Symra cinema when he was sixteen. There were no plants, no candles or cute knick-knacks. He had once hung up a notice-board he had thought he might use for postcards, photographs or any words of wisdom he might come across. In other people's homes he had seen boards like these. When he realised he never received postcards, and basically never took photos either, he cut out a quotation from Bjørneboe:

And this acceleration in the production of horsepower is again just one expression of acceleration in our understanding of the so-called laws of nature. This understanding = angst.

With a single glance Harry established that there were no messages on the answerphone (another unnecessary investment), unbuttoned his shirt, put it in the dirty-washing basket and took a clean one from the tidy pile in the cupboard.

Harry left the answering machine on (perhaps someone would call from the Norwegian Gallup organisation), locked the door and left again.

Without a trace of sentimentality he bought the last papers of the millennium from Ali's shop, then set off up Dovregata. In Waldemar Thranes gate people were hurrying home for the big night. Harry was shivering in his coat until he stepped into Schrøder's and the moist warmth of humanity hit him in the face. It was fairly full, but he saw that his favourite table was about to become free and he steered towards it. The old man who had got up from the table put on his hat, gave Harry a quick once-over from under white bushy eyebrows, a taciturn nod, and left. The table was by the window and during the day it was one of the few in the dimly lit room to have enough light to read by. No sooner had he sat down than Maja was by his side.

'Hi, Harry.' She smacked the tablecloth with a grey duster. 'Today's special?'

'If the cook's sober.'

'He is. Drink?'

'Now we're talking.' He looked up. 'What are you recommending today?'

'Right.' She placed one hand on her hip and proclaimed

in a loud, clear voice, 'Contrary to what people think, this city has in fact the purest drinking water in the country. And the least toxic pipes are to be found in the properties built around the turn of the century, such as this one.'

'And who told you that, Maja?'

'It was probably you, Harry.' Her laughter was husky and heartfelt. 'Being on the wagon suits you, by the way.' She said this under her breath, made a note of his order and was off.

The other newspapers were full of the millennium, so Harry tackled *Dagsavisen*. On page six his eyes fell on a large photograph of a wooden road sign with a sun cross painted on. *Oslo 2,611 km*, it said on one arm, *Leningrad 5 km* on the other.

The article beneath was credited to Even Juul, Professor of History. The subheading was concise: *The conditions for fascism seen in the light of increasing unemployment in Western Europe.*

Harry had seen Juul's name in newspapers before; he was a kind of *éminence grise* as far as the occupation of Norway and the *Nasjonal Samling* were concerned. He leafed through the rest of the paper but didn't find anything of interest. Then he flicked back to Juul's article. It was a commentary on an earlier report about the strong position held by neo-Nazism in Sweden. Juul described how neo-Nazism, which had seen a dramatic decline in the years of the economic upturn in the nineties, was now coming back with renewed vigour. He also wrote that a hallmark of the new wave was its firm ideological base. While neo-Nazism in the eighties had mostly been about fashion and group identification, a uniform code of dress, shaven heads and archaic slogans such as *'Sieg Heil'*, the new wave was better organised. There was a financial support network and it was not based to the same degree on wealthy leaders and sponsors. In addition, Juul wrote, the new movement was not merely a reaction to factors in the current social situation, such as unemployment and immigration; it wanted to set up an alternative to social democracy. The catchword was rearmament – moral, military and racial. The decline of Christianity was used as an example of moral decay, as well as HIV and the increase in drug abuse. And the image of the enemy was also to some extent new: champions of the EU who broke down national and racial boundaries; NATO people who held out a hand to Russian and Slav *Untermenschen*; and the new Asian capital barons who had taken on the Jews' role as world bankers.

Maja arrived with the lunch.

'Dumplings?' Harry asked, staring down at the grey lumps on a bed of Chinese cabbage sprinkled with thousand island dressing.

'Schrøder style,' Maja said. 'Leftovers from yesterday. Happy New Year.'

Harry held up the newspaper so that he could eat, and he had just taken the first bite of the cellulose dumpling when he heard a voice from behind the paper.

'It's dreadful, I say.'

Harry peeked beyond the newspaper. The Mohican was sitting at the neighbouring table, looking straight at him. Perhaps he had been sitting there the whole time, but Harry certainly hadn't noticed him come in. Presumably they called him the Mohican because he was the last of his kind. He had been a seaman during the war, was torpedoed twice, and all his pals were long since dead. Maja had told Harry that. His long, unkempt beard hung into his beer glass and he sat there with his coat on, as he always did, summer and winter alike. His face, so gaunt that it showed the contours of his skull, had a network of veins like crimson lightning on a background of bleached white. The red, watery eyes stared at Harry from behind a layer of limp skin folds.

'Dreadful!'

Harry had heard enough drunken babblings in his life not to take any particular notice of what regulars at Schrøder's had to say, but this was different. In all the years he had been

going there, these were the first comprehensible words he had
heard the Mohican speak. Even after the night last winter,
when Harry had found the Mohican sleeping against a house
wall in Dovregata and had most probably saved the old boy
from freezing to death, the Mohican had not even offered
him so much as a nod on the occasions they met. And now it
seemed that the Mohican had said his piece for the time being, as his lips were tightly pressed together and he was concentrating on his glass again. Harry looked around him before
leaning over to the Mohican's table.

'Do you remember me, Konrad Åsnes?'

The old man grunted and stared into space without answering.

'I found you asleep in a snowdrift in the street last year.
The temperature was minus eighteen.'

The Mohican rolled his eyes.

'There were no street lights, so I could easily have missed
you. You could have croaked, Åsnes.'

The Mohican screwed up one red eye and gave Harry a
furious look before raising his glass.

'Yes, I'd like to thank you for that.'

He drank carefully. Then he slowly put his glass down on
the table, placed it as if it were important that the glass should
stand in a particular spot on the table.

'Those gangsters should be shot,' he said.

'Really? Who?'

The Mohican directed a crooked finger towards Harry's
paper. Harry turned it over. The front page was emblazoned
with a large photograph of a shaven-headed Swedish neo-
Nazi.

'Up against the wall with them!' The Mohican smacked
the palm of his hand down on the table, and a few faces
turned towards him. Harry gestured with his hand to calm
him down.

'They're just young men, Åsnes. Try and enjoy yourself
now. It's New Year's Eve.'

'Young men? What do you think we were? That didn't stop the Germans. Kjell was nineteen. Oscar was twenty-two. Shoot them before it spreads, I say. It's an illness; you have to catch it early on.'

He pointed a trembling forefinger at Harry.

'One of them was sitting where you're sitting now. They don't bloody die out! You're a policeman, you go out and catch them!'

'How do you know I'm a policeman?' Harry asked in surprise.

'I read the newspapers. You shot someone in some country down south. That was good, but what about shooting a couple here too?'

'You're very talkative today, Åsnes.'

The Mohican clammed up and gave Harry a last surly glance before turning to the wall and studying the painting of Youngstorget. Harry, understanding that the conversation was over, waved to Maja for a cup of coffee and consulted his watch. A new millennium was just around the corner. Schrøder's would close at four o'clock because of a 'Private New Year's Eve Party', as the poster hanging on the entrance door said. Harry surveyed the familiar faces in the room. As far as he could see, all the guests had arrived.

25

Rudolf II Hospital, Vienna. 8 June 1944.

WARD 4 WAS FILLED WITH THE SOUNDS OF SLEEP-
ing. Tonight it was quieter than usual, no one moaning in
pain or waking from a nightmare with a scream. Helena
hadn't heard an air-raid warning in Vienna either. If they
didn't bomb tonight, she hoped it would make everything
easier. She had crept into the dormitory, stood at the foot of
his bed and watched him. There, in the cone of light from his
table lamp, he sat, so immersed in the book he was reading
that he didn't heed anything else. And she stood outside the
glow, in the dark. With all the knowledge of the dark.

As he was about to turn the page he noticed her. He
smiled and immediately put down his book.

'Good evening, Helena. I didn't think you were on duty
tonight.'

She placed her forefinger over her lips and went closer.

'What do you know about the night shifts?' she whispered.

He smiled. 'I don't know anything about the others. I
only know when you're on duty.'

'Is that right?'

'Wednesday, Friday and Sunday, then Monday and Tuesday. Then Wednesday, Friday and Sunday again. Don't be frightened, it's a compliment. There's not much else to use your brain on here. I also know when Hadler gets his enema.'

She laughed softly.

'But you don't know you've been declared fit for action, do you?'

He stared at her in surprise.

'You've been posted to Hungary,' she whispered. 'To the 3rd Panzer Division.'

'The Panzer Division? But that's the Wehrmacht. They can't enlist me. I'm a Norwegian.'

'I know.'

'And what am I supposed to be doing in Hungary? I —'

'Shhh, you'll wake the others. Uriah, I've read the orders. I'm afraid there's not much we can do about it.'

'But there has to be a mistake. It's . . .'

He accidentally knocked the book onto the floor and it landed with a bang. Helena bent down and picked it up. On the cover, under the title *The Adventures of Huckleberry Finn*, there was a drawing of a boy in rags on a timber raft. Uriah was clearly angry.

'This isn't my war,' he said through pursed lips.

'I know that too,' she whispered, putting the book in his bag under the chair.

'What are you doing?' he whispered.

'You have to listen to me, Uriah. Time is short.'

'Time?'

'The duty nurse will be doing her rounds in half an hour. You have to have your mind made up before then.'

He pulled the shade of the lamp down to see her better in the dark.

'What's going on, Helena?'

She swallowed.

'And why aren't you wearing your uniform today?' he asked.

This was what she had been dreading most. Not lying to her mother and saying she was going to her sister's in Salzburg for a couple of days. Not persuading the forester's son – who was now waiting in the road outside the gate – to drive her to the hospital. Not even saying goodbye to her possessions, the church and her secure life in the Viennese woods. But telling him everything: that she loved him and that she would willingly risk her life and future for him. Because she might be mistaken. Not about what he felt for her – of that she was certain – but about his character. Would he have the courage and the drive to do what she would suggest? At least he was clear it wasn't his war they were fighting against the Red Army in the south.

'We should have had time to get to know each other better,' she said, placing her hand over his. He grasped it and held it tight.

'But we don't have that luxury,' she said, squeezing his hand. 'There's a train for Paris leaving in an hour. I've bought two tickets. My teacher lives there.'

'Your teacher?'

'It's a long, complicated story, but he'll receive us.'

'What do you mean, receive us?'

'We can stay with him. He lives alone. And, as far as I know, he doesn't have a circle of friends. Have you got a passport?'

'What? Yes . . .'

He seemed lost for words, as if he was wondering whether he had fallen asleep while reading the book about the boy in rags and all this was just a dream.

'Yes, I've got a passport.'

'Good. The trip takes two days. We've got seats and I've brought lots of food.'

He took a deep breath.

'Why Paris?'

'It's a big city, a city you can disappear in. Listen, I've got some of my father's clothes in the car – you can change into civvies there. His shoe size —'

'No.' He held up his hand and her low, intense stream of words stopped momentarily. She held her breath and concentrated on his pensive face.

'No,' he repeated in a whisper. 'That's silly.'

'But . . .' She seemed to have a block of ice in her stomach.

'It's better to travel in uniform,' he said. 'A young man in civvies will only arouse suspicion.'

She was so happy she could hardly get the words out and squeezed his hand even harder. Her heart sang with such joy that she had to tell it to be quiet.

'And one more thing,' he said, swinging his legs out of bed.

'Yes?'

'Do you love me?'

'Yes.'

'Good.'

He already had his jacket on.

26

HARRY CAST HIS EYES AROUND. AT THE TIDY, well-organised shelves of ring-binders neatly displayed in chronological order. At the walls where diplomas and distinctions from a career in smooth ascent hung. A black and white photograph of a younger, uniformed Kurt Meirik, with the rank of major, greeting King Olav hung behind the desk and caught the eye of everyone who came in. This was the picture Harry sat studying when the door opened behind him.

'I apologise for keeping you waiting, Hole. Stay seated.'

It was Meirik. Harry hadn't made a move to stand up.

'Well,' said Meirik, taking a seat behind his desk. 'How has your first week with us been?'

Meirik sat upright in his chair and revealed a row of large yellow teeth, in a way which made you suspect he had overdone the smile training in his life.

'Fairly dull,' Harry said.

'Heh, heh. It hasn't been that bad, has it?' Meirik seemed surprised.

'Well, you've got better coffee than we have downstairs.'

'Crime Squad have, you mean?'

'Sorry,' Harry said. 'It takes time to get used to it. To "we" being POT now.'

'Yes, we'll just have to be a bit patient. That's true for a number of things. Isn't it, Hole, eh?'

Harry nodded assent. No point running at windmills. Not in the first month, anyway. As expected, he had been given an office at the end of a long corridor, which meant that he didn't see more of the others working there than was absolutely necessary. His job consisted of reading reports from regional POT offices and quite simply evaluating whether they were case files which should be passed up higher into the system. Meirik's instructions had been absolutely clear: unless it was rubbish, everything should be passed on. In other words, Harry's job was to filter out the dross. Last week, three reports had come in. He had tried to read them slowly, but there were limits to how long he could drag it out. One of the reports was from Trondheim and dealt with the new electronic monitoring equipment no one knew how to operate, as their monitoring expert had left. Harry passed it on. The second one concerned a German businessman in Bergen whom they now declared 'not suspicious' because he had delivered the consignment of curtain rails he said he was there to deliver. Harry passed that one on. The third was from the Østland region, from the police station in Skien. They had received some complaints from chalet owners in Siljan who had heard shooting the previous weekend. Since they weren't in the hunting season, an officer had gone up to investigate and had found empty cartridges of an unknown make in the woods. They had sent the cartridges to the forensics department within *Kripos*, the Norwegian CID, who had reported back that the ammunition was probably for a Märklin rifle, a very unusual weapon.

Harry had passed the report on, but not before taking a copy for himself.

'Right, what I wanted to talk to you about was a poster that has come into our possession. Neo-Nazis are planning to kick up a fuss outside mosques in Oslo on 17 May. There is some movable Muslim feast which falls on the seventeenth this year, and a great many foreign parents are refusing to allow their children to take part in the children's Independence Day parade because they want them to go to the mosque.'

'Eid.'

'I beg your pardon?'

'Eid. Their holy day. It's the Muslims' Christmas Eve.'

'So you're into this stuff?'

'No, but I was invited to a dinner by my neighbour last year. They're Pakistani. They thought it was so sad for me to sit alone on Eid.'

'Really? Hm.' Meirik put on his Oberinspektor Derrick glasses.

'I've got the poster here. They write that it is an insult to your host country to celebrate anything other than Norwegian Independence Day on 17 May. And they say that blacks are happy to claim benefits, but shirk every single Norwegian citizen's obligation.'

'To be obedient and shout "Hurrah" for Norway as the parade goes by,' Harry said, pulling out his pack of cigarettes. He had noticed the ashtray on top of the bookcase and Meirik nodded in response to Harry's enquiring glance. Harry lit up, drew the smoke deep into his lungs and tried to imagine the blood vessels in the lung wall greedily absorbing the nicotine. Life was becoming shorter and the thought that he would never stop smoking filled him with a strange satisfaction. Ignoring the warning on the cigarette packet might not be the most flamboyant act of rebellion a man could allow himself, but at least it was one he could afford.

'See what you can find out,' Meirik said.

'Fine, but I warn you I have a short fuse where skinheads are concerned.'

'Heh, heh.' Meirik showed his large yellow teeth again and Harry realised what he reminded him of: a dressage horse.

'Heh, heh.'

'There was another thing,' Harry said. 'It's about the report on the ammunition found in Siljan. It's for a Märklin rifle.'

'I have a vague recollection of hearing something about that, yes.'

'I've been doing a bit of checking of my own.'

'Oh?'

Harry picked up on the chill tone.

'I checked the National Firearms Registry for last year. No Märklin rifles have been registered in Norway.'

'That doesn't surprise me. The list must already have been checked by people here after you passed on the report, Hole. Not your job, you know.'

'Perhaps not. But I wanted to be sure that whoever was dealing with it followed up Interpol's reports on arms smuggling.'

'Interpol? Why should we do that?'

'No one is importing these rifles into Norway, so this one has been smuggled in.'

Harry took a print-out from his breast pocket.

'This is a copy of a list of consignments Interpol found during a raid on an illegal arms dealer in Johannesburg in November. Look here. A Märklin rifle. And there's the destination, Oslo.'

'Hm. Where did you get hold of this?'

'The Interpol file on the Net. Available to anyone in POT. Anyone who can be bothered.'

'Really?' Meirik's gaze settled on Harry for a moment before scrutinising the print-out more closely.

'This is all very well, but arms smuggling is not our business, Hole. If you knew how many illegal weapons the police confiscate in the course of one year —'

'Six hundred and eleven,' Harry said.

'Is that so?'

'Last year. And that's just the police authority in Oslo. Two out of three are taken off criminals, mainly small arms, pump guns and sawn-off shotguns. On average one gun is confiscated every day. In the nineties the number almost doubled.'

'Fine, so you understand that we in POT cannot prioritise an unregistered rifle in Buskerud.'

Meirik was struggling to maintain his composure. Harry exhaled smoke through his mouth and studied it as it rose to the ceiling.

'Siljan isn't in Buskerud,' he said.

Meirik's jaw muscles were working hard.

'Have you rung Customs & Excise, Hole?'

'No.'

Meirik looked at his watch, a lumpen, inelegant steel job Harry guessed he had been given for long and faithful service.

'Then I suggest you do. This is a case for them. Right now I have more pressing —'

'Do you know what a Märklin rifle is, Meirik?'

Harry watched the POT boss's eyebrows jump up and down and wondered if it was already too late. He could feel the swish of the windmills.

'Not my business, either, by the way, Hole. You'd better take this up with . . .'

Kurt Meirik suddenly seemed to realise that he was Hole's only line manager.

'A Märklin rifle,' Harry said, 'is a German semi-automatic hunting rifle which uses 16 mm bullets, bigger than those of any other rifle. It is intended for use on big game hunts, such as for water buffalo or elephants. The first rifle was made in 1970, but only three hundred were made before the German authorities banned the sale of the weapon in 1973. The reason was that the rifle is, with a couple of simple adjustments and Märklin telescopic sights, the ultimate professional murder weapon, and it had already become the world's most sought after assassination weapon by 1973. Of the three hundred rifles at least one hundred fell into the hands of contract killers and terrorist organisations like Baader Meinhof and the Red Brigade.'

'Hm. Did you say one hundred?' Meirik passed the printout back to Harry. 'That means that two out of three use the gun for what it was intended. Hunting.'

'This is not a weapon for hunting elk or any other kind of hunting common in Norway.'

'Really? Why not?'

Harry wondered what it was that held Meirik back. Why didn't he ask him to finish his cigarette and go? And why was he himself so keen to provoke such a reaction? Perhaps it was nothing, perhaps he was just getting old and grumpy. Whatever it was, Meirik was behaving like a well-paid childminder who didn't dare touch the brat. Harry observed the long column of ash bending towards the floor.

'First of all, hunting is not a millionaire's sport in Norway. A Märklin rifle with telescopic sights costs around 150,000 Deutschmarks – in other words, the same as a new Mercedes. And every cartridge costs 90 Deutschmarks. Secondly, an elk hit by a 16 mm bullet looks as if it has been in a collision with a train. A pretty messy business.'

'Heh, heh.' Meirik had obviously decided to change tactics. Now he was leaning back with his hands behind his shiny pate, as a sign that he wouldn't mind Hole entertaining him for a while yet. Harry stood up, took the ashtray down from the top shelf and returned to his seat.

'Of course the cartridges may belong to some fanatical arms collector who has tested out his new rifle and now keeps it hanging in a glass showcase in a big house somewhere in Norway, never to be used again. But dare we assume that?' Harry shook his head. 'I suggest I take a trip up to Skien and have a peep at this place. Besides, I doubt that it was a pro up there.'

'Really?'

'Pros clean up after themselves. Leaving empty cartridges

is like leaving a business card. But if it's an amateur with a Märklin rifle, that doesn't make me feel any more reassured.'

Meirik uttered a few hmm-sounds. Then he nodded.

'Fine. And keep me posted if you find out anything about the Independence Day plans of our neo-Nazis.'

Harry stubbed out his cigarette. *Venice, Italy*, it said on the side of the gondola-shaped ashtray.

27

Linz. 9 June 1944.

THE FAMILY OF FIVE GOT OFF THE TRAIN, AND they had the compartment to themselves. When they slowly moved off again, Helena had already taken her seat by the window, although she couldn't see a great deal in the dark, only the contours of buildings adjacent to the train. He sat opposite and studied her with a little smile playing on his lips.

'You Austrians are good at observing the blackout,' he said. 'I can't see a single light.'

She sighed, 'We're good at doing what we're told.'

She looked at her watch. It was almost two o'clock.

'The next town is Salzburg,' she said. 'It's close to the German border. And then . . .'

'Munich, Zürich, Basle, France and Paris. You've said that three times already.'

He leaned forward and squeezed her hand.

'It'll be fine, just you see. Sit over here.'

She moved without letting go of his hand and rested her head gently against his shoulder. He looked so different now he was in uniform.

'So this Brockhard has sent in another medical certificate, valid for a week?'

'Yes, he said he would send it by post yesterday afternoon.'

'Why such a short extension?'

'Well, so that he had the situation – and me – better under control. I would have had to give him a good reason to extend your sick leave each time. Do you understand?'

'Yes, I do,' he said and she saw his jaw muscles tensing.

'Let's not talk about Brockhard any more now,' she said. 'Tell me a story.'

She stroked his cheek and he gave a heavy sigh. 'Which one would you like to hear?'

'Whichever you like.'

The stories. That was how he had caught her attention at the Rudolf II Hospital. They were so different from the stories other soldiers told. Uriah's stories were about courage, comradeship and hope. Like the time he had come off duty and discovered a polecat on his best friend's chest ready to rip open his throat as he slept. The distance had been almost ten metres and the bunker with its black earthen walls almost pitch dark. But he had had no choice. He had put his gun to his cheek and kept firing until the magazine was empty. They had eaten the polecat for dinner the next day.

There were several stories like that one. Helena couldn't remember them all, but she remembered that she had started listening. His stories were lively and amusing; she wasn't sure if she could believe some of them. She wanted to, though, because they were an antidote to the other stories, stories about irredeemable fates and senseless deaths.

As the unlit train shook and juddered its way through the night on newly repaired rails, Uriah told about the time he had shot a Russian sniper in no man's land and had ventured out to give the atheistic Bolshevik a Christian burial, with psalms and everything.

'So beautifully did I sing that night,' Uriah said, 'I could hear them applauding from the Russian side.'

'Really?' she laughed.

'It was more beautiful than any singing you've heard in the *Staatsoper*.'

'Liar.'

Uriah pulled her over to him and sang softly into her ear:

> *Join the circle of men round the fire, gaze at*
> *torches so golden and bright,*
> *Urging soldiers to aim ever higher, pledge their*
> *beings to stand up and fight.*
> *In the flickering glistening flashes, see our*
> *Norway in years, of yore,*
> *See its people emerging from ashes, see your*
> *kinsfolk at peace and at war.*
>
> *See your fathers in action for freedom,*
> *suffer losses both woman and man,*
> *See the thousands arise to defeat them,*
> *giving all in their fight for our land.*
> *See the men out in snow every hour, proud and*
> *glad of the struggle and toil,*
> *Hearts aflame with the will and the power,*
> *standing firm on our forefathers' soil.*
>
> *See the names of the Norsemen appear, live in sagas*
> *of glittering words,*
> *Who though centuries dead are still here,*
> *still remembered from fells to fjords.*
> *But the man who has hoisted the penant,*
> *red and yellow the flag of the great,*
> *We salute you our fiery lieutenant: Quisling,*
> *ruler of soldier and state.*

Uriah was silent afterwards and stared blindly out of the window. Helena knew that his thoughts were far away, and let him remain with them. She put her arm around his chest.

Ra-ta-ta-tat – ra-ta-ta-tat – ra-ta-ta-tat.

It sounded as if someone was running beneath them, somebody was trying to catch them.

She was frightened. Not so much about the unknown territory that lay before them, but about the unknown man she was snuggling up to. Now that he was so close, everything she had seen and become used to from a distance seemed to disappear.

She listened for his heartbeat, but the rattle of the train on the rails was too loud, so she had to take it on trust that there was a heart in there. She smiled to herself and waves of pleasure washed over her. What a wonderful, wonderful insanity! She knew absolutely nothing about him; he had told her so little about himself, he had told her only these stories.

His uniform smelled of mildew, and for a second it struck her that it was probably the smell a soldier's uniform had when he had been lying dead on the battlefield for a while. Or had been buried. But where did these ideas come from? She had been so tense for so long that only now did she realise how tired she was.

'Sleep,' he said in response to her thoughts.

'Yes,' she said. She vaguely recalled hearing an air-raid siren in the distance as the world around her shrank.

'What?'

She heard her own voice, felt Uriah shaking her and she jumped. The first thing that came into her head when she saw the uniformed man in the doorway was that they had been caught.

'Tickets, please.'

'Oh,' she exclaimed. She tried to pull herself together and felt the ticket conductor's probing eyes on her as she rummaged feverishly in her bag. Finally she found the yellow cardboard tickets she had bought in Vienna and passed them to the conductor. He studied the tickets while rocking on his heels in rhythm with the train. It took longer than was comfortable for Helena.

'You're going to Paris?' he asked. 'Together?'

'Ganz genau,' Uriah said.

The conductor was an older man. He looked at them.

'You're not from Austria, I can hear.'

'No. I'm Norwegian.'

'Oh, Norway. I've heard it's beautiful.'

'Yes, thank you. You could say that.'

'So you voluntarily enlisted to fight for Hitler then?'

'I did. I've been on the Eastern Front. In the north.'

'Really? Where in the north?'

'Up by Leningrad.'

'Hm. And now you're going to Paris. Together with your . . . ?'

'Girlfriend.'

'Girlfriend, exactly. On leave?'

'Yes.'

The conductor punched their tickets.

'From Vienna?' he asked Helena, handing them back. She nodded.

'I can see you're Catholic,' he said, pointing to the crucifix she wore on a chain over her blouse. 'My wife is too.'

He leaned back and scanned the corridor. And then, turning to Uriah, he asked, 'Has your girlfriend shown you *Stephansdom* in Vienna?'

'No, I've been laid up in the hospital, so unfortunately I haven't had much of a chance to see the city.'

'Right. A Catholic hospital by any chance?'

'Yes, the Rudo—'

'Yes,' Helena interrupted. 'A Catholic hospital.'

'Hm.'

Why doesn't he go away? Helena wondered.

The conductor cleared his throat again.

'Yes?' Uriah said finally.

'It's none of my business, but I hope you've remembered your papers as proof that you're on leave.'

Papers? Helena thought. She had been to France twice before with her father, and it had never even occurred to her they might need anything other than a passport.

'Yes, it's not a problem for you, *Fräulein*, but for your uniformed friend here it's essential that he carries papers documenting where he's stationed and where he's going.'

'Of course we have papers,' she burst out. 'Surely you don't imagine that we would travel without them.'

'No, no, of course not,' the conductor responded hastily. 'I just wanted to remind you. A couple of days ago . . .' He shifted his attention to the Norwegian. '. . . they arrested a young man who clearly had no orders to go where he was going, and he was consequently treated as a deserter. They took him on to the platform and shot him.'

'You don't mean that.'

'I'm afraid I do. I don't mean to frighten you, but war is war. And since you have official papers, you shouldn't have any problems when we get to the border immediately after leaving Salzburg.'

The carriage lurched and the conductor had to grab hold of the door frame. The three people looked at each other in silence.

'So that's the first checkpoint?' Uriah asked finally. 'After Salzburg?'

The conductor nodded.

'Thank you,' Uriah said.

The conductor cleared his throat: 'I had a son your age. He fell at the front, by Dnerp.'

'I'm sorry to hear that.'

'Well, sorry to have woken you, *Fräulein. Mein Herr.*'

He saluted and was gone.

Helena made sure the door was completely closed. Then she hid her face in her hands.

'How could I have been so naive!' she sobbed.

'Don't cry now,' he said, putting his arm around her shoulder. 'I should have thought of the papers. After all, I knew I couldn't just move around freely.'

'But what if you tell them you're on sick leave and say you felt like going to Paris? That's a part of the Third Reich. It's —'

'Then they'll ring the hospital and Brockhard will say that I absconded.'

She leaned against him and sobbed in his lap. He caressed her sleek brown hair.

'Besides, I should have known that this was too good to be true,' he said. 'I mean – me and Schwester Helena in Paris?'

She could hear the smile in his voice.

'No, I'll wake up in my hospital bed soon, thinking that was one hell of a dream. And look forward to you bringing me my breakfast. Anyway, you're on night shift tomorrow. You haven't forgotten that, have you? Then I can tell you about the time Daniel filched twenty rations from the Swedish unit.'

She lifted a tear-stained face to him.

'Kiss me, Uriah.'

28

Siljan, Telemark. 22 February 2000.

HARRY CHECKED HIS WATCH AGAIN AND CAU-
tiously pressed his foot on the accelerator. The appointment
was for four o'clock. If he arrived after dusk, the whole trip
would be a waste of time. What was left of the winter tyre
tread keyed into the ice with a scrunch. Even though he had
only driven forty kilometres on the winding, icy forest path,
it seemed several hours since he had turned off the main
road. The cheap sunglasses he had bought at the petrol station hadn't helped much, and his eyes smarted from the
bright light reflecting off the snow.

At long last, he caught sight of the police car with the
Skien registration number at the edge of the road. He braked
warily, pulled over and took the skis off his roof rack. They
came from a Trondheim ski manufacturer who had gone
bankrupt fifteen years ago. That must have been roughly the
same time as he put on the wax, which was now a tough grey
mass underneath the skis. He found the track from the path
up to the chalet as it had been described. The skis stayed on
the track as if glued; he couldn't have moved sideways if he
had wanted to. The sun hung low over the spruce trees when
he reached his destination. On the steps of a black log chalet

sat two men in anoraks and a boy Harry, who didn't know any teenagers, guessed to be somewhere between twelve and sixteen.

'Ove Bertelsen?' Harry enquired, resting on his ski poles. He was out of breath.

'That's me,' one of the men said, standing up to shake hands. 'And this is Officer Folldal.'

The second man gave a measured nod.

Harry supposed it must have been the boy who found the cartridge shells.

'Wonderful to get away from the Oslo air, I imagine,' Bertelsen said.

Harry pulled out a pack of cigarettes.

'Even more wonderful to get away from the Skien air, I would think.'

Folldal took off his cap and straightened his back.

Bertelsen smiled: 'Contrary to what people say, the air in Skien is cleaner than in any other Norwegian town.'

Harry cupped his hands round a match and lit his cigarette.

'Is that right? I'll have to remember that. Have you found anything?'

'Over there.'

The other three put on their skis, and with Folldal in the lead they trudged along a track to a clearing in the forest. Folldal pointed with his pole to a black rock protruding twenty centimetres above the snow.

'The boy found the shells in the snow by that rock. I reckon it was a hunter out practising. You can see the ski tracks nearby. It hasn't snowed for over a week, so they could well be his. Looks like he was wearing those broad Telemark skis.'

Harry crouched down. He ran a finger along the rock where it met the broad ski track.

'Or old wooden skis '

'Oh yes?'

He held up a tiny splinter of wood.

'Well, I never,' Folldal said, looking across at Bertelsen.

Harry turned to the boy. He was wearing a pair of baggy hunting trousers with pockets everywhere and a woollen cap pulled down well over his head.

'Which side of the rock did you find the cartridges?'

The boy pointed. Harry took off his skis, walked round the rock and lay on his back in the snow. The sky was light blue now, as it is on clear winter days just before the sun goes down. Then he rolled on to his side and peered over the rock. He followed the clearing in the forest where they had come in. There were four tree stumps in the clearing.

'Did you find any bullets or signs of shooting?'

Folldal scratched the back of his neck. 'Do you mean, have we examined every tree trunk within a half-kilometre radius?'

Bertelsen discreetly placed a gloved hand over Folldal's mouth. Harry flicked his ash and studied the glowing end of his cigarette.

'No, I mean, did you check the tree stumps over there?'

'And why should we have examined those particular stumps?' Folldal asked.

'Because Märklin make the world's heaviest rifle. A gun weighing fifteen kilos is not an attractive option for a standing shot, so it would be natural to assume that he rested it on this rock to take aim. Märklin rifles eject bullet casings to the right. Since the spent shells were found on the right of the stone, he must have been shooting in the direction we have come from. So it would not be unreasonable to assume that he positioned something on one of the tree stumps to aim at, would it?'

Bertelsen and Folldal looked at each other.

'Well, we'd better check that out.'

'Unless this is a bloody big bark beetle . . .' Bertelsen said three minutes later, '. . . then this is a bloody big bullet hole.'

He kneeled down in the snow and poked his finger into one of the tree stumps. 'Shit, the bullet's gone in a long way. I can't feel it.'

'Take a look inside,' Harry said.

'Why?'

'To see if it's gone right through,' Harry answered.

'Right through that enormous spruce?'

'Just take a look and see if you can see daylight.'

Harry heard Folldal snort behind him. Bertelsen put his eye to the hole.

'Mother of Jesus . . .'

'Can you see anything?' Folldal shouted.

'Only half the course of the bloody Siljan river.'

Harry turned towards Folldal, who had turned his back to him to spit.

Bertelsen got to his feet. 'A bulletproof vest won't help much if you're shot with one of those bastards, will it,' he groaned.

'Not at all,' Harry said. 'The only thing that would help would be armour-plating.' He stubbed his cigarette against the tree stump and corrected himself: '*Thick* armour-plating.'

He stood on his skis, sliding them back and forth in the snow.

'We'll have to have a chat with the people in the neighbouring chalets,' Bertelsen said. 'They may have seen or heard something. Or they may feel like admitting they own this rifle from hell.'

'After we had the arms amnesty last year . . .' Folldal began, but changed his mind when Bertelsen eyeballed him.

'Anything else we can do to help?' Bertelsen asked Harry.

'Well,' Harry said, scowling in the direction of the forest path, 'you couldn't help me bump-start the car, could you?'

29

Rudolf II Hospital, Vienna. 23 June 1944.

IT WAS LIKE DÉJÀ VU FOR HELENA. THE WIN-
dows were open and the warm summer morning filled the
corridor with the perfume of newly mown grass. For two
weeks there had been air raids every night, but she didn't
even notice the smell of smoke. She was holding a letter in
her hand. A wonderful letter! Even the grumpy matron had
to smile when Helena sang out her *Guten Morgen*.

Dr Brockhard looked up from his papers in surprise
when Helena burst into his office.

'Well?' he said.

He took off his glasses and directed his stiff gaze at her.
She caught a glimpse of the wet tongue sucking the ends of
his glasses. She took a seat.

'Christopher,' she began. She hadn't used his Christian
name since they were small. 'I have something to tell you.'

'Good,' he said. 'That's exactly what I have been waiting
for.'

She knew what he had been waiting for: an explanation for
why she still hadn't complied with his wishes and gone to his
flat in the main building despite the fact that he had extended
Uriah's medical certificate twice. Helena had blamed the

bombing, saying that she didn't dare go out. Then he had offered to visit her in her mother's summer house, which she
flatly rejected.

'I'll tell you everything,' she said.

'Everything?' he queried with a little smile.

Well, she thought, *almost everything.*

'The morning Uriah —'

'His name is *not* Uriah, Helena.'

'The morning he disappeared and you raised the alarm,
do you remember that?'

'Naturally.'

Brockhard set down his glasses, parallel with the paper in
front of him. 'I considered reporting his disappearance to the
military police. However, he miraculously reappeared with
some story about wandering in the forest for half the night.'

'He wasn't in the forest. He was on the night train from
Salzburg.'

'Really?' Brockhard leaned back in his chair with a fixed
expression on his face, indicating that he was not a man who
liked to express surprise.

'He caught the night train from Vienna before midnight,
got off in Salzburg where he waited for an hour and a half
for the night train back again. He arrived at the *Hauptbahn-
hof* at nine that morning.'

'Hm.' Brockhard focused on the pen he held between his
fingertips. 'And what did he give as his reason for this idiotic
excursion?'

'Umm,' Helena said, unaware that she was smiling, 'you
may remember that I was also late that morning.'

'Yeess . . .'

'I was also returning from Salzburg.'

'Is that so?'

'That is so.'

'I think you will have to explain, Helena.'

She explained while staring at Brockhard's fingertips. A
drop of blood had formed under the pen nib.

'I see,' said Brockhard when she had finished. 'You thought you would go to Paris. And how long did you think you could hide there?'

'It's probably obvious that we didn't think much at all. Uriah thought we should go to America. To New York.'

Brockhard laughed drily. 'You're a very sensible girl, Helena. I can see that this turncoat must have blinded you with his beguiling lies about America. But do you know what?'

'What?'

'I forgive you.'

On seeing her gawp he continued, 'Yes, I forgive you. Perhaps you ought to be punished, but I know how restless young girls' hearts can be.'

'It's not forgiveness I —'

'How's your mother? It must be hard for her now that you are alone. Was it three years' imprisonment your father was given?'

'Four. Would you please listen, Christopher?'

'I beg of you, do not do or say anything you might come to regret, Helena. What you have told me changes nothing. The deal remains the same.'

'No!' Helena stood up so quickly that her chair toppled over and now she smacked the letter she had been kneading in her hand on to the desk.

'See for yourself! You no longer have any power over me. Or Uriah.'

Brockhard glanced at the letter. The opened brown envelope didn't mean a thing to him. He took out the letter, put on his glasses and began to read.

Waffen-SS
Berlin, 22 June

We have received a request from the Chief of Norwegian Police, Jonas Lie, to hand you over with immediate effect to the police in Oslo for further service. Since you are a Norwegian

citizen, we see no reason not to comply. This order therefore
countermands your previous orders to join the Wehrmacht.
You will be advised of details regarding the meeting point
and timing by the Norwegian police authorities.

Heinrich Himmler
Oberkommandierender der Schutzstaffel (SS)

Brockhard had to look at the signature twice. Heinrich Himmler in person! Then he held up the letter to the light.

'You can check it if you like, but I assure you it is genuine,' Helena said.

Through the open window she could hear birds singing
in the garden. Brockhard cleared his throat twice before
speaking.

'So you wrote a letter to the Chief of Police in Norway?'

'Uriah wrote to him. I simply posted it.'

'You posted it?'

'Yes. Or no, actually. I telegraphed it.'

'A whole application? That must have cost —'

'It was urgent.'

'Heinrich Himmler . . .' he said, more to himself than
to her.

'I'm sorry, Christopher.'

Again the dry laugh. 'Are you? Haven't you accomplished
exactly what you wanted, Helena?'

She forced a friendly smile.

'I have a favour to ask of you, Christopher.'

'Oh?'

'Uriah wants me to go with him to Norway. I need a recommendation from the hospital to be able to apply for a travel
permit.'

'And now you're afraid I'll put a spoke in your wheel?'

'Your father is on the governing board.'

'Yes, I could create problems for you.' He rubbed his chin.
The intense stare had fixed itself on to a point on her forehead.

'Whatever happens, Christopher, you can't stop us. Uriah and I love each other. Do you understand?'

'Why should I do a favour for a soldier's whore?'

Helena's mouth hung open. Even from someone she despised, someone who was clearly acting in passion, the word stung like a slap. But before she managed to answer, Brockhard's face had crumpled as if he were the one to have been hit.

'Forgive me, Helena. I . . . damn!' He abruptly turned his back on her. Helena wanted to get up and leave, but she couldn't find the words to liberate herself. His voice was strained as he added: 'I didn't mean to hurt you, Helena.'

'Christopher . . .'

'You don't understand. I'm not saying this out of arrogance, but I have qualities which in time I know you would grow to appreciate. I may have gone too far, but remember that I always acted with your best interests at heart.'

She stared at his back. The doctor's coat was a size too big for his narrow, sloping shoulders. She was reminded of the Christopher she had known as a child. He'd had delicate black curls and a real suit even though he was only twelve. One summer she had even been in love with him. Hadn't she?

He released a long, trembling breath. She took a pace towards him, then changed her mind. Why should she feel sympathy for this man? Yes, she knew why. Because her own heart was overflowing with happiness although she had done little to come by it. Yet Christopher Brockhard, who tried every day of his life to gain happiness, would always be a lonely man.

'Christopher, I have to go now.'

'Yes, of course. You have to do what you have to do, Helena.'

She stood up and walked to the door.

'And I have to do what I have to do,' he said.

30

Police HQ. 24 February 2000.

WRIGHT SWORE. HE HAD TRIED ALL THE KNOBS on the overhead projector to focus the picture, without any luck.

Someone coughed.

'I think perhaps the picture itself is unclear, Lieutenant. It's not the projector, I mean.'

'Well, at any rate, this is Andreas Hochner,' Wright said, shielding his eyes with his hand so that he could see those present. The room had no windows, so when, as now, the lights were switched off it was pitch black. According to what Wright had been told, it was bug-proof too, whatever that meant.

Besides himself, Andreas Wright, a lieutenant in the Military Intelligence Service, there were only three others present: Major Bård Ovesen from Military Intelligence, Harry Hole, the new man from POT, and Kurt Meirik, the head of POT. It was Hole who had faxed him the name of the arms dealer in Johannesburg. And had nagged him for information every day since. There was no doubt that a great number of people in POT seemed to think that Military Intelligence was merely a subsection of POT, but they obviously hadn't read the regulations, where it stated that they were equally ranked organisations working in partnership. But Wright had. So, in the end he had explained to the new man that low priority cases had to wait. Half an hour later Meirik had rung to say that this case was top priority. Why couldn't they have said that at the outset?

The blurred black and white image on the screen showed a man leaving a restaurant; it seemed to have been taken from a car window. The man had a broad, coarse face with dark eyes and a large, ill-defined nose with a thick, black, droopy moustache beneath.

'Andreas Hochner, born in 1954 in Zimbabwe, German parents,' Wright read from the print-outs he had brought with him. 'Ex-mercenary in the Congo and South Africa, probably involved with arms smuggling since the mideighties. At nineteen he was one of seven men accused of murdering a black boy in Kinshasa, but was acquitted for lack of evidence. Married and divorced twice. His employer in Johannesburg is suspected of being behind the smuggling of anti-air missiles to Syria and the purchase of chemical weapons from Iraq. Alleged to have supplied special rifles to Karadzic during the Bosnian war and to have trained snipers during the siege of Sarajevo. The last has not as yet been confirmed.'

'Please skip the details,' Meirik said, glancing at his watch. It was always slow, but there was a wonderful inscription from the Military High Command on the back.

'Alright,' Wright said, flicking through the rest of the papers. 'Yes, here. Andreas Hochner was one of four held during a raid on an arms dealer in Johannesburg in December. On that occasion a coded order list was found. One of the ordered items was a Märklin rifle, bound for Oslo. And a date: 21 December. That's all.'

There was silence, only the whirring of the overhead-projector fan could be heard. Someone in the dark coughed. It sounded like Bård Ovesen. Wright shaded his eyes.

'How can we be sure that Hochner is the key person in our case?' Ovesen asked.

Harry Hole's voice came out of the dark.

'I talked to an Inspector Isaiah Burne in Hillbrow, Johannesburg. He was able to tell me that after the arrests they searched the flats of those involved and found an interesting passport in Hochner's. The photo was of himself, but the name was completely different.'

'An arms dealer with a false name is not exactly . . . dynamite,' Ovesen said.

'I was thinking more of one of the stamps they found in it. Oslo, Norway, 10 December.'

'So he's been to Oslo,' Meirik said. 'There's a Norwegian on the company's list of customers, and we've found spent cartridges from this super-rifle. So Andreas Hochner came to Norway and we can assume a deal went ahead. But who is the Norwegian on the list?'

'The list does not, unfortunately, give a full name and address.' Harry's voice. 'The customer in Oslo is listed as Uriah. Bound to be a code name. And, according to Burne in Johannesburg, Hochner is not that interested in talking.'

'I thought the police in Johannesburg had effective methods of interrogation,' Ovesen said.

'Possibly, but Hochner probably risks more by talking than by keeping his mouth shut. It's a long list of customers . . .'

'I've heard they use electricity in South Africa,' Wright said. 'Under the feet, on nipples and . . . well. Bloody painful. Could someone switch on the light please?'

Harry: 'In a case which involves the purchase of chemical weapons from Saddam, a business trip to Oslo with a rifle is fairly trivial. I think, unfortunately, the South Africans are saving their electricity for more important issues, let's put it that way. Apart from that, it's not certain that Hochner knows who this Uriah is. And in the absence of any information about Uriah, we have to wonder: what are his plans? Assassination? Terrorism?'

'Or robbery,' Meirik said.

'With a Märklin rifle?' Ovesen said. 'That would be like shooting sparrows with a cannon.'

'A drugs killing maybe?' Wright suggested.

'Well,' Harry said. 'A handgun was all that was needed to kill the most protected person in Sweden. And the Olaf Palme assassin was never caught. So why a gun costing over half a million kroner to shoot someone here?'

'What do you suggest, Harry?'

'Perhaps the target isn't a Norwegian, but someone from outside. Someone who is a constant target for terrorists, but is too strongly protected in their home country for an assassination to succeed there. Someone they think they can kill more easily in a small, peaceful country where they reckon the security measures will be proportionate.'

'But who?' Ovesen asked. 'There's no one in the country who fits that profile.'

'And there's no one coming,' Meirik added.

'Perhaps it's longer term,' Harry said.

'But the weapon arrived two months ago,' Ovesen said. 'It doesn't make sense that foreign terrorists would come to Norway two months before they're due to carry out a mission.'

'Perhaps it's not foreigners, but a Norwegian.'

'There's no one in Norway capable of doing what you're suggesting,' Wright said, groping for a switch on the wall.

'Exactly,' Harry said. 'That's the point.'

'The point?'

'Imagine a high-profile foreign terrorist who wants to take the life of a person in his own country, and this person is going to Norway. The secret services in the country where he lives follow his every move, so instead of taking the risk himself he contacts a group of like-minded people in Norway. The fact that they may be amateurs is actually an advantage as the terrorist then knows the group in question will not be enjoying the attentions of the police.'

Meirik: 'The discarded cartridges would suggest they're amateurs, yes.'

'The terrorist and the amateur agree that the terrorist finances the purchase of an expensive weapon and afterwards all links are cut. There is nothing to be traced back to the terrorist. In this way he has set a process in motion, risking little more than some cash.'

'But what if this amateur is not capable of carrying out the job?' Ovesen asked. 'Or decides to sell the gun and run off with the money?'

'There is of course a certain risk involved, but we have to assume that the terrorist considers the amateur to be highly motivated. He may also have a personal motive that compels him to put his own life on the line in order to execute the mission.'

'Amusing hypothesis,' Ovesen said. 'How were you going to test it out?'

'You can't. I'm talking about a man we know nothing about. We don't know how he thinks; we can't rely on him acting rationally.'

'Nice,' Meirik said. 'Do we have any other theories as to how this weapon could have ended up in Norway?'

'Tons of them,' Harry said. 'But this is the worst possible scenario.'

'Hmmm,' Meirik sighed. 'Our job is to chase ghosts after all, so we'd better see if we can have a chat with this Hochner. I'll make a couple of calls to . . . aaahhh!'

Wright had found the switch and the room was filled with harsh white light.

31

The Lang Family's Summer Residence, Vienna. 25 June 1944.

HELENA WAS STUDYING HERSELF IN THE BED-room mirror. She would have preferred to have the window open so that she could listen for footsteps on the gravel drive, but Mother was very precise about the blackout. She contemplated the photograph of Father on the dresser. It always struck her how young and innocent he looked in the picture.

She had fastened her hair with a slide, as she always did. Should she do it differently? Beatrice had taken in Mother's red muslin dress so that it fitted Helena's tall, slim figure. Mother had been wearing this dress when she met Father. The thought was curious, remote and in a way quite painful. That might have been because when Mother told her about that time it was as if she were talking about two different people – two attractive, happy people who thought they knew where they were going.

Helena loosened the hairslide and shook her brown hair until it was in front of her face. The doorbell rang. She could hear Beatrice's footsteps in the hall. Helena fell backwards on to the bed and could feel the butterflies in her stomach. She couldn't help it – it was like being a love-sick fourteen-year-old in a summer romance again! She heard the muffled sound of talking from below, Mother's sharp, nasal voice, the clatter of coat-hangers as Beatrice hung his overcoat in the wardrobe. An overcoat! Helena thought. He had put on his overcoat even though it was one of these warm, sultry summer evenings they didn't usually have before August.

She waited and waited, then she heard Mother's voice calling:

'Helena!'

She got up from the bed, fixed the slide into position, looked at her hands, repeated to herself: *I have not got big hands, I have not got big hands.* Then she cast a final glance at the mirror – she *was* attractive! – took a trembling breath and went out of the door.

'Hele—'

Mother stopped calling as soon as Helena came into view at the top of the stairs. Helena cautiously placed one foot on the top step; the high heels she normally ran downstairs in suddenly seemed shaky and unsteady.

'Your guest has arrived,' Mother said.

Your guest. In another context Helena would probably have been annoyed by Mother's choice of expression to emphasise that she did not perceive the menial foreign soldier as a guest of the house. But these were exceptional times, and Helena could have kissed her mother for not being more difficult. At least she had gone to receive him before Helena herself made her entrance.

Helena looked across at Beatrice. The housekeeper smiled, but there was the same melancholic tinge to her eyes that her mother had. Helena shifted her gaze to Him. His eyes were shining and she seemed to feel the heat from them burning in her own cheeks. She had to lower her gaze to the brown, clean-shaven throat, the collar with the double 's's and the green uniform which had been so creased on the train but was now freshly pressed. He held a bouquet of roses in his hand, which she knew Beatrice would already have offered to put into a vase, but he had thanked her and asked her to wait so that Helena would see them first.

She took another step. Her hand rested lightly on the banister. It was easier now. She raised her head and encompassed all three of them in one look. And suddenly she realised in an odd way that this was the most beautiful moment of her life. For she knew what they saw and how they were reflected in it.

Mother saw herself, her own lost youth and her dreams coming down the stairs; Beatrice saw the girl she had brought up as her own; and he saw the woman he loved so much that he could not hide it behind Scandinavian embarrassment and good manners.

'You look wonderful,' Beatrice mouthed. Helena winked in return. Then she was down.

'So you found the way, even in the pitch dark?' she smiled at Uriah.

'Yes,' he answered in a loud, clear voice, and in the high, tiled hall the answer resounded as in a church.

Mother talked in her sharp, slightly piercing voice while Beatrice floated in and out of the dining room like a friendly ghost. Helena couldn't take her eyes off the diamond chain Mother wore around her neck, her most precious piece of jewellery which was only taken out on special occasions.

As an exception, Mother had left the door to the garden ajar. Cloud cover was so low that they might get away without any bombing tonight. The draught from the open door caused the flames of the stearin candles to flicker, and the shadows danced on the portraits of serious men and women bearing the surname of Lang. Mother had painstakingly explained to him who was who, what they had achieved and from which families they had selected their spouses. Uriah had listened with what Helena thought resembled a tiny sardonic smile, but it was difficult to be sure in the semi-darkness. Mother had explained that they felt a responsibility to save electricity with the war on. Naturally she didn't mention the family's present economic circumstances and that Beatrice was the last remaining servant of an original staff of four.

Uriah put down his fork and cleared his throat. Mother had placed them at the top of the long dining table. The young ones faced each other while she sat at the other end.

'That was delicious, Frau Lang.'

It had been a simple meal. Not so simple that it could be interpreted as an insult, but not so ostentatious that it might give him reason to believe he was a guest of honour.

'That's Beatrice,' Helena said with warmth. 'She makes Austria's best *Wienerschnitzel*. Have you tried it before?'

'Only once, as far as I know. And it doesn't bear comparison with this one.'

'*Schwein*,' Mother said. 'The one you ate was probably made with pork. In this house we only eat veal. Or, at a pinch, turkey.'

'I don't recall any meat,' he said with a smile. 'I think it was mostly egg and breadcrumbs.'

Helena laughed softly and received a swift glare from her mother.

The conversation had flagged on a couple of occasions during the meal, but after the long intervals Uriah tended to pick up the threads as often as Helena or her mother did. Helena had already decided before she invited him to dinner that she would not let what Mother thought bother her. Uriah was polite, but he was a man from a simple farming background, without the refinement of nature and manners that was concomitant with an upbringing in an elegant house. She had hardly needed to worry, however. Helena was amazed at Uriah's unconstrained, worldly wise deportment.

'You're probably planning to work when the war is over?'

the mother asked, putting the last bite of the potato into her mouth.

Uriah nodded and, while Frau Lang finished chewing, he patiently waited for the inevitable next question.

'And what work would that be, if I might ask?'

'Postman. At least, I was promised a job before the war broke out.'

'Delivering the post? Don't people live a terribly long distance from each other in your country?'

'It's not that bad. We settle where we can. Along the fjords, in the valleys and other places protected from the wind and weather. And then of course there are some towns and larger places too.'

'You don't say. Interesting. May I ask if you are a man of means?'

'Mother!' Helena stared at her mother in disbelief.

'Yes, my dear?' Mother dabbed her mouth with her napkin and waved to Beatrice to remove the plates.

'You make it sound like an interrogation.' Helena's dark eyebrows formed two 'v's in her forehead.

'Yes,' Mother said, raising her glass, with a beatific smile to Uriah. 'This is an interrogation.'

Uriah raised his glass and returned the smile.

'I understand you, Frau Lang. She is your only daughter. You are entirely within your rights. Well, I would say it is even your *duty* to be absolutely clear about what kind of man she has found herself.'

Frau Lang's narrow lips had formed into a pout to drink, but the wineglass stopped in mid-air.

'I am not well-off,' Uriah went on. 'But I am keen to work. I have a good head on me and I will manage to feed myself, Helena and undoubtedly several more. I promise to take care of her as well as I can, Frau Lang.'

Helena felt an intense desire to giggle and at the same time a strange excitement.

'Oh my goodness!' the mother exclaimed and put down her glass again. 'You're going a bit too far now, young man, aren't you?'

'Yes.' Uriah took a large swig and stared at the glass. 'And I have to say again that this is a really good wine, Frau Lang.'

Helena tried to kick his leg, but she couldn't reach under the wide oak table.

'These are strange times though. And there is so little of it.' He put down the glass, but continued to hold it in his gaze. The tiny hint of a smile Helena thought she had seen had disappeared.

'I have sat talking with my comrades on evenings like this, Frau Lang. About all the things we would do in the future, what the new Norway would be like and all the dreams we would realise, some great and some small. A few hours later they lay dead on the battlefield, without any future.'

He raised his eyes and looked directly at Frau Lang.

'I move quickly because I have found a woman I want and who wants me. A war is raging and all I can tell you about my future plans is so much eyewash. I have an hour to live a life in, Frau Lang. And perhaps that is all you have too.'

Helena shot a rapid glance at her mother. She seemed stunned.

'I received a letter from the Norwegian police today. I have to report to the field hospital at Sinsen school in Oslo for an examination. I'll be leaving in three days. And I was thinking of taking your daughter with me.'

Helena held her breath. The wall clock's ponderous tick boomed in the room. Mother's diamonds continued to glitter as the muscles under the wrinkled skin of her neck tightened and relaxed. A sudden gust of wind from the garden door caused the flames to lie flat and the shadows to leap between the dark furniture. Only the shadow of Beatrice at the kitchen door seemed to stand completely still.

'*Apfelstrudel*,' Mother said with a wave to Beatrice. 'A Viennese speciality.'

'I would like you to know that I am really looking forward to it,' Uriah said.

'Yes, and so you should be,' said Mother, forcing another sardonic smile. 'It's made with apples from our own garden.'

32

Johannesburg. 28 February 2000.

HILLBROW POLICE STATION WAS IN THE CENTRE of Johannesburg and looked like a fortress with barbed wire on top of the walls and steel mesh in front of windows, which were so small that they were more like gun slits.

'Two men, black, killed last night, in this police district alone,' Officer Isaiah Burne said as he led Harry through a labyrinth of corridors with peeling white walls and worn linoleum. 'Did you see the big Carlton Hotel? Closed. The whites moved out to the suburbs a long time ago, so now we only have each other to shoot at.'

Isaiah hitched up his pants. He was black, tall, knock-kneed and more than a little overweight. The white nylon shirt had dark rings of sweat in the armpits.

'Andreas Hochner is usually held in a prison we call Sin City out of town,' he said. 'We brought him in today for these interviews.'

'Are there others apart from mine?' Harry asked.

'Here we are,' Isaiah said, swinging open a door. They went into a room where two men were standing with folded arms and staring through a brown window.

'Two-way mirror,' Isaiah whispered. 'He can't see us.'

The two men in front of the window nodded to Isaiah and Harry and moved away.

They looked into a small, dimly lit room with one chair and one small table. On the table there was an ashtray full of cigarette ends and a microphone on a stand. The man sitting on the chair had dark eyes and a thick black moustache which hung down over the corners of his mouth. Harry immediately recognised him from Wright's blurred photographs.

'The Norwegian?' one of the two men mumbled, inclining his head towards Harry. Isaiah gave a nod of assent.

'OK,' the man said, turning to Harry, but without letting the man at the table out of his sight. 'He's yours, Norwegian. You got twenty minutes.'

'The fax said —'

'Screw the fax, Norwegian. Do you know how many countries want to interrogate this guy or have him handed over?'

'Well, no.'

'Just be happy you can talk to him at all,' the man said.

'Why has he agreed to talk to me?'

'How should we know? Ask him yourself.'

Harry tried to breathe from his stomach when he came into the cramped, airless interview room. On the wall, where red stripes of rust ran to form a kind of grille pattern, there was a clock. It showed 10.30. Harry's mind was on the policemen following him, Argus-eyed; that was what must have been making his hands clammy. The figure on the chair was hunched, his eyes half closed.

'Andreas Hochner?'

'Andreas Hochner?' the man in the chair repeated in a whisper, raised his eyes and gave the impression that he had just spotted something he wanted to crush under his heel. 'No, he's at home banging your mother.'

Warily, Harry took a seat. He thought he could hear guffaws of laughter from the other side of the black mirror.

'I'm Harry Hole from the Norwegian police,' he said softly. 'You agreed to talk to us.'

'Norway?' Hochner said with some scepticism. He leaned forward and inspected the ID card Harry held up. Then he smiled a little sheepishly.

'Sorry, Hole. They didn't tell me it was Norway today, you see. I've been waiting for you.'

'Where's your lawyer?' Harry put the briefcase on the table, opened it and took out a sheet of questions and a notepad.

'Forget him. I don't trust the guy. Is the mike on?'

'I don't know. Does it matter?'

'I don't want the niggers to hear. I'm interested in making a deal. With you. With Norway.'

Harry looked up from the question sheet. The clock on the wall over Hochner's head was ticking. Three minutes gone. Something told him he wasn't going to get his allotted time.

'What sort of deal?'

'Is the mike on?' Hochner whispered between his teeth.

'What sort of deal?'

Hochner rolled his eyes. Then he leaned forward over the table and said in a rapid whisper, 'In South Africa it's the death penalty for the things they maintain I've done. Do you understand what I'm getting at?'

'Maybe. Go on.'

'I can tell you certain things about the man in Oslo so long as you can guarantee your government will ask the nigger government for a reprieve. Because I helped you, right. Your Prime Minister, she was here, right? Her and Mandela went round hugging each other. The ANC honchos in charge now, they like Norway. You support them. You boycotted us when the nigger commies wanted us to be boycotted. They'll listen to you, right?'

'Why can't you make the same deal by helping the police here?'

'For fuck's sake!' Hochner's fist hit the table so hard the ashtray jumped and it rained cigarette butts. 'Don't you understand anything, you fucking oinker! They think I've killed nigger kids.'

His hands grabbed the edge of the table and he glowered at Harry with wide eyes. Then it was as if his face cracked, it crumpled like a punctured football. He hid it in his hands.

'They just want to see me swing, don't they!'

There was a bitter sob. Harry studied him. He wondered how many hours the two of them in there had kept Hochner awake with questions before he arrived. He took a deep breath. Then he leaned across the table, grabbed the microphone with one hand and pulled the lead out with the other.

'Deal, Hochner. We've got ten seconds. Who's Uriah?'

Hochner watched him between his fingers.

'What?'

'Quick, Hochner. They'll be here in a moment!'

'He's . . . he's an old guy, over seventy for sure. I only met him once, at the handover.'

'What did he look like?'

'Old, as I said.'

'Description!'

'He was wearing a coat and hat. It was the middle of the night in a badly lit container port. Blue eyes, I think, medium height . . . mm.'

'What did you talk about? Quick!'

'This and that. We spoke English at first, but changed when he realised that I could speak German. I told him that my parents came from Elsass. He said he'd been there, somewhere called Sennheim.'

'What's his game?'

'Don't know, but he's an amateur. He talked a lot, and when he got the gun, he said it was the first time he'd held a weapon for more than fifty years. He said he hates —'

The door to the room was torn open.

'Hates what?' Harry shouted.

At that moment he felt a hand tighten around his collarbone. A hoarse voice close to his ear.

'What the hell are you doing?'

Harry held Hochner's gaze as they dragged him backwards

towards the door. Hochner's eyes had glazed over and his Adam's apple bobbed up and down. Harry could see his lips move, but didn't hear what he said.

Then the door slammed in front of him.

Harry rubbed his neck as Isaiah drove him to the airport. They had been driving for twenty minutes before Isaiah spoke.

'We've been working on this case for six years. The list of arms deliveries covers twenty countries. We've been worried about precisely what happened today; that someone would dangle diplomatic help in front of him in order to get information.'

Harry shrugged his shoulders.

'So what? You've caught him and you've done your job, Isaiah. All that's left is to pick up the medals. Whatever deals anyone makes between Hochner and the government has nothing to do with you.'

'You're a policeman, Harry. You know what it's like to see criminals go free, people who don't blink an eyelid about killing, who you know will continue where they left off as soon as they're out on the street again.'

Harry didn't answer.

'You do know, don't you? Good, because this is the deal. It sounded like you got your end of the bargain with Hochner. That means it's up to you whether you want to keep your part. Or let it go. Is that right?'

'I'm just doing my job, Isaiah, and I could use Hochner at some point as a witness. Sorry.'

Isaiah banged the steering wheel so hard it made Harry jump.

'Let me tell you something, Harry. Before the elections in 1994, when we still had white minority rule, Hochner shot two black girls, both eleven years old, from a water tower outside the school grounds in a black township called Alexandra. We think someone in *Afrikaner Volkswag,* the apartheid party, was behind it. There was some controversy surrounding the school because it had three white pupils. He used Singapore bullets, the same type they use in Bosnia. They open after a hundred metres and bore their way through everything in their way, like a drill. Both girls were hit in the neck and for once it didn't matter that the ambulances, as usual, took over an hour to turn up in a black township.'

Harry didn't answer.

'But you're wrong if you think it's revenge we're after, Harry. We've understood that you can't build a new society on revenge. That's why the first black majority government set up a commission to uncover assaults and harassment during apartheid times. It wasn't about revenge; it was about owning up and forgiving. It has healed a lot of wounds and done the whole society some good. At the same time, though, we're losing the fight against criminality, and particularly here in Jo'burg where everything is completely out of control. We're a young, vulnerable nation, Harry, and if we want to make any progress we have to show that law and order means something, that chaos can be used as a pretext for crime. Everyone remembers the killings in 1994. Everyone is following the case in the papers now. That's why it is more important than your personal agenda or mine, Harry.'

He clenched his fist and hit the steering wheel again.

'It's not about being judges of life and death, but about giving a belief in justice back to ordinary people. Sometimes it takes the death penalty to give them that belief.'

Harry tapped a cigarette out of the packet, opened the window a little and stared at the yellow slagheaps that broke the monotony of the arid landscape.

'So what do you say, Harry?'

'You'll have to put your foot down if I'm going to make that flight, Isaiah.'

Isaiah punched the steering column so hard Harry was amazed it survived.

33

Lainz Zoo, Vienna. 27 June 1944.

HELENA SAT ALONE IN THE BACK SEAT OF ANDRÉ
Brockhard's black Mercedes. The car pitched gently between
the large horse-chestnut trees lining both sides of the avenue. They were on their way to the stables at Lainz Zoo.

She looked out on to the green clearings. A cloud of dust
rose behind them from the dry gravel track, and even with
the window open it was almost unbearably hot in the car.

A herd of horses grazing in the shade from the edge of a
beech wood raised their heads as the car passed.

Helena loved Lainz Zoo. Before the war she had often
spent her Sundays in the large wooded area to the south of the
Vienna Woods, picnicking with her parents, aunts and uncles
or riding with her friends.

Early this morning when the hospital matron passed on a
message to her that André Brockhard wanted to talk to her she
had been prepared for everything and anything. He was going
to send a car before lunch. Ever since she had received the
recommendation from the hospital and her travel permit, she
had been walking on cloud nine and the first thing she thought
was that she would use the opportunity to thank Christopher's
father for the help the governing board had given her. Her sec-

ond thought was that it was hardly likely that André Brockhard had summoned her to receive her gratitude.

Calm down, Helena, she said to herself. *They can't stop us now. Early tomorrow morning we'll be gone.*

The day before she had packed some clothes and her treasured belongings into two suitcases. The crucifix over her bed was the last thing she put into her case. The music box her father had bought her was still on the dressing-table. Things she had never believed she would part with lightly; it was strange how little they meant now. Beatrice had helped her and they had talked about old times as they listened to Mother's pacing of the floor beneath them. It was going to be an awkward, difficult parting. Now she was only looking forward to the evening. Uriah had said it would be a terrible shame if he didn't see anything of Vienna before leaving, so he had invited her out to dinner. Where, she didn't know. He had simply winked confidentially and asked if she thought they would be able to borrow the forester's car.

'Here we are, Fräulein Lang,' the chauffeur said, pointing to the fountain where the avenue came to an end. A gilt cupid balanced on one leg atop a soapstone globe over the water. A large mansion in grey stone stood behind it. Connected to the two sides of the main house were long, low, red wooden buildings which together with a simple stone house formed an inner courtyard.

The chauffeur stopped the car, got out and opened the door for Helena.

André Brockhard had been standing on the front steps of the mansion. Now he came towards them, his shiny riding boots glinting in the sun. André Brockhard was in his midfifties, but there was as much spring in his step as in a young man's. He had unbuttoned his red woollen jacket, fully aware that his athletic upper torso would thus be seen to its advantage. His riding breeches were tight against muscular thighs. Brockhard Snr could hardly have been less like his son.

'Helena!' The voice was precisely as hearty and warm as it

is with men who are so powerful that they are the ones who determine when a situation is going to be hearty and warm. It was a long time since she had seen him, but he looked as he always did, Helena thought: white-haired, erect, two blue eyes looking at her from either side of a large, majestic nose. The heart-shaped mouth did suggest that the man had a softer side, but for most this was something that still had to be proved.

'How is your mother? I do hope it was not too impertinent of me to take you away from your work like this,' he said, passing his hand to her for a brief, dry handshake. He continued without waiting for an answer.

'I had to have a word with you, and I thought it couldn't wait.' He motioned towards the house. 'Yes, you've been here before.'

'No,' Helena said, peering up at him with a smile.

'No? I assumed Christopher would have brought you here. You were as thick as thieves when you were younger.'

'Your memory must be playing tricks on you, Herr Brockhard. Christopher and I knew each other well enough, but —'

'Really? In that case I'll have to show you around. Let's go down to the stables.'

He placed a hand lightly against the middle of her back and steered her in the direction of the wooden buildings. The gravel crunched as they walked.

'What happened to your father is sad, Helena. I'm really sorry. I wish there were something I could do for you and your mother.'

You could have invited us to the Christmas party last winter as you used to, Helena thought, but she said nothing. She would have been pleased because then she wouldn't have had to put up with her mother's insistence on going.

'Janjic!' Brockhard shouted to a black-haired boy standing in the sun and polishing saddle gear. 'Go and fetch Venezia.'

The boy went into the stable while Brockhard stood still, whacking his whip lightly against his knee and rocking on his boot heels. Helena cast a glance at her wristwatch.

'I'm afraid I cannot stay here long, Herr Brockhard. My shift . . .'

'No, of course. I understand. Let me come to the point.'

From inside the stable they heard fierce whinnying and the sound of hooves clattering on wooden boards.

'Your father and I used to do a fair amount of business together. Before the sad bankruptcy, of course.'

'I know.'

'Yes, and you probably also know that your father was in a lot of debt. Indirectly, that was why things happened as they did. I mean this unfortunate . . .' He searched for the right word. And found it. ' . . . *affinity* with the Jewish loan sharks was of course very damaging for him.'

'You mean Joseph Bernstein?'

'I can't remember the names of these people.'

'You should do, he went to your Christmas party.'

'Joseph Bernstein?' André Brockhard smiled, but the smile didn't reach his eyes. 'That must have been many years ago.'

'Christmas 1938. Before the war.'

Brockhard nodded and darted an impatient glance towards the stable door.

'You have a good memory, Helena. That's good. Christopher could do with a good head. Since he occasionally loses his own, I mean. Apart from that, he's a good boy, you'll see that.'

Helena could feel her heart beginning to pound. Had something gone wrong after all? Brockhard Snr was talking to her as if she were his future daughter-in-law. Instead of feeling terror, she felt anger gaining the upper hand. When she spoke again, she meant to sound friendly, but anger had her larynx in a stranglehold and made her voice sound hard and metallic.

'I hope there has not been a misunderstanding, Herr Brockhard.'

Brockhard must have noticed the timbre in her voice; at

any rate there was not much left of the warmth he had
greeted her with when he said:

'In that case let us clear up these misunderstandings. I
would like you to look at this.'

He pulled a sheet from the inside pocket of his red jacket,
straightened it and passed it to her.

Bürgschaft, it said at the head of what appeared to be a
contract. Her eyes ran across the dense text. She didn't understand much of what was written there except that the house in
the Vienna Woods was mentioned and that her father's and
André Brockhard's names were at the bottom with their re-
spective signatures. She sent him a quizzical look.

'This appears to be a surety.'

'It is a surety,' he acknowledged. 'When your father
thought that the Jews' loans were going to be called in, and
thereby his own, he approached me and asked me if I would
stand security for quite a large refinancing loan in Germany.
Which, unfortunately, I was soft-hearted enough to do. Your
father was a proud man, and to ensure that the security did
not appear as pure charity, he insisted that the summer house
you and your mother live in now should be used as a surety
against the security.'

'Why against the security and not against the loan?'

Brockhard was taken aback.

'Good question. The answer is that the value of the house
was not enough as a guarantee against the loan that your
father needed.'

'But André Brockhard's signature was enough?'

He smiled and ran his hand down his powerful bull neck
which, in the heat, was now covered in a shiny layer of sweat.

'I own the odd property in Vienna.'

A massive understatement. Everyone knew that André
Brockhard had large holdings of shares in two of the largest
Austrian industrial companies. After the *Anschluss* – Hitler's
'occupation' in 1938 – the companies had transferred their production of toys and machines to production of weapons for the

axis powers, and Brockhard had become a multi-millionaire. And now Helena knew that he also owned the house she was living in. She felt a large lump growing in her stomach.

'Don't look so worried, my dear Helena,' Brockhard exclaimed, and the warmth was suddenly back in his voice. 'I wasn't considering taking the house from your mother, you understand.'

But the lump in Helena's stomach continued to grow and grow. He might as well have added: 'Or from my own daughter-in-law.'

'Venezia!' he shouted.

Helena turned towards the stable door where the groom emerged from the shadows, leading a shining white horse. Even though a storm of ideas was raging through her mind, the sight made Helena forget for a moment. It was the most beautiful horse she had ever seen; it was like a supernatural creature standing in front of her.

'A Lipizzaner,' Brockhard said. 'The world's best-trained breed of horse. Imported from Spain in 1562 by Maximilian II. You and your mother must have seen them performing at the *Spanische Reitschule* in town, haven't you?'

'Yes, of course.'

'It's like watching ballet, isn't it?'

Helena nodded. She couldn't take her eyes off the animal.

'They take their summer holiday here in the *Lainzer Tiergarten* until the end of August. Unfortunately, no one else apart from the riders at the Spanish Riding School is allowed to ride them. Untrained riders could inculcate bad habits. Years of punctilious dressage would go to waste.'

The horse was saddled. Brockhard grabbed the halter and the groom moved away. The animal stood stock still.

'Some consider it cruel to teach horses dance steps. They say the animals suffer from having to do things which are contrary to their nature. People who say this kind of thing haven't seen these horses in training, but I have. And, believe me, horses love it. Do you know why?'

He stroked the horse's muzzle.

'Because that is the order of nature. In His wisdom God so ordained it that an inferior creature is never happier than when serving and obeying a superior creature. You only have to look at children and adults. At women and men. Even in so-called democratic countries the weak willingly concede power to an elite which is stronger and wiser than they. That is just the way it is. And because we're all God's creatures it is the responsibility of superior beings to ensure that inferior beings submit.'

'To make them happy?'

'Precisely, Helena. You understand a lot for . . . such a young woman.'

She couldn't determine which of the two words he gave greater stress.

'To know your place is important, both for high and low. If you resist it, in the long term you will never become happy.'

He patted the horse on the neck and looked into Venezia's large brown eyes.

'You're not the type to resist, are you?'

Helena knew that the question was directed at her and closed her eyes while she tried to breathe deeply and calmly. She was aware that what she said now or what she didn't say could be crucial for the rest of her life; she couldn't afford to let the anger of the moment be the deciding factor.

'Are you?'

Suddenly Venezia whinnied and shook her head to the side, causing Brockhard to slip and lose balance. He hung on to the halter under the horse's neck. The groom dashed to his aid, but before he could get there, Brockhard, his face red and sweat-stained, had struggled to his feet and angrily waved him away. Helena could not stifle a smile, and perhaps Brockhard saw it. In any event, he raised his whip to the horse, then came to his senses and let it fall again. He articulated a few words with his heart-shaped mouth, which amused Helena even more. Then he went over to Helena, placing his hand lightly but imperiously against the small of her back again:

'We've seen enough, and you have important work awaiting you, Helena. Allow me to accompany you to the car.'

They stood by the steps to the house while the chauffeur got into the car and drove forward.

'I hope and assume we will see each other again soon, Helena,' he said, taking her hand. 'Incidentally, my wife asked me to pass on her regards to your mother. Indeed, I believe she said she would invite you over one weekend soon. I don't remember when, but you will be hearing from her.'

Helena waited until the chauffeur had got out and opened the door for her before saying, 'Do you know why the dressage horse threw you to the ground, Herr Brockhard?'

She could see in his eyes that his temperature was rising again.

'Because you looked it in the eye, Herr Brockhard. A horse perceives eye contact as provocative, as if it and its status in the herd are not being respected. If it cannot avoid eye contact, it will react in a different way, by rebelling for example. In dressage you don't get anywhere by not showing respect, however superior your species might be. Any animal trainer can tell you that. In the mountains in Argentina there's a wild horse which will jump off the nearest precipice if any human tries to ride it. Goodbye, Herr Brockhard.'

She took a seat at the back of the Mercedes and, trembling, breathed in deeply as the car door was gently closed behind her. As she was driven down the avenue in Lainz Zoo, she closed her eyes and saw André Brockhard's stiff figure obscured by the cloud of dust behind them.

34

Vienna. 28 June 1944.

'*GUTEN ABEND, MEINE HERRSCHAFTEN.*'

The small, slim head waiter made a deep bow and Helena tweaked Uriah's arm as he couldn't stop laughing. They had been laughing all the way from the hospital because of the commotion they had been causing. It turned out Uriah was a terrible driver and so Helena had told him to stop whenever they met a car on the narrow road down to the Hauptstraße. Instead Uriah had leaned on the horn, with the result that the oncoming cars had driven into the verge or had pulled over. Fortunately there were not that many cars still on the road in Vienna, so they arrived safe and sound at Weihburggasse in the centre before 7.30.

The head waiter glanced at Uriah's uniform before checking, with a deeply furrowed brow, the reservations book. Helena looked over his shoulder. The buzz of conversation and laughter under the crystal chandeliers hanging from the arched yellow ceilings supported on white Corinthian pillars was only just drowned out by the orchestra.

So this is Zu den drei Husaren, she mused with pleasure. It was as if the three steps outside had magically led them from a war-ravaged city into a world where bombs and other tribulations were of minor importance. Richard Strauss and Arnold Schönberg must have been regular patrons here, for this was the place where the rich, the cultivated and the free-thinkers of Vienna met. So free-thinking that it had never crossed her father's mind to take the family there.

The head waiter cleared his throat. Helena realised that he had been unimpressed by Uriah's rank of *Vizekorporal* and was perhaps puzzled by the strange foreign name in the book.

'Your table is ready. Please follow me,' he said with a strained smile, picking up two menus on his way. The restaurant was packed.

'Here you are.'

Uriah smiled at Helena with resignation. They had been given an unlaid table beside the swing door into the kitchen.

'Your waiter will be with you in a moment,' the head waiter said and evaporated into thin air.

Helena looked around and began to chuckle.

'Look,' she said. 'That was our original table.'

Uriah turned. Absolutely right: in front of the orchestra a waiter was already clearing a table set for two.

'Sorry,' he said. 'I think I might have put *Major* before my name when I phoned to book. I was relying on your radiance to outshine my lack of rank.'

She took his hand and at that moment the orchestra struck up a merry Hungarian *Csardas*.

'They must be playing for us,' he said.

'Maybe they are.' She lowered her eyes. 'If not, it doesn't matter. They're playing gypsy music. It's wonderful when it's played by gypsies. Can you see any?'

He shook his head, his eyes intent on studying her face as if it were important he registered every feature, every crease of skin, every strand of hair.

'They've all gone,' she said. 'Jews, too. Do you think the rumours are true?'

'Which rumours?'

'About the concentration camps.'

He shrugged.

'There are all sorts of rumours during war. As for myself, I would feel quite safe in Hitler's captivity.'

The orchestra began to play a song for three voices in a strange language. A couple of people in the audience sang along.

'What's that?' Uriah asked.

'A *Verbunkos*,' Helena said. 'A kind of soldiers' song, just like the Norwegian one you sang on the train. Songs to recruit young Hungarian men to the Rákóczi war of independence. What are you laughing at?'

'At all the unusual things you know. Can you understand what they are singing too?'

'A little. Stop laughing,' she sniggered. 'Beatrice is Hungarian, and she used to sing to me. It's all about forgotten heroes and ideals.'

'Forgotten.' He squeezed her hand. 'As this war will be one day.'

A waiter had arrived unobtrusively at their table and coughed discreetly to signal his presence.

'*Meine Herrschaften*, are you ready to order?'

'I think so,' Uriah said. 'What would you recommend today?'

'*Hähnchen*.'

'Chicken. Sounds good. Could you choose a good wine for us? Helena?'

Helena's eyes scanned the list.

'Why are there no prices?' she asked.

'War, *Fräulein*. They vary from day to day.'

'And what does *Hähnchen* cost?'

'Fifty schillings.'

Out of the corner of her eye she saw Uriah blanch.

'Goulash soup,' she said. 'We have already eaten today, and I hear that your Hungarian dishes are very good. Wouldn't you like to try it too, Uriah? Two dinners in one day is not healthy.'

'I . . . ,' Uriah began.

'And a light wine,' Helena said.

'Two goulash soups and a light wine?' the waiter asked with a raised eyebrow.

'I'm sure you understand what I mean,' she gave him the menu and a beaming smile, 'waiter.'

She and Uriah held each other's gaze until the waiter had disappeared behind the kitchen door, then they began to giggle.

'You're crazy,' he laughed.

'Me? It wasn't me who booked *Zu den drei Husaren* with less than fifty schillings in my pocket!'

He pulled out a handkerchief and leaned across the table. 'Do you know what, Fräulein Lang?' he said while drying her tears of laughter. 'I love you. I really do.'

At that moment the air-raid siren sounded.

When Helena thought back to that evening she always had to ask herself how accurately she remembered it; whether the bombs fell as close as she recalled, whether everyone had turned round as they walked up the aisle in the Stephansdom. Even though their last night in Vienna remained veiled in unreality, on cold days it didn't stop her warming her heart on the memory. And she could think about the same tiny moment that summer's night and one day it would evoke laughter and the next tears, without her ever understanding why.

When the air-raid siren sounded, all other sounds died. For a second the whole restaurant seemed to be frozen in time, then the first curses resounded beneath the gilt vaulted ceiling.

'*Hunde!*'

'*Scheiße!* It's only eight o'clock.'

Uriah shook his head.

'The English must be out of their minds,' he said. 'It's not even dark yet.'

The waiters instantly busied themselves at the tables while the head waiter shouted curt orders to the diners.

'Look,' Helena said. 'Soon this restaurant will be in ruins too and all they are interested in is getting customers to settle their bills before they run for cover.'

A man in a dark suit jumped up on to the podium where the orchestra was packing away its instruments.

'Listen!' he shouted. 'All those who have settled their bills are requested to make their way immediately to the nearest shelter, to the underground near Weihburggasse 20. Please be quiet and listen! Turn right when you leave and then walk two hundred metres. Look for the men with red armbands. They'll show you where to go. And stay calm. The planes won't be here for a while yet.'

At that moment they heard the boom of the first bombs falling. The man on the podium tried to say something else, but the voices and screams drowned him out. He gave up, crossed himself, jumped down and made for the shelter.

There was a rush for the exit where a crowd of terrified people had already gathered. A woman was standing in the cloakroom screaming, *'Mein Regenschirm!* – my umbrella!' But the cloakroom attendants were nowhere to be seen. More booms, closer this time. Helena looked over at the abandoned table next to them where two half-full glasses of wine rattled against each other as the whole room vibrated in a loud two-part harmony. A couple of young women with a merry walrus-like man in tow were on their way towards the exit. His shirt had ridden up and a beatific smile played around his lips.

Within minutes the restaurant was deserted and an eery silence fell over the place. All they could hear was low sobs from the cloakroom, where the woman had stopped shouting for her umbrella and had rested her forehead on the counter. Half-eaten meals and open bottles were left on the white tablecloths. Uriah was still holding Helena's hand. A new boom made the chandeliers shake and the woman in the cloakroom came to and ran out screaming.

'Alone at last,' Uriah said.

The ground beneath them shook and a fine sprinkling of plaster from the gilt ceiling glittered in the air. Uriah stood up and held out his arm.

'Our best table has just become free, *Fräulein*. If you wouldn't mind . . .'

She took his arm, stood up and together they walked to the podium. She barely heard the whistling sound. The crash of the explosion that followed was deafening, the plaster from the walls turned into a sandstorm and the large windows giving on to Weihburggasse were blown in. The lights went out.

Uriah lit the candles in the candelabrum on the table, pulled the chair out for her, held up the folded napkin between thumb and first finger and flipped it open to lay it gently on her lap.

'*Hähnchen und Prädikatwein?*' he asked, discreetly brushing fragments of glass off the table, the dinner plates and her hair.

Perhaps it was the candles and the golden dust glittering in the air as dark fell outside, perhaps it was the cooling draught from the open windows giving them a breather from the hot Pannonian summer, or perhaps it was simply her own heart, whose blood seemed to be raging through her veins in an attempt to experience these moments more intensely. But she could remember music, and that was not possible as the orchestra had packed up and fled. Was she dreaming it, this music? It was only many years later, before she was about to give birth to a daughter, that she realised what it must have been. Over the new cradle the father of her child had hung a mobile with coloured glass marbles, and one evening she had run her hand through the mobile and had immediately recognised the sound. And knew where it came from. It was

the crystal chandelier in *Zu den drei Husaren* which had
played for them. The clear, delicate wind chimes of the chandelier as it swung to the pounding of the ground, and Uriah
marching in and out of the kitchen with *Salzburger Nockerl*
and three bottles of Heuriger wine from the cellar, where he
had also found one of the chefs sitting in the corner with a
bottle. The chef didn't move a muscle to prevent Uriah from
taking provisions; on the contrary, he had inclined his head
to show his approval when Uriah showed him which wine
he had chosen.

Then he placed his forty-odd schillings under the candelabrum, and they went out into the mild June evening. In
Weihburggasse it was totally still, but the air was thick with
the smell of smoke, dust and earth.

'Let's go for a walk,' Uriah said.

Without either of them saying a word about where to go,
they turned right, up Kärntner Straße, and were suddenly
standing in front of a darkened, deserted Stephansplatz.

'My God,' Uriah said. The enormous cathedral before
them filled the young night sky.

'Stephansdom?' he asked.

'Yes.' Helena leaned her head backwards and her eyes
followed the *Südturm*, the green-black church spire, up, up
towards the sky where the first stars had crept out.

The next thing Helena remembered they were standing
inside the cathedral, surrounded by the white faces of the
people who had sought refuge there, the sounds of crying
children and organ music. They walked towards the altar,
arm in arm, or had she only dreamed that? Had it really
happened? Had he not suddenly taken her in his arms and
said she would be his? Hadn't she whispered, *Ja, Ja, Ja*, as
the void in the church seized her words and flung them up to
the vaulted ceiling, the dove and Christ on the cross, where
the words were repeated and repeated until it had to be true?
Whether it had happened or not, the words were truer than

those she had carried with her since her conversation with André Brockhard.

'I cannot go with you.'

They were said, but when and where?

She had told her mother the same afternoon, that she wasn't leaving, although she didn't give a reason. Her mother had tried to comfort her, but Helena couldn't stand the sound of her sharp, self-righteous voice and had locked herself in her bedroom. Then Uriah had come, knocked on the door, and she had decided not to think any more, but to let herself fall without any fear, without imagining anything except an eternal abyss. Perhaps he had seen that immediately she opened the door. Perhaps the two of them standing in the doorway had made a tacit agreement to live the rest of their lives in the hours they had before the train left.

'I cannot go with you.'

The name of André Brockhard had tasted like gall on her tongue, and she had spat it out. Together with the rest: the surety, the mother who was in danger of being thrown on to the street, the father who didn't want a decent life to return to, Beatrice who had no other family. Yes, all that was said, but when? Had she told him everything in the cathedral? Or after they had run through the streets down to Filharmoni-kerstraße? Where the pavement was littered with bricks and shards of glass, and the yellow flames licked out of the windows in the old *Konditorei*, lighting their way to where they rushed into the opulent but now deserted blacked-out hotel reception, lit a match, arbitrarily took a key from the wall and sprinted up the stairs with carpeting so thick that they made no noise at all, ghosts who flitted along the corridors searching for Room 342. Then they were in each other's arms, tearing off each other's clothes as if they too were on fire, his breath burning against her skin; she scratched him till he bled and put her lips to the cuts afterwards. She repeated the words until it sounded like an incantation: 'I cannot go with you.'

When the air-raid siren sounded, signalling that the bombing was over for this time, they were lying entwined in the bloody sheets, and she wept and wept.

Afterwards everything merged into a maelstrom of bodies, sleep and dreams. When they had been making love and when she had only dreamed that they were making love, she didn't know. She had awoken in the middle of the night to the sound of rain, and knew instinctively that he was not by her side; she had gone to the window and stared down at the streets below being washed clean of the ash and soil. The water was already running over the edges of the pavement and an opened, ownerless umbrella sailed down the street towards the Danube. Then she had gone back to bed. When she awoke again it was light outside, the streets were dry and he was lying beside her, holding his breath. She looked at the clock on the bedside table. Two hours until the train left. She stroked his forehead.

'Why aren't you breathing?' she whispered.

'I've just woken up. You aren't breathing, either.'

She snuggled up to him. He was naked, but hot and sweaty.

'So we must be dead.'

'Yes,' he said.

'You went somewhere.'

'Yes.'

She could feel him trembling.

'But you're back now,' she said.

Part Four

PURGATORY

35

Container Port, Bjørvika.
29 February 2000.

HARRY PARKED BESIDE A WORKMEN'S HUT ON top of the only hill he could find in the flat quay area of Bjørvika. A sudden spell of mild weather had started to melt the snow, the snow was shining and it was simply a wonderful day. He walked between the containers piled up like gigantic Lego bricks in the sun, casting jagged shadows on the tarmac. The letters and symbols declared that they came from such distant climes as Taiwan, Buenos Aires and Cape Town. Harry stood on the edge of the quay, closed his eyes and imagined himself there as he sniffed in the mixture of sea water, sun-warmed tar and diesel. When he opened his eyes again, the ferry to Denmark slipped into his field of vision. It looked like a refrigerator. A fridge transporting the same people to and fro in a recreational shuttle service.

He knew it was too late to pick up on any leads from the meeting between Hochner and Uriah. It wasn't even certain that this was the container port where they had met; it could equally as well have been Filipstad. Nevertheless, he had still had hopes that the place would be able to tell him something, give his imagination the necessary prod.

He kicked a tyre that was protruding over the edge of the

quay. Perhaps he should buy a boat so that he could take Dad and Sis out to sea in the summer? Dad needed to get out. The man who had once been so sociable had become a loner since Mum died eight years ago. And though Sis didn't get far under her own steam, you could often forget that she had Down's syndrome.

A bird dived with glee between the containers. The blue tit can reach a speed of twenty-eight kilometres an hour. Ellen had told him that. A mallard can reach sixty-two kilometres an hour. They both managed equally well. No, Sis wasn't a problem; he was more concerned about his father.

Harry tried to concentrate. Everything Hochner had said, he had written in his report, word for word, but now he focused on the man's face to try and remember what he hadn't said. What did Uriah look like? Hochner hadn't managed to say a great deal, but when you have to describe someone you usually begin with the most striking features, whatever stands out. And the first thing Hochner had said about Uriah was that he had blue eyes. Unless Hochner thought having blue eyes was particularly unusual, it would suggest that Uriah did not have any visible handicap or walked or talked in a particular way. He spoke both German and English, and had been to somewhere in Germany called Sennheim. Harry followed the Denmark ferry, which was making for Drøbak. Well-travelled. Had Uriah been to sea? he wondered. Harry had looked it up in an atlas, even a German one, but he hadn't found anywhere called Sennheim. Hochner might have been making it up. Probably of no significance.

Hochner said that Uriah nurtured a hatred. So perhaps what he had guessed was right – that the person they were looking for had a personal motive. But what did he hate?

The sun disappeared behind the island of Hovedøya and there was an instant bite in the breeze off the Oslo fjord. Harry wrapped his coat tighter round him and walked back to his car. And the half a million? Had Uriah received it from a Mr Big or was this a solo job with his own funds?

He took out his mobile phone. A Nokia, a tiny thing, only two weeks old. He had fought against it for a long time, but in the end Ellen had persuaded him to buy one. He tapped in her number.

'Hi, Ellen. Harry here. Are you alone? OK. I want you to concentrate. Yes, it's a little game. Are you ready?'

They had played often enough before. The 'game' started with him giving her verbal cues. No background information, no clues as to where he was stuck, just scraps of information – of five words maximum – in any order. It had taken them time to work out the method. The most important rule was that there had to be at least five scraps of information, but no more than ten. Harry had got the idea when he bet Ellen a shift that she couldn't remember the order of the cards in a pack after seeing them for two minutes, two seconds per card. He had lost three times before he gave in. Afterwards she had told him the method she used. She didn't think of the cards as cards, but associated a person or action with every card and made up a story as they were turned over. Afterwards he had tried to use her association skills on the job. Sometimes the results were amazing.

'Man, seventy,' Harry said slowly. 'Norwegian. Half a million kroner. Bitter. Blue eyes. Märklin rifle. Speaks German. Able-bodied. Arms smuggling at container port. Shooting practice in Skien. That's it.'

He got into the car.

'Nothing? Thought so. OK. Reckoned it was worth a try. Thanks, anyway. Take care.'

Harry was on the raised intersection – known locally as the traffic machine – in front of the Post House when he suddenly had a thought and called Ellen back.

'Ellen? It's me again. There was one thing I forgot. Still with me? *Hasn't held a weapon for more than fifty years*. Repeat. *Hasn't held a . . .* Yes, I know it's more than five words. Still nothing? Damn, now I've missed my turning! Catch you later, Ellen.'

He put his phone on the passenger seat and concentrated on driving. He had just turned off the roundabout when his mobile bleeped.

'Harry here. What? What on earth made you think of that? Right, right, now don't get angry, Ellen. Now and then I forget that you don't know what goes on in your own noodle. Brain. In your great big, beautiful, bouffant brain, Ellen. And yes, now you say it, it's obvious. Thanks very much.'

He put down the phone and at that moment remembered he owed her three night shifts. Now that he was no longer in Crime Squad, he would have to find something else. He considered what he could do, for approximately three seconds.

36

Irisveien. 1 March 2000.

THE DOOR OPENED AND HARRY PEERED INTO A pair of piercing blue eyes in a lined face.

'Harry Hole, police,' he said. 'I rang this morning.'

'Right.'

The old man's grey-white hair was brushed smoothly across his high forehead, and he was wearing a tie under a knitted cardigan. It had said EVEN & SIGNE JUUL on the post-box outside the entrance to this red duplex house in the quietly affluent suburb in north Oslo.

'Please, come in, Inspector Hole.'

His voice was calm and firm, and there was something about his bearing that made Professor Even Juul look younger than, by rights, he had to be. Harry had done his research and knew that the history professor had been in the Resistance movement. Although Even Juul was retired, he was still considered to be Norway's foremost expert on the history of the German Occupation and the *Nasjonal Samling*.

Harry bent down to take off his shoes. On the wall directly in front of him hung old, slightly faded black and white photographs in small frames. One of them showed a young lady in nurse's uniform. Another, a young man in a white coat.

They went into the sitting room where a greying Airedale stopped barking and instead dutifully sniffed Harry's crotch before walking over and lying down beside Juul's armchair.

'I've been reading some of your articles about Fascism and National Socialism in *Dagsavisen*,' Harry said after they had sat down.

'My goodness, so *Dagsavisen* readers do exist then?' Juul smiled.

'You seem keen to warn us against today's neo-Nazism?'

'Not to warn, I am merely pointing out some historical parallels. It's an historian's duty to uncover, not to judge.' He lit his pipe. 'Many people believe that right and wrong are fixed absolutes. That is incorrect, they change over time. The job of the historian is primarily to find the historical truth, to look at what the sources say and present them, objectively and dispassionately. If historians were to stand in judgment on human folly, our work would seem to posterity like fossils – the remnants of the orthodoxy of their time.'

A blue column of smoke rose into the air. 'But this isn't what you came here to ask, I imagine?'

'We're wondering if you can help us to find a man.'

'You mentioned that on the telephone. Who is this man?'

'We don't know. But we have deduced that he has blue eyes, he's Norwegian and is seventy years old. And he speaks German.'

'And?'

'That's it.'

Juul laughed. 'Well, there are a few to choose from then.'

'Right. There are 158,000 men in this country over seventy, and I would guess around 100,000 of them have blue eyes and can speak German.'

Juul raised an eyebrow. Harry gave a sheepish smile.

'Office for National Statistics. I checked, for fun.'

'So how do you think I can help?'

'I'm coming to that. This person reportedly said that he hasn't handled a weapon in over fifty years. I thought, that is, my colleague thought, that over fifty is more than fifty, but less than sixty.'

'Logical.'

'Yes, she's very . . . er, logical. So, let's assume it was fifty-five years ago. Then we'd be smack in the middle of the Second World War. He's around twenty and uses a weapon. All Norwegians privately owning a gun had to hand them over to the Germans. So where is he?'

Harry counted on three fingers: 'Either he's in the Resistance, or he's fled to England, or he's at the Eastern Front fighting alongside the Germans. He speaks better German than English. Accordingly . . .'

'So this colleague of yours came to the conclusion that he must have been fighting at the front, did she?' Juul asked.

'She did.'

Juul sucked on his pipe.

'Many of the Resistance people had to learn German,' he said, 'in order to infiltrate, monitor and so on. And you're forgetting the Norwegians in the Swedish police force.'

'So the conclusion doesn't stand up?'

'Well, let me think aloud a bit,' Juul said. 'Roughly fifteen thousand Norwegians volunteered for service at the front, of whom seven thousand were called up and were thus allowed to use a weapon. That's a lot more than those who escaped to England and joined up there. And even though there were more men in the Resistance at the end of the war, very few of them ever held a weapon.'

Juul smiled.

'For the time being, let's assume you're right. Now obviously these men fighting at the front are not listed in the telephone directory as ex-Waffen SS, but I imagine you have found out where to search?'

Harry nodded.

'The Traitors' Archives. Filed according to name, along with all the data from the court cases. I've been through it in the course of the last few days. I was hoping that enough of them would be dead to make it a manageable total, but I was wrong.'

'Yes, they're tough old birds,' Juul laughed.

'And so I come to why we called you. You know the background of these soldiers better than anyone. I would like you to help me to understand how men like that think, to understand what makes them tick.'

'Thank you for your confidence, Inspector, but I'm a historian and know no more than anyone else about individual motivation. As you perhaps know, I was in the Resistance, in *Milorg*, and that doesn't exactly qualify me to get into the head of someone who volunteers for the Eastern Front.'

'I think you know a great deal, anyway, herr Juul.'

'Is that right?'

'I think you know what I mean. My research has been very thorough.'

Juul sucked on his pipe and looked at Harry. In the silence that followed Harry became aware that someone was standing in the sitting-room doorway. He turned and saw an elderly woman. Her gentle, calm eyes were looking at Harry.

'We're just having a chat, Signe,' Even Juul said.

She gave Harry a cheery nod, opened her mouth as if to say something, but stopped when her eyes met Even Juul's. She nodded again, quietly closed the door and was gone.

'So you know?' Juul asked.

'Yes. She was a nurse on the Eastern Front, wasn't she?'

'By Leningrad. From 1942 to the retreat in March of 1944.' He put down his pipe. 'Why are you hunting this man?'

'To be honest, we don't know that, either. But there might be an assassination brewing.'

'Hm.'

'So what should we look for? An oddball? A man who's still a committed Nazi? A criminal?'

Juul shook his head.

'Most of the men at the front served their sentence and then slipped back into society. Many of them made out sur-

prisingly well, even after being branded traitors. Not so sur-
prising maybe. It often turns out that the gifted ones are those
who make decisions in critical situations like war.'

'So the person we're looking for may well be one of those
who did alright for himself.'

'Absolutely.'

'A pillar of society?'

'The door to positions of national importance in finance
and politics would probably have been closed to him.'

'But he could have been an independent businessman, an
entrepreneur. Definitely someone who has earned enough
money to buy a weapon for half a million. Who could he possibly be after?'

'Does this necessarily have anything to do with his having fought at the front?'

'I have a sneaking feeling it might.'

'A motive for revenge then?'

'Is that so unreasonable?'

'No, not at all. Many men from the front see themselves
as the real patriots in the war. They think that, given the way
the world looked in 1940, they acted in the best interests of
the nation. They consider the fact that we sentenced them as
traitors to be a total travesty of justice.'

'So?'

Juul scratched behind his ear.

'Well. The judges involved in bringing them to justice
are by and large dead now. And the same is true of the politicians who laid the basis for the trials. The revenge theory
seems thin.'

Harry sighed. 'You're right. I'm only trying to form a
picture with the few pieces of the puzzle I have.'

Juul glanced quickly at his watch. 'I promise I'll give it
some thought, but I really don't know if I can help you.'

'Thanks anyway,' Harry said, getting up. Then he remembered something and pulled out a pile of folded sheets
of paper from his jacket pocket.

'By the way, I took a copy of my report of the interview with a witness in Johannesburg. If you could have a look to see whether there's anything of significance in it?'

Juul said yes, but shook his head as if meaning no.

As Harry was putting on his shoes in the hall, he pointed to the photograph of the man in the white coat.

'Is that you?'

'In the first half of the previous century, yes,' Juul laughed. 'It was taken in Germany before the war. I was supposed to follow in my father's and grandfather's footsteps and study medicine there. When the war broke out I made my way home and in fact got my hands on my first history books on the boat. After that it was too late: I was hooked.'

'So you gave up medicine?'

'Depends on how you look at it. I wanted to try to find an explanation of how one man and one ideology could bewitch so many people. And perhaps find an antidote, too.' He laughed. 'I was very, very young.'

37

First Floor, Continental Hotel.
1 March 2000.

'NICE THAT WE COULD MEET LIKE THIS,' BERNT
Brandhaug said, raising his wineglass.

They toasted and Aud Hilde smiled at the Under Secretary for Foreign Affairs.

'And not only on official business,' he said, holding her gaze until she looked down. Brandhaug studied her. She wasn't exactly attractive, her features were a little too coarse for that and she was certainly plump, but she had a charming, flirty way about her and she was *young* plump.

She had rung him from the staff office this morning saying they needed his advice on an unusual case, but before she could say any more he had asked her up to his office. And when she was there he had immediately decided he didn't have the time and they could discuss it over a meal after work.

'We civil servants should also have a few perks,' he had said. She presumed he meant the meal.

So far everything had gone well. The head waiter had given them Brandhaug's regular table and, to the best of his knowledge, there was no one he knew in the room.

'Yes, there's this strange case we had yesterday,' she said, letting the waiter unfold the napkin over her lap. 'We had a visit from an elderly man who maintained that we owed him money. The Foreign Office, that is. Almost two million kroner, he said, referring to a letter he had sent in 1970.'

She rolled her eyes. She shouldn't wear so much make-up, Brandhaug thought.

'So what did we owe him money for?'

'He said he was a merchant seaman during the war. It was something to do with Nortraship. They had withheld his pay.'

'Oh, yes, I think I know what it was about. What else did he say?'

'That he couldn't wait any longer. That we had cheated him and all the other merchant seamen. God would punish us for our sins. I don't know if he had been drinking or he was ill, but he looked under the weather. He brought a letter with him, signed by the Norwegian Consul General in Bombay in 1944, who guaranteed, on behalf of the Norwegian state, the back payment of the war-risk bonus for four years' service as an officer in the Norwegian merchant navy. Had it not been for the letter, we would have just given him the heave-ho of course, and we wouldn't have bothered you with this trivial matter.'

'You can come to me any time you wish, Aud Hilde,' he said, with a sudden stab of panic: her name was Aud Hilde, wasn't it?

'Poor man,' Brandhaug said, gesturing to the waiter to bring more wine. 'The sad thing about this case is that he is actually right. Nortraship was established to administer the boats in the merchant fleet that the Germans had not already captured. It was an organisation with partly political and partly commercial interests. The British, for example, paid large sums in risk bonuses to Nortraship to use Norwegian shipping. But the money, instead of being used to pay the crews, went straight into the ship-owners' pockets and the state's coffers. We're talking about several hundred million kroner here. The merchant seamen tried to get their money back through legal proceedings, but they lost their case in the Supreme Court in 1954. The Storting passed an act in 1972, establishing that merchant seamen had a right to this money.'

'This man doesn't seem to have received anything. Because he was in the China Sea and was torpedoed by the Japanese and not by the Germans, he said.'

'Did he say what his name was?'

'Konrad Åsnes. Wait a moment and I'll show you the letter. He had worked out how much was owed with compound interest.'

She bent to look in her bag. Her upper arms quivered. She should do a bit more exercise, Brandhaug thought. Four kilos less and Aud Hilde would simply be well-rounded instead of . . . fat.

'It's alright,' he said. 'I don't need to see it. Nortraship comes under the Ministry of Commerce.'

She looked up at him.

'He insisted we were the ones who owed him the money. He gave us a deadline of two weeks.'

Brandhaug laughed.

'Did he? And what's the rush now, after sixty years?'

'He didn't say. He only said that we would have to take the consequences if we didn't pay.'

'My goodness.' Brandhaug waited until the waiter had poured out more wine for them before leaning forward. 'I hate taking the consequences, don't you?' She flashed him a hesitant smile.

Brandhaug raised his glass.

'I was wondering what we should do about this case?' she said.

'Forget it,' he said. 'But I was also wondering one thing, Aud Hilde.'

'What's that?'

'If you've seen the hotel room we have at our disposal here.'

Aud Hilde smiled again and said she hadn't.

38

Focus Fitness Centre, Ila. 2 March 2000.

HARRY WAS PEDALLING AND SWEATING. THE cardiovascular room was equipped with eighteen hypermodern ergometric exercise bikes, all occupied by 'urban', generally speaking, attractive people staring at the mute TV monitor hanging from the ceiling. Harry was watching Elisa in *The Robinson Expedition* mouthing that she couldn't stand Poppe. Harry knew. It was a repeat.

That don't impress me much! rang out from the loudspeakers.

No, well, there's a surprise, Harry thought, who liked neither the loud music nor the rasping sounds that could be heard coming from somewhere in his lungs. He could have worked out for nothing in the gym at Police HQ, but Ellen had persuaded him to join the Focus centre. He had gone along with that, but drew the line when she tried to get him to join an aerobics class. Moving in time to canned music with a troupe of people who all liked canned music while an instructor with a rictus smile encouraged greater exertion with such verbal wit as 'no pain, no gain' was for Harry an incomprehensible form of voluntary self-abasement. The way he saw it, the biggest advantage of Focus was that he could work out and watch

The Robinson Expedition without having to be in the same room as Tom Waaler, who appeared to spend most of his free time in the police gym. Harry cast a quick glance around and confirmed that tonight, as usual, he was the oldest person there. Most people in the room were girls, with Walkmans plugged into their ears, sneaking a look in his direction at regular intervals. Not because they were looking at him, but because Norway's most popular stand-up comic sat next to him in a grey hoodie without a drop of sweat beneath his jaunty forelock. A message flashed up on Harry's speedometer console: *You're training well.*

But dressing badly, Harry thought, looking down at his limp, faded jogging bottoms, which he had to keep hitching up because of the mobile phone hanging on the waistband. And his tired Adidas trainers were neither new enough to be modern or old enough to be trendy again. The Joy Division T-shirt which had once held some kind of street cred just sent out the signal that he hadn't been following what was happening on the music scene for a number of years. But Harry didn't feel completely – completely – in the cold until his phone began to bleep and he noticed that seventeen reproachful pairs of eyes, including the stand-up comic's, were directed at him. He unhooked the tiny black devil's machine from his waistband.

'Hole.'

That don't impress me much! again.

'It's Juul. Am I disturbing?'

'No, it's just music.'

'You're wheezing like a walrus. Ring me back when it's more convenient.'

'It's convenient now. I'm at the gym.'

'Alright. I have good news. I've read your report from Johannesburg. Why didn't you say he'd been to Sennheim?'

'Uriah? Is that important? I wasn't even sure I had the name right. I looked for it on a map of Germany but I couldn't find any Sennheim.'

'The answer to your question is yes, it is important. If you've been in any doubt as to whether he fought at the front, you can be reassured now. It's one hundred per cent certain. Sennheim is a little place and the only Norwegians I've heard of who have been there went during the war. To the training camp before leaving for the Eastern Front. The reason you didn't find Sennheim on a map of Germany is because it isn't in Germany, but in French Alsace.'

'Yes, but . . .'

'Alsace has alternated between being French and German throughout its history, that's why they speak German there. The fact that our man has been to Sennheim reduces the number of potential candidates drastically. You see, only men from the *Nordland* and *Norge* regiments received their training there. And even better – I can give you the name of a person who was in Sennheim and would almost certainly be willing to help.'

'Really?'

'A soldier from the *Nordland* regiment who fought at the front. He joined us in the Resistance as a volunteer in 1944.'

'Wow.'

'He grew up on a remote farm with his parents and elder brothers, who were all fanatical NS people, and was forced to sign up for service at the front. He himself was never a convinced Nazi, and in 1943 he deserted near Leningrad. He was briefly in Russian captivity and fought alongside the Russians before managing to get back to Norway via Sweden.'

'Did you trust a soldier from the Eastern Front?'

Juul laughed. 'Absolutely.'

'Why are you laughing?'

'It's a long story.'

'I've got plenty of time.'

'We ordered him to eliminate a member of his family.'

Harry stopped pedalling. Juul cleared his throat.

'When we found him in Nordmarka, just north of Ullevålseter, at first we didn't believe his story. We thought he was an infiltrator and we were of a mind to shoot him. We had connections in the Oslo police archives, which meant that we could check his story, and it turned out in fact that he had been reported missing at the front. He was presumed to have deserted. His family background checked out and he had papers showing he was who he said he was. All of this could have been fabricated by the Germans, of course, so we decided to put him to the test.'

Pause.

'And?'

'We hid him in a hut, away from both us and the Germans. Someone suggested that we should order him to eliminate one of his brothers in the *Nasjonal Samling*. The main idea was to see how he would react. He didn't say a word when we gave him the orders, but the next day he was gone when we went down to his hut. We were sure he had backed out, but two days later he reappeared. He said he had been to the family farm in Gudbrandsdalen. A few days later we received reports from our people up there. One brother had been found in the cowshed, the other in the barn. The parents on the sitting-room floor.'

'My God,' Harry said. 'The man must have been out of his mind.'

'Probably. We all were. It was war. Besides, we never talked about it, not then and not since. You shouldn't either . . .'

'Of course not. Where does he live?'

'Here in Oslo. Holmenkollen, I think.'

'And his name is?'

'Fauke. Sindre Fauke.'

'Great. I'll contact him. Thank you, herr Juul.'

On the TV screen, there was a very close close-up of Poppe sending a tearful greeting home. Harry secured the mobile phone in the waistband of his tracksuit bottoms, hitched them up and strode off to the weights room.

Shania Twain remained unimpressed.

39

Gentlemen's Outfitter, Hegdehaugsveien.
2 March 2000.

'Wool quality, super 110,' the shop assistant said, holding the suit jacket for the old man. 'The best. Light and hard-wearing.'

'It will only be worn once,' the old man said with a smile.

'Oh,' she said, slightly nonplussed. 'Well, we have some cheaper —'

He studied himself in the mirror. 'This one is fine.'

'Classic cut,' the shop assistant assured him. 'The most classic cut we have.'

She looked aghast at the old man, who was bent double. 'Are you ill? Shall I . . . ?'

'No, it was a little twinge. It'll go.' The old man straightened up. 'How soon can you have the trousers taken up?'

'By Wednesday next week. If there's no hurry. Do you need them for a special occasion?'

'I do, but Wednesday is fine.'

He paid her in 100-kroner notes.

As he counted them out, she said, 'Well, I can tell you that you will have a suit for the rest of your life.'

His laughter was reverberating in her ears long after he had gone.

40

Holmenkollen. 3 March 2000.

IN HOLLMENKOLLVEIEN IN BESSERUD, HARRY found the house number he was looking for in the dark, on a large black timbered house beneath some very tall fir trees. A gravel drive led to the house, and Harry drove right up to a level area where he swung round. The idea was to park on the slope, but as he changed down into first gear, the car gave an almighty cough and breathed its last. Harry cursed and turned the ignition key, but the starter motor just groaned.

He got out of the car and walked up to the house as a woman came out of the door. She obviously hadn't heard him coming and paused on the steps with an enquiring smile.

'Good morning,' Harry said, nodding towards the car. 'Bit off colour, needs . . . some medicine.'

'Medicine?' Her voice was warm and deep.

'Yes, I think it's caught a touch of that flu going round at the moment.'

Her smile widened. The woman seemed to be about thirty and was wearing a black coat of the plain, effortlessly elegant kind which Harry knew cost an arm and a leg.

'I was on my way out,' the woman said. 'Are you coming here?'

'I think so. Sindre Fauke?'

'Almost,' she said. 'But you're a few months late. My father has moved into town.'

Harry went closer and could see she was attractive. And there was something about the relaxed way she spoke, the way she looked him straight in the eye, that suggested that she was also self-assured. A professional woman, he guessed. Something requiring a cool, rational mind. Estate agent, head of a department in a bank, politician or something like that. Well-off at any rate, of that he was fairly sure. It wasn't just the coat and the colossal house behind her, but something in the attitude and the high, aristocratic cheekbones. She walked down the steps as if walking along a straight line, made it seem easy. Ballet lessons, Harry thought.

'Is there anything I can help with?'

The consonants were clearly articulated, the intonation with the stress on 'I' so over-distinct that it was almost theatrical.

'I'm from the police.' He started to search through his jacket pockets for his ID card, but she dismissed it with a wave.

'Yes, well, I would have liked to have a chat with your father.'

To his irritation, Harry noticed that his intonation involuntarily became rather more formal than it usually was.

'Why is that?'

'We're looking for someone. And I was hoping your father might be able to help.'

'Who are you looking for?'

'I'm afraid I can't say.'

'OK.' She nodded as if it had been a test Harry had just passed.

'But if you're telling me he doesn't live here . . .' Harry said, shading his eyes. She had slim hands. Piano lessons,

Harry thought. And she had laughter wrinkles around her eyes. Perhaps she was over thirty after all?

'He doesn't,' she said. 'He's moved to Majorstuen. Vibes gate 18. You'll find him either there or in the University Library, I imagine.'

University Library. She articulated it so clearly that not a syllable went to waste.

'Vibes gate 18. I see.'

'Good.'

'Yes.'

Harry nodded. And kept nodding. Like a dog. She smiled with compressed lips and raised both eyebrows as if to say that was that, if there were no more questions the meeting was adjourned.

'I see,' Harry repeated.

Her eyebrows were black and uniform. Plucked probably, Harry thought. Not noticeably plucked though.

'I have to go now,' she said. 'My tram . . .'

'I see,' Harry said for the third time without making a move to go.

'I hope you find him. My father.'

'We will.'

'Bye.' The gravel crunched beneath her heels as she began to walk away.

'Um . . . I've got a little problem . . .' Harry said.

'Thanks for your help.'

'Not at all,' she said. 'You're sure it isn't too big a detour for you?'

'Absolutely not, I'm going the same way,' Harry said, peeking at the delicate, beyond-any-shadow-of-a-doubt pricey leather gloves which were now a dirty grey from pushing his Escort.

'The question is whether the car will stay the distance,' he said.

'It does seem to have had a colourful past,' she said, pointing to the hole in the dashboard and a protruding tangle of red and yellow wires where the radio should have been.

'A break-in,' Harry said. 'That's why the door won't lock. They broke that as well.'

'So it's open season for all and sundry now?'

'Yes, that's what it's like when you're old enough.'

She laughed. 'Is it?'

He threw her a quick glance. Perhaps she was the type whose appearance doesn't change as they age, who looks thirty from the time she's twenty till fifty. He liked her profile, the soft lines. Her skin had a warm, natural glow and not the dry, dull suntan women of her age like to buy in February. She had buttoned up her coat and he could see her long, slim neck. He saw her hands resting lightly in her lap.

'It's red,' she said calmly.

Harry jumped on the brakes.

'Sorry,' he said.

What was he doing? Looking at her hands to find out if she was wearing a wedding ring? My God.

He looked around and suddenly realised where they were.

'Something wrong?' she asked.

'No, no.' The lights changed to green and he accelerated. 'I have bad memories of this place.'

'Me too,' she said. 'I came through here on the train a few years ago, directly after a police car had driven across the rails and right into the wall over there.' She pointed. 'It was harrowing. One policeman was still hanging from the fence pole, like a crucifixion. I didn't sleep for several nights afterwards. It was said the policeman who was driving was drunk.'

'Who said that?'

'Someone I was studying with. From police college.'

They passed Frøen. Vinderen lay behind them. A long way, Harry decided.

'So you went to police college?' he asked.

'No, are you out of your mind?' She laughed again. Harry liked the sound. 'I studied law at university.'

'Me too,' he said. 'When were you there?'

Very crafty, Hole.

'I finished in '92.'

Harry did the maths. At least thirty, then.

'And you?'

'In '90,' Harry said.

'Can you remember the gig with the Raga Rockers during the Law Festival in '88?'

'Yes, of course. I was there. In the garden.'

'Me too! Wasn't it fantastic!' She looked at him, her eyes shining.

Where? he thought. *Where were you?*

'Yes, it was wonderful.' Harry didn't remember much of the concert. But he was suddenly reminded of all the great West End women who used to turn up when Raga played.

'If we studied at the same time, we must have lots of mutual acquaintances,' she said.

'Doubt it. I was a policeman then and didn't really hang out with students.'

They crossed Industrigata in silence.

'You can drop me here,' she said.

'Is this where you want to go?'

'Yes, this is fine.'

He pulled into the kerb and she turned towards him. A stray strand of hair hung in front of her face. Her gaze was both gentle and fearless. Brown eyes. A totally unexpected but instant thought struck him: he wanted to kiss her.

'Thank you,' she said with a smile.

She pulled down the door handle. Nothing happened.

'Sorry,' Harry said, leaning over and breathing in her aroma. 'The lock . . .' he gave the door a hefty thump and it swung open. He felt as if he was drowning. 'Perhaps we'll see each other again?'

'Perhaps.'

He had an urge to ask her where she was going, where she worked, whether she liked it, what else she liked, whether she had a partner, whether she fancied going to a concert even if it wasn't Raga. Luckily, however, it was too late. She was already taking those ballet steps of hers along the pavement in Sporveisgata.

Harry sighed. He had met her half an hour ago and he didn't even know her name. He must be going through the menopause prematurely.

Then he looked into the mirror and did a highly irregular U-turn. Vibes gate was close by.

41

Vibes Gate, Majorstuen. 3 March 2000.

A MAN STOOD AT THE DOOR WITH A BROAD SMILE as Harry came puffing and panting up to the third floor.

'Sorry about the stairs,' the man said, stretching out his hand. 'Sindre Fauke.'

His eyes were still young, but otherwise his face looked as if it had been through two world wars. At least. What was left of his white hair was combed back and he was wearing a red lumberjack shirt under the open Norwegian cardigan. His handshake was warm and firm.

'I've just made some coffee,' he said. 'And I know what you're after.'

They went into the sitting room, which had been converted into a study with a bureau and a PC. Papers were strewn everywhere, and piles of books and journals covered the tables and the floor alongside the walls.

'I haven't quite got things in order yet,' he explained, making room for Harry on the sofa.

Harry studied the room. No pictures on the wall, only a supermarket calendar with pictures of Nordmarka.

'I'm working on a large project which I hope will become a book. A war book.'

'Hasn't someone already written that one?'

Fauke laughed out loud. 'Yes, you could certainly say that. They just haven't written it quite right yet. And this is about *my* war.'

'Uh-huh. Why are you doing it?'

Fauke shrugged.

'At the risk of sounding pretentious – those of us who were involved have a duty to record our experiences for posterity before we depart this life. At any rate, that's how I see it.'

Fauke went into the kitchen and shouted into the sitting room.

'It was Even Juul who rang and told me I would be receiving a visit. POT, I was led to understand.'

'Yes, but Juul told me you lived in Holmenkollen.'

'Even and I don't have that much contact, and I kept my telephone number as my move is only temporary. Until I finish this book.'

'Right. I went up there. I met your daughter and she gave me this address.'

'So she was at home? Well, she must be having time off.'

From what? Harry was about to ask, but he decided it would be too obvious.

Fauke came back with a large steaming pot of coffee and two mugs.

'Black?' He put one of the mugs in front of Harry.

'Great.'

'Good. Because you have no choice.' Fauke laughed, almost spilling the coffee as he poured it out.

Harry thought it was remarkable how little Fauke reminded him of the daughter. He didn't have her cultivated way of speaking or conducting herself, or any of her features or dark complexion. Only the forehead was the same. High with a thick blue vein running across.

'You've got a big house up there,' he said instead.

'Endless maintenance and clearing snow,' Fauke answered, tasting the coffee and smacking his lips with approval. 'Dark, gloomy and too far away from everything. I can't stand Holmenkollen. On top of that, just snobs living there. Nothing for a migrant Gudbrandsdalen man like me.'

'So why don't you sell it?'

'I suppose my daughter likes it. She grew up there, of course. You wanted to talk about Sennheim, I understood.'

'Your daughter lives there alone?'

Harry could have bitten off his tongue. Fauke took a swig from his mug. Rolled the coffee round in his mouth. For a long time.

'She lives with a boy. Oleg.'

His eyes were vacant and he wasn't smiling any longer.

Harry drew a couple of quick conclusions. Too quick perhaps, but if he was right Oleg must have been one of the reasons Sindre Fauke was living in Majorstuen. Anyway, that was that. She lived with someone, no point thinking about it any more. Just as well, actually.

'I can't tell you too much, herr Fauke. As I'm sure you understand, we're working . . .'

'I understand.'

'Good. I'd like to hear what you know about the Norwegians in Sennheim.'

'Ooh. There were lots of us, you know.'

'Those still alive today.'

Fauke broke into a smile.

'I don't mean to be morbid, but that makes it considerably easier. Men dropped like flies at the front. On average 60 per cent of my company died every year.'

'Well I never. The death rate of the hedge sparrow is . . . erm.'

'Yes?'

'Sorry. Please continue.'

Harry, abashed, stared down into his coffee mug.

'The point was that the learning curve in war is steep,' Fauke said. 'Should you survive the first six months, the chances of survival become many times greater. You don't step on mines, you keep your head down in the trenches, you wake up when you hear the cocking of a Mosin–Nagant rifle. And you know that there is no room for heroes, and that fear is your best friend. Hence, after six months I was among a small group of Norwegians who realised we might survive the war. And most of us had been to Sennheim. Gradually, as the war went on, they moved the training camp to places deeper in Germany. Or the volunteers came directly from Norway. The ones who came without any training . . .' Fauke shook his head.

'They died?' Harry asked.

'We didn't even bother to learn their names when they arrived. What was the point? It's hard to understand, but as late as 1944 volunteers were still streaming to the Eastern Front, long after those of us who were there knew which way the war was going to go. They thought they were going to save Norway, the poor things.'

'I understood you were no longer there in 1944?'

'That's right. I deserted. New Year's Eve, 1942. I betrayed my country twice.' Fauke smiled. 'And ended up in the wrong camp both times.'

'You fought for the Russians?'

'In a way. I was a prisoner of war. We were starving to death. One morning they asked in German if anyone knew anything about telecommunications. I had a rough idea, so I put up my hand. It turned out that all the communications people in one of the regiments had died. Every single one! The next day I was operating a field telephone as we attacked my former comrades in Estonia. That was near Narva . . .'

Fauke raised his coffee mug, with both hands wrapped round it.

'I lay on a hillock watching the Russians attack a German machine gun post. They were just mown down by the Germans. One hundred and twenty men and four horses lay in heaps before the machine gun finally overheated. Then

the remaining Russians killed them with bayonets to save ammunition. Half an hour, maximum, passed from the time the
attack was launched until it finished. A hundred and twenty
men dead. Then it was on to the next post. And the same procedure there.'

Harry could see the mug was shaking slightly.

'I knew I was going to die. And for a cause I didn't believe in. I didn't believe in Stalin or Hitler.'

'Why did you go to the Eastern Front if you didn't believe
in the cause?'

'I was eighteen years old. I had grown up on a farm way
up in Gudbrandsdalen where as a rule we never saw anyone
except our nearest neighbours. We didn't read papers, didn't
have any books – I knew nothing. All I knew about politics
was what my father told me. We were the only ones left in
the family; the rest emigrated to the USA in the twenties.
My parents and the neighbouring farms on both sides were
sworn Quisling supporters and members of the NS. I had
two older brothers who I looked up to in absolutely all matters. They were part of *Hirden*, the uniformed political
activists and it had been their task to recruit young people to
the party at home, otherwise they would have volunteered to
go to the front as well. That was what they told me at least.
I only discovered later that their job was to recruit informers. But then it was too late as I was already on my way to
the front.'

'So you were converted at the front?'

'I wouldn't call it a conversion. Most of the volunteers
thought mainly of Norway and little of politics. The turning
point for me came when I realised I was fighting another
country's war. In fact, it was that simple. And actually it was
no better fighting for the Russians. In June 1944 I had unload-
ing duties on the quay in Tallinn, where I managed to sneak
on board a Swedish Red Cross boat. I buried myself in the
coke hold and hid there for three days. I had carbon monox-
ide poisoning, but I recovered in Stockholm. From there I

travelled to the Norwegian border where I crossed on my own. It was August by then.'

'Why on your own?'

'The few people I had contact with in Sweden didn't trust me; my story was a little too fantastic. That was fine, though. I didn't trust anyone, either.'

He laughed aloud again.

'So I lay low and coped in my own way. The border-crossing itself was child's play. Believe me, going from Sweden to Norway during the war was considerably less dangerous than picking up food rations in Leningrad. More coffee?'

'Please. Why didn't you simply stay in Sweden?'

'Good question. And one which I've asked myself many times.'

He ran a hand across his thin white hair.

'I was obsessed by the thought of revenge, you see. I was young, and when you're young you tend to have this delusion about the ideals of justice, you think it is something we humans are born with. I was a young man with internal conflicts when I was at the Eastern Front, and I behaved like a shit to many of my comrades. Despite that, or precisely because of it, I swore I would avenge all those who had sacrificed their lives for the lies they had fed us back home. And I would take revenge for my own ruined life which I thought would never be whole again. All I wanted was to settle a score with all those who had really betrayed our country. Nowadays psychologists would probably call it war psychosis and have me locked up immediately. Instead I went to Oslo, not knowing anyone or having a place to stay, carrying papers that would have me shot on the spot as a deserter. The day I arrived in Oslo by lorry I went up to Nordmarka. I slept under some spruce branches and ate nothing but berries for three days before they found me.'

'The Resistance people?'

'I understand from Even Juul that he told you the rest.'

'Yes.' Harry fidgeted with the mug. The killings. It was an

incomprehensible action which meeting the man had not made any more comprehensible. It had been there all the time, at the front of his brain, ever since Harry saw Fauke standing there smiling in the doorway and he shook his hand. *This man executed his parents and two brothers.*

'I know what you're thinking,' Fauke said. 'But I was a soldier who had been given orders to kill. If I hadn't been given the orders, I wouldn't have done it. But this I do know: my family were among the ranks of those who cheated our country.'

Fauke looked straight at Harry. His hands round the coffee mug were no longer shaking.

'You're wondering why I killed them all when my orders were to kill only one,' he said. 'The problem was they didn't say which one. They left it to me to be the judge of life or death. And I couldn't do it. So I killed them all. There was a guy at the front we called the redbreast. Like the bird, the robin redbreast. He had taught me that killing with the bayonet was the most humane method. The carotid artery runs from the heart to the brain and when you sever the link, the brain receives no oxygen and the victim is instantly brain-dead. The heart pumps three, maybe four times, but then it stops beating. The problem is that it is difficult. Gudbrand – that was his name – was a master of his art, but I struggled with my mother for what seemed an age and only managed to cause her flesh wounds. In the end I had to shoot her.'

Harry's mouth was dry. 'I see,' he said.

The meaningless words hung in the air. Harry shoved the coffee mug across the table and pulled out a notebook from his leather jacket.

'Perhaps we could talk about the men you were with in Sennheim?'

Sindre Fauke stood up immediately.

'I apologise, Inspector. I hadn't intended to present it so coldly and brutally. Let me just explain to you before we go on: I am not a brutal man. This is only my way of dealing with things. I needn't have told you about it, but I did so because I cannot afford to duck the issue. That is also why I'm writing this book. I have to go through it every time the topic is brought up, explicitly or implicitly. To be absolutely sure that I am not hiding from it. The day I hide, fear will have won its first battle. I don't know why it's like this. A psychologist could probably explain it.'

He sighed.

'But now I've said all I'm going to say on the matter. Which is probably already too much. More coffee?'

'No, thank you,' Harry said.

Fauke sat down again. He supported his chin on clenched fists.

'OK. Sennheim. The hard kernel of the Norwegians. In fact, a mere five people, including me. And one of them, Daniel Gudeson, died the same night I deserted. So, four then: Edvard Mosken, Hallgrim Dale, Gudbrand Johansen and me. The only one I've seen since the war is Edvard Mosken, our section leader. That was the summer of 1945. He was given three years for treason. I don't even know if the others survived. But let me tell you what I know about them.'

Harry turned over a fresh page in his notebook.

42

POT. 3 March 2000.

G-u-d-b-r-a-n-d J-o-h-a-n-s-e-n. HARRY TYPED the letters with his index fingers. A country boy. According to Fauke, a nice, somewhat feeble character, whose idol and big-brother surrogate was Daniel Gudeson, who was shot during the night watch. Harry pressed ENTER and the program started.

He stared in the direction of the wall. At the wall. At a small picture of Sis. She was pulling a face; she always did when she was being photographed. One summer holiday many years ago. The shadow of the photographer was on her white T-shirt. Mum.

A little peep from the PC signalled that the search was over and he focused on the computer screen again.

The national registration office had two Gudbrand Johansens registered, but the birth dates showed they were under sixty. Sindre Fauke had spelled the names for him, so it was unlikely he had got them wrong. That could only mean either Johansen had changed his name, or he lived abroad, or he was dead.

Harry tried the next one. The section leader from Mjøndalen. The one with small children back home. E-d-v-a-r-d

M-o-s-k-e-n. Disowned by his family because he had gone to the front. Double click on SEARCH.

The ceiling lights suddenly came on. Harry turned round.

'You should switch on the lights when you're working late.' Kurt Meirik stood in the doorway with his finger on the switch. He came in and perched on the edge of the table.

'What have you found out?'

'That we're looking for a man well over seventy. Who probably fought at the front.'

'I mean about these neo-Nazis and Independence Day.'

'Oh.' There was a new peep from the PC. 'I haven't had time to look into that yet, Meirik.'

There were two Edvard Moskens on the screen. One was born in 1942, the other in 1921.

'We're having a department party next Saturday,' Meirik said.

'I've got the invitation in my pigeon-hole.' Harry double-clicked on 1921 and the address of the older Mosken came up. He lived in Drammen.

'Personnel said you hadn't responded yet. I just wanted to make sure you were coming.'

'Why's that?'

Harry tapped Edvard Mosken's ID number into Criminal Records.

'We like people to get to know each other across departmental boundaries. I haven't even seen you in the canteen once yet.'

'I'm quite happy here in the office.'

No hits. He brought up the Central National Register for everyone who'd had formal dealings with the police for any reason. Not necessarily prosecuted – they might, for instance, have been arrested, reported or themselves been a victim of a criminal act.

'It's good to see you immersed in cases, but don't wall yourself in here. Will I see you at the party, Harry?'

ENTER.

'I'll see. I have another arrangement I made a long time ago,' Harry lied.

No hits again. While he was in the Central National Register he might as well put in the third name Fauke had given him. H-a-l-l-g-r-i-m D-a-l-e. An opportunist, in Fauke's view. Relied on Hitler winning the war and rewarding those who had chosen the right side. Had already regretted it by the time he got to Sennheim, but it was too late to turn back. Harry had thought there was something vaguely familiar about the name when Fauke had said it, and now the same feeling resurfaced.

'Let me put it a little stronger,' Meirik said. 'I am instructing you to come.'

Harry looked up. Meirik smiled.

'A joke,' he said. 'But it would be nice to see you there. Have a good evening.'

'Bye,' Harry mumbled, returning to the screen. One Hallgrim Dale. Born 1922. ENTER.

The screen filled with text. One more page. And then another.

They didn't all do well after the war then, Harry thought. Hallgrim Dale – place of residence: Schweigaards gate, Oslo – was what newspapers loved to describe as 'no stranger to the police'. Harry's eyes ran down the list. Vagrancy, drunkenness, harassment of neighbour, petty larceny, affray. A lot, but nothing of any real consequence. The most impressive thing was that he was still alive, Harry thought, as he noted down that he had been taken in to sober up as recently as last August. He found the Oslo telephone directory, looked up Dale's number and rang. While he was waiting for an answer he searched the register and found the other Edvard Mosken, born in 1942. He had an address in Drammen, too. He took down the ID number and went back to Criminal Records.

'This is a message from Telenor. You have reached a telephone number which is no longer in use. This is a me —'

Harry wasn't surprised. He put down the phone.

Edvard Mosken Junior had been given a prison sentence. A long sentence; he was still inside. What for? Drugs, Harry guessed, and pressed ENTER. A third of all prisoners had been on a drugs charge. There. Yes indeed. Smuggling hash. Four kilos. Four years, unconditional sentence.

Harry yawned and stretched. Was he getting anywhere or was he just sitting here wasting time because the only other place he felt like going was Schrøder's, and he didn't feel like sitting there drinking coffee? What a shit day. He summed up: Gudbrand Johansen doesn't exist, at least not in Norway; Edvard Mosken lives in Drammen and has a son with a drugs conviction; and Hallgrim Dale is a drunk and hardly the type to have half a million kroner to blow.

Harry rubbed his eyes.

Should he look up Fauke in the telephone directory to see if there was a number for Homenkollveien? He groaned.

She has a partner. And she has money. And class. In short: everything you don't have.

He put Hallgrim Dale's ID number into the Register, ENTER. The machine whirred and churned.

Long list. More of the same. Poor old alkie.

You both studied law. And she likes the Raga Rockers, too.

Wait a moment. On the last record, Dale was coded as 'victim'. Had he been beaten up? ENTER.

Forget her. That's it, now she was forgotten. Should he ring Ellen and ask if she fancied going to the cinema? Let her choose the film. No, he'd better go to Focus. Sweat it out.

It flashed at him from the screen.

HALLGRIM DALE. 151199. MURDER.

Harry took a deep breath. He was surprised, but why wasn't he more surprised? He double-clicked on DETAILS.

The computer droned and vibrated. But for once the convolutions of his brain were quicker than the computer, and by the time the picture came up he had already managed to place the name.

43

Focus Gym. 3 March 2000.

'ELLEN HERE.'

'Hi, it's me.'

'Who?'

'Harry. And don't pretend there are other men who ring you and say "it's me".'

'You sod. Where are you? What's that dreadful music?'

'I'm at Focus.'

'What?'

'I'm cycling. Soon have done eight kilometres.'

'Let me just get this absolutely straight, Harry: you're sitting on a bike at Focus at the same time as talking on your mobile?' She stressed the words 'Focus' and 'mobile'.

'Is there anything wrong with that?'

'Honestly, Harry.'

'I've been trying to get hold of you all evening. Do you remember that murder case you and Tom Waaler had in November, name of Hallgrim Dale?'

'Naturally. Kripos took over almost immediately. Why's that?'

'Not sure yet. It may have something to do with this ex-front man I'm after. What can you tell me?'

'This is work, Harry. Ring me at the office on Monday.'

'Just a little, Ellen. Come on.'

'One of the cooks in Herbert's Pizza found Dale in the back alley. He was lying between the large rubbish bins with his throat cut. The crime scene people found *nada*. The doctor who did the autopsy, by the way, thought that the cut around the throat was just fantastic. Surgical precision, he said.'

'Who do you think did it?'

'No idea. Might have been one of the neo-Nazis of course, but I don't think so.'

'Why not?'

'If you kill someone right on your doorstep, you're either foolhardy or just plain foolish. But everything about this murder seems so tidy, so thought through. There were no signs of a struggle, no clues, no witnesses. Everything suggests that the murderer knew exactly what he was doing.'

'Motive?'

'Hard to say. Dale certainly had debts, but hardly amounts worth squeezing out of him. As far as we know, he didn't do drugs. We searched his flat – nothing there, apart from empty bottles. We talked to some of his drinking pals. For some reason or other he had taken up with these drinking ladies.'

'Drinking ladies?'

'Yes, the ones who stick to the soaks. You've seen them, you know what I mean.'

'Yes indeed, but . . . *drinking ladies*.'

'You always get hung up on the craziest things, Harry, and it can be very irritating. Do you know that? Perhaps you should —'

'Sorry, Ellen. You're forever right and I'll do my best to improve. You were saying?'

'There's a lot of partner-swapping in alkie circles, so we can't rule out a jealousy killing. Incidentally, do you know who we had in for questioning? Your old friend Sverre Olsen. The cook had seen him at Herbert's Pizza around the time of the murder.'

'And?'

'Alibi. He'd been sitting there all day, had only been out for ten minutes to buy something. The shop assistant confirmed.'

'He could have —'

'Yes, you would have liked it to be him, but Harry . . .'

'Dale might have had something other than money.'

'Harry . . .'

'He might have had information. About someone.'

'You like conspiracy theories up there on the sixth floor, don't you? But can't we deal with this on Monday, Harry?'

'Since when have you been so particular about working hours?'

'I'm in bed.'

'At half past ten?'

'I'm not on my own.'

Harry stopped pedalling. It hadn't occurred to him until now that people around him might be listening to the conversation. He swivelled round. Luckily there were only a handful of people training at this late hour.

'Is that the artist guy from Tørst?' he whispered.

'Mm.'

'And how long have you two been bed pals?'

'A while.'

'Why didn't you tell me?'

'You didn't ask.'

'Is he lying next to you now?'

'Mm.'

'Is he good?'

'Mm.'

'Has he told you he loves you yet?'

'Mm.'

Pause.

'Do you think about Freddie Mercury when you—'

'Goodnight, Harry.'

44

Harry's Office. 6 March 2000.

THE CLOCK IN RECEPTION SHOWED 8.30 AS HARRY
arrived at work. It wasn't much of a reception area, more an
entrance which functioned as a funnel. The funnel boss was
Linda, who looked up from her computer and greeted him
with a cheery 'Good morning'. Linda had been in POT
longer than anyone and, strictly speaking, she was the only
person in security Harry needed to have any contact with in
order to carry out his daily work. Apart from being the 'funnel boss', the tiny fast-talking woman of fifty functioned as
a kind of communal secretary, receptionist and general fac-
totum. It had occurred to Harry a couple of times that if he
were a spy for a foreign power and had to tap someone in
POT for information, he would choose Linda. Furthermore,
she was the only person in POT, apart from Meirik, who
knew what Harry was doing there. He had no idea what the
others thought. During his extremely rare visits to the canteen to buy a yoghurt or cigarettes (which they didn't sell,
it turned out) he had caught the looks from the tables. He
hadn't tried to interpret them, however; he had merely scut-
tled back to his office.

'Someone phoned for you,' Linda said. 'Spoke English. I'll just have a look . . .'

She took a yellow Post-it off her computer monitor.

'Hochner.'

'Hochner?' Harry exclaimed.

Linda looked at the slip of paper, uncertain. 'Yes, that was what she said.'

'*She?* He, don't you mean?'

'No, it was a woman. She said she would call back . . .' Linda turned and looked at the clock behind her, '. . . now. She seemed pretty keen to get hold of you. While I've got you here, Harry – have you been round to introduce yourself yet?'

'Haven't had time. Next week, Linda.'

'You've been here for a whole month. Yesterday Steffensen asked me who the tall blond guy was he'd met in the toilet.'

'Really? And what did you tell him?'

'I said it was on a need-to-know basis.' She laughed. 'And you have to come to the department do on Saturday.'

'So I understand,' he mumbled, picking up two pieces of paper from his pigeon-hole. One was a reminder about the party, the other an internal note about the new arrangement for reps. Both sailed into the bin as soon as he had closed his office door.

Then he sat down, pressed REC and PAUSE on the answerphone and waited. After about thirty seconds the telephone rang. Harry picked up, expecting Hochner.

'Harry Hole speaking.'

'Herry? Spicking?' It was Ellen.

'Sorry. I thought it was someone else.'

'He's an animal,' she said before he could say anything else. 'Føcking ønbelivebel, he is.'

'If you're talking about what I think you're talking about, I would prefer you to stop right there, Ellen.'

'Wimp. Who were you expecting a call from, by the way?'

'A woman.'

'At last!'

'Forget it. It's probably a relative or the wife of a guy I've interviewed.'

She sighed. 'When are you going to meet someone, Harry?'

'You're in love now, are you?'

'Well guessed! Aren't you?'

'Me?'

Ellen's joyous screech pierced his eardrum.

'You didn't deny it! I've caught you, Harry Hole! Who is it, who, who?'

'Stop it, Ellen.'

'Tell me I'm right!'

'I haven't met anyone, Ellen.'

'Don't lie to Mummy.'

Harry laughed. 'Tell me more about Hallgrim Dale. How far has the investigation got now?'

'Don't know. Talk to Kripos.'

'I will, but what does your intuition tell you about the murder?'

'That he's a pro. It isn't a passion killing. And despite the fact that I said the murder seemed neat and tidy, I don't believe that it was carefully planned in advance.'

'No?'

'The killing was efficient and there were no clues left behind, but the scene of the crime was a poor choice. He could easily have been seen from the street or in the back alley.'

'The other line is bleeping. I'll call you back.'

Harry pressed the PAUSE button on the answering machine and checked that the tape was now running before he switched to the other line.

'Harry.'

'Hello, my name is Constance Hochner?'

'How do you do, Ms Hochner.'

'I'm Andreas Hochner's sister.'

'I see.'

Even on the bad line he could hear she was nervous. Nevertheless, she went straight to the point.

'You had an agreement with my brother, Mr Hole. And you haven't kept your part of the deal.'

She spoke with a strange accent, the same as Andreas Hochner's. Automatically, Harry tried to visualise her, a habit he had adopted early on as a detective.

'Well, Ms Hochner, I can't do anything for your brother before I have verified the information he gave us. For the time being, we have not found anything to corroborate what he said.'

'But why should he lie, Mr Hole? A man in his predicament?'

'That is precisely why, Ms Hochner. If he doesn't know anything he could be desperate enough to pretend that he does.'

There was a pause on the crackly line from . . . where? Johannesburg?

Constance Hochner was speaking again.

'Andreas warned me that you might say something like that. That's why I'm calling you, to tell you I have more information from my brother that you may be interested in.'

'Oh, yes?'

'But you cannot have the information unless your government does something about my brother's case first.'

'We'll do what we can.'

'I'll contact you again when there is evidence that you're helping us.'

'As you know, Ms Hochner, it doesn't work like that. First of all, we have to see the results of the information we receive. Then we can help him.'

'My brother must have guarantees. The legal proceedings against him start in two weeks.'

Her voice failed her somewhere in the middle, and Harry knew she was close to tears.

'The only thing I can give you is my word that I'll do as much as I can.'

'I don't know you. You don't understand. They intend to sentence Andreas to *death*. They —'

'Nevertheless, that is all I can offer you.'

She began to cry. Harry waited. After a while she was quiet.

'Do you have children, Ms Hochner?'

'Yes,' she sniffled.

'And you know what your brother has been accused of?'

'Obviously.'

'Then you'll also know that he will need all the absolution he can get. As he can help us, via you, to stop a killer, he will have done some good. And you will have too, Ms Hochner.'

She was breathing heavily over the telephone. Harry thought she was going to cry again.

'Do you promise to do as much as you can, Mr Hole? My brother hasn't done all the things they are accusing him of.'

'I promise.'

Harry heard his own voice. Calm and steady. While crushing the receiver.

'OK,' Constance Hochner said softly. 'Andreas says that the person who took delivery of the weapon and paid for it at the harbour that night is not the same as the person who ordered it. The man who ordered it was a fairly regular customer, a youngish man. He spoke good English with a Scandinavian accent. And he insisted that Andreas used the code name 'the Prince' with him. Andreas said you should start by focusing on groups of guys fixated with guns.'

'Is that everything?'

'Andreas has never seen him, but he says that he would recognise his voice immediately if you sent him a tape.'

'Excellent,' Harry said, hoping she wouldn't hear how disappointed he was. He instinctively straightened his shoulders as if to steel himself before serving up the lie.

'If I discover anything, I'll start pulling the strings here.'
The words smarted like caustic soda in his mouth.

'Thank you, Mr Hole.'

'Nothing to thank me for, Ms Hochner.'

He repeated the last phrase a couple of times to himself after putting down the receiver.

'That's too much,' Ellen said on hearing the story about the Hochner family.

'See if your brain can forget it's in love for a while and let it perform some of its tricks,' Harry said. 'Now at least you've got your cues.'

'Illegal importation of arms, regular customer, the Prince, arms freaks. That's only four.'

'That's all I have.'

'Why do I agree to this?'

'Because you love me. Now I have to be off.'

'Wait. Tell me about the woman you —'

'Hope your intuition is better with solving crime, Ellen. Take care.'

Harry rang the Drammen number directory enquiries had given him.

'Mosken speaking.' A self-assured voice.

'Edvard Mosken?'

'Yes. To whom am I speaking?'

'Inspector Hole, POT. I have a couple of questions.'

It struck Harry that this was the first time he had introduced himself as an inspector. For some reason it felt like a lie.

'Has something happened to my son?'

'No. Would it be convenient to visit you at midday tomorrow, herr Mosken?'

'I'm a pensioner. And single. There's hardly a moment when it wouldn't be convenient, Inspector.'

Harry called Even Juul and brought him up to date on what had happened.

Harry was considering what Ellen had said about the murder of Hallgrim Dale as he walked to the canteen to buy a yoghurt. He would ring Kripos to find out more about the case, although he had a strong feeling that Ellen had already told him everything worth knowing. Nevertheless. The statistical probability of being murdered in Norway was about one in ten thousand. When a person you're looking for turns up dead in a four-month-old murder case, it is difficult to believe that it is a coincidence. Could the murder be linked in any way with the purchase of the Märklin rifle? It was barely 9 a.m. and Harry already had a headache. He hoped Ellen would be able to come up with something on the Prince. Anything at all. If nothing else, it would be a place to begin.

45

Sogn. 6 March 2000.

AFTER WORK HARRY DROVE UP TO THE SHEL-
tered housing in Sogn. Sis was waiting for him. She had put
on a bit of weight in the last year, but her boyfriend Henrik,
who lived further down the corridor, liked her like that, she
claimed.

'But then Henrik is a mongo.'

She usually said that when she had to explain Henrik's
minor idiosyncrasies. She, for her part, was not a mongo.
There was obviously an almost invisible though sharp distinction somewhere. And Sis liked to explain to Harry
which of the residents were mongos, and those who were
only almost.

She told Harry about the usual things: what Henrik had
said last week (which could on occasion be quite remarkable),
what they had seen on TV, what they had eaten and where
they planned to go on holiday. They were always planning
holidays. This time it was Hawaii and Harry could only smile
at the thought of Sis and Henrik in Hawaiian shirts at the airport in Honolulu

He asked if she had talked to Dad, and she said he had
visited her two days ago.

'That's good,' Harry said.

'I think he's forgotten Mum now,' Sis said. 'That's good.'

Harry stayed in his chair for a moment, thinking about what she had said. Then Henrik knocked on the door and said *Hotel Caesar*, a soap opera, was beginning on TV2 in three minutes, so Harry put on his coat and promised to phone soon.

The traffic by the lights at Ullevål Stadium was as sluggish as usual, and he realised too late that he would have to turn right at the ring road because of roadworks. He thought about what Constance Hochner had told him. Uriah had used a middleman, probably a Norwegian. It meant there was someone out there who knew who Uriah was. He had already asked Linda to go through the secret archives to find someone with the nickname 'the Prince', but he was fairly sure she wouldn't find anyone. He had a definite feeling that this man was smarter than the average criminal. If it was true what Andreas Hochner said – that the Prince was a regular customer – it meant that he had managed to build up his own clientele without POT or anyone else finding out. Something like that takes time and requires care, cunning and discipline – none of which were characteristics of the gangsters Harry knew. Of course, he might have had more than his share of good fortune, since he hadn't been arrested. Or he might have a position which protected him. Constance Hochner had said that he spoke good English. He could be a diplomat, for example – someone who could travel in and out of the country without being stopped at customs.

Harry came off the ring road at Slemdalsveien and drove up towards Holmenkollen.

Should he ask Meirik if he could have Ellen provisionally transferred to POT? Meirik seemed more intent on him counting neo-Nazis and going to social events than chasing wartime ghosts.

Harry had driven right up to her house before he realised where he was. He stopped the car and stared between the trees. It was fifty or so metres to the house from the main road. There was light in the windows on the ground floor.

'Idiot,' he said aloud and started at the sound of his own voice. He was about to drive off when he saw the front door open and light fall on the steps. The thought that she might see and recognise his car put him in a state of panic. He slotted the car into reverse so that he could back quietly and discreetly up the hill and out of sight, but he didn't have his foot hard enough on the accelerator and the engine died. He heard voices. A tall man in a long, dark coat had come out on to the steps. He was talking, but the person he was talking to was hidden by the door. Then he leaned in towards the door opening and Harry could no longer see them.

They're kissing, he thought. *I've driven up to Holmenkollen to spy on a woman I've talked to for fifteen minutes kissing her boyfriend.*

Then the door closed, and the man got into an Audi and drove past him down to the main road.

On his way home Harry wondered how he should punish himself. It had to be something severe, something that would have a deterrent effect for the future. An aerobics class at Focus.

46

Drammen. 7 March 2000.

HARRY HAD NEVER UNDERSTOOD EXACTLY WHY Drammen came in for so much criticism. The town wasn't a beauty, but was it so much uglier than most of the other overgrown villages in Norway? He considered stopping for a cup of coffee at Børsen, but a quick check of his watch revealed that he didn't have enough time.

Edvard Mosken lived in a red wooden house with a view of the trotting track. An oldish Mercedes estate was parked outside the garage. Mosken himself was standing at the front door. He examined Harry's ID carefully before saying anything.

'Born in 1965? You look older than that, Inspector Hole.'

'Bad genes.'

'Bad luck for you.'

'Well, they let me into eighteen-certificate films when I was fourteen.'

It was impossible to discern whether Edvard Mosken appreciated the joke or not. He motioned for Harry to go in.

'You live alone?' Harry asked as Mosken led the way to the sitting room. The flat was clean and well-kept; few personal ornaments and just as exaggeratedly neat as some men like to be when they are allowed to choose for themselves. It reminded Harry of his own flat.

'Yes. My wife left me after the war.'

'Left?'

'Upped sticks. Cleared off. Went on her way.'

'I see. Children?'

'I had a son.'

'Had?'

Edvard Mosken stopped and turned round.

'Am I not expressing myself clearly, Inspector Hole?'

One white eyebrow was raised, forming a sharp angle on the high, open forehead.

'No, it's me,' Harry said. 'I have to be spoonfed.'

'OK. I *have* a son.'

'Thank you. What did you do before you retired?'

'I owned a few lorries. Mosken Transport. Sold the business seven years ago.'

'Did it go well?'

'Well enough. The buyers kept the name.'

They sat down, each on their own side of the coffee table. Harry knew that there would be no question of coffee. Edvard sat on the sofa, leaning forward with his arms crossed as if to say: *Let's get this over with.*

'Where were you on the night of 21 December?'

Harry had decided on the way over to open with this question. By playing the only card he had before Mosken had a chance to sound out the terrain and deduce that they didn't have anything, Harry could at least hope to flush out a reaction, which might tell him something. If Mosken had anything to hide, that was.

'Am I under suspicion for anything?' Mosken asked. His face betrayed no more than mild surprise.

'It would be good if you could just answer the question, Mosken.'

'As you wish. I was here.'

'That was quick.'

'What do you mean?'

'You didn't exactly have to think about it.'

Mosken grimaced. It was the kind of grimace where the mouth makes a parody of a smile while the eyes look at you in despair.

'When you get to be as old as I am, it's the evenings when you *didn't* sit on your own that you remember.'

'Sindre Fauke has given me a list of the Norwegians who were together at the Sennheim training camp. Gudbrand Johansen, Hallgrim Dale, you and Fauke.'

'You forgot Daniel Gudeson.'

'Did I? Didn't he die before the war was over?'

'Yes, he did.'

'So, why do you mention his name?'

'Because he was with us at Sennheim.'

'My understanding from Fauke was that many Norwegians went through Sennheim, but that you four were the only ones to survive.'

'That's right.'

'So why mention Gudeson in particular?'

Edvard Mosken stared at Harry. Then he shifted his gaze into a void.

'Because he was with us for such a long time. We thought he would survive. Well, we almost believed Daniel Gudeson was indestructible. He was no ordinary person.'

'Do you know that Hallgrim Dale is dead?'

Mosken shook his head.

'You don't seem very surprised.'

'Why should I be? Nowadays I'm more surprised to hear who is still alive.'

'What about if I tell you that he was murdered?'

'Oh, well, that's different. Why are you telling me this?'

'What do you know about Hallgrim Dale?'

'Nothing. The last time I saw him was in Leningrad. He was suffering from shell-shock.'

'You didn't travel back together?'

'How Dale and the others got home I have no idea. I was wounded in winter 1944 as the result of a grenade thrown from a Russian fighter plane into the trench.'

'A fighter plane? From a plane?'

Mosken smiled laconically and nodded.

'When I woke up in the field hospital the retreat was in full swing. Later that summer I ended up in the field hospital in Sinsen School, Oslo. Then came the capitulation.'

'So you didn't see any of the others after you were wounded?'

'Just Sindre. Three years after the war.'

'After you had served your time?'

'Yes. We ran into each other in a restaurant.'

'What do you think about him deserting?'

Mosken shrugged.

'He must have had his reasons. At least he took sides at a time when no one knew how the war would end. That's more than you can say about most Norwegian men.'

'What do you mean?'

'There was a saying during the war: *Those who decide late will always decide right.* At Christmas in 1943 we could see that our front was moving backwards, but we had no real idea how bad it was. Anyway, no one could accuse Sindre of changing like a weather-vane. Unlike those at home who sat on their backsides during the war and suddenly rushed to join the Resistance in the last months. We used to call them the "latter-day saints". A few of them today swell the ranks of those who make public statements about the Norwegians' heroic efforts for the right side.'

'Is there anyone in particular you're thinking about?'

'Of course you always think about the odd person who has been given the shining hero treatment afterwards. It's not that important, though.'

'What about Gudbrand Johansen? Do you remember him?'

'Of course. He saved my life at the end there. He . . .'

Mosken bit his lower lip. As if he had already said too much, Harry wondered.

'What happened to him?'

'Gudbrand? Damned if I know. The grenade . . . Gudbrand, Hallgrim Dale and I were in the trench when it came bouncing across the ice and hit Dale on the helmet. I can only remember that Gudbrand was closest to it when it exploded. I came out of the coma later and no one could tell me what had happened to Gudbrand or Dale.'

'What do you mean? Had they disappeared?'

Mosken's eyes searched for the window.

'This happened the same day the Russians launched their full offensive. It was chaotic, to put it mildly. Our trenches had long since passed into Russian hands when I woke up and the regiment had been transferred. If Gudbrand survived, he would probably have ended up in the *Nordland* regiment field hospital, in the Northern Sector. The same would be true of Dale if he had been wounded. I suppose I must have been there too, but when I woke up I was somewhere else.'

'Gudbrand Johansen's name isn't in the Civil Register.'

Mosken shrugged. 'So he must have been killed by the grenade. That was what I assumed.'

'And you've never tried to trace him?'

Mosken shook his head.

Harry looked around for something, anything, that might suggest Mosken had coffee in the house – a coffee pot, a coffee cup. There was a photograph of a woman in a gold frame on the hearth.

'Are you bitter about what happened to you and the other Eastern Front soldiers after the war?'

'As far as the punishment goes, no. I'm a realist. People had to be brought to justice because it was a political necessity. I had lost a war. I'm not complaining.'

Edvard Mosken suddenly laughed – it sounded like a

magpie's cackle. Harry had no idea why he had laughed.
Then Mosken became serious again.

'What smarted was being labelled a traitor. But I console
myself with the fact that we know that we defended our
country with our lives.'

'Your political views at that time . . .'

'If they are the same today?'

Harry nodded, and Mosken said with a dry smile, 'That's
an easy question to answer, Inspector. No. I was wrong. Simple as that.'

'You haven't had any contact with neo-Nazis since?'

'God forbid – no! There was a meeting in Hokksund a
few years ago and one of the idiots rang me up to ask if I
would go and talk about the war. I think they called themselves "Blood and Honour". Something like that.'

Mosken leaned across the coffee table. On one corner
there was a pile of magazines, neatly stacked and aligned
with the edge.

'What is POT actually looking for? Are you trying to
monitor the neo-Nazis? If that's the case, you've come to the
wrong place.'

Harry was unsure how much to tell him at this point. His
answer was honest enough though.

'I don't really know what we're looking for.'

'That sounds like the POT I know.'

He laughed his magpie cackle again. It was an unpleasant, high-pitched sound.

Harry later concluded it must have been the combination of
the scornful laugh and the fact that he wasn't offered any coffee that made him ask the next question in the way that he did.

'How do you think it must have been for your son to grow
up with an ex-Nazi as a father? Do you think that's why Edvard Mosken Jr is doing time for a drugs offence?'

Harry regretted it the second he saw the anger and pain
in the old man's eyes. He knew that he could have found out
what he wanted without hitting beneath the belt.

'The trial was a farce!' Mosken fizzed. 'The defence law-yer they gave my son is the grandson of the judge who sen-tenced me after the war. They're punishing my child to hide their own shame at what they did during the war. I —'

He stopped abruptly. Harry waited for him to go on, but nothing came. Without any prior warning, he suddenly felt the pack of hounds in the pit of his stomach tug at the chains. They hadn't stirred for quite a while now. They needed a drink.

'One of the "latter-day saints"?' Harry asked.

Mosken shrugged. Harry knew the topic was closed for now. Mosken angled his watch.

'Planning to go somewhere?' Harry asked.

'Going on a walk to my chalet.'

'Oh yes? Far away?'

'Grenland. I need to be off before it gets dark.'

Harry stood up. In the hall they stood searching for suit-able parting words when Harry suddenly remembered some-thing.

'You said you were wounded in Leningrad during winter 1944 and were sent to Sinsen School later that summer. What did you do in the intervening period?'

'What do you mean?'

'I've just been reading one of Even Juul's books. He's a war historian.'

'I'm quite aware who Even Juul is,' Mosken said with an inscrutable smile.

'He writes that the *Norge* regiment was dissolved in Krasnoje Selo in March 1944. Where were you from March to the time you arrived at Sinsen School?'

Mosken held Harry's gaze for a long while. Then he opened the front door and peered out.

'Almost down to zero now,' he said. 'You'll have to drive carefully.'

Harry nodded. Mosken straightened up, shaded his eyes and squinted in the direction of the empty trotting stadium where the grey, oval, gravel track stood out against the dirty snow.

'I was in places that once had names,' Mosken said, 'but were so transformed that no one could recognise them. Our maps only showed paths, water and minefields, no names. If I tell you I was in Pärnu in Estonia, that might be true. I don't know and nor does anyone else. During the spring and summer of '44 I was lying on a stretcher, listening to machine-gun fire and thinking about death. Not about where I was.'

Harry drove slowly alongside the river and stopped at the red lights in front of the town bridge. The other bridge, which crossed the E18 motorway, ran like a dental brace through the countryside and obstructed a view of Drammen fjord. Well, OK, perhaps not everything had been a success in Drammen. Harry had actually decided he would stop for a coffee in Børsen on the way back, but he changed his mind. He remembered they served beer too.

The lights changed to green. Harry accelerated.

Edvard Mosken had reacted furiously to the question about his son. Harry made up his mind to find out more about who the judge in the Mosken trial had been. Then he took a last look at Drammen in the mirror. Of course there were worse towns.

47

Ellen's Office. 7 March 2000.

ELLEN HADN'T MANAGED TO COME UP WITH ANY-thing.

Harry had wandered down to her office and sat in her creaky old office chair. They had recruited a new man, a young policeman from the station in Steinkjer, and he would be here in a month's time.

'I'm not clairvoyant,' she said on seeing Harry's disappointed face. 'And I checked with the others at the morning meeting today, but no one had heard of the Prince.'

'What about the Firearms Registry? They ought to have some idea about arms smugglers.'

'Harry!'

'Yes?'

'I don't work for you any longer.'

'*For* me?'

'*With* you, then. It's just that it felt like I was working for you. Bully.'

Harry shoved himself off with his foot and span round on the swivel chair. Four complete turns. He had never managed more. Ellen rolled her eyes.

'OK, so I rang the Firearms Registry too,' she said. 'They

hadn't heard of the Prince, either. Why don't they give you an assistant up in POT?'

'The case doesn't have high priority. Meirik lets me get on with it, but actually he wants me to discover what the neo-Nazis are planning to do on Eid.'

'One of the cues was "arms freaks". I can hardly imagine bigger arms freaks than the neo-Nazis. Why not start there and kill two birds with one stone?'

'I wondered about that myself.'

48

Café Ryktet, Grensen. 7 March 2000.

EVEN JUUL WAS STANDING ON THE STEPS AS
Harry pulled up in front of his house.

Burre stood beside him, pulling at his lead.

'That was quick,' Juul said.

'I got into the car as soon as I put down the phone,' Harry
said. 'Is Burre coming too?'

'I was just taking him for a little walk while I waited. Go
inside, Burre.'

The dog looked up at Juul with pleading eyes.

'Now!'

Burre jumped backwards and scurried in. Harry also recoiled at the sudden command.

'Let's go,' Juul said.

Harry caught a glimpse of a face behind the kitchen curtains as they drove away.

'It's getting lighter,' Harry said.

'Is it?'

'The days are, I mean. They're longer now.'

Juul nodded without answering.

'There's one thing I've been wondering about a bit,' Harry
said. 'Sindre Fauke's family, how did they die?'

'I've told you already. He killed them.'

'Yes, but how?'

Even Juul stared at Harry before answering.

'They were shot. Through the head.'

'All four?'

'Yes.'

Eventually they found a car park in Grensen and from there they walked to the place Juul had insisted on showing Harry when they had talked on the telephone.

'So, this is Ryktet then,' Harry said on entering the poorly lit, almost empty café with only a few people sitting round well-worn plastic tables. Harry and Juul got themselves a coffee and sat at one of the window tables. Two elderly men further back in the room stopped speaking and scowled at them.

'Reminds me of a café I go to sometimes,' Harry said, inclining his head towards the two old men.

'The old incorrigibles,' Juul said. 'Old Nazis and Eastern Front types who still think they were right. Here they sit pouring out their bitterness against the great betrayal, the Nygaardsvold government and the general state of things in the world. Those of them who still have breath in their bodies, at least. The ranks are thinning, I can see.'

'Still politically committed?'

'Oh, yes, they're still angry. At Third World aid, cuts in the defence budget, women priests, marriages for homosexuals, our new countrymen, all the things you would guess would upset these old boys. In their hearts they're still fascists.'

'And you think Uriah might frequent this place?'

'If Uriah is on some kind of crusade of vengeance against society, he would certainly find like-minded people here. Naturally, there are other meeting places for the ex-Eastern Front comrades, yearly gatherings here in Oslo, for example, for comrades-in-arms and others from all over the country. But those meetings are of a completely different order from the ones at this watering hole – they are purely social events to commemorate the dead, and there is a ban on talking politics. No, if I were hunting for an Eastern Front man with revenge on his mind, this is the place I would start.'

'Has your wife been to any of these, what did you call them . . . gatherings of comrades-in-arms?'

Juul stared at Harry in surprise. Then he slowly shook his head.

'Just an idea,' Harry said. 'Wondered if she might have anything to tell me?'

'She hasn't,' Juul said curtly.

'Fine. Is there any connection between those you call the "old incorrigibles" and the neo-Nazis?'

'Why do you ask?'

'I've had a tip-off which suggests that Uriah used a middleman to get hold of the Märklin rifle, someone who moves in arms circles.'

Juul shook his head.

'Most ex-Eastern Front men would be annoyed to hear you put them in the same category. Even though neo-Nazis generally hold them in very high regard. For them, fighting at the front is the ultimate dream – protecting their country and race with a firearm in their hand.'

'So if one of these old soldiers wanted to acquire a weapon he could reckon on support from the neo-Nazis?'

'He would probably meet with goodwill, yes. But he would have to know who to approach. Not just anyone would be able to provide him with such an advanced weapon as the one you are after. It's fairly indicative that the police in Hønefoss, during a raid on a neo-Nazi garage, found a rusty old Datsun full of home-made clubs, wooden spears and a couple of blunt axes. The majority of these people are literally Stone Age types.'

'So where do I begin to look for a person in this milieu who has contacts with international arms dealers?'

'The problem is not that the milieu is particularly large. In fact, *Fritt Ord*, the nationalists' newspaper, claims that

there are approximately fifteen hundred national socialists
and national democrats in Norway, but if you call the *Monitor*, the voluntary organisation which keeps an eye on fascist
nests, they'll tell you that there are fifty active members at
most. No, the problem is that the wealthy backers who really
hold the reins are invisible. They don't wear boots or have
swastikas tattooed on their upper arms, let's put it like that.
They may have a position in society they can exploit to serve
the cause, but to do that they have to keep a low profile.'

A deep voice rumbled behind them: 'How dare you come
here, Even Juul.'

49

Gimle Cinema, Bygdøy Allé.
7 March 2000.

'So what do I do?' Harry asked Ellen, nudging her forward in the queue. 'I'm just sitting wondering whether I should go and ask one of the old moaners if they know anyone who might be entertaining assassination plans and has purchased a rifle priced way above the norm for this special occasion. And at that very instant one of them comes over to our table and says in a funereal voice: *How dare you come here, Even Juul*'

'So what did you do?' Ellen asked.

'Nothing. I just sit there and see Even Juul's face drop. He looks as if he's seen a ghost. It's obvious the two of them know each other. By the way, that was the second person I've met today who knows Juul. Edvard Mosken also said he knew him.'

'Is that so strange? Juul writes for the newspapers, he's on TV, he's high profile.'

'You're probably right. At any rate, Juul stands up and simply marches out. I have to run after him. Juul's face is ashen when I catch up with him in the street. But when I ask what happened, he claims he doesn't know the man. Afterwards I drive him home and he barely says goodbye before leaving. He looks totally stunned. Is row ten alright?'

Harry stooped at the box-office window to buy two tickets.

'I have my doubts about this film,' he said.

'Why?' Ellen asked. 'Because it was my choice?'

'I heard a gum-chewing girl on the bus say to her friend that *Todo sobre mi madre* was nice. As in *naaiice*.'

'What's that supposed to mean?'

'When girls say that a film is *nice*, I get this *Fried Green Tomatoes* feeling. When you girls are served up some schmalz with even less content than *The Oprah Winfrey Show* you think you've seen a *warm, intelligent* film. Popcorn?'

He nudged her forward in the popcorn queue.

'You're a damaged human being, Harry. A damaged human being. By the way, do you know what? Kim was jealous when I said I was going to the cinema with a colleague from work.'

'Congratulations.'

'Before I forget,' she said. 'I found the name of Edvard Mosken Jr's defence counsel you were asking about. And his grandfather who was working on the postwar trials.'

'Yes?'

Ellen smiled.

'Johan Krohn and Kristian Krohn.'

'Bingo.'

'I talked to the Public Prosecutor in the trial against Mosken Jr. Mosken Snr went ballistic when the court found his son guilty and physically attacked Krohn. He screamed that Krohn and his grandfather were conspiring against the Mosken family.'

'Interesting.'

'I deserve a big bag of popcorn, don't you think?'

Todo sobre mi madre was a great deal better than Harry had feared. But in the middle of the scene where Rosa is buried he still had to pester a tear-streaked Ellen to ask where Grenland was. She answered that it was the area around Porsgrunn and Skien, and was then allowed to see the rest of the film in peace.

50

Oslo. 11 March 2000.

HARRY COULD SEE THE SUIT WAS TOO SMALL. HE could see it, but he couldn't understand it. He hadn't put on any weight since he was eighteen and the suit had fitted perfectly when he had bought it at Dressmann for the post-exams celebrations in 1990. Nevertheless, standing in front of the mirror in the lift, he saw that his socks were visible between the suit trousers and the black Dr Martens shoes. It was just one of those unsolvable mysteries.

The lift doors slid to the side and Harry could already hear the music, loud male chatter and female twittering emanating from the open doors in the canteen. He looked at his watch. It was 8.15. Eleven should do it and then he could go home.

He inhaled, stepped into the canteen and scanned the room. The canteen was the traditional Norwegian kind – a square room with a glass counter, at one end of which you ordered food, light-coloured furniture from some fjord in Sunnmøre and a smoking ban. The party committee had done their best to camouflage the daily backdrop with balloons and red tablecloths. Even though men were in the majority, the male-female mix was much more evenly distributed than

when Crime Squad threw a party. Most people seemed to
have already imbibed quite a bit of alcohol. Linda had talked
about various pre-party looseners, and Harry was glad that no
one had invited him.

'You look so good in a suit, Harry.'

That was Linda. He hardly recognised the woman in the
tight dress, which emphasised not only the extra kilos but
also her womanly exuberance. She was carrying a tray of
orange-coloured drinks which she held up in front of him.

'Er . . . no thanks, Linda.'

'Don't be so boring, Harry. This is a party!'

Prince was howling on the car stereo again.

Ellen bent forward in the driver's seat and turned down
the volume.

Tom Waaler gave her a sideways glance.

'A little too loud,' she said, thinking that it was only three
weeks until the policeman from Steinkjer arrived, and she
wouldn't have to work with Waaler any more.

It wasn't the music. He didn't bother her. And he definitely
wasn't a bad policeman.

It was the telephone calls. Not that Ellen Gjelten didn't have
some sympathy for a certain nurturing of your sex life, but half
the times his mobile phone rang she gathered from the conversations that a woman had already been spurned, was being
spurned or was about to be spurned. The latter conversations
were the most unpleasant. They were the women he had not
yet rejected, and he had a special voice for them which made
Ellen want to scream out loud: *Don't do it! He won't bring you
any good! Run for it!* Ellen Gjelten was a generous person who
found it easy to forgive human weakness. She had not detected
many human weaknesses in Tom Waaler, but not much humanity either. To put it bluntly, she didn't like him.

They drove past Tøyen Park. Waaler had received a tip-
off that someone had seen Ayub, the Pakistani gang leader

they had been after since the assault in the Palace Gardens
in December, in Aladdin, the Persian restaurant in Haus-
manns gate. Ellen knew they were already too late; they would
only be asking people if they knew where Ayub was. They
wouldn't get an answer, but at least they would have put in
an appearance, shown they weren't going to leave him in
peace.

'Wait in the car, I'll go in and check,' Waaler said.

'OK.'

Waaler pulled down the zip of his leather jacket.

To show off the muscles he had acquired pumping iron in
the gym at Police HQ, Ellen thought. Or enough of the shoulder holster for them to know that he was carrying a weapon.
The police officers in Crime Squad were always entitled to
carry weapons, but she knew that Waaler carried more than a
service revolver. A large bore number; she didn't have it in her
to ask what. Right after cars, Waaler's favourite topic of conversation was handguns, and she preferred cars. She didn't
carry a weapon herself. Not unless she was forced to, as she
was during the presidential visit in the autumn.

Something stirred, at the back of her brain. But it was
soon interrupted by a digital bleep-bleep version of 'Napoleon with his Army'. It was Waaler's mobile telephone. Ellen
opened the door to shout after him, but he was already on
his way into the restaurant.

It had been a boring week. Ellen couldn't remember such
a boring week since she had started in the police force. She
feared it had something to do with her finally having a private life. Suddenly there was a point in getting home before
it was late and Saturday shifts like this evening's had become
a sacrifice. The mobile played 'Napoleon . . .' for the fourth
time.

One of the spurned women? Or one who still had that to
come? If Kim dumped her now . . . but he wouldn't do that.
She just knew it.

'Napoleon with his Army' for the fifth time.

The shift would be over in a couple of hours and she would go home, take a shower and nip up to Kim's in Helgesens gate, five minutes in her charged sexual state. She giggled.

Six times! She grabbed the phone from under the handbrake.

'This is Tom Waaler's answerphone. Unfortunately herr Waaler is not here. Please leave a message.'

She meant it as a joke. Actually she had meant to say who she was afterwards, but for some reason she just sat listening to the heavy breathing at the other end. Perhaps for a thrill, perhaps she was just curious. At any rate, she suddenly twigged that the person at the other end thought he had reached the answerphone and was waiting for the bleep! She pressed one of the keys. *Bleep.*

'Hi, this is Sverre Olsen.'

'Hi, Harry, this is . . .'

Harry turned, but the rest of Kurt Meirik's sentence was swallowed up in the bass as the self-elected DJ cranked up the volume of the music blasting out of the loudspeaker directly behind Harry.

That don't impress me much . . .

Harry had been at the party for barely twenty minutes, had already checked his watch twice and managed to ask himself the following questions four times: *Did the murder of Dale have anything to do with the Märklin rifle deal? Who would be capable of cutting someone's throat so quickly and efficiently that he could do it in broad daylight in a back alley in the centre of Oslo? Who is the Prince? Could the sentencing of Mosken's son have anything to do with this case? What had happened to the fifth Norwegian soldier at the front, Gudbrand Johansen? And why hadn't Mosken made an effort to find him after the war if, as he maintained, Johansen had saved his life?*

He was standing in the corner now beside one of the

loudspeakers, with a Munkholm – in a glass to avoid questions about why he drank non-alcoholic beer – while watching a couple of the youngest POT employees dancing.

'Sorry, I didn't catch that,' Harry said.

Kurt Meirik was twirling the stem of an orange-coloured drink between his fingers. He seemed more erect than ever, standing there in his blue striped suit. Fitted perfectly, as far as Harry could see. Harry pulled his jacket sleeves down, aware that his shirt was sticking out way beyond his cuff links. Meirik leaned in closer.

'I'm trying to tell you this is the head of our foreign department, Inspector . . .'

Harry noticed the woman by his side. Slim figure. Plain red dress. He experienced a faint premonition.

So she had the looks, but did she have the touch?

Brown eyes. High cheekbones. Dark complexion. Short, dark hair framing a narrow face. Her smile was already in her eyes. He remembered she was good-looking, but not so . . . ravishing. It was the only word that occurred to him to cover the meaning: *ravishing*. He knew the fact that she was standing opposite him now ought to have rendered him speechless with astonishment, but there was somehow a kind of logic about it, something that made him inwardly acknowledge the whole situation with a nod.

'. . . Rakel Fauke,' Meirik said.

'We've already met,' Harry said.

'Oh?' Kurt Meirik exclaimed in surprise.

Rakel and Harry looked at each other.

'We have,' she said, 'but I don't think we got as far as exchanging names.'

She extended her hand with a slightly angled wrist, which once again made him think of piano and ballet lessons.

'Harry Hole,' he said.

'Aha,' she said. 'Of course you are. From Crime Squad, isn't that right?'

'Right.'

'I didn't realise you were the new inspector in POT when we met. Had you said that then . . .'

'Then what?' Harry asked.

She cocked her head to one side.

'Yes, then what?' She laughed. Her laughter forced the idiotic word to pop up into Harry's brain again: *ravishing*.

'Then at least I would have told you that we work in the same place,' she said. 'I don't usually tell people what I do for a living. You get so many strange questions. I'm sure it's the same for you.'

'Yes, of course.'

She laughed again. Harry wondered what it would take to make her laugh like that all the time.

'How is it I haven't seen you in POT before?' she asked.

'Harry's office is down at the end of the corridor,' Kurt Meirik said.

'Aha.' She nodded as if she understood, still with the sparkling smile in her eyes. 'The office right at the end, really?'

Harry inclined his head gloomily.

'Yes, well,' Meirik said. 'So now you've been introduced. We were on our way to the bar, Harry.'

Harry waited for the invitation. It didn't come.

'Talk to you later,' Meirik said.

Understandable, Harry thought. The head of POT and the inspector probably had lots of collegial boss-to-subordinate backslaps to give tonight. He leaned against the loudspeaker, but cast a furtive glance after them. She had recognised him. She had remembered that they hadn't exchanged names. He downed his beer in one draught. It tasted of nothing.

Waaler slammed the door after him.

'No one has seen, talked to or ever heard of Ayub,' he said. 'Drive.'

'Right,' Ellen said, checked the mirror and swung out from the kerb.

'You've begun to like Prince, too, I hear.'

'Have I?'

'You turned up the volume while I was away, anyway.'

'Oh.' *She had to ring Harry.*

'Is something the matter?'

Ellen stared rigidly ahead of her, at the wet black tarmac glistening in the light from the street lamps.

'The matter? What could be the matter?'

'I don't know. You look as if something has happened to you.'

'Nothing has happened, Tom.'

'Did anyone ring? Hey!' Tom stiffened in his seat and placed both palms firmly on the dashboard. 'Didn't you see that car or what?'

'Sorry.'

'Shall I take over?'

'Driving? Why?'

'Because you're driving like a . . .'

'Like a what?'

'Forget it. I asked if anyone had rung.'

'No one rang, Tom. If anyone had rung, I would have said, wouldn't I?'

She had to ring Harry. Quick.

'Why did you turn off my mobile?'

'What?' Ellen eyed him aghast.

'Keep your eyes on the road, Gjelten. I asked: Why —'

'No one rang. You must have switched off the phone yourself.'

Unconsciously, her voice had risen. She heard it screech in her own ears.

'OK, Gjelten,' he said. 'Relax, I was just wondering.'

Ellen tried to do as he instructed. Breathing evenly and concentrating on the traffic in front of her. She took a left off the roundabout down Vahls gate. Saturday evening, but the streets in this part of town were practically deserted. The lights were green. To the right along Jens Bjelkes gate. Left, down Tøyengata. Into the Police HQ car park. She could feel Tom's eyes studying her the whole way.

Harry hadn't looked at his watch once since meeting Rakel Fauke. He had even joined Linda for a round of introductions to some of his colleagues. The conversation had been stiff. They asked him what his position was, and once he answered the conversation petered out. Probably an unwritten rule in POT that you mustn't ask too much. Or they didn't give a toss. Fair enough, he wasn't particularly interested in them either. He had resumed his position by the speaker. He had seen a glimpse of her red dress a couple of times. As far as he could judge, she was circulating and didn't spend much time with anyone. She hadn't danced, he was fairly sure of that.

My God, I'm behaving like a teenager, he thought.

Then he did look at his watch: 9.30. He could go over to her, say a few words, see what happened. And if nothing happened, he could slink off, get the promised dance with Linda out of the way, and then off home. *Nothing happened?* What sort of self-delusion was this? Another inspector, as good as married. He could do with a drink. No. He stole one more look at his watch. He shuddered at the thought of the dance he had promised. Back home to his flat. Most of them were good and drunk now. Even in a sober state they would hardly have noticed the new inspector disappearing down the corridor. He could just stroll out the door and take the lift down. Outside his Ford Escort was loyally waiting for him. Linda looked as if she was having fun on the dance floor where she had a tight hold on a young officer who was swinging her round with a sweaty smile on his lips.

'There was a bit more buzz at the Raga gig at the Law Festival, don't you think?'

He felt his heart race as he heard her dark voice beside him.

Tom had positioned himself beside Ellen's chair in her office.

'Sorry if I was a bit rough in the car in town.'

She hadn't heard him coming and gave a start. She was holding the receiver, but hadn't yet dialled the number.

'Don't worry,' she said. 'It's me who is a little, well . . . you know.'

'Premenstrual?'

She peered up at him and knew it was not a joke. He was actually trying to be understanding.

'Maybe,' she said. Why was he in her office now when he had never come in before?

'Shift's over, Gjelten.' He inclined his head towards the clock on the wall. It said 10.00. 'I've got the car here. Let me drive you home.'

'Thank you very much, but I have to make a call first. You go on.'

'Private call?'

'No, it's just . . .'

'Then I'll wait here.'

Waaler settled into Harry's old office chair, which screamed in protest. Their eyes met. Damn! Why hadn't she said it was a private call? Now it was too late. Did he know that she had stumbled on to something? She tried to read his expression, but she seemed to have lost the ability since the panic had seized her. Panic? Now she knew why she had never felt comfortable with Tom Waaler. It wasn't because of his coldness, his views on women, blacks, flashers and homosexuals or his tendency to grab every legal opportunity to use violence. Off the top of her head, she could list the names of ten other policemen who would run Tom Waaler close on such matters, but still she had been able to find

some positives about them which allowed her to get on with
them. With Tom Waaler, though, there was something else
and now she knew what it was: she was scared of him.

'Well,' she said. 'It can wait until Monday.'

'Fine.' He stood up again. 'Let's get going.'

Waaler had one of those Japanese sports cars which Ellen
thought looked like cheap Ferrari imitations. It had bucket
seats which scrunched your shoulders up and loudspeakers
that seemed to fill half the car. The engine purred affection-
ately and the light from the street lamps swept through the
compartment as they drove up Trondheimsveien. A falsetto
voice she was becoming familiar with sidled out of the loudspeakers.

Prince. The Prince.

'I can get out here,' Ellen said, trying to make her voice
sound natural.

'Out of the question,' Waaler said, looking in the mirror.
'Door-to-door service. Where are we going?'

She resisted the impulse to tear open the door and jump
out.

'Turn left here,' Ellen said, pointing.

Be at home, Harry.

'Jens Bjelkes gate,' Waaler read out the street sign on the
wall and turned.

The lighting here was frugal and the pavements deserted.
Out of the corner of her eye Ellen saw small squares of light
flit across his face. Did he know she knew? And could he
see she was sitting with her hand in her bag? Did he realise
she was clutching the black gas spray she had bought in Germany? She had shown it to him in the autumn when he had
insisted she was putting herself and her colleagues at risk
by refusing to carry a weapon. Hadn't he discreetly intimated
that he could get hold of a neat little gun which could be hidden anywhere on the body? It wasn't registered and therefore
couldn't be traced back to her, should there be an 'accident'.

She hadn't taken his words so seriously at that time; she had thought it was one of those semi-macabre macho jokes and laughed it off.

'Stop next to the red car there.'

'But number 4 is in the next block,' he said.

Had she told him she lived at number 4? Possibly. She might have forgotten. She felt transparent, like a jellyfish, as if he could see her heart thumping away much too fast.

The engine purred in neutral. He had stopped. She hunted feverishly for the door handle. Bloody Japanese nerds! Why couldn't they just design a plain, easy-to-recognise handle for the door?

'See you Monday,' she heard Waaler's voice say behind her as she found the handle, stumbled out and inhaled the toxic March Oslo air as if coming to the surface after a long time under water. When she slammed her heavy front door she could still hear the smooth, well-lubricated sound of Waaler's car idling outside.

She charged up the stairs, her boots stamping down hard on every step, holding the keys in front of her like a divining rod. Then she was in her flat. As she dialled Harry's number she memorised Sverre Olsen's message word for word.

This is Sverre Olsen. I'm still waiting for the ten big ones as commission for the shooter for the old guy. Ring me at home.

Then he rang off.

It had taken her a nanosecond to realise the connection. The fifth clue to the puzzle about who the middleman was in the Märklin deal. A policeman. Tom Waaler. Of course. Ten thousand in commission to a nobody like Olsen – that had to be a big job. The old man. Arms freaks. Sympathies with the extreme right. The Prince who would soon be a chief inspector. It was crystal clear, so self-evident that for a moment she had been shocked that she, with her ability to register sub-tones inaudible to others, had not realised it before. She knew paranoia had had her in its grip for some time, but still she hadn't managed to refrain from thinking the thought through to the end as she waited for him to come out of the restaurant: Tom Waaler had every possibility of climbing higher, of pulling strings from ever-more important positions, sheltering beneath the wings of power. Who knows what alliances he had already struck and with whom at Police HQ. If she put her mind to it, there were of course several people she could never imagine becoming involved. But the only person she could count on 100 – *one hundred* – per cent was Harry.

Got through. It wasn't engaged. It was never engaged at his place. Come on, Harry!

She also knew it was only a question of time before Waaler would talk to Olsen and find out what had happened, and she didn't doubt for a second that her life would be in jeopardy from that moment on. She would have to act fast, but she couldn't afford to make a single mistake. A voice interrupted her reasoning.

'This is Hole. Speak to me.'

Bleep.

'Sod you, Harry! This is Ellen. We've got him now. I'll ring you on your mobile.'

She held the receiver between shoulder and chin as she flicked through the index of numbers for H, dropped the book on to the floor with a bang, swore and finally found Harry's mobile number. Fortunately he always had his mobile on him.

Ellen Gjelten lived on the second floor of a recently renovated block of flats together with a tame great tit called Helge. The walls of the flat were half a metre thick and the windows were double-glazed. Nevertheless, she could have sworn that she heard the purring sound of a car in neutral.

Rakel Fauke laughed.

'If you've promised Linda a dance, you won't get away with a quick sweep of the floor.'

'Mm. The alternative is to make a run for it.'

A pause ensued and Harry realised that what he had said was open to misinterpretation. He hurriedly filled the silence with a question.

'How did you start at POT?'

'Via Russian,' she said. 'I joined the Ministry of Defence Russian course and worked for two years as an interpreter in Moscow. Kurt Meirik recruited me then and there. After finishing my law degree I went straight into pay grade thirty-five. I thought I'd caught the goose that laid the golden egg.'

'Hadn't you?'

'Are you kidding? Today the students I studied with earn three times more than I'll ever get.'

'You could stop, and do what they do.'

She arched her shoulders forward. 'I like what I do. Not all of them can say the same.'

'Good point.'

Silence.

Good point. Was that really the best he could muster?

'What about you, Harry? Do you like what you do?'

They stood facing the dance floor, but Harry could feel her eyes on him, measuring him up. All sorts of thoughts scurried through his brain. She had small laughter lines next to her eyes. Mosken's chalet was not far from where they had found the empty cartridges from the Märklin rifle. According to *Dagbladet*, 40 per cent of women living in towns were unfaithful. He should ask Even Juul's wife if she remembered three Norwegian soldiers in the *Norge* regiment being wounded or killed by a hand-grenade thrown from a plane, and he should have gone for it at the New Year menswear sales Dressman advertised on TV3. But did he like what he did?

'Some days I do,' he said.

'What do you like about it?'

'I don't know. Does that sound stupid?'

'I don't know.'

'I'm not saying that because I haven't thought about why I'm a policeman. I have. And I don't know. Perhaps I just enjoy catching naughty boys and girls.'

'So what do you do when you're not catching naughty boys and girls?' she asked.

'Watch *The Robinson Expedition*.'

She laughed again. And Harry knew he was prepared to say the silliest things if there was a chance he could make her laugh like that. He pulled himself together and talked relatively seriously about his current situation, but since he took care not to mention the unpleasant aspects of his life, there wasn't a great deal to tell. When she still seemed interested he went on to talk about his father and Sis. Why did he always end up talking about Sis when someone asked him to talk about himself?

'Sounds like a nice girl,' she said.

'The nicest,' Harry said. 'And the bravest. Never afraid of new things. A test pilot of life.'

Harry told her about the time Sis had put in a spontaneous offer for a flat in Jacob Aalls gate – because the wallpaper in the picture she had seen on the property page in *Aftenposten* reminded her of her childhood room in Oppsal – and had been told the asking price was two million kroner, a record square-metre price for Oslo that summer.

Rakel Fauke laughed so much she spilled tequila on Harry's suit jacket.

'The best thing about her is that after a crash landing she picks herself up, brushes herself down and is immediately ready for the next kamikaze mission.'

She dried the lapels of his jacket with a handkerchief.

'And you, Harry, what do you do when you crash land?'

'Me? Well. I probably lie still for a second. And then I get up because there's no other option, is there?'

'Good point.'

He looked up smartly to see if she was making fun of him. Amusement was dancing in her eyes. She radiated strength, but he doubted that she had had much experience of crash landings.

'Your turn to tell something about yourself.'

Rakel had no sister to fall back on, she was an only child. So she talked about her work instead.

'But we rarely catch anyone,' she said. 'Most cases are settled amicably with a telephone call or at a cocktail party at an embassy.'

Harry smiled sardonically.

'And how was the matter of the Secret Service agent I shot smoothed over?' he asked. 'Telephone call or cocktail party?'

She studied him pensively while putting her hand in the glass to fish out a lump of ice. She held it up, between two fingers. A drop of melted water ran slowly down her wrist, under a thin gold chain towards the elbow.

'Dance, Harry?'

'As far as I remember, I've just spent at least ten minutes explaining how much I hate dancing.'

She angled her head again.

'I mean – would you dance with me?'

'To this music?'

An almost inert pan pipe version of 'Let it Be' oozed like thick syrup out of the speakers.

'You'll survive. Look on it as a warm-up for the great Linda test.'

She placed a hand lightly on his shoulder.

'Are we flirting now?' Harry asked.

'What did you say, Inspector?'

'Sorry, but I'm so bad at reading hidden signals that I asked if we were flirting.'

'Highly improbable.'

He placed his hand around her waist and took a tentative dance step.

'It feels like losing my virginity, this does,' he said. 'But it's probably inevitable – sooner or later every Norwegian male has to go through something like this.'

'What are you talking about?' she laughed.

'Dancing with a colleague at an office party.'

'I'm not forcing you.'

He smiled. It could have been anywhere, they could have been playing 'The Birdie Song' backwards on a ukulele – he would have killed for this dance.

'Wait – what have you got there?' she asked.

'Well, it's not a pistol and I *am* glad to see you, but . . .'

Harry unclipped his mobile from his belt and released his hand from her waist to go over and put the mobile on the speaker. Her arms were raised towards him when he returned.

'Hope we haven't got any thieves here,' he said. It was a hoary old joke at Police HQ, she must have heard it a hundred times before, but she laughed softly into his ear anyway.

Ellen let the phone ring until it stopped before putting down the receiver. Then she tried again. She stood by the window, looking down on to the street. No car. Of course not. She was overwrought. Tom was probably on his way home to bed. Or someone else's bed.

After three attempts she gave up on Harry, and rang Kim instead. He sounded tired.

'I took the taxi back at seven this evening,' he said. 'I've done twenty hours' driving today.'

'I'll just have a shower first,' she said. 'Only wanted to know if you were there.'

'You sound stressed.'

'It's nothing. I'll be there in three quarters of an hour. I'll have to use your phone by the way. And stay the night.'

'Fine. Would you mind nipping into the 7-Eleven in Markveien and buying some cigarettes?'

'Sure. I'll take a cab.'

'Why?'

'Explain to you afterwards.'

'You know it's Saturday night? You'll never get through to Oslo Taxis. And it'll take you four minutes to run up here.'

She wavered.

'Kim?' she said.

'Yes?' he said.

'Do you love me?'

She heard his low chuckle and could imagine the half-closed, sleepy eyes and that lean, almost emaciated body of his under the duvet in the miserable flat in Helgesens gate. He had a view of the river Akerselva. He had everything she wanted. And for an instant she almost forgot Tom Waaler. Almost.

'Sverre!'

Sverre Olsen's mother stood at the bottom of the stairs, shouting at the top of her lungs, as she had done for as long as he could remember.

'Sverre! Telephone!'

She shouted as if she needed help, as if she was drowning or something like that.

'I'll take it up here, Mum!'

He swung his legs down from the bed, picked the phone up from the desk and waited for the click that told him his mother had put down the receiver.

'Hello?'

'It's me.' Prince in the background. Always Prince.

'I guessed it had to be,' Sverre said.

'Why's that?'

The question came like greased lightning. So quickly that Sverre was immediately on the defensive, as if it was he who owed money and not the other way around.

'You're probably ringing because you got my message?' Sverre said.

'I'm ringing because I'm looking at a list of calls received on my mobile. I see that you talked to someone at 20.32 this evening. What message were you wittering on about?'

'About the cash. I'm getting short, and you promised —'

'Who did you talk to?'

'Eh? The lady on your answerphone, I suppose. Pretty neat. Is it a new one of . . . ?'

No answer. Just Prince on low volume. *You sexy mother-fucker . . .* The music abruptly came to an end.

'Tell me what you said exactly.'

'I just said that —'

'No! Exactly. Word for word.'

Sverre repeated it as exactly as he was able.

'I guessed as much,' the Prince said. 'You've just given away our whole operation to an outsider, Olsen. If we don't plug the leak right away, we've had it. Do you understand?'

Sverre Olsen didn't understand anything.

The Prince was utterly composed as he explained that his mobile phone had fallen into the wrong hands.

'It was no answering machine you heard, Olsen.'

'Who was it then?'

'Let's say the enemy.'

'*Monitor.* Is there someone sniffing around?'

'The person in question is on her way to the police. It's your job to stop her.'

'Me? I just want my money and —'

'Shut your mouth, Olsen.'

Olsen shut his mouth.

'This is about the Cause. You're a good soldier, aren't you?'

'Yes, but . . .'

'And a good soldier clears up afterwards, doesn't he?'

'I've just been running messages between you and the old codger. You're the one who —'

'Especially when the soldier has a three-year rap hanging over him, made conditional on a technicality.'

Sverre could hear himself swallow.

'How do you know that?' he started.

'Don't you bother about that. I only want you to realise

that you have as much to lose because of this as the rest of
the brotherhood.'

Sverre didn't answer. He didn't need to.

'Look on the bright side, Olsen. This is war. And there's
no place for cowards and traitors. Furthermore, the brotherhood rewards its soldiers. On top of the ten thousand you'll
get forty more when the job's done.'

Sverre mulled it over. Mulled over what clothes he should
wear.

'Where?' he asked.

'Schous plass in twenty minutes. Bring whatever you
need with you.'

'Don't you drink?' Rakel asked.

Harry looked around him. Their last dance had been so
tight it might have caused eyebrows to rise. Now they had
withdrawn to a table at the back of the canteen.

'I've given it up,' Harry said.

She nodded.

'It's a long story,' he added.

'I've got plenty of time.'

'This evening I only feel like hearing funny stories,' he
smiled. 'Let's talk about you instead. Have you had the kind
of childhood you can talk about?'

Harry had half expected her to laugh, but he received
only a tired smile.

'My mother died when I was fifteen. Apart from that, I
can talk about the rest.'

'I'm sorry to hear that.'

'There's nothing to be sorry about. She was an exceptional
woman, but funny stories were on the agenda this evening . . .'

'Have you any brothers or sisters?'

'No, there's only me and Father.'

'So you had to take care of him on your own?'

She eyed him with surprise.

'I know what it's like,' he said. 'I've also lost my mother. My dad sat in a chair staring at the wall for years. I had to feed him, literally.'

'My father ran a large building-supplies chain he had started from scratch, and I believed it was his whole life. But when Mother died he lost all interest overnight. He sold it before it went to pieces. And he pushed everyone he knew away from him. Including me. He became a bitter, lonely old man.'

She spread out her hand.

'I had my own life to live. I had met a man in Moscow, and father felt betrayed because I wanted to marry a Russian. When I brought Oleg back to Norway, the relationship between me and my father became very problematical.'

Harry stood up and came back with a margarita for her and a Coke for himself.

'Shame we never met on the law course, Harry.'

'I was a muppet at the time,' Harry said. 'I was aggressive towards everyone who didn't like the same records or films as I did. No one liked me. Not even I did.'

'Now I don't believe that.'

'I pinched it from a film. The guy who said it was chatting up Mia Farrow. In the film, that is. I've never tried it out in real life.'

'Well,' she said, cautiously tasting the margarita. 'I think that was a good start. But are you sure you didn't pinch the bit about pinching it too?'

They laughed and discussed good and bad films, good and bad gigs they had been to, and after a while Harry was aware that he would have to amend his first impressions of her. For instance, she had travelled round the world on her own when she was twenty, at an age when all Harry had to show, in terms of adult experiences, was a failed Inter-Railing trip and a growing alcohol problem.

She checked her watch.

'Eleven. I have someone waiting for me.'

Harry felt his heart sink.

'Me too,' he said, getting up.

'Oh?'

'Just a monster I keep under the bed. Let me drive you home.'

She smiled. 'That's not necessary.'

'It's practically on the way.'

'You also live in Holmenkollen?'

'Close by. Or quite close by. Bislett.'

She laughed.

'On the other side of the city then. I know what you're after.'

Harry smiled sheepishly. She put a hand on his arm. 'You need someone to push the car, don't you?'

'Looks like he's gone, Helge,' Ellen said.

She stood by the window with her coat on, peeping out between the curtains. The street below was empty; the taxi which had been waiting there had gone off with three high-spirited party girls. Helge didn't answer. The one-winged bird blinked twice and scratched its stomach with a foot.

She tried Harry's mobile once again, but the same woman's voice repeated that the phone was switched off or was in an area with poor coverage.

Then Ellen put the cloth over the cage, said goodnight, turned off the light and let herself out. Jens Bjelkes gate was still deserted as she hurried towards Thorvald Meyers gate, which she knew would be teeming with people at this time on a Saturday night. Outside Fru Hagen restaurant she nodded to a couple of people she must have exchanged a few words with one damp evening here in Grünerløkka's well-lit streets. She suddenly remembered she had promised to buy Kim some cigarettes and turned to go down to the 7-Eleven in Markveien. She saw a new face she vaguely recognised and automatically smiled when she saw him looking at her.

In the 7-Eleven she paused and tried to recall whether Kim smoked Camel or Camel Lights, realising how little time they had spent together. And how much they still had to learn about each other. And that for the first time in her life it didn't frighten her, but it was something she was looking forward to. She was so utterly happy. The thought of him lying naked in bed, three blocks away from where she was standing filled her with dull, delicious cravings. She opted for Camel, waited impatiently to be served. Outside in the street, she opted for the short cut along the Akerselva.

It struck her how little distance there was between a seething mass of people and total desolation in a large city. Suddenly all she could hear was the gurgle of the river and the sound of snow groaning beneath her boots. And it was too late to rue taking the short cut when she became aware that it was not only her own steps she could hear. Now she could hear breathing too, heavy, panting. Frightened and angry, Ellen thought that, no, she knew, at that moment her life was in danger. She didn't turn, she simply started to run. The steps behind her immediately fell into the same tempo. She tried to run calmly, tried not to panic or run with flailing arms and legs. *Don't run like an old woman,* she thought, and her hand moved for the gas spray in her coat pocket, but the steps behind her were relentless, coming ever closer. She thought that if she could reach the single cone of light on the path, she would be saved. She knew it wasn't true. She was directly under the light when the first blow hit her shoulder and knocked her sideways into the snowdrift. The second blow paralysed her arm and the gas spray slipped out of her unfeeling hand. The third smashed her left kneecap; the pain obstructed the scream muted deep in her throat and caused her veins to bulge out in the winter-pale skin of her neck. She saw him raise the wooden baseball bat in the yellow street light. She recognised him now, the same man she had seen turn round outside Fru Hagen. The policewoman in her noticed that he was wearing a short green jacket, black boots and a black combat cap. The first blow to the head destroyed the optic nerve and now all she saw was the pitch black night.

Forty per cent of hedge sparrows survive, she thought. *I'll get through this winter.*

Her fingers fumbled in the snow for something to hold on to. The second blow hit her on the back of the head.

There's not long to go now, she thought. *I'll survive this winter.*

Harry pulled up by the drive to Rakel Fauke's house in Holmenkollveien. The white moonlight lent her skin an unreal, wan sheen and even in the semi-darkness inside the car he could see from her eyes that she was tired.

'So that was that,' Rakel said.

'That was that,' Harry said.

'I would like to invite you up, but . . .'

Harry laughed. 'I assume Oleg would not appreciate that.'

'Oleg is sleeping sweetly, but I was thinking of his babysitter.'

'Babysitter?'

'Oleg's babysitter is the daughter of someone in POT. Please don't misunderstand me, but I don't want any rumours at work.'

Harry stared at the instruments on the dashboard. The glass over the speedometer had cracked and he suspected that the fuse for the oil lamp had gone.

'Is Oleg your child?'

'Yes, what did you think?'

'Well, I may have thought you were talking about your partner.'

'What partner?'

The cigarette lighter must have been either thrown out of the window or stolen along with the radio.

'I had Oleg when I was in Moscow,' she said. 'His father and I lived together for two years.'

'What happened?'

She shrugged.

'Nothing happened. We simply fell out of love. And I came back to Oslo.'

'So you are . . .'

'A single mum. What about you?'

'Single. Only single.'

'Before you began with us, someone mentioned something about you and the girl you shared an office with in Crime Squad.'

'Ellen? No. We just got on well. *Get* on well. She still helps me out now and then.'

'What with?'

'The case I'm working on.'

'Oh, I see, the case.'

She looked at her watch again.

'Shall I help you to get the door open?' Harry asked.

She smiled, shook her head and gave it a shove with her shoulder. The door squealed on its hinges as it swung open.

The Holmenkollen slopes were quiet, except for a gentle whistling in the fir trees. She placed a foot in the snow outside.

'Goodnight, Harry.'

'Just one thing.'

'Yes?'

'When I came here last time, why didn't you ask me what I wanted from your father?'

'Professional habit. I don't ask about cases I'm not involved in.'

'Aren't you curious anyway?'

'I'm always curious. I just don't ask. What's it about?'

'I'm looking for an ex-soldier your father may have

known at the Eastern Front. This particular man has bought a Märklin rifle. By the way, your father didn't give the impression of being at all bitter when I talked to him.'

'The writing project seems to have excited him. I'm surprised myself.'

'Perhaps one day you'll get closer again?'

'Perhaps,' she said.

Their eyes met, hooked on to each other almost and couldn't let go.

'Are we flirting now?' she asked.

'Highly improbable.'

He could see her laughing eyes long after he had parked illegally in Bislett, chased the monster back under the bed and fallen asleep without noticing the little red flashing light on the answerphone.

Sverre Olsen quietly closed the door behind him, took off his shoes and crept up the stairs. He skipped the step he knew would creak, but he knew this was a waste of effort.

'Sverre?'

The shout came from the open bedroom door.

'Yes, Mum?'

'Where have you been?'

'Just out, Mum. I'm going to bed now.'

He closed his ears to her words; he knew more or less what they would be. They fell like slushy sleet and were gone as soon as they hit the ground. Then he closed the door to his room and was alone. He lay down on the bed, stared at the ceiling and went through what had happened. It was like a film. He scrunched up his eyes, tried to shut it out, but the film continued to run.

He had no idea who she was. As arranged, the Prince had met him in Schous plass and they had driven to the street where she lived. They had parked so that they weren't visible from her flat, but they would be able to see her if she left the

building. He had said it could take all night, told him to relax, put on that bloody nigger music and lowered the back of
his seat. But the front door had opened after just half an
hour and the Prince had said, 'That's her.'

Sverre had loped after her, but he didn't catch up until
they were in the dark street and there were too many people
around them. She had suddenly turned and looked straight at
him. For a moment he was sure he had been sussed, that she
had seen the baseball bat up his sleeve sticking out over his
jacket collar. He had been so frightened that he had not been
able to control the twitches in his face, but later when she had
run out of 7-Eleven, the terror had turned into anger. He remembered, and yet didn't remember, details from when they
were under the light on the path. He knew what had happened, but it was as if fragments had been removed, like in
one of those quiz games on TV where you are given pieces of
a picture and you have to guess what the picture is.

He opened his eyes again. Stared at the bulging plaster-
board on the ceiling. When he had the money, he would get
a builder to fix the leak Mum had been nagging him about
for so long. He tried to think about roof repairs, but he knew
it was because he was attempting to drive the other thoughts
away. He knew something was wrong. It had been different
this time. Not like with slit-eyes at Dennis Kebab. This girl
had been a normal Norwegian woman. Short brown hair,
blue eyes. She could have been his sister. He tried to repeat
to himself what the Prince had instilled in him: he was a
soldier, it was for the Cause.

He looked at the picture he had pinned on the wall under
the flag with the swastika on. It was of the *Reichsführer-SS
und Chef der Deutschen Polizei* Heinrich Himmler speaking on the rostrum when he was in Oslo in 1941. He was talking to the Norwegian volunteers taking their oaths for the
Waffen SS. Green uniform. The initials SS on the collar. Vidkun Quisling in the background. Himmler. An honourable
death, 23 May 1945. Suicide.

'Fuck!'

Sverre placed his feet on the floor, stood up and began to pace restlessly.

He stopped in front of the mirror by the door. Clutched his head. Then he searched through his jacket pockets. Damn, what had happened to his combat cap? For a moment, panic seized him as he wondered if he might have left it beside her in the snow, but then he remembered he had been wearing it when he went back to the Prince's car. He breathed out.

He had got rid of the baseball bat, as the Prince had said. Wiped off the fingerprints and thrown it in the Akerselva. Now it was just a question of lying low and waiting to see what transpired. The Prince had said he would sort everything out, as he had done before. Sverre didn't know where the Prince worked, but it was obvious he had good connections with the police. He undressed in front of the mirror. His tattoos were a grey colour in the moonlight as it shone in between the curtains. He fingered the Iron Cross hanging around his neck.

'You whore,' he mumbled. 'You fucking commie whore.'

When he finally fell asleep, it had already begun to cloud over in the east.

51

Hamburg. 30 June 1944.

My dearest beloved Helena,

I love you more than I love myself. You know that now.
Even though we had only a short time together, and you
have a long and happy life in front of you (I know you will
have!), I hope you will never forget me completely. It is evening here. I'm sitting in sleeping quarters by the harbour in
Hamburg and the bombs are falling outside. I'm alone. The
others are sheltering in bunkers and cellars. There's no electricity, but the raging fires outside give more than enough
light to write by.

We had to get off the train before arriving in Hamburg as
the railway tracks had been bombed the night before. We
were loaded on to trucks and taken to town. It was a terrible
sight that met us. Every second house seemed to be in ruins,
dogs slunk alongside the smoking debris and everywhere I
saw emaciated children in rags staring at the trucks with their
large vacant eyes. I travelled through Hamburg on my way to
Sennheim only two years ago, but now it is hardly recognis-
able. At that time I thought the Elbe was the most beautiful
river I had seen, but now bits of planks and the flotsam from
wrecked shipping drift past in the filthy brown water, and I

heard someone say that it has been contaminated by all the dead bodies floating in it. People were also talking about more night-time bombing raids and getting out of the city by any means possible. My plan is to take the train to Copenhagen tonight, but the railway lines to the north have also been bombed.

I apologise for my awful German. As you can see, my hand is a bit uncertain too, but it's because the bombs are making the whole house shake. And not because I'm afraid. What should I be afraid of? From where I'm sitting I am witness to a phenomenon I've heard about, but I've never seen – a firestorm. The flames on the other side of the harbour seem to be sucking everything in. I can see loose timber and whole lead roofs taking off and flying into the flames. And the sea – it's boiling! Steam is rising up from under the bridges over there. If some poor soul were to try jumping into the water to escape the bombs, they would be fried alive. I opened the windows and it felt as if the air had been deprived of oxygen. And then I heard the roar – it's as if someone is standing in the flames shouting, 'More, more, more.' It is uncanny and frightening, yes, but also strangely attractive.

My heart is so full of love that I feel invulnerable – thanks to you, Helena. If one day you should have children (I know you want them and I want you to have them) I want you to tell them the stories about me. Tell them as fairy tales, for that is what they are – true fairy tales. I have decided to go out into the night to see what I will find, who I will meet. I'll leave this letter on the table in my metal canteen. I've scratched your name and address into it with my bayonet so that those who find it will know what to do.

Your beloved Uriah.

Part Five

SEVEN DAYS

52

Jens Bjelkes Gate. 12 March 2000.

'*HI, THIS IS ELLEN AND HELGE'S ANSWERPHONE. Please leave a message.*'

'Hi Ellen, this is Harry. As you can hear, I've been drinking and I apologise. Really. But if I were sober, I probably wouldn't be phoning you now. You know that, I'm sure. I went to the crime scene today. You were lying on your back in the snow by a path along the Akerselva. You were found by a young couple on the way to a dance at the Blå just after midnight. Cause of death: serious injuries to the front part of the brain as a result of violent blows from a blunt instrument. You had also been hit on the back of the head and received three fractures to the cranium as well as a smashed left kneecap and signs of a blow to the right shoulder. We assume that it was the same instrument which caused all the injuries. Doctor Blix puts the time of death between eleven and twelve at night. You seemed . . . I . . . Wait a moment.

'Sorry. Right. The Crime Scene Unit found around twenty different types of boot print in the snow on the path and a couple in the snow beside you, but the latter had been kicked to pieces, possibly with the intention of removing clues. No witnesses have come forward so far, but we're doing the usual rounds of the neighbourhood. Several houses overlook the path, so Kripos think there's a chance that someone saw something. Personally, I think the chances are negligible. You see, there was a repeat of *The Robinson Expedition* on Swedish TV between 11.15 and 12.15. Joke. I'm trying to be funny, can you hear that? Oh, yes, we found a black cap a few metres away from where you were lying. There were bloodstains on it. If it is your blood, the cap may, ergo, belong to the murderer. We've sent the blood for analysis, and the cap is at the forensics lab where they are checking it for hair and skin particles. If the guy isn't losing hair, I hope he's got dandruff. Ha, ha. You haven't forgotten Ekman and Friesen, have you? I haven't got any more clues for you yet, but let me know if you come up with anything. Was there anything else? Yes, there was. Helge has found a new home with me. I know this is a change for the worse, but it is for all of us, Ellen. With the possible exception of you. Now I'm going to have another drink and reflect on precisely that.'

53

Jens Bjelkes Gate. 13 March 2000.

'*HI, THIS IS ELLEN AND HELGE'S ANSWERPHONE. Please leave a message.*'

'Hi, this is Harry again. I didn't go to work today, but at any rate I called Doctor Blix. I'm happy to be able to tell you that you were not sexually assaulted and that, as far as we've been able to establish, all your earthly goods were untouched. This means that we do not have a motive, although there can be reasons for him not completing what he had set out to do. Or why he couldn't bring himself to do it. Today two witnesses reported seeing you outside Fru Hagen. A payment from your card was registered at 22.55 at the 7-Eleven in Markveien. Your pal Kim has been at the station for questioning all day. He said you were on your way up to his and he had asked you to buy some cigarettes for him. One of the Kripos guys got hung up on the fact that you had bought a different brand from those your friend smokes. On top of that, your pal has no alibi. I'm sorry, Ellen, but at the moment he's their main suspect.

'By the way, I've just had a visitor. She's called Rakel and works for POT. She popped up to see how I was, she said. She sat here for a while, although we didn't say much. Then she left. I don't think it went very well.

'Helge says hello.'

54

Jens Bjelkes Gate. 14 March 2000.

'*Hi, this is Ellen and Helge's answerphone. Please leave a message.*'

'It's the coldest March in living memory. The thermometer reads minus eighteen and the windows in this block are from the turn of the century. The popular notion that you don't freeze when you're drunk is a total fallacy. Ali, my neighbour, knocked on the door this morning. It turns out I had a nasty fall down the stairs coming home yesterday and he helped me to bed.

'It must have been lunchtime before I got to work because the canteen was full of people when I went to get my morning cup of coffee. I had the impression they were staring at me, but perhaps I was imagining it. I miss you terribly, Ellen.

'I checked your friend's record. I saw he had been given a short sentence for possession of hash. Kripos still think he's the one. I've never met him and, God knows, I'm no judge of character, but from what you told me about him, he doesn't strike me as the type. Do you agree? I rang Forensics and they said they hadn't found a single hair on the cap, just some skin particles. They're sending it off for a DNA test and reckon the results will be back within four weeks. Do you know how many hairs an adult loses every single day? I checked. Approximately 150. And not one strand of hair on that cap. Afterwards, I went down to Møller and asked him to get a list drawn up of all the men who have been sentenced for GBH over the last four years and at present have shaven heads.

'Rakel came to my office with a book: *Our Small Birds*. Strange book. Do you think Helge likes millet cobs? Take care.'

55

Jens Bjelkes Gate. 15 March 2000.

'HI, THIS IS ELLEN AND HELGE'S ANSWERPHONE. *Please leave a message.*'

'They buried you today. I wasn't there. Your parents deserved a dignified commemorative service and I wasn't particularly presentable today, so instead I thought of you at Schrøder's. At eight o'clock last night I got in the car and drove up to Holmenkollveien. It wasn't a good idea. Rakel had a visitor, the same guy I've seen there before. He introduced himself as something or other from the Ministry of Foreign Affairs and gave the impression he was on business there. I think he was called Brandhaug. Rakel didn't seem very pleased to receive his visit, but then again perhaps that's just me. So I beat a hasty retreat before it became too embarrassing. Rakel insisted I should take a taxi. But, looking out of the window now, I can see the Escort parked in the street, so I can't have followed her advice.

'Things are, as you know, a little chaotic right now. But at least I went to the pet shop and bought some bird seed. The lady behind the counter suggested Trill, so that's what I took.'

56

Jens Bjelkes Gate. 16 March 2000.

'*HI, THIS IS ELLEN AND HELGE'S ANSWERPHONE.
Please leave a message.*'
   'I went for a walk to Ryktet today. It's a bit like Schrøder's.
At least they don't give you a funny look when you order a
Pils for breakfast. I sat down at a table with an old man and
after a struggle managed to get some sort of conversation
off the ground. I asked him what he had against Even Juul.
He gave me a long, searching look; it was obvious he didn't
recognise me from the previous time I had been there. But
after buying him a beer I got the whole story. The old boy
had fought at the Eastern Front – I had already guessed that –
and he knew Juul's wife, Signe, from when she was a nurse
there. She had volunteered because she was engaged to one
of the soldiers in the *Norge* regiment. Juul clapped eyes on
her when she was found guilty of treason in 1945. She was
given two years, but Juul's father, who had a high position in
the Socialist Party, arranged for her to be released after only
a few months. When I asked the old boy why that bothered
him so much, he mumbled that Juul wasn't the saint he appeared to be. That was precisely the word he used – "saint".
He said that Juul was like all the other historians – he wrote

myths about Norway during the war in the way the victors
wanted them presented. The man couldn't remember the name
of her first fiancé, only that he had been a kind of hero to the
others in the regiment.

'Afterwards I went to work. Kurt Meirik dropped by to
see me. He didn't say anything. I called Bjarne Møller, and
he informed me that there were thirty four names on the list
I had requested. Are men with no hair more prone to violence, I wonder? Anyway, Møller has put an officer on the
case to ring round and check the alibis to get the number
down. I can see from the preliminary report that Tom Waaler
drove you home and that when he dropped you off at 22.15
you were in a calm frame of mind. He also testifed that you
had talked about trivialities. Nevertheless, when you left me
a message, at 22.16 according to Telenor – in other words as
soon as you had got in the door – you were obviously pretty
excited that you were on the track of something. I think that's
odd. Bjarne Møller didn't think so. Perhaps it's just me.

'Get in touch with me soon, Ellen.'

57

Jens Bjelkes Gate. 17 March 2000.

'*HI, THIS IS ELLEN AND HELGE'S ANSWERPHONE. Please leave a message.*'

'I didn't go to work today. It's minus twelve outside, marginally warmer in the flat. The telephone has been ringing all day and when I finally decided to answer it, it was Doctor Aune. Aune is a good man, for a psychologist; at least he doesn't behave as if he is less confused than the rest of us with respect to what goes on in our heads. Aune's old contention that every alcoholic's nightmare begins where the last drunken spree ended is a great warning, but not necessarily accurate. He was surprised that I was more or less together this time. Everything is relative. Aune also talked about an American psychologist who has discovered that the lives we lead are to a certain extent hereditary. When we step into our parents' roles, our lives begin to resemble theirs. My father became a hermit after my mother died, and now Aune is frightened that I will be the same because of a couple of tough experiences I've had – the shooting accident in Vinderen, you know. And in Sydney. And now this. Right. I've told you about my days, but had to laugh when Doctor Aune told me that Helge, a great tit, was preventing me from letting my life go down the chute. As I said, Aune is a good man, but he should cut out all that psycho-stuff.

'I called Rakel and asked her out. She said she would give it some thought and ring me back. I don't know why I do this to myself.'

58

Jens Bjelkes Gate. 18 March 2000.

'. . . IS A *TELENOR ANNOUNCEMENT. THE NUMBER you have dialled is no longer available. This is a Telenor announcement. The number . . .*'

Part Six

BATHSHEBA

59

Møller's Office. 25 April 2000.

THE FIRST SPRING OFFENSIVE CAME LATE. IT wasn't until the end of March that the gutters began to gurgle and flow. By April all the snow had disappeared as far as Sognsvann. But then the spring had to retreat again. The snow came swirling down and lay in huge drifts, even in the centre of town, and weeks passed before the sun melted it again. Dogs' turds and refuse from the previous year lay stinking in the streets; the wind picked up speed across the open stretches in Grønlandsleiret and by Galleri Oslo, swept up the sand and made people go round rubbing their eyes and spitting. The talk of the town was the single mother who would perhaps become Queen one day, the European football championship and the unseasonal weather. At Police HQ, the talk was about what people did over Easter and the miserable increase in pay, and they went on as if everything was as before.

Everything was not as before.

Harry sat in his office with his feet on the table, looking out at the cloudless day, the retired ladies in their ugly hats out for the morning and taking up the whole of the pavement, delivery vans going through the lights on amber, all the small details which lent the town the false veneer of normality. He had been wondering about that for some time now – if he was the only one who was not allowing himself to be duped. It was six weeks since they had buried Ellen, but when he looked out, he saw no change.

There was a knock at the door. Harry didn't answer, but it opened anyway. It was the head of Crime Squad, Bjarne Møller.

'I heard you were back.'

Harry watched one of the red buses glide into a bus stop. The advertisement on the side of the vehicle was for Storebrand Life Insurance.

'Can you tell me, boss,' he asked, 'why they call it life insurance when they obviously mean death insurance?'

Møller sighed and perched on the edge of the desk.

'Why haven't you got an extra chair in here, Harry?'

'If people don't sit down, they get to the point quicker.' He was still staring out of the window.

'We missed you at the funeral, Harry.'

'I had changed my clothes,' Harry said, more to himself than Møller. 'I'm sure I was on my way, too. When I looked up and caught sight of the miserable gathering around me, I even thought for a moment that I had arrived. Until I saw Maja standing there in her pinny and waiting for my order.'

'I guessed it was something like that.'

A dog wandered across the brown lawn with its nose along the ground and its tail in the air. At least someone appreciated spring in Oslo.

'What happened then?' Møller asked. 'We haven't seen much of you for a while.'

Harry gave a shrug.

'I was busy. I've got a new lodger – a one-winged great tit. And I sat listening to old messages on my answerphone. It turned out all the messages I've been left over the last two years fit on to one thirty-minute tape. And they were all from Ellen. Sad, isn't it? Well, perhaps not so sad. The only sad thing is that I wasn't at home when she made her last call. Did you know that Ellen had found him?'

For the first time since Møller had come in Harry turned round to face him.

'You do remember Ellen, don't you?'

Møller sighed.

'We all remember Ellen, Harry. And I remember the message she left on your answerphone, and you telling Kripos you thought this was a reference to the middleman in the arms deal. Because we haven't managed to catch the killer doesn't mean we've forgotten her, Harry. Kripos and the Crime Squad have been on the go for weeks, we've hardly slept. If you had come to work, perhaps you would have seen how hard we were working.'

Møller immediately regretted what he had said. 'I didn't mean . . .'

'Yes, you did. And, of course, you're right.'

Harry ran his hand across his face.

'Last night I listened to one of her messages. I have no idea why she rang. The message was full of advice about the things she thought I should eat and concluded by reminding me to feed small birds, to do stretching exercises after training and to remember Ekman and Friesen. Do you know who Ekman and Friesen are?'

Møller repeated his shake of the head.

'They are two psychologists who have discovered that when you smile the facial muscles set off some chemical reactions in your brain, which gives you a more positive attitude towards the world around you, makes you more satisfied with your existence. What they did was to prove the old adage that if you smile at the world, the whole world smiles at you. For a while she got me to believe that.'

He looked up at Møller.

'Sad or what?'

'So sad.'

They broke into smiles and sat without speaking.

'I can see from your face that you've come to tell me something, boss. What is it?'

Møller jumped down from the desk and started pacing the room.

'The list of thirty-four baldie suspects was reduced to twelve after we checked their alibis. OK?'

'OK.'

'We can determine the blood type of the owner of the cap from the DNA tests on the skin particles we found. Four of the twelve have the same blood type. We took blood samples from these four and sent them for DNA testing. The results came today.'

'And?'

'Nada.'

The office went quiet. All that could be heard was Møller's rubber soles, which made a little squeak every time he did an about-turn.

'And Kripos have rejected the theory that Ellen's boyfriend did it?' Harry asked.

'We checked his DNA too.'

'So we're back to square one?'

'More or less, yes.'

Harry faced the window again. A flock of thrushes took off from a large elm tree and flew west, towards the Plaza Hotel.

'Perhaps the cap is meant to mislead us?' Harry said. 'It doesn't make sense to me that a man who leaves no other traces and who covers over his boot prints is so clumsy that he could lose his cap just a few metres from the victim.'

'Maybe. But the blood on the cap is Ellen's. We have established that much.'

Harry's attention was caught by the dog returning, sniffing at the same trail. It stopped roughly in the middle of the lawn, stood for a moment with its nose on the ground, undecided, before taking a decision, going off to the left and disappearing from view.

'We have to follow the cap,' Harry said. 'As well as the convictions, check anyone who has been brought in for or charged with GBH. Over the last ten years. Include Akershus too. And make sure that —'

'Harry . . .'

'What is it?'

'You don't work for Crime Squad now. And anyway, the investigation is being led by Kripos. You're asking me to tread on their toes.'

Harry didn't say a word. Just nodded slowly. His gaze was fixed on somewhere in Ekeberg.

'Harry?'

'Have you ever thought you should be somewhere else, boss? I mean, just look at this shit spring.'

Møller stopped pacing and smiled.

'Since you ask, I've always thought that Bergen could be a wonderful town to live in. For the kids and so on, you know.'

'But you'd still be a policeman, wouldn't you?'

'Of course.'

'Because people like us are no good at anything else, are we?'

Møller rolled back his shoulders. 'Maybe not.'

'But Ellen was good at other things. I often thought what a waste of human resources it was having her work for the police. Catching naughty boys and girls. That's enough for the likes of us, but not for her. Do you know what I mean?'

Møller went over to the window and stood beside Harry.

'It'll be better when we get into May,' he said.

'Mm,' Harry said.

The clock on Grønland church struck two.

'I'll see if I can have Halvorsen put on to the case,' Møller said.

60

Ministry of Foreign Affairs. 27 April 2000.

BERNT BRANDHAUG'S LONG AND VARIED EXPERI-
ence with women had taught him that on the rare occasions
he decided that there was a woman he not only wanted but
had to have, it was for one of the following four reasons:
she was more beautiful than all the others; she satisfied him
sexually more than any others; she made him feel more of a
man than any others; or, more crucially, she wanted someone else.

Brandhaug had realised that Rakel Fauke was that type
of woman.

He had rung her one January day under the pretext of
needing an assessment of the new military attaché at the Russian embassy in Oslo. She had told him that she could send a
memo, but he had insisted on a face-to-face report. Since it
was Friday afternoon, he had suggested meeting over a glass
of beer at the bar in the Continental. That was how he had
found out that she was a single parent. In fact, she had turned
down the invitation, saying she had to pick up her son from
the nursery, and he had brightly asked, 'I assume a woman of
your generation has a man to take care of such things?'

Although she didn't give a direct answer he had intuited from her response that there was not a man on the scene.

When he rang off he was generally pleased with his gains, even though he was mildly irritated that he had said *your generation* and thus emphasised the age difference between them.

The next thing he did was to ring Kurt Meirik and discreetly pump him for information about Ms Fauke. The fact that he was less than discreet and Meirik smelled a rat didn't bother him in the slightest.

Meirik was his usual, well-informed self. Rakel had worked as an interpreter in Brandhaug's own department for two years at the Norwegian embassy in Moscow. She had married a Russian, a young professor of gene technology who had taken her by storm and had immediately converted theory into practice by making her pregnant. However, the professor had been born with a gene that predisposed him to alcoholism, combined with a predilection for physical discussion, and so their wedded bliss was brief. Rakel Fauke had not repeated the mistake of many in her sisterhood: she didn't wait, forgive or try to understand; she marched right out of the door with Oleg in her arms the second the first blow fell. Her husband and his relatively influential family had appealed for custody of Oleg, and had it not been for her diplomatic immunity she would not have succeeded in leaving Russia with her son.

As Meirik was telling him that the husband had taken out a lawsuit against her, Brandhaug vaguely recalled a summons issued by a Russian court passing through his in-tray. But she had only been an interpreter at that time and he had delegated the whole business, without making a mental note of her name. When Meirik mentioned that the custody suit was still being chewed over by the Russian and Norwegian authorities, Brandhaug abruptly broke off the conversation and rang down to the legal department.

* * *

The next call, to Rakel, was an invitation to dinner, no pretext this time, and upon her friendly but firm refusal he dictated a letter addressed to her, signed by the head of the legal department. The letter, in brief outline, told her that the Ministry of Foreign Affairs, since the business had dragged on, was now attempting to reach a compromise solution with the Russian authorities on custody 'out of humane consideration for Oleg's Russian family.' That would require Rakel and Oleg to appear before a Russian court and comply with the court's ruling.

Four days later Rakel phoned Brandhaug and asked to meet him concerning a private matter. He answered that he was busy, which was true, and asked if the meeting could be postponed for a couple of weeks. When, with a hint of shrillness behind her courteous professional tones, she begged him for a meeting as soon as possible, he discovered, after lengthy reflection, that Friday at six at the bar in the Continental was the only option. Once there, he ordered gin and tonic as she elucidated her problem with what he could only assume was a mother's biologically determined desperation. He nodded gravely, did his utmost to express his sympathy with his eyes and was finally emboldened to place a fatherly, protective hand over hers. She stiffened, but he went on as if nothing had happened, telling her that unfortunately he was not in a position to overrule a department head's decisions. Naturally, though, he would do whatever was in his power to prevent her having to appear before the Russian court. He also stressed that, bearing in mind the political influence of her ex-husband's family, he fully shared her concern that the Russian court's ruling might go against her. He sat there, staring spellbound into her tear-filled brown eyes, and it seemed to him that he had never seen anything to surpass her beauty. Nevertheless, when he suggested extending the evening to include dinner in the restaurant, she thanked him and declined. The rest of the evening, spent in the company of a glass of whisky and pay-TV, was an anticlimax.

The next morning Brandhaug called the Russian ambassador, explaining that the Norwegian Foreign Ministry had had an internal discussion about Oleg Fauke-Gosev's custody case. Would he send him an update on the Russian authorities' wishes in the matter? The ambassador had never heard of the case, but promised to accede to the Foreign Office head's request and also to send the letter in the form of an urgent summons. The letter in which the Russians requested Rakel and Oleg to appear before a Russian court arrived a week later. Brandhaug immediately sent a copy to the head of the legal department and one to Rakel Fauke. This time her phone call came one day later. After listening to her Brandhaug said that it would be contrary to his diplomatic code of behaviour to try to influence the matter, and in any case it was injudicious of them to discuss this on the telephone.

'As you know, I don't have any children myself,' he said. 'But from the way you describe Oleg he sounds like a wonderful boy.'

'If you had met him, you would —' she began.

'That shouldn't be a problem. By chance I saw in the correspondence that you live in Holmenkollveien, and that is only a stone's throw from Nordberg.'

He noticed the hesitation at the quiet end of the telephone line, but he felt the momentum was with him.

'Shall we say nine o'clock tomorrow evening?'

A long pause ensued before she answered.

'No six-year-old is up at nine o'clock.'

So they agreed on six o'clock instead. Oleg had brown eyes like his mother and was a well-behaved boy. However, it annoyed Brandhaug that the mother would not drop the topic of the court summons or send Oleg to bed. Yes, one might almost suspect that she was keeping the boy there on

the sofa as a hostage. And he did not like the boy staring at
him either. Brandhaug knew, ultimately, that Rome was not
going to be built in a day, but he still tried as he stood on the
step to go. He looked deep into her eyes and said, 'You are
not only a beautiful woman, Rakel, you are also a very brave
person. I would just like you to know that I hold you in great
esteem.'

He wasn't sure how he was to interpret her expression,
but he took the risk anyway and leaned forward to plant a
kiss on her cheek. Her reaction was ambivalent. The mouth
smiled and she thanked him for the compliment, but her
eyes were cold as she added, 'I apologise for keeping you so
long, herr Brandhaug. Your wife must be waiting.'

His invitation had been so unambiguous that he decided
to give her a few days to reflect, but no telephone call came
from Rakel Fauke. On the other hand, unexpectedly, a letter
from the Russian embassy did come, requesting an answer,
and Brandhaug realised that his enquiry had breathed new
life into the Oleg Fauke-Gosev case. Regrettable, but now it
had happened he saw no reason not to exploit the opportunity. He immediately rang Rakel in POT and acquainted her
with the latest developments in the case.

Some weeks later he found himself once more in the timbered house in Holmenkollveien, which was larger and even
darker than his own. *Their* own. This time after bedtime.
She seemed a lot more relaxed in his company than before.
Furthermore, he had manoeuvred the conversation on to a
more personal track, which meant that it did not appear alto-
gether too obtrusive when he mentioned how platonic the
relationship between him and his wife had become and how
important it was to forget the brain occasionally and listen
to your body and your heart. Then the doorbell rang, provid-
ing an unwelcome interruption. Rakel went out to answer it
and returned with a tall man with a close-shaven head and

bloodshot eyes. She introduced him as a colleague from
POT. Brandhaug had definitely heard the name before, he
just couldn't remember when and in what context. He took
an immediate dislike to everything about him. He disliked
the interruption, the fact that the man was drunk and that he
sat down on the sofa and stared at him, like Oleg, without
uttering a word. But what he disliked most was the change
in Rakel, who brightened up, ran to make coffee and laughed
with abandon at this man's cryptic monosyllable answers
as if they contained brilliant flashes of wit. And there was
genuine concern in her voice when she refused to allow him
to drive his own car home. The only redeeming feature Brandhaug could discern in the man was that he suddenly went on
his way and immediately afterwards they heard his car
starting up, which might of course mean that he would have
the decency to kill himself. The damage he had done to the
atmosphere was irreparable, however, and not long afterwards
Brandhaug was sitting in his own car on his way home. It
was then that his old hypothesis came back to him – there
are four possible causes for men deciding that they *have* to
possess a woman. And the most crucial one is that you know
she desires someone else.

When he rang Kurt Meirik the following day to ask who
the tall, fair-haired policeman was, he was initially very surprised, then he started to laugh. Because it was the very
person he had promoted and deployed in POT. An irony of
fate, naturally, but fate is also on occasion subject to the
counsel of the Royal Norwegian Ministry for Foreign Affairs.
When Brandhaug put down the receiver, he was already in
better spirits. He strode through the corridors to the next
meeting, whistling on his way, and reached the conference
room in under seventy seconds.

61

Police HQ. 27 April 2000.

HARRY STOOD IN THE DOORWAY OF HIS OLD OF-
fice, looking at a blond-haired young man sitting in Ellen's
chair. He was concentrating so hard on the computer screen
he didn't notice Harry until he coughed.

'So you're Halvorsen then, are you?'

'Yes,' the young man said with an inquisitive expression
on his face.

'From the police station in Steinkjer?'

'Correct.'

'Harry Hole. I used to sit where you're sitting now, but in
the other chair.'

'It's knackered.'

Harry smiled. 'It's always been knackered. Bjarne Møller
asked you to check a couple of details with regard to the Ellen Gjelten case?'

'A couple of details?' Halvorsen exclaimed in protest. 'I've
been working non-stop for three days.'

Harry sat down on his old chair, which had been shifted
to Ellen's table. It was the first time he had seen what the
office looked like from her position.

'What have you found out, Halvorsen?'

Halvorsen frowned.

'Don't worry,' Harry said. 'I was the one who asked for this information. Check it out with Møller, if you like.'

Halvorsen's face suddenly lit up.

'Of course! You're Hole from POT! Sorry, I was a bit slow on the uptake.' A big smile spread across his boyish face. 'I remember the case in Australia. How long ago is that now?'

'A while. As I said . . .'

'Oh yes, the list!' He tapped a pile of computer print-outs with his knuckles. 'These are all the guys who have been brought in, charged with or convicted of GBH over the last ten years. There are over a thousand names. That part was easy; the problem is finding out which ones are skinheads. The info says nothing about that. This could take weeks . . .'

Harry leaned back in his chair.

'I know. But criminal records have codes for the weapons used. Run searches for the codes for firearms and see how many you're left with.'

'In fact, I was going to suggest that to Møller when I saw how many names there were. Most of them used knives, guns or fists. I should have a new list ready in a few hours.'

Harry stood up.

'Fine,' he said. 'I don't remember my internal number, but you'll find it on the telephone list. And next time you have a good suggestion, don't hesitate to make it. We aren't *that* smart down here in Oslo.'

Halvorsen, a little unsure of himself, sniggered.

62

POT. 2 May 2000.

THE RAIN HAD BEEN LASHING DOWN ALL MORN-
ing before the sun made an unanticipated, brash appearance,
and in the blinking of an eye it burned off all the clouds in
the sky. Harry was sitting with his feet on the desk and his
hands behind his head, kidding himself that he was thinking
about the Märklin rifle. But his thoughts had wandered outside
the window, along the newly washed streets which smelled
warm now, along the wet tarmac and the tramlines up to the
top of Holmenkollen, to the grey smudges of snow still lying
in the shadow of the spruce forest, where Rakel, Oleg and he
had hopped around on the muddy paths to avoid the deepest
puddles. Harry had vague memories of going on Sunday
walks like that even when he was Oleg's age. If they were
long walks, and he and Sis were lagging behind, his father
had put pieces of chocolate on the lowest branches. Sis was
still convinced that *Kvikklunsj* bars grew on trees.

Oleg hadn't said a lot to Harry the first two times he visited. But that was fine. Harry didn't know what to say to
Oleg either. Their discomfort had eased slightly when Harry
discovered he had Tetris on his GameBoy. With neither mercy
nor shame, Harry had played at his best and beaten the six-

year-old boy by over 40,000 points. After that Oleg had begun to ask Harry about cases, and why snow was white, and all the other things that give grown men deep furrows in their foreheads and make them concentrate so hard that they forget to be embarrassed. Last Sunday Oleg had seen a hare in its winter coat and had run on ahead, leaving Harry to hold Rakel's hand. It was cold on the outside and warm on the inside. She had twisted her head round and smiled at him as she swung her arms high, forwards and backwards, as if to say: *We're playing games, this isn't for real.* He had noticed she became tense when people approached and he had let go of her hand. Afterwards they had drunk cocoa on the Frogner slopes and Oleg had asked why it was spring.

He had invited Rakel out for a meal. This was the second time. The first time she had said she would think about it and rang back to say no. This time she had also said she would think about it, but at least she hadn't said no. Yet.

The telephone rang. It was Halvorsen. He sounded sleepy.

'I've checked 70 out of the 110 suspected of using a weapon in GBH assaults,' he said. 'So far, I've found eight skinheads.'

'How did you find that out?'

'I rang them. It's amazing how many of them are at home at four in the morning.'

Halvorsen laughed a little insecurely as Harry's end went quiet.

'You rang each one?' Harry asked.

'Of course,' Halvorsen said. 'Or their mobiles. It's amazing how many of them have —'

Harry interrupted him.

'And so you asked these violent criminals if they wouldn't mind giving an up-to-date description of themselves to the police?'

'Not exactly. I said we were looking for a suspect with long red hair and asked if they had dyed their hair recently,' Halvorsen said.

'I don't follow you.'

'If you'd shaved your head, what would you answer?'

'Hm,' Harry said. 'There are obviously a few canny types up there in Steinkjer.'

The same nervous laugh.

'Fax me up the list,' Harry said.

'You'll have it as soon as I'm back.'

'Back?'

'One of the officers down here was waiting for me when I got in. Needed to see the case notes I've been working on. Must be urgent.'

'I thought Kripos was working on the Gjelten case now,' Harry said.

'Obviously not.'

'Who is it?'

'I think he's called Vole, or something like that,' Halvorsen said.

'There's no Vole in Crime Squad. Do you mean Waaler?'

'That's it,' Halvorsen said and, a little ashamed, added, 'There are so many new names right now . . .'

Harry felt like giving the young constable a bollocking for handing over case material to people whose names he hardly knew, but this wasn't the time to be sharp with him. The boy had been up for three nights in a row and was probably dead on his feet.

'Good work,' Harry said, and was about to put down the phone.

'Wait! Your fax number?'

Harry stared out the window. The clouds had begun to draw in over Ekeberg Ridge again.

'You'll find it on the telephone list,' he said.

The phone rang the second he put it down. It was Meirik, who asked him to go to his office *straight away*.

'How's it going with the report on the neo-Nazis?' he asked as soon as he saw Harry in the doorway.

'Badly,' Harry said, sinking into the chair. In the picture above Meirik's head the Norwegian King and Queen peered down at him. 'The E on my keyboard has got stuck,' Harry added.

Meirik forced a smile, much like the man in the picture, and asked Harry to forget the report for the time being.

'I need you to do something else. The Chief Information Officer from the trade unions has just called. Half the trade union leaders have been faxed death threats today. Signed 88, a short form for *Heil Hitler*. It's not the first time, but this time it's been leaked to the press. They've already started ringing us. We've managed to trace the death threats to a public fax machine in Klippan. That's why we have to take the threat seriously.'

'Klippan?'

'A little place three miles east of Helsingborg. Sixteen thousand inhabitants and the worst Nazi nest in Sweden. You'll find families there who have been Nazis in unbroken lineage since the thirties. Some Norwegian neo-Nazis go on pilgrimages there to see and learn. I want you to pack a big bag, Harry.'

Harry had an unpleasant premonition.

'We're sending you there to do some undercover work, Harry. You have to infiltrate the local network. Job, identity and other details we'll sort out for you bit by bit. Be prepared to stay there for quite some time. Our Swedish colleagues have already sorted out somewhere for you to live.'

'Undercover work,' Harry repeated. He could hardly believe his ears. 'I know diddle about spying, Meirik. I'm a detective. Or had you forgotten?'

Meirik's smile had become dangerously thin.

'You'll learn fast, Harry. That's not a problem. Look upon it as an interesting, useful experience.'

'Hm. For how long?'

'A few months. Maximum six.'

'Six?' Harry yelled.

'Be positive, Harry. You've got no family ties, no —'

'Who else is in the team?'

Meirik shook his head.

'No team. You're on your own. It seems more plausible that way. And you report directly to me.'

Harry rubbed his chin.

'Why me, Meirik? You have a whole department of experts here on infiltration and the extreme right.'

'There's always a first time.'

'And what about the Märklin rifle? We've traced it to an old Nazi and now there are these threats signed *Heil Hitler*. Isn't it better that I continue my work here . . . ?'

'I have made up my mind, Harry.' Meirik didn't bother to smile any more.

Something stank. Harry could smell it a long way off, but he didn't know what it was or where it was coming from. He stood up and Meirik followed suit.

'You leave after the weekend,' Meirik said. He put out his hand.

It struck Harry that was an odd thing to do and the same thought seemed to have crossed Meirik's mind at that moment too – there was self-consciousness in his expression. But now it was too late. The hand hung in the air, helpless, with splayed fingers, and Harry quickly pressed flesh to get the embarrassing situation over with.

As Harry passed Linda in reception, she shouted that there was a fax for him in his pigeon-hole and Harry nabbed it on his way past. It was Halvorsen's list. He ran his eye down the list of names while trudging up the corridor trying to work out which part of him would benefit from six months' socialising with neo-Nazis in some hole in southern Sweden. Not the part of him that was trying to stay sober. Not the part of him that was waiting for Rakel's response to his dinner invitation. And definitely not the part trying to find Ellen's murderer. He stopped in his tracks.

The last name . . .

There was no reason for him to be surprised that old acquaintances popped up on the list, but this was quite different. This was the sound he heard when he had cleaned his Smith & Wesson and then put it together again. The smooth click that told him everything fitted.

He was in his office and on the phone to Halvorsen in seconds. Halvorsen noted down his questions and promised to ring back as soon as he had something.

Harry leaned back. He could hear his heart beating. As a rule, this was not his forte, putting together small pieces of information which didn't seem to have anything in common. Must have been a moment of inspiration. When Halvorsen rang a quarter of an hour later, Harry had the feeling he had been waiting for hours.

'That's right,' Halvorsen said. 'One of the boot prints the Crime Scene Unit found on the path was from a combat boot, size 45. They could specify the brand because the print was made by a boot which had hardly been worn.'

'And do you know who wears combat boots?'

'Oh yes, they're NATO certified. Quite a few people order them, especially in Steinkjer. I've seen a number of these English football hooligans wearing them too.'

'Right. Skinheads. Bootboys. Neo-Nazis. Did you find any photos?'

'Four. Two from Aker Community Workshop and two of a demo outside Blitz, the youth centre, in 1992.'

'Is he wearing a cap in any of them?'

'Yes, in the ones taken at Aker.'

'Combat cap?'

'Let me see.'

Harry could hear Halvorsen's breathing crackle against the membrane of the microphone. Harry said a silent prayer.

'Looks like a beret,' Halvorsen said.

'Are you sure?' Harry asked, with no attempt to disguise his disappointment.

Halvorsen was fairly sure and Harry swore aloud.

'Perhaps the boots can help?' Halvorsen suggested cautiously.

'The murderer will have thrown away the boots unless he's an idiot. And the fact that he kicked over the prints in the snow imply that he isn't.'

Harry was undecided. Again he had this sensation, this sudden certainty that he knew who the killer was, and he knew it was dangerous. Dangerous because it made you reject the nagging doubts, the small voices whispering the contradictions, telling you that despite everything the picture was not perfect. Doubts are like cold water, and you don't want cold water when you are close to apprehending a murderer. Yes, Harry had been certain before. And had been wrong.

Halvorsen spoke.

'Officers in Steinkjer bought combat boots directly from America, so there can't be many places that sell them. And if these boots were almost new . . .'

Harry immediately followed his line of thought.

'Good, Halvorsen! Find out who stocks them. Start with army surplus places. Afterwards, go round showing the photographs, and ask if anyone remembers recently selling him a pair of boots.'

'Harry . . . Er . . .'

'Yeah, I know. I'll clear it with Møller first.'

Harry knew that the chances of finding a salesman who remembered all the customers he sold shoes to was minimal. The chances were, of course, slightly better when customers had *Sieg Heil* tattooed on their necks, but anyway – Halvorsen might as well learn that 90 per cent of all murder investigations were spent looking in the wrong places. Harry rang off and called Møller. The Crime Squad chief listened to all his arguments and when Harry was finished, cleared his throat.

'Good to hear that you and Waaler finally agree on something,' he said.

'Oh?'

'He called me half an hour ago and said almost exactly the same as you have just said. I gave him permission to bring Sverre Olsen in for questioning.'

'Wow.'

'Absolutely.'

Harry wasn't sure what to do. So when Møller asked him if he had any more to say, Harry mumbled a 'Bye' and put down the receiver. He stared out of the window. The rush hour was beginning to get into gear in Schweigaards gate. He picked out a man in a grey coat and old-fashioned hat, and watched him slowly walk past until he was out of sight. Harry could feel that his pulse was almost normal again. Klippan. He had almost forgotten, but now it returned like a pounding hangover. He wondered whether to call Rakel's internal number, but rejected that idea right away.

Then something weird happened.

At the margin of his field of vision, outside the window, a movement caught his eye. He couldn't make out what it was at first; he could only see it closing in fast. He opened his mouth, but the word, the shout or whatever it was his brain was trying to formulate, never passed his lips. There was a soft thud, the glass in the window vibrated lightly and he sat staring at a wet patch where a grey feather was stuck, quivering in the spring wind. He didn't move. Then he grabbed his jacket and sprinted for the lift.

63

Krokliveien, Bjerke. 2 May 2000.

SVERRE OLSEN TURNED UP THE RADIO. HE FLICKED slowly through his mother's latest women's magazine while listening to the newsreader talk about the threatening letters trade-union leaders had received. The gutter directly above the sitting-room window was still dripping. He laughed. The threats sounded like one of Roy Kvinset's numbers. Hopefully there wouldn't be so many spelling mistakes this time.

He glanced at his watch. This afternoon the tables at Herbert's would be buzzing. He was flat broke, but he had repaired the old Wilfa vacuum cleaner this week, so perhaps Mum wouldn't mind lending him a hundred. Fuck the Prince! It was now two weeks since he last promised that Sverre would get his money 'in a couple of days'. In the meantime, a couple of the guys he owed money to were beginning to use an unpleasantly menacing tone. And worst of all, his table at Herbert's Pizza had been commandeered by someone else. It would soon be a long time since the raid on Dennis Kebab.

The last time he was at Herbert's he had felt an irresistible desire to stand up and yell that he was the one who had killed the police bitch in Grünerløkka. Blood had spurted out like a geyser following his final lunge. She had died screaming. He wouldn't have considered it necessary to add that he hadn't known she was a policewoman. Or that the sight of the blood had almost made him throw up.

Fuck the Prince! He had known the whole time she was a cop.

Sverre had earned the money. No one could tell him any different, but what could he do? After what had happened, the Prince had forbidden him to phone. As a precaution, until the worst of the furore had quietened down.

The gate hinges outside screeched. Sverre got to his feet, switched off the radio and hurried into the hall. On the way up the stairs he heard his mother's footsteps on the gravel. Then he was in his own room and he heard her keys jangling in the lock. As she rummaged around downstairs, he stood in the middle of his room and studied himself in the mirror. He ran a hand across his scalp and felt the millimetre high prickles rub against his fingers like a brush. He had made up his mind. Even with the forty grand he would get himself a job. He was pissed off with staying at home and, to tell the truth, he was pissed off with 'the comrades' at Herbert's too. Sick of tagging along with people who were going nowhere. He had taken the Heavy Current course at technical college and he was good at repairing electrical things. Lots of electricians needed apprentices and assistants. In a few weeks his hair would have grown over the *Sieg Heil* tattoo at the back of his head.

His hair, yes. He suddenly remembered the telephone call he had received during the night, the policeman with the Trondheim accent who had asked him about red hair! When Sverre woke up in the morning he had imagined it was a dream, until his mother had asked him over breakfast what kind of person would ring at four in the morning.

Sverre shifted his focus of attention from the mirror to the walls. The picture of the Führer, the posters of Burzum gigs, the flag with the swastika on, the Iron Cross and the Blood & Honour poster which was a copy of Joseph Goebbels' old propaganda poster. For the first time it struck him that his room was like a boy's room. If you replaced the Swedish White Aryan Resistance banner with a Manchester United scarf and the picture of Heinrich Himmler with one of David Beckham you would have thought it was a teenager's room.

'Sverre!' It was Mum.

He closed his eyes.

'Sverre!'

It wouldn't go away. It would never go away.

'Yes!' he screamed out so loud that the scream filled his head.

'There's someone here who wants to talk to you.'

Here? To him? Sverre opened his eyes again and stared ir-resolutely at himself in the mirror. No one came here. As far as he knew, no one even knew he lived here. His heart began to beat faster. Could it be that policeman with the Trondheim accent again?

He was walking towards his bedroom door when it slid open.

'Hello, Olsen.'

Because the spring sun was low and shone right in through the window on the landing he could only see a silhouette fill-ing the doorway. But he knew perfectly well whose voice it was.

'Aren't you happy to see me?' the Prince said, closing the door behind him.

He scanned the walls inquisitively. 'Quite a place you have here.'

'Why did she let you . . . ?'

'I showed your mother this.' The Prince waved around a card with a Norwegian coat of arms in gold on a light blue background. It said POLITI on the other side.

'Oh fuck,' Sverre said with a gulp. 'Is that genuine?'

'Who knows? Relax, Olsen. Take a seat.'

The Prince pointed to the bed and sat the wrong way round on the desk chair.

'What are you doing here?' Sverre asked.

'What do you think?' He beamed a broad smile at Sverre, who was sitting on the very edge of the bed. 'The day of reckoning.'

'The day of reckoning?'

Sverre still had not collected himself completely. How did the Prince know he lived here? And the police ID card. Looking at him now, it struck Sverre that the Prince could easily be a policeman – the well-groomed hair, the cold eyes, the solarium-brown face and the well-trained upper body, the short jacket in soft black leather and the blue jeans. Strange he hadn't noticed before.

'Yes,' the Prince said, still smiling. 'The day of reckoning has come.' He pulled out an envelope from his inside pocket and passed it to Sverre.

'About time,' Sverre said, flashing a fleeting nervous smile and sticking his fingers into the envelope. 'What's this?' he asked, pulling out a folded A4 sheet.

'It's a list of the eight people Crime Squad will soon be visiting, and almost certainly taking blood from, to send for DNA testing to find a match for the skin particles they found on your cap at the scene of the crime.'

'My cap? You said you'd found it in your car and burned it?'

Sverre stared in horror as the Prince shook his head in regret.

'It seems I went back to the scene of the crime. A young couple was waiting for the police, frightened out of their wits. I must have "lost" the cap in the snow a few metres from the body.'

Sverre ran both hands across his head several times.

'You seem baffled, Olsen?'

Sverre nodded and attempted a smile, but the corners of his mouth didn't seem to want to obey.

'Do you want me to explain?'

Sverre nodded again.

'When a police officer is murdered the case has top priority until the murderer is caught, however long it takes. It isn't written in any instruction manual, but when the victim is one of our own, no questions are asked about resources. That's the problem with killing police officers – detectives simply won't give up until they have . . .' he pointed to Sverre, '. . . found the guilty party. It's just a question of time – so I took the liberty of giving the detectives a helping hand so the waiting time would not be too long.'

'But . . .'

'You might be wondering why I helped the police to find you when the odds are that you would report me in order to have your own sentence commuted?'

Sverre swallowed. He tried to think, but it was too much and everything was blocked.

'I can understand that this must be a hard nut to crack,' the Prince said, stroking a finger along the imitation Iron Cross hanging from a nail on the wall. 'Of course, I could have shot you right after the murder. But then the police would have known that you were in league with someone trying to cover their tracks and would have continued the hunt.'

He unhooked the chain from the nail and hung it round his neck, over his leather jacket.

'Another alternative was to "solve" the crime on my own, to shoot you while arresting you and make it look as if you had resisted arrest. The problem with that is that it might seem suspiciously clever for one person to solve a case on their own. People might start thinking, especially since I was the last person to see Ellen Gjelten alive.'

He paused and laughed.

'Don't look so scared, Olsen! I'm telling you these are alternatives I rejected. What I've done is to sit on the sidelines, keep myself informed about progress and watch them close in on you. The plan has always been to jump in when they get close, take over the baton and do the last lap myself. By the way, a piss artist working in POT tracked you down.'

'Are you . . . a policeman?'

'Does it suit me?' The Prince was pointing to the Iron Cross. 'No, to hell with that. I'm a soldier like you, Olsen. A ship has to have watertight bulkheads, otherwise the slightest leak will cause it to sink. Do you know what it would mean if I betrayed my identity to you?'

Sverre's mouth and throat were so dry he could no longer swallow. He was frightened. Frightened for his life.

'It would mean that I couldn't let you leave this room alive. Do you understand?'

'Yes.' Sverre's voice was hoarse. 'My m-money . . .'

The Prince put his hand inside his jacket and pulled out a pistol.

'Sit still.'

He walked over to the bed, sat beside Sverre and, holding the pistol in both hands, pointed it at the door.

'This is a Glock, the world's most reliable handgun. I was sent it from Germany yesterday. The manufacture number has been filed off. The street value is about eight thousand kroner. Look on it as the first instalment.'

Sverre jumped as it went off with a bang. He stared with large eyes at the little hole at the top of the door. The dust danced in the stripe of sunlight which ran like a laser beam from the hole through the room.

'Feel it,' the Prince said, dropping the gun in his lap. Then he stood up and went to the door. 'Hold it tight. Perfect balance, isn't it?'

Sverre reluctantly curled his fingers around the stock of the gun. He could feel he was sweating inside his T-shirt. *There's a hole in the ceiling.* That was all he could think. And that the bullet had made a new hole and they still hadn't got hold of a builder. Then what he had been expecting happened. He closed his eyes.

'Sverre!'

She sounds as if she's drowning. He gripped the gun. *She always sounds as if she's drowning.* Then he opened his eyes again and saw the Prince turn by the door, in slow motion. He swung up his arms; both hands were held round a shiny black Smith & Wesson revolver.

'Sverre!'

A yellow flame spat out of the muzzle of the gun. He could see her standing at the bottom of the stairs. Then the bullet hit him, bored through the top of his forehead, out through the back, taking the *Heil* from the *Sieg Heil* tattoo with it, into and through the wooden studwork in the wall, through the insulation before stopping behind the Eternit cladding panel on the outside wall. But by then Sverre Olsen was already dead.

64

Krokliveien. 2 May 2000.

HARRY HAD SCROUNGED A COFFEE OFF SOMEONE in the Crime Scene Unit with a thermos. He was standing in front of the ugly little house in Krokliveien in Bjerke, peering at a young officer up a ladder who was marking the hole in the roof where the bullet had exited. Curious onlookers had already begun to gather and for the sake of security the police had cordoned off the area around the house with yellow tape. The man on the ladder was bathed in the afternoon sunlight, but the house lay in a hollow in the ground and it was already cold where Harry stood.

'So you arrived immediately after it happened?' Harry heard a voice behind him ask. He turned round. It was Bjarne Møller. He had become an increasingly rare sight at crime scenes, but Harry had heard several people say he had been a good detective. Some even suggested that he should have been allowed to continue. Harry offered him the cup of coffee, but Møller shook his head.

'Yes, I must have arrived about four to five minutes afterwards,' Harry said. 'Who told you?'

'Central switchboard. They said you had rung and asked for reinforcements after Waaler reported the shooting.'

Harry motioned with his head towards the red sports car in front of the gateway.

'When I arrived I saw Waaler's Jap car. I knew he was coming here, so that was fine. But when I got out of my car I heard a terrible howling noise. At first I thought there was a dog somewhere in the neighbourhood. As I walked up the gravel path, however, I knew it was coming from inside the house and that it wasn't a dog. It was human. I didn't take any chances and rang for assistance from Økern police district.'

'It was the mother?'

Harry nodded. 'She was completely hysterical. It took them almost half an hour before they had her in a calm enough state to say something sensible. Weber is still talking to her now, in the sitting room.'

'Good old sensitive Weber?'

'Weber's fine. He's a bit of an old sourpuss at work, but he's pretty good with people in this kind of situation.'

'I know. I was just joking. How's Waaler taking it?'

Harry shrugged his shoulders.

'I know,' Møller said. 'He's a cold fish. Fair enough. Shall we go in and take a dekko?'

'I've been in.'

'Well, give me a guided tour then.'

They made their way up to the first floor as Møller mumbled greetings to colleagues he hadn't seen for ages.

The bedroom was full of specialists from the Crime Scene Unit and cameras were flashing. Black plastic, on which the outline of a body had been drawn, covered the bed.

Møller let his gaze wander round the walls. 'Jesus Christ,' he mumbled.

'Sverre Olsen didn't vote for the Socialists,' Harry said.

'Don't touch anything, Bjarne,' shouted an inspector Harry recognised from Forensics. 'You know what happened last time.'

Apparently Møller did; at any rate he laughed good-naturedly.

'Sverre Olsen was sitting on the bed when Waaler came in,' Harry said. 'According to Waaler, he was standing by the door and he asked Olsen about the night Ellen was killed. Olsen pretended he couldn't remember the date, so Waaler asked a few more questions and gradually it became obvious that Olsen did not have an alibi. According to Waaler, he asked Olsen to go to the station with him and give a statement, and that was when Olsen suddenly grabbed the revolver that he must have kept hidden under the pillow. He fired and the bullet passed above his shoulder and through the door – here's the hole – and through the ceiling in the hall. According to Waaler, he pulled out his service revolver and got Olsen before he could fire off any more shots.'

'Quick reactions. Good shot, too, I heard.'

'Smack in the forehead,' Harry said.

'Not so strange perhaps. Waaler got top results in the shooting test last autumn.'

'You're forgetting my results,' Harry said drily.

'How's it going, Ronald?' Møller shouted, turning to the inspector dressed in white.

'Plain sailing, I reckon.' The inspector stood up and straightened his back with a groan. 'We found the bullet that killed Olsen behind the Eternit panel here. The one that went through the door continued on up through the ceiling. We'll have to see if we can find that one as well so that the ballistics boys have something to play with tomorrow. The angles fit anyway.'

'Hm. Thanks.'

'Don't mention it. How's your wife by the way?'

Møller told him how his wife was, omitted to ask how the inspector's was, but for all Harry knew, he didn't have one. Last year four of the boys in Forensics had separated from their wives in the same month. They had joked in the canteen that it must have been the smell of corpses.

They saw Weber outside the house. He was standing on

his own with a cup of coffee in his hand, watching the man on the ladder.

'Was it alright, Weber?' Møller asked.

Weber squinted at them as if he first had to check whether he could be bothered to answer them.

'She won't be a problem,' he said, peering up at the ladder man again. 'Of course she said she couldn't understand it because her son hated the sight of blood and so on, but we won't have any problems as far as the factual things that happened here are concerned.'

'Hm.' Møller placed a hand behind Harry's elbow. 'Let's take a little walk.'

They strolled down the road. It was an area with small houses, small gardens and blocks of flats at the end. Some children, their faces red with effort, pedalled past them on their way up to the police cars with the sweeping blue lights. Møller waited until they were well out of the others' hearing.

'You don't seem particularly happy that we've caught Ellen's killer,' he said.

'Well, depends what you mean by happy. First of all, we don't know if it *is* Sverre Olsen yet. The DNA tests —'

'The DNA tests will show it's him. What's up, Harry?'

'Nothing, boss.'

Møller stopped. 'Really?'

Møller inclined his head towards the house.

'Is it because you think Olsen got away too lightly with a quick bullet?'

'I'm telling you, it's nothing!' Harry said with a sudden vehemence.

'Spit it out!' Møller bellowed.

'I just think it's bloody funny.'

Møller frowned. 'What's funny?'

'An experienced policeman like Waaler . . .' Harry had lowered his voice. He spoke slowly, stressing every word. '. . . deciding to take off alone to talk to and possibly arrest a suspect. It breaks all the written and unwritten rules.'

'So what are you saying? That Tom Waaler provoked it? Do you think he made Olsen go for his gun so that he could avenge Ellen's killing? Is that it? Is that why you stood there saying *according to Waaler* this and *according to Waaler* that, precisely as if we in the police don't trust a colleague's words? While half the Crime Scene Unit is listening?'

They glared at each other. Møller was almost as tall as Harry.

'I'm just saying it's bloody funny,' Harry said, turning away. 'That's all.'

'That's enough, Harry! I don't know what made you come out here after Waaler or whether you suspected that something was going to happen, but I know that I don't want to hear any more about it. I don't want to hear another damned word insinuating anything. Understood?'

Harry's eyes lingered on the Olsen family's yellow house. It was smaller than the other houses and it didn't have the same high hedge around it as the rest in this quiet-afternoon residential street. The other hedges made this ugly, Eternit-cladded home seem unprotected. The neighbouring houses seemed to be cold-shouldering it. There was the acidic smell of bonfires, and the distant metallic voice of the commentator from Bjerke trotting track came and went with the wind.

Harry shrugged.

'Sorry. I . . . you know.'

Møller put his hand on his shoulder.

'She was the best. I know that, Harry.'

65

Schrøder's. 2 May 2000.

THE OLD MAN WAS READING *AFTENPOSTEN*. HE
was deeply engrossed, studying the form for the trotting races
when his attention was caught by the waitress standing by
his table.

'Hello,' she said, putting the large glass in front of him.
As usual, he didn't answer, merely observed her as she counted
his change. Her age was indefinable, but he guessed somewhere between thirty-five and forty. And she looked as if the
years had been as hard to her as to the clientele she served.
But she had a nice smile. Could knock back a drink or two.
She left and he downed the first swig of his beer as his eyes
wandered round the room.

He looked at his watch. Then he got up, went over to the
coin-operated phones at the back of the room, deposited three
one-krone coins, punched in the number and waited. After
three rings the phone was picked up.

'Juul.'

'Signe?'

'Yes.'

He could hear from her voice that she was already frightened, she knew who was ringing. This was the sixth time, so

perhaps she had worked out the pattern and knew he would ring today.

'This is Daniel,' he said.

'Who is that? What do you want?' Her breath came in quick, successive pants.

'I just told you, it's Daniel. I only want you to repeat what you said years ago. Do you remember?'

'Please stop this. Daniel is dead.'

'Until death us do part, Signe. Until *death* us do part.'

'I'll phone the police.'

He put down the receiver. Then he donned his hat and coat and walked slowly out into the sunshine. In Sankthanshaugen Park the first buds had appeared. It wouldn't be long now.

66

Dinner. 5 May 2000.

RAKEL'S LAUGHTER PENETRATED THE CONSTANT buzz of voices, cutlery and busy waiters in the packed restaurant.

'. . . and I was almost scared when I saw that there was a message on the answerphone,' Harry said. 'You know that small flashing eye. And then your voice of authority.'

He lowered his voice into a deep key.

'This is Rakel. Dinner at eight on Friday. Don't forget, nice suit and wallet. Helge was scared out of his wits. I had to give him two millet cobs before he calmed down.'

'I *didn't* say that!' she protested between bursts of laughter.

'It was similar.'

'No, it wasn't! And it was your fault. It was the message you've got on your answerphone.'

She tried to find the same deep key: *'This is Hole. Speak to me.* That is just so . . . so . . .'

'Harry-like?'

'Exactly.'

It had been a perfect dinner, a perfect evening, and now it was time to ruin it, Harry thought.

'Meirik has given me my orders. I have to go to Sweden on

an undercover assignment,' he said, fidgeting with his glass of Farris water. 'Six months. I'm leaving after the weekend.'

'Oh.'

He was surprised when he didn't see a reaction register on her face.

'I rang Sis and my father and told them earlier today,' he went on. 'My father spoke. He even wished me good luck.'

'That's nice.' She gave him a fleeting smile and busied herself with the dessert menu.

'Oleg will miss you,' she said in a low voice.

He looked at her, but couldn't catch her eye.

'And what about you?' he asked.

A wry smile flitted across her face.

'They've got Banana Split à la Szechuan,' she said.

'Order two.'

'I'll miss you too,' she said and her eyes found the next page of the menu.

'How much?'

She shrugged.

He repeated the question. And watched her take a breath. She was poised to speak, but let the air out. Then she started again. In the end it came.

'Sorry, Harry, but right now there's only space for one man in my life. A little man of six.'

It felt like having a bucket of freezing cold water poured over your head.

'Come on,' Harry said. 'I can't be *that* wrong.'

She raised her eyes from the menu with a quizzical expression on her face.

'You and me,' Harry said, leaning across the table. 'Here, this evening. We're flirting. We're having fun. But we want more than that. *You* want more than that.'

'Perhaps.'

'Not perhaps. Absolutely certain. You want everything.'

'So what.'

'*So what? You* have to tell me, *that's what,* Rakel. I'm off to some dump in southern Sweden in a few days' time. I'm not a spoiled man. I just want to know if I have anything to come back to in the autumn.'

Their eyes met and this time he held her gaze. For a long time. She finally put down the menu.

'I'm sorry. I don't mean to be like this. I know this will sound strange, but . . . the alternative won't work.'

'What alternative?'

'Doing what I feel like doing. Taking you home and taking off all your clothes and making love to you all night.'

She whispered the last part softly and quickly. As if it were something she had wanted to wait until the very last minute to say, but when it had to be said, it had to be said exactly like that. Blunt and unadorned.

'What about one more night?' Harry said. 'What about several nights? What about tomorrow night and the night after that and next week and . . . ?'

'Stop it!' She had an angry line over the bridge of her nose. 'You have to understand, Harry. It won't work.'

'Right.' Harry flicked out a cigarette and lit it. He allowed her to stroke his chin, his mouth. The gentle touch ran like an electric shock along his nerve fibres, leaving a dull pain.

'It's not you, Harry. For a while I thought I might be able to do it again. I've been through all the arguments. Two adults. No one else involved. Non-committal and simple. And a man I feel more for than anyone since . . . since Oleg's father. That's why it won't stop with just the once. And that . . . that is no good.'

She fell silent.

'Is it because Oleg's father is an alcoholic?'

'Why do you ask about that?'

'I don't know. It could explain why you don't want to get involved with me. Not that you need to have been with another alkie to know that I'm not a good catch, but . . .'

She rested her hand on his.

'You're a good catch, Harry. It's not that.'

'So what is it then?'

'This is the last time. That's what it is. We won't meet again.'

Her eyes rested on him. And he saw it now. They weren't tears of laughter gleaming in the corners of her eyes.

'And the rest of the story?' he asked, trying to force a smile. 'Is that like everything else in POT, on a need-to-know basis?'

She nodded.

The waiter came to their table, but must have sensed his timing was off and went away again.

She opened her mouth to say something. Harry could see that she was on the verge of tears. She bit her lower lip. Then she put the napkin down on the tablecloth, shoved her chair back, stood up without a word and left. Harry remained, sitting and staring at the napkin. She must have been squeezing it in her hand for some time, he mused, because it was crumpled up into a ball. He watched it slowly unfold like a white paper flower.

67

Halvorsen's Flat. 6 May 2000.

WHEN HALVORSEN WAS WOKEN BY THE TELE-phone ringing, the luminous figures on the digital alarm clock showed 1.30 a.m.

'Hole speaking. Were you asleep?'

'Nope,' Halvorsen said, without the slightest idea why he should lie.

'I had a couple of things on my mind, about Sverre Olsen.'

From the breathing and the traffic in the background it sounded as if Harry was out walking.

'I know what you want to know,' Halvorsen said. 'Sverre Olsen bought a pair of combat boots at Top Secret in Henrik Ibsens gate. They recognised him from the photo and fur-thermore they could give us the date. You see, Kripos had been there to check his alibi in connection with the Hall-grim Dale case before Christmas. But I faxed all that up to your office earlier today.'

'I know. I've just come from there now.'

'Now? I thought you were going out for dinner this eve-ning?'

'Well, we finished early.'

'And you went back to work?' Halvorsen asked, in disbelief.

'Yes, I suppose I did. It was your fax which started me thinking. I was wondering if you could check a couple of other things for me tomorrow.'

Halvorsen groaned. First of all, Møller had told him in a way that brooked no misunderstanding: Harry was to have nothing to do with the Ellen Gjelten case. And second: tomorrow was Saturday.

'Are you there, Halvorsen?'

'Yes.'

'I can imagine what Møller said. Don't take any bloody notice. Now you've got the chance to learn a little more about detective work.'

'The problem is, Harry —'

'Keep quiet and listen, Halvorsen.'

Halvorsen cursed to himself. And listened.

68

Vibes Gate. 8 May 2000.

THE SMELL OF FRESHLY BREWED COFFEE WAFTED
into the hall where Harry was hanging his jacket on an over-
loaded coat stand.

'Thank you for receiving me at such short notice, herr
Fauke.'

'Not at all,' Fauke mumbled from the kitchen. 'An old
man like me is only too happy to help. If I *can* help.'

He poured coffee into two large mugs and put them on
the kitchen table. Harry ran the tips of his fingers along the
rough surface of the dark, heavy oak table.

'From Provence,' Fauke said without any prompting. 'My
wife liked French peasant furniture.'

'Wonderful table. Your wife had good taste.'

Fauke smiled.

'Are you married? No? Never been married? You shouldn't
wait too long, you know. You become difficult, on your own
all the time.'

He laughed.

'I know what I'm talking about. I was past thirty when I
got married. That was late for the time. May 1955.'

He pointed to one of the photographs hanging on the wall over the kitchen table.

'Is that really your wife?' Harry asked. 'I thought it was Rakel.'

'Oh yes, of course,' after first looking at Harry in surprise. 'I forgot that you and Rakel knew each other from POT.'

They went into the sitting room, where the piles of paper had grown since his last visit and occupied all the chairs except the one at the desk. Fauke cleared a place for them to sit by the overflowing coffee table.

'Did you find out anything about the names I gave you?' he asked.

Harry summarised what he had discovered.

'However, there are a few new elements,' he said. 'A policewoman has been murdered.'

'I read something about it in the paper.'

'That case has been solved. We're waiting for the results of a DNA test. Do you believe in coincidences, herr Fauke?'

'Not really.'

'Neither do I. That's why I ask myself questions when the same people keep cropping up in cases which are apparently unrelated. On the same evening Ellen Gjelten was murdered, she left a message on my answer-phone saying "We've got him now". She was helping me to search for the person who had ordered the Märklin gun from Johannesburg. Of course, there doesn't have to be any connection between this person and the killer, but they are adjacent thoughts. Especially since she was clearly very concerned to get hold of me. This was a case I had been dealing with for weeks, yet she tried to contact me several times that night. And she sounded very agitated. That may suggest that she felt threatened.'

Harry placed his forefinger on the coffee table.

'One of the people on your list, Hallgrim Dale, was murdered last autumn. In the alley where he was found there were also, among other things, the remains of vomit. A link was not made immediately since the blood group didn't match that of the victim, and the image of an extremely cold-blooded professional murderer didn't square with someone who throws up at the scene of a crime. Kripos, however, did not exclude the possibility that the vomit belonged to the murderer and sent off a saliva sample for DNA testing. Earlier today one of my colleagues compared these results with the tests done on the cap we found by the murdered policewoman. They are identical.'

Harry paused and looked at the other man.

'I see,' Fauke said. 'You think the perpetrators could be one and the same.'

'No, I don't think so. I just think there may be a connection between the murders and it is no chance that Sverre Olsen was close by both times.'

'Why couldn't he have killed both of them?'

'He might have done that, of course, but there is a crucial difference between the kind of violence Sverre Olsen used and the murder of Hallgrim Dale. Have you ever seen the physical damage that a baseball bat can do? The soft wood smashes bones and causes internal organs like the liver and kidneys to burst. The skin's often as not unscathed and the victim generally dies of internal bleeding. In the case of Hallgrim Dale the carotid artery was severed. As a result of *this* kind of killing, blood gushes out. Do you understand?'

'Yes, but I don't see where you're going.'

'Sverre Olsen's mother told one of the officers that Sverre couldn't stand the sight of blood.'

Fauke's cup of coffee stopped on its way to his mouth. He put it down again.

'Yes, but . . .'

'I know what you're thinking – that he could still have done it and the fact that he couldn't stand the sight of blood may explain why he threw up. But the point is that the killer wasn't using a knife for the first time. According to the pathologist's report, it was a perfect surgical cut, which only someone who knew what he was doing could have carried out.'

Fauke nodded slowly.

'I understand what you mean,' he said.

'You look pensive,' Harry said.

'I think I know why you're here. You're wondering if one of the soldiers from Sennheim was capable of executing such a killing.'

'Right. Was there anyone?'

'Yes, there was.' Fauke grasped his mug with both hands and his eyes wandered into the distance. 'The one you didn't find. Gudbrand Johansen. I told you we called him the redbreast, didn't I?'

'Can you tell me any more about him?'

'Yes, but we'll have to have more coffee first.'

69

Irisveien. 8 May 2000.

'WHO'S THAT?' CAME A SHOUT FROM INSIDE THE door. The voice was small and frightened. Harry could see her outline through the frosted glass.

'Harry Hole. We spoke on the phone.'

The door was opened a fraction.

'Sorry, I . . .'

'That's alright.'

Signe Juul opened the door wide and Harry walked into the hallway.

'Even's out,' she said with an apologetic smile.

'Yes, you said on the phone,' Harry said. 'It was actually you I wanted to talk to.'

'Me?'

'If that's OK, fru Juul?'

The elderly lady led the way in. Her hair, thick and steely grey, was twisted into a knot and held in place with an old-fashioned hairslide. And her round, swaying body was the kind that made you think of a soft embrace and good food.

Burre raised his head when they came into the sitting room.

'So, your husband has gone for a walk on his own?' Harry asked.

'Yes, he can't take Burre into the café,' she said. 'Please, do sit down.'

'The café?'

'Something he's started doing recently,' she smiled. 'To read the papers. He says he thinks better when he's not sitting at home.'

'There's probably something in that.'

'Absolutely. And you can daydream too, I suppose.'

'What kind of daydreams, do you think?'

'Well, I've no idea. You can perhaps imagine you're young again, drinking coffee at a pavement café in Paris or Vienna.' Again that same quick, apologetic smile. 'Enough of that. Coffee?'

'Yes, please.'

Harry studied the walls while Signe Juul went into the kitchen. Above the fireplace was a portrait of a young man wearing a black cloak. Harry hadn't noticed the picture when he had been here previously. The cloak-clad man was standing in a dramatic pose, apparently scanning distant horizons beyond the painter's view. Harry walked over to the picture. A little framed copper plaque read: *Overlege Kornelius Juul, 1885–1969.* Medical consultant.

'That's Even's grandfather,' Signe Juul said, arriving with a tray of coffee things.

'Right. You have a lot of portraits here.'

'Yes,' she said, putting down the tray. 'The picture beside it is Even's maternal grandfather, Dr Werner Schumann. He was one of the founders of Ullevål Hospital in 1885.'

'And this?'

'Jonas Schumann. Consultant at the Rikshospital.'

'And your relatives?'

She looked at him in bewilderment. 'What do you mean?'

'Where are your relatives?'

'They . . . are elsewhere. Cream in your coffee?'

'No, thank you.'

Harry sat down. 'I wanted to talk to you about the war,' he said.

'Oh no,' she burst out.

'I understand, but this is important. Is it alright to ask?'

'We'll see,' she said, pouring herself coffee.

'You were a nurse during the war . . .'

'At the Eastern Front, yes. A traitor.'

Harry looked up. Her eyes watched him calmly.

'There were around four hundred of us. We were all sentenced to imprisonment afterwards. Despite the fact that the international Red Cross sent in an appeal to the Norwegian authorities to stop all criminal proceedings. The Norwegian Red Cross didn't apologise until 1990. Even's father, in the picture over there, had connections and managed to get my sentence commuted . . . partly because I had helped two injured Resistance men in the spring of 1945. And because I was never a member of the *Nasjonal Samling*. Is there anything else you would like to know?'

Harry stared into his coffee cup. It struck him how quiet it could be in some of Oslo's better residential areas.

'It's not your past I'm after, fru Juul. Do you remember a Norwegian soldier at the front called Gudbrand Johansen?'

Signe Juul flinched, and Harry knew he had stumbled on to something.

'What is it you actually want to know?' she asked, her face taut.

'Hasn't your husband told you?'

'Even never tells me anything.'

'Right. I'm trying to identify the Norwegian soldiers who went through Sennheim on the way to the front.'

'Sennheim,' she repeated softly. 'Daniel was there.'

'Yes, I know you were engaged to Daniel Gudeson. Sindre Fauke told me that.'

'Who's he?'

'A veteran of the front and the Resistance whom your

husband knows. It was Fauke who suggested I talk to you about Gudbrand Johansen. Fauke deserted, so he doesn't know what happened to Gudbrand afterwards. But another soldier from the front, Edvard Mosken, told me about a hand-grenade exploding in the trenches. Mosken wasn't able to account for all the events following the explosion, but if Johansen survived it would be natural to assume that he ended up in the field hospital.'

Signe Juul made a smacking noise with her lips. Burre ambled over and she buried her fingers in the dog's thick, wiry coat.

'Yes, I can remember Gudbrand Johansen,' she said. 'Daniel occasionally wrote about him, in the letters from Sennheim and in the notes I got from him at the field hospital. They were very different. I think Gudbrand Johansen became like a younger brother to him.' She smiled. 'Most men in Daniel's presence tended to behave like younger brothers.'

'Do you know what happened to Gudbrand?'

'He ended up in the hospital with us, as you said. This was at the time when our section of the front was falling into Russian hands and there was a full-scale retreat. We couldn't get any medicine to the front because all the roads were blocked by traffic coming from the other direction. Johansen was badly injured with, among other things, a shell splinter in his thigh, just above the knee. Gangrene was spreading in his foot and there was a risk we might have to amputate. So, instead of waiting for medicine which wasn't coming, he was sent with the stream of traffic to the west. The last I saw of him was a bearded face sticking up from under a blanket at the back of a lorry. The spring mud was up to the middle of the wheels and it took them an hour to move round the first bend and out of sight.'

The dog had rested its head in her lap and looked up at her with sad eyes.

'And that was the last you saw or heard of him?'

She slowly raised the delicate porcelain cup to her lips,

took a tiny sip and put it down. Her hand didn't shake much, but it was trembling.

'I received a card from him a few months later,' she said. 'He wrote that he had some of Daniel's personal effects, a Russian cap that I understood to be some kind of trophy of war. The writing was rather confused, but that is not at all unusual among recent war casualties.'

'The card, do you . . . ?'

She shook her head.

'Do you remember where it was sent from?'

'No. I can only remember that the name made me think it was somewhere green and rural and that he was well.'

Harry stood up.

'How did this Fauke know about me?' she asked.

'Well —' Harry didn't quite know how to put it, but she broke in.

'All the soldiers at the front have heard of me,' she said and her mouth smiled. 'The woman who sold her soul to the Devil for a shorter sentence. Is that what they think?'

'I don't know,' Harry said. He knew he had to get out. They were only two blocks away from the circular road round Oslo, but it was so quiet they could have been by a lake in the mountains.

'You know I never saw him again,' she said. 'Daniel. After they told me he was dead.'

She had focused on an imaginary point in front of her.

'I received a New Year's greeting from him via an orderly and three days later I saw Daniel's name on a list of the fallen. I didn't believe it was true. I told them I would refuse to believe it until they showed me his body. So they took me to the mass grave in the Northern Sector where they were burning the dead. I went down into the grave, trod over dead bodies as I searched, going from one burned corpse to the next, staring into the blackened, empty eye sockets. But none of them was Daniel. They said it would be impossible for me to recognise him, but I told them they were wrong. Then they said

that he might have been put in one of the graves that had
been covered over. I don't know, but I never saw him again.'

She started when Harry cleared his throat.

'Thank you for the coffee, fru Juul.'

She followed him out to the hall. As he stood by the
wardrobe, buttoning up his coat, he couldn't help looking
for her features in the faces peering out of the framed photographs hanging on the wall, but in vain.

'Do we have to tell Even any of this?' she asked, opening
the door for him.

Harry looked at her in surprise.

'I mean, does he have to know that we talked about this?'
she added hurriedly. 'About the war and . . . Daniel?'

'Well, not if you don't want him to, of course.'

'He'll see that you've been here. But can't we just say that
you waited for him and you had to go to another appointment?'

Her eyes were imploring, but there was something else
there too.

Harry couldn't put his finger on what it was until he was in
Ringveien and had opened the window to let in the liberating,
deafening roar of cars, which blew the silence out of his head.
It was horror. Signe Juul was terrifed of something.

70

Brandhaug's House, Nordberg.
8 May 2000.

BERNT BRANDHAUG TAPPED THE EDGE OF THE crystal glass with his knife, pushed his chair back and dabbed his mouth with his napkin while gently clearing his throat. A tiny smile flitted across his lips, as if he were already amused by the points he was going to make in this speech to his guests: Chief Constable Størksen with husband and Kurt Meirik with wife.

'Dear friends and colleagues.'

Out of the corner of his eye he could see his wife smiling stiffly to the others as if to say: *Sorry we have to go through this, but it is beyond my control.*

This evening Brandhaug talked about friendship and collegiality. About the importance of loyalty and summoning positive energy as a defence against the scope democracy will always allow for mediocrity, the abrogation of responsibility and incompetence at leadership level. Of course you couldn't expect politically elected housewives and farmers to understand the complexity of the areas of responsibility they were designated to manage.

'Democracy is its own reward,' Brandhaug said, a formulation he had plagiarised and made his own. 'But that doesn't mean that democracy doesn't come at a price. When we make a sheet-metal worker a minister of finance . . .'

At regular intervals he checked that the Chief Constable was listening and interjected a witticism about the democratisation process in various ex-colonies in Africa where he had once been an ambassador himself. But the speech, which he had given several times before in other forums, did not inspire him this evening. His mind was somewhere else, where it had been for the last few weeks: with Rakel Fauke.

She had become an obsession with him and he had on occasion considered forgetting her. He had been trying too hard to have her.

He thought about his recent manipulations. If it hadn't been for the fact that Kurt Meirik was the head of POT, it would never have worked. The first thing he'd had to do was get this Harry Hole off the scene, out of the way, out of the city, to some place where he couldn't be contacted by Rakel or anyone else.

Brandhaug had rung Kurt and said that his contact at *Dagbladet* had told him that there were rumours doing the rounds in press circles about 'something' having happened during the presidential visit in the autumn. They had to act before it was too late, hide Harry somewhere the press couldn't get hold of him. Didn't Kurt think so too?

Kurt had humm-ed and haa-ed. At least until it all blew over, Brandhaug had insisted. To tell the truth, Brandhaug doubted that Meirik had believed what he said for one moment. Not that he was unduly worried. A few days later Kurt called him to say that Harry Hole had been sent to the front, to some God-forsaken place in Sweden. Brandhaug had literally rubbed his hands with glee. Nothing could upset the plans he had made for Rakel and him now.

'Our democracy is like a beautiful, smiling, but slightly naive daughter. The fact that the powers for good in a society stick together has nothing to do with elitism or power games; it is simply the only guarantee we have that our daughter,

Democracy, will not be violated and that the government
will not be taken over by undesirable forces. Hence loyalty,
this almost forgotten virtue, between people like us is not
only desirable but also absolutely vital. Yes, it is a duty
which . . .'

They had moved to the deep armchairs in the sitting room
and Brandhaug had passed round his box of Cuban cigars, a
gift from the Norwegian consulate in Havana.

'Rolled on the inside of Cuban women's thighs,' he had
whispered to Anne Størksen's husband and winked, but he
didn't appear to have understood the point. He made a dry,
stiff impression, this husband of hers, what was his name
again? A double name – my God, had he forgotten? Tor Erik!
That was it, Tor Erik.

'More cognac, Tor Erik?'

Tor Erik smiled a thin, compressed smile and shook his
head. Probably the ascetic type who jogs fifty kilometres a
week, Brandhaug thought. Everything about the man was
thin – the body, the face, the hair. He had seen the look he
had exchanged with his wife during the speech, as if reminding her of a private joke. It didn't necessarily have anything to do with the speech.

'Sensible,' Brandhaug said sourly. 'Better safe than sorry?'

Elsa appeared in the door to the sitting room.

'There's a telephone call for you, Bernt.'

'We have guests, Elsa.'

'It's someone from *Dagbladet*.'

'I'll take it up in my office.'

It was from the newsdesk, some woman whose name he
didn't know. She sounded young and he tried to picture her.
It was about the demonstration that evening outside the Austrian embassy in Thomas Heftyes gate, against Jörg Haider
and the extreme right Freedom Party, who had been elected

to help form the government. She only wanted a few brief comments for the morning paper.

'Do you think this would be an appropriate time to review Norway's diplomatic links with Austria, herr Brandhaug?'

He closed his eyes. They were fishing, as they were wont to do from time to time, but both he and they knew that they wouldn't get a bite; he was too experienced. He could feel that he had been drinking; his head was light and his eyes danced on the back of his eyelids, but it was no problem.

'That is a political judgment and it is not up to civil servants in the Foreign Office to decide,' he said.

There was a pause. He liked her voice. She was blonde, he could sense it.

'I wonder whether with your broad experience of foreign affairs you might predict what the Norwegian government will do?'

He knew what he ought to answer. It was very simple.

I don't make predictions about that sort of thing.

No more, no less. You didn't need to be in a job like his for very long before you had the feeling you had already answered all the questions in existence. Young journalists generally thought they were the first to ask him precisely the question they asked because they had spent half the night working it out. And they were all impressed when he seemed to pause for thought before answering a question he had probably answered a dozen times before.

I don't make predictions about that sort of thing.

He was surprised he hadn't said these words to her already, but there was something about her voice, something which made him feel like being a trifle more obliging. *Your broad experience*, she had said. He felt like asking her if it had been her idea to call him, Bernt Brandhaug, in particular.

'As the most senior civil servant in the Ministry of Foreign Affairs I ensure that our usual diplomatic relations with

Austria are maintained,' he said. 'That is clear – we are of course aware that other countries in the world are reacting to what is going on in Austria now. However, having diplomatic relations with a country does not mean that we like what is happening there.'

'No, we do have diplomatic links with several military regimes,' the voice answered at the other end. 'So why do you think there are such violent reactions to precisely this government?'

'I suppose it must be based on Austria's recent history.' He should have stopped there. He should have stopped. 'The links with Nazism are there. After all, most historians agree that during the Second World War Austria was in reality an ally of Hitler's Germany.'

'Wasn't Austria occupied, like Norway?'

It struck him that he had no idea what they learned at school about the Second World War nowadays. Very little apparently.

'What did you say your name was?' he asked. Perhaps he *had* drunk a bit too much. She told him her name.

'Well, Natasja, let me help you a little before you start ringing anyone else. Have you heard of the Anschluss? It means that Austria wasn't occupied in the normal understanding of the word. The Germans marched on Austria in March 1938. There was almost no resistance and that was how it stayed for the remainder of the war.'

'Like Norway then?'

Brandhaug was shocked. She had said it in such an assured way, without a tinge of shame about her ignorance.

'No,' he said slowly, as if talking to a dull-witted child. 'Not like in Norway. In Norway we defended ourselves and we had the Norwegian King and Norwegian government in London ready and waiting, making radio programmes and . . . giving encouragement to those back home.'

He could hear that his phraseology was slightly unfortunate and added, 'In Norway the whole population stood shoulder to shoulder against the occupying forces. The few Norwegian traitors who donned Waffen SS uniforms and fought for the Germans were the scum of society that you have to accept exists in every country. But in Norway the power for good held up, the strong individuals who led the Resistance movement were the nucleus which paved the way for the democracy. These people were loyal to each other and in the final analysis that is what saved Norway. Democracy is its own reward. Scrub what I said about the King, Natasja.'

'So you think that everyone who fought alongside the Nazis was scum?'

What was she really after? Brandhaug decided to bring the conversation to a close.

'I simply mean to say that those who were traitors during the war should be happy they were let off lightly with imprisonment. I've been an ambassador in countries where each and every one of them would have been shot and I'm not so damned sure that wouldn't have been right in Norway too. But back to the comment you wanted, Natasja. The Ministry for Foreign Affairs has no comment to make on the demonstration or on Austria's new members of Parliament. I have guests here, so if you wouldn't mind excusing me, Natasja . . .'

Natasja excused him and he put down the phone.

Back in the sitting room people were making moves to go.

'Already?' he said with a broad smile, but limited his objections to that. He was tired.

He accompanied his guests to the door. He applied particular pressure to the Chief Constable's hand and said she should not hesitate to ask should there be anything he could do to help. It was all very well going through work channels but . . .

The last thing he thought about before falling asleep was Rakel. And her policeman he had removed from the scene. He fell asleep with a smile, but awoke with a splitting headache.

71

Fredrikstad to Halden. 9 May 2000.

THE TRAIN WAS BARELY HALF FULL AND HARRY
had found a seat by the window.

The girl in the seat directly behind him had taken out the
earplugs from her Walkman and he could make out the vocal-
ist but none of the instruments. The monitoring expert they had
used in Sydney had explained to Harry that at low volumes the
human ear amplifies the frequencies human voices use.

Harry thought there was something comforting about the
fact that the last thing you heard before everything went
quiet was the human voice.

Streaks of quivering raindrops fought their way across
the carriage windows. Harry peered out at the flat, wet fields
and the electric cables rising and falling between the posts
alongside the track.

On the platform in Fredrikstad a Janizary band had been
playing. The conductor on the train had explained to him
that they were practising for Independence Day on 17 May.

'Every Tuesday, every year at this time,' he said. 'The
band leader thinks that rehearsals are more realistic when
they are surrounded by people.'

Harry had thrown a few clothes in a bag. The apartment

in Klippan was supposed to be simple, but very well furnished. A television, a stereo, even some books.

'*Mein Kampf* and that sort of thing,' Meirik had said with a grin.

He had not called Rakel. Even though he could have done with hearing her voice. A last human voice.

'The next station is Halden,' came the nasal crackle from the loudspeaker, interrupted by the strident, off-key tone of the train's brakes.

Harry ran a finger across the window as he juggled the sentence in his head. A strident, off-key tone. An off-key strident tone. A tone which is strident . . .

A tone can't be off-key, he thought. *A tone isn't off-key until it is set alongside other tones.* Even Ellen, the most musical person he had known, needed a few moments, a few tones, to hear the music. Even she was unable to pinpoint a single moment and say with total certainty that it was off-key. It was wrong, it was a lie.

And yet this tone sang in his ear, high-pitched and gratingly off-key. He was going to Klippan to stake out a potential sender of a fax which as yet had provoked no more than a couple of newspaper headlines. He had combed the day's newspapers and it was obvious that they had already forgotten the story about the threatening letters of which they had made so much a mere four days ago. Instead, *Dagbladet* wrote about the skier Lasse Kjus, who hated Norway, and Bernt Brandhaug, the Under Secretary of State at the Foreign Office, who, if quoted correctly, had said that traitors should be given the death sentence.

There was another tone that was off-key. But perhaps because he wanted it to be. Rakel's departure from the restaurant, the expression in her eyes, almost a declaration of love before she cut it short, leaving him in free fall and with a bill of eight hundred kroner that she had boasted *she* would pay. It didn't make sense. Or did it? Rakel had been in Harry's flat, seen him drinking, heard him talking tearfully about a dead colleague he had known for barely two years as if she was the only person he had ever had a close relationship with. Pathetic. Humans should be spared the sight of each other stripped bare. So why hadn't she called it a day then and there? Why hadn't she said to herself that this man was more trouble than she could handle?

As usual, he had escaped into his work when his private life became too much of a burden. It was typical of a certain type of man, he had read. That was probably why he had spent the weekend brewing conspiracy theories and scenarios which placed all the various elements – the Märklin rifle, Ellen's murder, the murder of Hallgrim Dale – in one pot so that he could stir it up into one foul-smelling broth. That was pathetic too.

He ran an eye over the paper spread out over the collapsible table in front of him, focused on the photograph of the FO head. There was something familiar about that face.

He rubbed his chin with his hand. From experience he knew that the brain tended to make its own associations when an investigation was in a rut. And the investigation into the rifle was a closed chapter. Meirik had made that clear – he had called it a non-case. Meirik had wanted him to write reports about neo-Nazis and do undercover work among rootless youths in Sweden. Well, fuck him!

'. . . the platform is on the right hand side.'

What if he simply got off the train? What was the worst that could happen? As long as the Foreign Office and POT were frightened that the shooting incident at the toll barrier last year would leak out, Meirik couldn't give him the boot. And as far as Rakel was concerned . . . as far as Rakel was concerned, he didn't know.

The train came to a halt with a final groan and the carriage fell quiet. Outside in the corridor, doors slammed. Harry remained in his seat. He could hear the song from the Walkman more clearly. It was one he had heard many times before; he just couldn't remember where.

72

Nordberg and the Continental Hotel.
9 May 2000.

THE OLD MAN WAS CAUGHT COMPLETELY UNPRE-
pared; the sudden stabbing pains took his breath away. He
curled up on the ground where he lay and forced his fist into
his mouth to stop himself screaming. He lay like that, trying
to retain consciousness as waves of light and dark surged
through him. Opening and closing his eyes. The sky rolled in
over him. It was as if time were accelerating: the clouds sped
across the sky, the stars shone through the blue. Day turned
into night, into day, night, day, and back to night again. Then
it was over and he could smell the aroma of wet earth beneath him and he knew he was alive.

He remained in the same position until he had got his
breath back. The sweat had stuck his shirt to his body. Then
he rolled over on to his stomach and looked down towards
the house again.

It was a large black timber house. He had been lying there
since the morning and he knew the wife was the only one
home. Nevertheless, all the windows were lit on the ground
and the first floor. He had seen her walking round to switch
all the lights on as soon as there was a suspicion of dusk, from
which he assumed that she was frightened of the dark.

He was frightened himself – not of the dark though, he had never been afraid of that. He was frightened of time accelerating. And the pain. It was a new experience and he hadn't learned to control it yet. Nor did he know if he could. And the time? He did his best not to think about cells dividing and dividing and dividing.

A pale moon appeared in the sky. He checked his watch: 7.30. Soon it would be too dark and he would have to wait until the morning. In that case he would have to spend the whole of the night in the bivouac. He looked at the construction he had made. It consisted of two Y-shaped branches he had pushed into the earth leaving half a metre above the ground. Between these, in the fork of the branches, was a stripped branch from a pine tree. Then he had cut three long branches which he placed on the ground and rested against the pine branch. He had covered them with a thick layer of spruce twigs. Thus he had a kind of roof which would protect him from the rain, retain some warmth and camouflage his presence from walkers, should they unexpectedly stray from the path. It had taken him barely half an hour to make the windbreak.

He calculated the risk of being seen from the road or by anyone in the nearby houses as negligible. It would have to be an unusually sharp-eyed person to make out the bivouac between the tree trunks in the dense spruce forest from a distance of almost three hundred metres. For safety's sake he had covered nearly the whole of the opening with spruce twigs too and tied rags around the barrel of the rifle so that the low afternoon sun would not catch the steel.

He checked his watch again. Where the hell was he?

Bernt Brandhaug twirled the glass in his hand and checked his watch again. Where the hell was she?

They had arranged to meet at 7.30 and now it was getting

on for 7.45. He downed the rest of his drink and poured himself another from the bottle of whisky room service had brought up: Jameson. The only good thing ever to come out of Ireland. He poured himself another. It had been one hell of a day. The headlines in *Dagbladet* had meant that the telephone never stopped ringing. He had received a fair amount of support, but in the end he had called the news editor at *Dagbladet*, an old friend from university, and made it clear that he had been misquoted. As a quid pro quo he had promised them inside information about the Foreign Minister's major blunder at the European Finance Committee meeting. The editor had asked for some time to think. After half an hour he rang back. It seemed that this Natasja was new to the paper and she had admitted that she might have misunderstood Brandhaug. They wouldn't issue a disclaimer, but they wouldn't follow up the matter either. The damage limitation exercise had been successful.

Brandhaug took a large gulp, rolled the whisky around his mouth and tasted the rough yet smooth aroma deep down in the nasal channel. He looked around him. How many nights had he spent here? How many times had he woken up in the slightly too soft king-size bed with a bit of a headache after one drink too many? How many times had he asked the woman by his side – if she was still there – to take the lift to the breakfast lounge on the first floor and walk down the stairs to the reception, so that it looked as if she was coming from a breakfast meeting, and not from one of the bedrooms. Just to be on the safe side.

He poured himself another drink.

It would be different with Rakel. He wouldn't send her down to the breakfast lounge.

There was a light knock at the door. He stood up, took a last look at the exclusive bedspread of yellow and gold, sensed a tiny rush of fear, which he instantly brushed aside, and covered the four strides to the door. He inspected himself in the hall mirror, slid his tongue across his white front teeth, moistened a finger and ran it along his eyebrows and opened the door.

She was leaning against the wall with her coat unbuttoned. She was wearing a red woollen dress underneath. He had asked her to wear something red. Her eyelids were heavy and she gave him a wry smirk. Brandhaug was surprised – he had never seen her looking like this before. She must have been drinking or taking some kind of pills – her eyes studied him apathetically and he hardly recognised her voice when she mumbled something incoherent about almost not finding the place. He took her arm but she wriggled free, so he guided her into the room with his hand against the small of her back. She slumped down on to the sofa.

'A drink?' he asked.

'Yes, please,' she said, her speech slurred. 'Or would you rather I stripped off immediately?'

Brandhaug poured her a glass without answering. He knew what she was playing at. But if she thought she could ruin his pleasure by assuming the role of soiled goods, she was mistaken. Alright, he might have preferred it if she had chosen the role his conquests in the Foreign Department went for – the innocent girl falling for her boss's irresistible charm and his self-assured masculine sensuality. But the most important thing was that she succumbed to his desires. He was too old to believe in humanity's romantic motives. The only thing that separated them was what they were both after: power, career or custody of a son.

It had never bothered him that women were dazzled by his position as head. After all, he was too. He was Bernt Brandhaug, the Under Secretary of State at the Foreign Office. For Christ's sake, he had spent all his life becoming the Under Secretary. If Rakel wanted to dope herself up and present herself as a whore, that didn't change the facts.

'I apologise, but I have to have you,' he said, dropping two ice cubes in her drink. 'When you get to know me, you'll understand all this better. But let me give you a kind of first lesson anyhow, an idea of what makes me tick.'

He passed her the glass.

'Some men crawl through life with their noses to the ground and are content with the scraps. The rest of us rise up on two legs, walk to the table and take our rightful places. We are in the minority because our lifestyle demands of us that occasionally we have to be brutal, and this brutality requires strength. We have to extricate ourselves from our social democratic, egalitarian upbringing. If it is a choice between that and crawling, I prefer to break with a short-sighted moralism which is not capable of placing individual actions in context. And it's my belief that, deep down, you will come to respect me for that.'

She didn't answer; she just knocked back the drink.

'Hole didn't pose any threat for you,' she said. 'He and I are only good friends.'

'I think you're lying,' he said, reluctantly filling the glass she proffered. 'And I have to have you to myself. Don't misunderstand me. When I made it a condition that you immediately broke all contact with Hole, it had less to do with jealousy and more to do with a principle of purity. Nevertheless, a few weeks in Sweden, or wherever it is Meirik sent him, will do him no harm.'

Brandhaug chuckled.

'Why are you looking at me like that, Rakel? It is not as if I were King David and Hole . . . what was his name again, the one King David made the generals send to the front lines?'

'Uriah,' she mumbled.

'Exactly. He died, didn't he?'

'Otherwise it wouldn't have been much of a story,' she said into her glass.

'Fine. But nobody is going to die here. And if I'm not much mistaken, King David and Bathsheba lived quite happily ever after, didn't they?'

Brandhaug took a seat beside her on the sofa and raised her chin with his finger.

'Tell me, Rakel, how come you know so many Bible stories?'

'A good upbringing,' she said, tearing herself away and pulling her dress over her head.

He swallowed as he gazed at her. She was attractive. She was wearing white underwear. He had specifically asked her to wear white underwear. It brought out the golden glow of her skin. You couldn't tell that she had given birth. But the fact that she had, the fact that she was demonstrably fertile and the fact that she had nourished a child at her breast made her even more attractive in Bernt Brandhaug's eyes. She was perfect.

'We aren't in any hurry,' he said, resting a hand on her knee. Her face did not betray any emotion, but he felt her flinch.

'Do whatever you like,' she said, shrugging her shoulders.

'Would you like to see the letter first?'

He inclined his head in the direction of the brown envelope embossed with the Russian embassy's seal, lying in the middle of the table. Ambassador Vladimir Aleksandrov's brief letter to Rakel Fauke informed her that the Russian authorities requested her to ignore the previous summons to the custody hearing on behalf of Oleg Fauke-Gosev. The whole matter was to be postponed indefinitely on account of the backlog of cases at the law courts. It had not been easy. Brandhaug had been obliged to remind the Russian ambassador of a couple of favours he owed him. And, in addition, to offer further favours. A couple of them were on the very margins of what was permissible for a Norwegian Foreign Office head.

'I trust you,' she said. 'Can we get this over with?'

She hardly blinked as his palm hit her cheek, but her head danced as if attached to a rag doll.

Brandhaug rubbed his hand while thoughtfully contemplating her.

'You're not stupid, Rakel,' he said. 'So I assume you know that this is only a provisional arrangement. There are six months to wait before the case becomes time-barred. A new summons could come at any moment; all it takes is a phone call from me.'

She stared at him and finally he registered signs of life in her dead eyes.

'I think an apology would not be out of place,' he said.

Her bosom heaved, her nostrils quivered. Her eyes filled slowly with tears.

'Well?' he asked.

'Sorry.' Her voice was barely audible.

'You'll have to speak up.'

'Sorry.'

Brandhaug beamed.

'There, there, Rakel.' He dried a tear from her cheek. 'This will be fine. You only have to get to know me. I want us to be friends. Do you understand, Rakel?'

She nodded.

'Sure?'

She sniffled and nodded again.

'Excellent.'

He stood up and loosened his belt buckle.

It was an unusually cold night and the old man had slipped into his sleeping-bag. Even though he was lying on a thick layer of spruce twigs the cold from the ground penetrated his body. His legs had gone stiff, and every now and then he had to rock from side to side to prevent his upper body from losing feeling too.

The windows in the house were still lit, but it was now so dark outside that he could no longer see much through the rifle sights. The situation wasn't hopeless yet though. If the man returned home this evening the outside lamp above the garage entrance, facing the forest, was lit. The old man looked through the sights. Even though the lamp did not give off much light, the colour of the garage door was bright enough to outline him clearly against it.

The old man turned over on to his back. It was quiet here; he would hear the car coming. Provided he didn't fall asleep. The bout of stomach pains had drained him, but he couldn't sleep. He had never slept on duty before. Never. He could feel the hatred and tried to warm himself on it. This was different, this was not like the other hatred which burned on a low, steady flame, which had been there for years, consuming and clearing the undergrowth of small thoughts, creating a perspective and allowing him to see things better. This new hatred burned with such ferocity that he wasn't sure whether he was controlling it or it was controlling him. He knew he must not let himself be dragged along; he had to stay cool.

He looked at the starry sky between the spruce trees above him. It was quiet. So still and cold. He was going to die. They were all going to die. It was a good thought; he tried to keep it in mind. Then he closed his eyes.

Brandhaug stared at the chandelier on the ceiling. A strip of blue light from a Blaupunkt advert outside was reflected in the prisms. So still. So cold.

'You can go now,' he said.

He didn't look at her, just heard the sound of the duvet being folded back and felt the bed rise. Then he heard the sound of clothes being pulled on. She hadn't said a word. Not when he touched her, not when he had ordered her to touch him. She lay there with these large, wide-open, black eyes. Black with fear. Or hatred. That was what had made him so uncomfortable that he hadn't . . .

At first he had ignored it. He had waited for the feeling. Thought of other women he had had, all the times it had worked. But the feeling didn't come and after a while he had asked her to stop touching him. There was no reason why she should be allowed to humiliate him.

She obeyed like a robot. Made sure she kept her end of the bargain, no more, no less. There were six months to wait until Oleg's custody case became time-barred. He had plenty of time. No point getting het up; there would be other days, other nights.

He had gone back to the beginning, but he clearly shouldn't have had the drinks. They had numbed him, made him unresponsive to her caresses and his own.

He had ordered her into the bathtub and made a drink for them both. Hot water, soap. He had held long monologues about how beautiful she was. She hadn't said a word. So quiet. So cold. In the end the water had gone cold too and he had dried her and taken her to bed again. Her skin afterwards was bumpy and dry. She had started to tremble and he had felt her beginning to respond. Finally. His hand had moved downwards, downwards. Then he had seen her eyes again. Big, black, dead. Her gaze fixed on a point on the ceiling. And the magic was gone again. He felt like slapping her, slapping life into her lifeless eyes, slapping her with the flat of his hand, seeing the skin flare up, become inflamed and red.

He heard her taking the letter from the table and opening the clasp on her bag.

'We'll have to drink less next time,' he said. 'That goes for you too.'

She didn't answer.

'Next week, Rakel. Same place, same time. You won't forget, will you?'

'How could I?' she said. The door closed and she was gone.

He got up, mixed himself another drink. Jameson and water, the only good thing to . . . He drank it slowly. Then he lay back.

Soon it was midnight. He closed his eyes, but sleep wouldn't come. From the adjacent room he could hear someone had put on pay-TV. If it was pay-TV, that is. The groans sounded fairly lifelike. A police siren cut through the night. Damn! He tossed and turned. The soft bed had already made his back go stiff. He always had problems sleeping here, not solely because of the bed. The yellow room was and always would be a hotel room, an alien place.

A meeting in Larvik, he had told his wife. And, as usual, when she asked he couldn't remember the name of the hotel they were staying in. Was it Rica, he wondered? If it finished late, he would ring, he had said. But you know how it is with these late-night suppers, darling.

Well, she had nothing to grumble about. He had provided her with a life that was more than she could ever have hoped for with her background. Thanks to him, she had travelled the world, lived in luxurious embassy residences staffed with servants in some of the world's most beautiful cities, learned foreign languages and met exciting people. She had never had to lift a finger all her life. What would she do if she were left on her own, never having worked? He was the basis of her existence, her family, in short everything she had. No, he wasn't that bothered about what Elsa might or might not think.

Nevertheless, it was her he was thinking about right now. He should have been there, with her. A warm, familiar body against his back, an arm round him. Yes, a little warmth after all that coldness.

He looked at his watch again. He could say the supper had finished early and he had decided to drive home. Not only that, she would be happy. She absolutely hated being on her own at night in that big house.

He lay there listening to the sounds coming from the neighbouring room.

Then he got up and quickly began to dress.

* * *

The old man is no longer old. And he is dancing. It is a slow waltz and she has rested her cheek against his neck. They have been dancing for a long time, they are sweaty and her skin is so hot it burns against his. He can feel her smiling. He wants to continue dancing like this, to go on simply holding her until the building burns down, until time stands still, until they can open their eyes and see that they have come to a different place.

She whispers something, but the music is too loud.

'What?' he says, bending his head. She places her lips against his ear.

'You have to wake up,' she says.

He thrust open his eyes. He blinked in the dark before seeing his breath hang rigid and white in front of him. He hadn't heard the car arrive. He turned over, gave a low groan and tried to pull his arms from underneath him. It was the noise of the garage door that had awoken him. He heard the car revving up and just caught the blue Volvo being swallowed up by the dark garage. His right arm had gone to sleep. In a few seconds the man would come out again, stand in the light, close the garage door and then . . . it would be too late.

The old man fumbled desperately with the zip on the sleeping-bag and pulled out his left arm. The adrenaline was coursing through his veins, but sleep wouldn't let go, like a layer of cotton wool muffling all the sounds and preventing him from seeing clearly. He heard the sound of the car door being closed.

Now he had both arms out of the sleeping-bag and fortunately the starlit sky gave him enough light quickly to locate the rifle and put it in position. Hurry, hurry! He rested his cheek against the cold rifle butt. He squinted through the sights. Blinked, couldn't see a thing. With trembling fingers he took off the cloth he had wrapped around the sights to keep the frost off the lens. That's it! Rested his cheek against the butt again. What now? The garage was out of focus, he must have moved the rangefinder. He heard the bang of the garage

door as it was closed. He twisted the rangefinder and the man
below came into focus. He was a tall, broad-shouldered man
wearing a wool coat and standing with his back to him. The
old man blinked twice. The dream still hung like a thin mist
in front of his eyes.

He wanted to wait until the man turned, until he could establish beyond all doubt that he was the right one. His finger
curled around the trigger, pressed it carefully. It would have
been easier with the weapon he had trained on for years, when
the trigger pressure had been in his blood and all the movements had been automatic. He concentrated on his breathing.
Killing someone is not difficult. Not if you have trained to
do it. At the opening of the Battle of Gettysburg in 1863 two
newly recruited companies had stood fifty metres apart and
fired off round after round at each other without anyone being
hit – not because they were bad marksmen, but because they
had aimed above one another's heads. They simply had not
been able to cross the threshold to killing another person. But
when you have done it once . . .

The man in front of the garage turned. He seemed to be
looking directly at the old man. It was him, no doubt about
it. His upper body almost filled the whole of the rifle sights.
The mist in the old man's head was beginning to disperse.
He held his breath and increased the pressure on the trigger
slowly and calmly. The first shot had to hit because it was
pitch-black away from the circle of light by the garage. Time
froze. Bernt Brandhaug was a dead man. The old man's brain
was utterly clear now.

That was why the feeling that he had done something wrong
came a thousandth of a second before he knew what it was.
The trigger wouldn't move. The old man pressed harder, but
the trigger wouldn't budge. The safety catch. The old man
knew it was too late. He found the safety catch with his thumb,
flicked it open. Then he stared through the sights at the empty
cone of light. Brandhaug was gone, was walking towards the
front door on the other side of the house, facing the road.

The old man blinked. His heart was beating against the inside of his ribs like a hammer. He let the air out of his aching lungs. He had fallen asleep. He blinked again. His surroundings seemed to be swimming in a kind of haze now. He had failed. He punched the ground with his clenched fist. It wasn't until the first hot tear fell on to the back of his hand that he realised he was crying.

73

Klippan, Sweden. 10 May 2000.

HARRY WOKE UP.

It took a second before he knew where he was. After he had let himself into the flat the first thing that had occurred to him was that it would be impossible to sleep. There was only a thin wall and a single pane of glass separating the bedroom from the busy road outside. But as soon as the supermarket on the other side of the road had closed for the night, the place seemed to go dead. Hardly a car had passed and the local population seemed to have been swallowed up.

In the supermarket Harry had bought a pizza grandiosa which he heated in the oven. He thought how odd it was to be sitting in Sweden, eating Italian food made in Norway. Afterwards, he switched on the dusty TV which was standing on a beer crate in the corner. There was obviously something wrong with the TV because all the people's faces had this strange green shimmer. He sat watching a documentary. A girl had put together a personal account of her brother, who had spent her entire childhood in the 1970s travelling the world and sending her letters. From the homeless milieu in Paris, a kibbutz in Israel, a train journey through India and the verge of despair in Copenhagen. It had been made very simply. A few film-clips, but mostly stills, a voiceover and a strangely melancholic, sad story. He must have dreamed about it because when he woke up the characters and places were still playing on his retina.

The sound that had woken him came from the coat he had left hanging over the kitchen chair. The high-pitched bleeps bounced off the walls of the bare room. He had switched on the electric panel radiator to full, but he was still freezing under the thin duvet. He placed his feet on the cold lino and took the mobile phone out of his inside coat pocket.

'Hello?'

No answer.

'Hello?'

All he could hear at the other end was breathing.

'Is that you, Sis?'

She was the only person he could immediately think of who had his number and who might conceivably ring him in the middle of the night.

'Is something the matter? With Helge?'

He'd had doubts about giving the bird to Sis, but she had seemed so happy and had promised she would take good care of it. But it wasn't Sis. She didn't breathe like that. And she would have answered.

'Who is it?'

Still no answer.

He was about to hang up when there was a little whimper. The breathing began to quiver; it sounded as if the person at the other end was going to cry. Harry sat down on the sofa bed. In the gap between the thin blue curtains he could see the neon sign of the ICA supermarket.

Harry eased a cigarette out of the packet on the coffee table beside the sofa, lit it and lay back. He inhaled deeply as he heard the quivering breathing change into low sobbing.

'Don't cry now,' he said.

A car passed outside. Had to be a Volvo, Harry thought. Harry covered his legs with the duvet. Then he told the story

about the girl and her elder brother, more or less as he remembered it. When he had finished she wasn't crying any
more and right after he said goodnight, the line was cut.

When the mobile phone rang again it was past 8.00 and
light outside. Harry found it under the duvet, between his
legs. It was Meirik. He sounded stressed.

'Come back to Oslo immediately,' he said. 'Looks like
that Märklin rifle of yours has been used.'

Part Seven

BLACK CLOAK

74

Rikshospital. 10 May 2000.

HARRY RECOGNISED BERNT BRANDHAUG AT ONCE. He had a broad smile on his face and was staring at Harry with wide-open eyes.

'Why's he smiling?' Harry asked.

'Don't ask me,' Klemetsen said. 'The facial muscles go stiff and people have all sorts of weird expressions. Now and then we have parents here who can't recognise their own children because they've changed so much.'

The autopsy table stood in the middle of the room. Klemetsen removed the sheet so they could see the remains of the body. Halvorsen did a swift about-turn. He had rejected Harry's offer of menthol cream before they went in. As the room temperature in Autopsy Room No. 4 in the forensics department at the Rikshospital was twelve degrees, the smell wasn't the worst thing. Halvorsen couldn't stop retching.

'Agreed,' Knut Klemetsen said. 'He's not a pretty sight.'

Harry nodded. Klemetsen was a good pathologist and a considerate man. He was aware that Halvorsen was new and didn't want to embarrass him. Brandhaug looked no worse than most bodies. In other words, he looked no worse than the twins who had lain in water for a week, the eighteen-year-old

who had crashed at 200 kph escaping from the police or the
junkie who had set fire to herself, sitting naked except for a
quilted anorak. Harry had seen most things and as far as his
top ten nasties were concerned, Bernt Brandhaug was well
out of the running. But one thing was clear: for a bullet
through the back Bernt Brandhaug looked horrific. The gaping exit wound in his chest was big enough for Harry to stick
his fist in.

'So the bullet entered through his back?' Harry said.

'Right between his shoulder-blades, angled downwards. It
smashed the vertebral column on entry and the sternum on
its way out. As you can see, parts of the sternum are missing.
They found traces of it on the car seat.'

'On the car seat?'

'Yes, he had just opened the garage door, probably on his
way to work, and the bullet went through him at an angle,
through the front and the rear windscreens, and lodged in
the wall at the back of the garage, no less.'

'What kind of bullet could it be?' asked Halvorsen, who
seemed to have recovered.

'The ballistics experts will have to answer that one,' Klemetsen said. 'But its performance was like a cross between
a dumdum and a tunnel drill. The only place I have ever
seen anything like this was when I was working on a UN
assignment in Croatia in 1991.'

'A Singapore bullet,' Harry said. 'They found the remains
embedded half a centimetre into the wall. The cartridge they
found in the trees nearby was the same kind as the one I found
in Siljan last winter. That was why they contacted me straight
away. What else can you tell us, Knut?'

There wasn't much. He said that the autopsy had already
been carried out, with Kripos present as required by law. The
cause of death was obvious and otherwise there were only
two points he considered worthy of mention – there were
traces of alcohol in Brandhaug's blood and vaginal secretions
had been found under the nail of his right middle finger.

'His wife's?' Halvorsen asked.

'Forensics will establish that,' Klemetsen said, looking at the young policeman over his glasses. 'If they think it necessary. There may not be any need to ask her that sort of thing now, unless you consider it relevant for the investigation.'

Harry shook his head.

They drove up Sognsveien and then up Peder Ankers vei before arriving at Brandhaug's house.

'Ugly house,' Halvorsen said.

They rang the bell and some time passed before a heavily made-up woman in her fifties opened the door.

'Elsa Brandhaug?'

'I'm her sister. What's it about?'

Harry showed his ID.

'More questions?' the sister asked with suppressed anger in her voice. Harry nodded and knew more or less what was about to come.

'Honestly! She's completely worn out and it won't get her husband back, all your —'

'I apologise, but we're not thinking about her husband,' Harry interrupted politely. 'He's dead. We're thinking about the next victim. We're hoping no one else will have to go through what she is experiencing now.'

The sister stood there with her mouth open, unsure how she should continue her sentence. Harry helped her out of her quandary by asking if they should take off their shoes before entering.

Fru Brandhaug didn't seem as worn out as the sister would have had them believe. She was sitting on the sofa staring into thin air, but Harry noticed the knitting protruding from under a cushion. Not that there was anything wrong with knitting when your husband has just been murdered. On reflection, Harry thought it was even quite natural. Something familiar to cling to while the rest of the world crashed around your ears.

'I'm leaving tonight,' she said. 'For my sister's.'

'I understand the police will be here standing guard until further notice,' Harry said. 'In case . . .'

'In case they're after me too,' she said with a nod.

'Do you think they are?' Halvorsen asked. 'And if so, who is "they"?'

She shrugged her shoulders. Stared out of the window at the pale daylight coming into the room.

'I know Kripos have been here and asked you about this,' Harry said. 'But I was wondering if you knew whether your husband was receiving any threats after the newspaper article in yesterday's *Dagbladet.*'

'No one rang here,' she said. 'But then you can only find *my* name in the telephone book. That was how Bernt wanted it. You'll have to ask the Foreign Office if anyone rang.'

'We have done,' Halvorsen said, briefly exchanging glances with Harry. 'We're trying to trace the calls received by his office yesterday.'

Halvorsen asked several questions about any possible enemies her husband might have had, but she didn't have a lot to help them with.

Harry sat down and listened for a while until he suddenly had an idea. He asked, 'Were there absolutely no phone calls yesterday?'

'Yes, there probably were,' she said. 'A couple, anyway.'

'Who phoned?'

'My sister. Bernt. And some opinion poll or other, if I remember correctly.'

'What did they ask about?'

'I don't know. They asked to speak to Bernt. They've got lists of names, haven't they. Along with your age and gender . . .'

'They asked to speak to Bernt Brandhaug, did they?'

'Yes . . .'

'They don't use names for opinion polls. Did you hear any noise in the background?'

'What do you mean?'

'They usually work from those open plan offices with lots of other people.'

'There was something,' she said, 'but . . .'

'But?'

'Not the kind of noise you're thinking of. It was . . . different.'

'When did you receive this call?'

'At about midday, I think. I said he was coming home in the afternoon. I had forgotten Bernt had to go to Larvik for a meal with the Exports Council.'

'Since Bernt's name is not in the telephone directory, did it occur to you that it might have been someone calling everyone called Brandhaug to find out where Bernt lived? And to find out when he was coming home?'

'I don't follow you . . .'

'Opinion pollsters don't phone a man of working age at home in the middle of the working day.'

Harry turned to Halvorsen.

'Check with Telenor to see if you can get hold of the number they rang from.'

'Excuse me, fru Brandhaug,' Halvorsen said. 'I noticed that you have a new Ascom ISDN telephone out in the hallway. I've got the same setup myself. The last ten calls are stored in the memory with number and time. May I . . . ?'

Harry sent Halvorsen an approving look before he got to his feet. Fru Brandhaug's sister accompanied him into the hallway.

'Bernt was old-fashioned in some ways,' fru Brandhaug told Harry with a crooked smile. 'But he liked buying modern things when they came out. Telephones and that sort of thing.'

'How old-fashioned was he with regard to fidelity, fru Brandhaug?'

Her head shot up.

'I thought we could deal with this one while we were alone,' Harry said. 'Kripos checked out what you told them earlier today. Your husband wasn't at any meeting with the Exports Council in Larvik yesterday. Did you know that the Foreign Office has a room at the Continental at its disposal?'

'No.'

'My boss in the Secret Service tipped me off about it this morning. It turns out that your husband checked in there yesterday afternoon. We don't know whether he was alone, but of course you begin to get certain ideas when a husband lies to his wife and goes to a hotel.'

Harry studied her face as it went through a metamorphosis from fury to despair to resignation to . . . laughter. It sounded like low weeping.

'I really shouldn't be surprised,' she said. 'If you absolutely have to know, he was . . . very *modern* in that area too. Though I fail to see what it has to do with the case.'

'It might have given a jealous husband a motive for killing him,' Harry said.

'It gives me a motive too, herr Hole. Have you considered that? When we lived in Nigeria a contract killing cost two hundred Norwegian kroner.' She laughed the same wounded laugh. 'I thought you said the motive was the statement that appeared in *Dagbladet*.'

'We're covering all the options.'

'As a rule they were women he met through work,' she said. 'Of course, I don't know everything that went on, but I caught him red-handed once. And then I saw the pattern and how he had been doing it. But murder?' She shook her head. 'You don't shoot anyone for that sort of thing nowadays, do you?'

She looked at Harry, who didn't know how to respond. Through the glass door to the entrance hall he could hear Halvorsen's deep voice. Harry cleared his throat:

'Do you know if he was conducting a relationship with any particular woman recently?'

She shook her head. 'Ask around in the Foreign Office. It's a strange environment, you know. Bound to be someone there who would be more than willing to give you a pointer.'

She said this without rancour, purely as a matter of information.

They both looked up when Halvorsen came into the room.

'Odd,' he said. 'You did receive a telephone call at 12.24, fru Brandhaug, but not yesterday. The day before.'

'Oh dear, perhaps I mixed up the days,' she said. 'Yes, well, so it has nothing to do with the case, then.'

'Maybe not,' Halvorsen said. 'I checked the number with enquiries anyway. The call came from a pay phone. At Schrøder's café.'

'Café?' she said. 'Yes, that would probably explain the noises in the background. Do you think . . . ?'

'It doesn't necessarily have anything to do with the murder of your husband,' Harry said, getting up. 'There are lots of strange people at Schrøder's.'

She accompanied them to the front steps. It was a grey afternoon outside with low-lying clouds sweeping across the hill behind them.

Fru Brandhaug stood with her arms crossed, as if she were freezing cold.

'It's so dark here,' she said. 'Have you noticed that?'

The Crime Scene Unit was still busy combing the area around the bivouac where they had found the cartridge when Harry and Halvorsen approached from across the heath.

'Hey, you there!' they heard a voice shout as they ducked under the yellow police tape.

'Police,' Harry answered.

'Makes no difference!' the same voice shouted back. 'You'll have to wait until we've finished.'

It was Weber. He was wearing high rubber boots and a comical yellow raincoat. Harry and Halvorsen ducked back under the tape.

'Hey, Weber,' Harry shouted.

'Got no time,' he answered with a dismissive wave.

'It'll take one minute.'

Weber went closer with long strides and an obviously irritated expression on his face.

'What do you want?' he yelled from a distance of twenty
metres.

'How long had he been waiting?'

'The bloke up here? No idea.'

'Come on Weber. A guess.'

'Who's working on this case? Kripos or you?'

'Both. We haven't co-ordinated yet.'

'And are you trying to kid me you're going to?'

Harry smiled and took out a cigarette.

'You've come up with some good guesses before, Weber.'

'Cut out the flattery, Hole. Who's the lad?'

'Halvorsen,' Harry said before Halvorsen had a chance to
introduce himself.

'Listen to me, Halvorsen,' Weber said, regarding Harry
with a disgust he made no attempt to disguise. 'Smoking is a
revolting habit and the ultimate proof that humans are here on
earth for one thing only – enjoyment. The bloke who was here
left eight dog-ends in a half-full pop bottle. Teddy cigarettes,
no filter. And Teddy smokers are not content with two a day, so
unless he ran out, by my reckoning he was here for twenty-
four hours at most. He had cut sprigs of spruce down from
the lowest branches which the rain couldn't get at. But there
were drops of rain on the spruce covering the bivouac. The
last time it rained was three o'clock yesterday afternoon.'

'So he was lying here from somewhere between eight
a.m. and three p.m. yesterday?' Halvorsen asked.

'I think Halvorsen could go far,' Weber said laconically,
with his eyes still on Harry. 'Especially considering the com-
petition he'll have in the force. It's getting bloody worse and
worse. Have you seen what they're recruiting at the police
college now? Even the teacher training colleges are getting
geniuses in comparison with the rubbish we get.'

All of a sudden it seemed that Weber wasn't in a hurry

after all and he set off on a long diatribe about the gloomy prospects for the police force.

'Did anyone living nearby see anything?' Harry quickly asked as Weber paused to draw breath.

'We've got four men doing house to house now, but most of the people won't be back till later. They won't dig up anything.'

'Why not?'

'I don't think he showed himself round here. Earlier today we had a dog following his footsteps for about a kilometre into the forest, to one of the paths. But we lost him there. I would guess he took the same route here and back, following the network of paths between Sognsvann and Lake Maridal. He could have parked a car in at least a dozen car parks for walkers in this area. And there are thousands of them using the paths every day, at least half of them with a rucksack. You see?'

'We see.'

'And now you're probably going to ask me if there are any fingerprints.'

'Well . . .'

'Come on.'

'What about the bottle of pop?'

Weber shook his head.

'No prints. Nothing. Considering how long he was here, he has left surprisingly few traces. We'll keep searching, but I'm pretty positive that the shoe print and a few fibres from his clothing are all we'll find.'

'Plus the cartridge.'

'He left that on purpose. Everything else has been removed a little too thoroughly.'

'Hm. As a warning perhaps. What do you think?'

'What do I think? I thought it was only you young blokes who had been blessed with a bit of brainpower. That's the impression they're trying to promote in the force nowadays.'

'Right. Thanks for your help, Weber.'

'And pack the fags in, Hole.'

'Bit of a stickler,' Halvorsen said in the car on the way down to the city centre.

'Weber can be hard to take sometimes,' Harry conceded. 'But he knows his job.'

Halvorsen drummed the beat to a soundless song on the dashboard. 'What now?' he asked.

'Continental.'

Kripos had phoned the Continental fifteen minutes after they had washed and changed the bedding in Brandhaug's room. No one had noticed Brandhaug had had a visitor, only that he had checked out at around midnight.

Harry stood in reception, pulling at his last cigarette while the duty head receptionist from the previous night wrung his hands and looked unhappy.

'We didn't know that herr Brandhaug had been shot until late morning,' he said. 'Otherwise we wouldn't have touched his room.'

Harry gave a sign of acknowledgement and took a drag of his cigarette. The hotel room was not the scene of any crime; it would simply have been interesting to know if there was any blonde hair on the pillow and to contact whoever may have been the last person to talk to Brandhaug.

'Well, if that's everything then,' the man said with a smile and a faint suggestion he was going to cry.

Harry didn't respond. He had noticed that the head receptionist had become more and more nervous the less he and Halvorsen said. So he said nothing; he waited and watched the glow of his cigarette.

'Er . . .' said the receptionist, running a hand along the lapel of his jacket.

Harry waited. Halvorsen studied the floor. The head receptionist held out for barely fifteen seconds before cracking.

'Of course, he did occasionally have visitors up there,' he said.

'Who?' Harry said without taking his eyes off the glow of his cigarette.

'Women and men . . .'

'Who?'

'As a matter of fact, I don't know. It's none of our business who the Under Secretary of State chooses to spend his time with.'

'Really?'

Silence.

'Of course, if a woman comes here who is obviously not a guest, we do take note which floor she takes the lift to.'

'Would you recognise her?'

'Yes.' The answer came like a shot, no hesitation. 'She was very attractive. And very drunk.'

'Prostitute?'

'If so, then a high-class one. And they tend to be sober. Well, not that I know much about them. This hotel is no —'

'Thank you,' Harry said.

A southerly wind brought in warm weather and, as Harry left the police HQ after the meeting with Meirik and the Chief Constable, he instinctively knew that something had finished. A new season was on its way.

The Chief Constable and Meirik had both known Brandhaug. Only professionally, they both found it necessary to stress. It was clear that the two had discussed the matter in private. Meirik opened the meeting by definitively drawing a line under the undercover job in Klippan. He almost seemed relieved, Harry noted. The Chief Constable then put forward her proposal, and Harry realised that his dashing exploits in Sydney and Bangkok had even left a mark on the upper echelons of the police force.

'Typical sweeper,' the Chief Constable had called Harry. And then she explained the role they were now going to play him in.

A new season. The warm Föhn wind made Harry feel light-headed and he permitted himself a taxi since he was still dragging around a heavy bag. The first thing he did on walking into his flat in Sofies gate was to check the answerphone. The red eye was lit. No blinking. No messages.

He had asked Linda to copy the case file and he spent the rest of the evening going through everything they had on the murders of Hallgrim Dale and Ellen Gjelten. Not that he was expecting to find anything new, but it might stimulate his imagination. He glanced over from time to time at the telephone, wondering how long he would manage to wait before he called her. The Brandhaug case was the main item on the TV news. At midnight he went to bed. At one o'clock he got up, pulled out the telephone jack and put the phone in the fridge. At three o'clock he fell asleep.

75

Møller's Office. 11 May 2000.

'WELL?' MØLLER SAID, AFTER HARRY AND HAL-vorsen had taken their first sip of coffee and Harry, with a grimace, had told him what he thought of it.

'I think the connection between the newspaper article and the killing is a dead duck.'

'Why?' Møller stretched back in his chair.

'In Weber's opinion, the killer had been hiding in the forest since early in the day, so at most a few hours after *Dagbladet* had hit the stands. This was not a spontaneous action; it was a well-planned attack. The killer had known he was going to shoot Brandhaug for some days. He had been out to recce the area; he knew about Brandhaug's comings and goings; he had found the best place to fire from, with the least risk of being seen; he knew how he was going to get in and out, hundreds of tiny details.'

'So you think this is the murder he bought the Märklin rifle for?'

'Maybe. Maybe not.'

'Thanks. That got us a long way,' Møller said acidly.

'I only mean that it is a possibility. On the other hand, it's all completely out of proportion. It seems slightly over the top to smuggle in the world's most expensive assassination rifle to kill a high-ranking though relatively nondescript bureaucrat without a bodyguard or any security staff. Any hitman could literally ring the doorbell and shoot him with a handgun at close range. This is a little like . . . like . . .'

Harry made circle movements with his hands.

'Shooting sparrows with a cannon,' Halvorsen said.

'Exactly,' Harry said.

'Hm.' Møller closed his eyes. 'And what kind of role do you see for yourself in the continuing investigation, Harry?'

'As a kind of sweeper,' Harry smiled. 'I'm the guy from POT who does his own thing, but can request assistance from all other departments whenever necessary. Who reports to Meirik, but has access to all the documents in the case. Who asks questions, but can't be questioned. That sort of thing.'

'What about a licence to kill as well?' Møller said. 'And a very fast car?'

'In fact, this is not my idea,' Harry said. 'Meirik has just been talking to the Chief Constable.'

'The Chief Constable?'

'Yup. I suppose you'll get an email about it during the course of the day. The Brandhaug case has top priority from this minute and the Chief Constable does not want to leave any stone unturned. This is one of those FBI deals where investigation teams have to some degree overlapping duties in order to avoid the standardisation of ideas you get on big cases. You must have read about it.'

'No.'

'The point is that even if you have to duplicate a few of the jobs, and even if the same investigative work is carried out several times by different teams, this is more than outweighed by the advantages of different approaches and different lines of investigation.'

'Thank you,' Møller said. 'What has this got to do with me? Why are you sitting here now?'

'Because, as I said, I can request assistance from all other —'

'. . . departments if necessary. I heard that. Spit it out, Harry.'

Harry angled his head towards Halvorsen, who was smiling somewhat sheepishly at Møller. Møller groaned.

'Please, Harry! You know we're down to the bare bones in Crime Squad.'

'I promise you'll get him back in good condition.'

'I said no!'

Harry said nothing. He waited, entwining his fingers and studying the cheap reproduction of Kittelsen's *Soria Maria Castle* hanging on the wall over the book shelves.

'When will I get him back?' Møller asked.

'As soon as the case is over.'

'As soon . . . That's how a section head answers an inspector, Harry. Not the other way around.'

Harry shrugged.

'Sorry, boss.'

76

Irisveien. 11 May 2000.

HER HEART WAS ALREADY BEATING LIKE A SEW-
ing machine gone wild when she picked up the receiver.

'Hi, Signe,' the voice said. 'It's me.'

She felt the tears coming immediately.

'Stop this,' she whispered. 'Please.'

'Until death us do part. That's what you said, Signe.'

'I'm getting my husband.'

The voice gave a chuckle.

'But he's not there, is he.'

She was squeezing the telephone so tight that her hand
hurt. How could he know that Even wasn't at home? And how
come he only called when Even was out?

The next thought made her throat constrict; she couldn't
breathe and she began to feel faint. Was he calling from a
place where he could see the house, where he could see when
Even went out? No, no, no. With an effort of will, she pulled
herself together and concentrated on breathing. Not too
quickly, deep breaths. *Calm*, she told herself, as she had told
the injured soldiers who were brought in to them from the
trenches; crying, panic-stricken and hyperventilating. She
had her terror under control. And she could hear from the

sounds in the background that he was calling from somewhere with a lot of people. Her house was in a residential
area.

'You were so beautiful in your nurse's uniform, Signe,'
the voice said. 'So shining white and pure. White, exactly
like Olaf Lindvig in his white leather tunic. Do you remember him? You were so pure that I thought you could never
betray us, that you didn't have it in your heart. I thought you
were like Olaf Lindvig. I saw you touch him, his hair, Signe.
One moonlit night. You and he, you looked like angels, as if
you were sent from heaven. But I was mistaken. There are,
by the way, angels which are not heaven-sent, Signe. Did you
know that?'

She didn't answer. Her thoughts churned around her head
in a maelstrom. Something he said had set them in motion.
The voice. She could hear it now. He was distorting his voice.

'No,' she forced herself to answer.

'No? You should do. I am such an angel.'

'Daniel's dead,' she said.

The other end went quiet. Only his breath wheezing
against the membrane. Then the voice again.

'I have come to pass judgment. On the living and the dead.'

Then he rang off.

Signe closed her eyes. She got up and went into the bedroom. She stood behind the drawn blinds and saw herself reflected in the window. She was shaking as if she had a high
temperature.

77

Harry's Old Office. 11 May 2000.

IT TOOK HARRY TWENTY MINUTES TO MOVE BACK
into his old office. Everything he needed found space in a
bag from the 7-Eleven. The first thing he did was to cut out
a picture of Bernt Brandhaug from *Dagbladet*. Then he
pinned it on to the notice-board, beside the archive pictures
of Ellen, Sverre Olsen and Hallgrim Dale. Four clues. He
had sent Halvorsen up to the Department of Foreign Affairs
to make enquiries and see if he could find out who the woman
at the Continental was. Four people. Four lives. Four stories.
He sat down in the wrecked chair and studied them, but they
just stared past him, vacantly.

He rang Sis. She really wanted to keep Helge, at least
for a while. They had become such good friends, she said.
Harry said that was fine as long as she remembered to feed
him.

'It's a her,' Sis said.

'Oh, yes. How do you know that?'

'Henrik and I checked.'

He was going to ask how they had checked, but decided
he preferred not to know.

'Have you talked to Dad?'

She had. She asked Harry if he was going to meet the girl again.

'Which girl?'

'The one you said you'd been for a walk with, I suppose. The one with a little boy.'

'Oh, her. No, I don't think so.'

'Very stupid.'

'Stupid? You've never met her, Sis.'

'I think it's stupid because you're in love with her.'

Now and then Sis was capable of saying things Harry had no idea how to answer. They agreed to go to the cinema one day. Harry wondered if that meant Henrik would be joining them. Sis said it did. That was the way it was when you had a partner.

They rang off and Harry sat deep in thought. He and Rakel had never met in the corridors yet, but he knew where her office was. He made up his mind and got up – he had to talk to her now, he couldn't wait any longer.

Linda flashed him a smile as he came in the door to POT.

'Back already, handsome?'

'I was just going to nip in to see Rakel.'

'Just, was it, Harry? I saw you two at the office party, you know.'

To his irritation, Harry could feel her mischievous smile making his ears burn and could hear that his attempt at a dry laugh didn't quite come off.

'But you can save yourself the walk, Harry. Rakel is at home today. Off sick. One moment, Harry . . .' She picked up the telephone. 'POT. Can I help you?'

Harry was on his way out of the door when Linda called after him.

'It's for you. Do you want to take it here?' She passed him the telephone.

'Is that Harry Hole?' It was a woman's voice. She sounded out of breath. Or terrified.

'That's me.'

'This is Signe Juul. You have to help me, Inspector Hole. He's going to kill me.'

Harry could hear barking in the background.

'Who's going to kill you, fru Juul?'

'He's on his way here now. I know it's him. He . . . he . . .'

'Try to stay calm, fru Juul. What are you talking about?'

'He's distorted his voice, but this time I recognised it. He knew that I had stroked Olaf Lindvig's hair at the field hospital. That was when I knew. My God, what shall I do?'

'Are you alone?'

'Yes,' she said. 'I'm alone. I'm totally, totally alone. Do you understand?'

The barking in the background had become frenzied now.

'Can't you run over to your neighbour's and wait for us there, fru Juul? Who —'

'He'll find me! He finds me everywhere.'

She was hysterical. Harry placed his hand over the receiver and asked Linda to call the central switchboard to tell them to send the closest patrol car available to fru Juul in Irisveien in Berg. Then he talked to Signe Juul and hoped she wouldn't notice his own agitation.

'If you don't go out, then at least lock every door, fru Juul. Who —'

'You don't understand,' she said. 'He . . . he . . .' Beep. The engaged signal. The line was broken.

'Fuck! Sorry, Linda. Tell them the car is urgent. And they have to be careful. There may be an armed intruder.'

Harry rang directory enquiries, got Juul's number and dialled it. Still engaged. Harry threw the phone over to Linda.

'If Meirik asks after me, tell him I'm on my way to Even Juul's house.'

78

WHEN HARRY SWUNG INTO IRISVEIEN HE IMME-
diately saw the police car outside Juul's house. The quiet street
with the timber houses, the puddles of melted ice, the blue
light slowly turning, two inquisitive children on bicycles – it
was like a repetition of the scene outside Sverre Olsen's house.
Harry prayed the similarities would stop there.

He parked, got out of the Escort and walked slowly towards the house. As he closed the door behind him he heard
someone come out on to the stairs.

'Weber,' Harry said in surprise. 'Our paths cross again.'

'Indeed they do.'

'I didn't know you were on patrol duty too.'

'You know bloody well I'm not. But Brandhaug lives
nearby and we had only just got into the car when the message came through on the radio.'

'What's going on?'

'Your guess is as good as mine. There's no one at home.
But the door was open.'

'Have you had a look around?'

'From cellar to loft.'

'Strange. The dog isn't here, either, as far as I can see.'

'Dogs and people, all gone. But it looks as if someone has been in the cellar because the window in the door there is smashed.'

'Right,' Harry said, looking across Irisveien. He caught sight of a tennis court between the houses.

'She may have gone to one of the neighbours,' Harry said. 'I asked her to.'

Weber followed Harry into the hallway where a young police officer was standing looking at the mirror above the telephone table.

'Well, Moen, can you see any signs of intelligent life?' Weber asked sarcastically.

Moen turned and gave Harry a brief nod.

'Well,' Moen said. 'I don't know if it's intelligent or merely weird.'

He pointed to the mirror. The other two came closer.

'Well, I'll be blowed,' Weber said.

The large red letters appeared to have been written with lipstick.

GOD IS MY JUDGE.

Harry's mouth felt like the inside of orange peel.

The glass in the front door rattled as it was torn open.

'What are you doing here?' asked the silhouette standing in front of them with his back to the light. 'And where's Burre?'

It was Even Juul.

Harry sat at the kitchen table with a clearly very worried Even Juul. Moen did the rounds of the neighbours, searching for Signe Juul and asking if anyone had seen anything. Weber had pressing things to do on the Brandhaug case and had to go off in the patrol car, but Harry promised Moen a lift.

'She usually told me when she was going out,' Even Juul said. 'Tells me, I mean.'

'Is that her writing on the mirror in the hall?'

'No,' he said. 'I don't think so, anyway.'

'Is it her lipstick?'

Juul looked at Harry without answering.

'She was terrified when I talked to her on the phone,' Harry said. 'She kept saying someone was trying to kill her. Have you any idea who that could have been?'

'Kill?'

'That's what she said.'

'But no one wants to kill Signe.'

'No?'

'Are you crazy, man?'

'Well, in that case, I'm sure you'll understand that I have to ask you if your wife was unstable. Hysterical.'

Harry wasn't sure that Juul had heard him when Juul shook his head.

'Fine,' Harry said, getting up. 'You'll have to rack your brains for anything at all that might help us. And you should call all your friends and relatives to see if she has gone there for protection. I have started a search – Moen and I will check the immediate vicinity. For the time being, there's not a lot else we can do.'

As Harry closed the door behind him, Moen came walking towards him. He was shaking his head.

'No one even saw a car?' Harry asked.

'At this time of day there are only pensioners and mothers with small children at home.'

'Pensioners are good at noticing things.'

'Not this time, apparently. If there was anything remotely worth noticing, that is.'

Worth noticing. Harry didn't know why, but there was something about Moen's phrasing that resonated at the back of his brain. The children on the bicycles had vanished. He sighed.

'Let's be off.'

79

Police HQ. 11 May 2000.

HALVORSEN WAS ON THE TELEPHONE WHEN Harry went into the office. He put a finger against his lips to show someone was talking. Harry guessed he was still trying to trace the woman at the Continental, and that could only mean he hadn't had any luck at the Foreign Office. Apart from a pile of case notes on Halvorsen's desk, the office was free of paper. Everything but the Märklin case had been cleared away.

'No,' Halvorsen said. 'Let me know if you hear anything, OK?'

He put down the receiver.

'Did you get hold of Aune?' Harry asked, dropping down on to his chair.

Halvorsen nodded and raised two fingers. Two o'clock. Harry consulted his watch. Aune would be there in twenty minutes.

'Get me a picture of Edvard Mosken,' Harry said, picking up the receiver. He tapped in Sindre Fauke's number and they agreed to meet at three. Then he told Halvorsen about Signe Juul's disappearance.

'Do you think it has anything to do with the Brandhaug case?' Halvorsen asked.

'I don't know, but it makes it all the more important that we talk to Aune.'

'Why's that?'

'Because this is beginning to look more and more like the work of someone unhinged. So we need an expert.'

Aune was a big man in many ways. Overweight, almost two metres tall, and he was considered to be the best psychologist in his field. This field was not abnormal psychology, but Aune was a clever man and he had helped Harry on other cases.

He had a friendly, open face and it had often struck Harry that Aune was actually too human, too vulnerable, too *alright* to be able to operate on the battlefield of the human psyche without being damaged by it. When Harry asked him about this, Aune had replied that of course he was affected, but then who wasn't?

Now he was listening attentively to Harry as he spoke. About the slitting of Hallgrim Dale's throat, the murder of Ellen Gjelten and the assassination of Bernt Brandhaug. Harry told him about Even Juul, who thought they should be looking for a soldier who had fought on the Russian Front, a theory which may have been strengthened by Brandhaug being killed after the report in *Dagbladet*. Finally, he told him about Signe Juul's disappearance.

Afterwards Aune sat deep in thought. He grunted as he alternated between nodding and shaking his head.

'I regret to say that I am not sure I can help you much,' he said. 'The only thing I have to work on is the message on the mirror. It's reminiscent of a calling card and it is quite normal for serial killers, especially after several killings when they begin to feel secure enough to want to up the ante by provoking the police.'

'Is he a sick man, Aune?'

'Sick is a relative concept. We're all sick. The question is, what degree of functionality do we have with respect to the rules society sets for desirable behaviour? No actions are in themselves symptoms of sickness. You have to look at the context within which these actions are performed. Most people, for instance, are equipped with an impulse control in the midbrain which attempts to prevent us from killing our fellow creatures. This is just one of the evolutionary qualities with which we are equipped to protect our own species. But if you train long enough to overcome these inhibitions, the inhibition is weakened. As with soldiers, for example. If you or I suddenly began to kill, there is a good chance we would become sick. But that is not necessarily the case if you are a contract killer or a . . . policeman for that matter.'

'So, if we're talking about a soldier – someone who has been fighting for either side during a war – the threshold for killing is much lower than with someone else, assuming both are of sound mind?'

'Yes and no. A soldier is trained to kill in a war situation, and in order for the inhibitions not to kick in, he has to feel that the action of killing is taking place in the same context.'

'So he must feel he is still fighting a war?'

'Put simply, yes. But supposing that is the situation, he can continue killing without being sick in a medical sense. No sicker than any normal soldier, at any rate. Then it is just a matter of a divergent sense of reality, and now we're all skating on thin ice.'

'Why's that?' Halvorsen asked.

'Who is to say what is true or real, moral or immoral? Psychologists? Courts of law? Politicians?'

'Right,' said Harry. 'But there are those who do.'

'Exactly,' Aune said. 'But if you feel that those who have been invested with authority judge you high-handedly or unjustly, in your eyes they lose their moral authority. For instance, if anyone is imprisoned for being a member of a

wholly legal party, you look for another judge. You appeal
against the sentence to a higher authority, so to speak.'

' "God is my judge",' Harry said.

Aune nodded.

'What do you think that means, Aune?'

'It might mean that he wants to explain his actions. Despite everything, he feels a need to be understood. Most
people do, you know.'

Harry dropped in at Schrøder's on his way to meet Fauke.
It wasn't a busy morning and Maja was sitting at the table
under the TV with a cigarette and the newspaper. Harry
showed her the picture of Edvard Mosken which Halvorsen
had managed to produce in an impressively short time, probably via the authority which had issued an international driver's licence to Mosken two years before.

'I think I've seen that prune face before, yes,' she said.
'But how can I remember where or when? He must have
been here a few times since I recognise him. He's not a regular though.'

'Could anyone else have spoken to him?'

'Now you're asking me tricky stuff, Harry.'

'Somebody rang from the pay phone here at 12.30 last
Monday. I'm not expecting you to remember, but *could* it have
been this person?'

Maja shrugged.

'Of course it could. But it *could* have been Father Christmas too. You know what it's like, Harry.'

On his way to Vibes gate Harry rang Halvorsen and
asked him to get hold of Edvard Mosken.

'Should I arrest him?'

'No, no. Check his alibis for the Brandhaug murder and
Signe Juul's disappearance today.'

Sindre Fauke's face was grey when he opened the door to
Harry.

'A friend turned up with a bottle of whisky yesterday,' he explained and pulled a face. 'My body can't take that sort of thing any more. No, if only I were sixty again . . .'

He laughed and went to take the whistling coffee pot off the stove.

'I read about the murder of this man from the Foreign Office,' he shouted from the kitchen. 'It said in the paper that the police are not ruling out the possibility of a link with what he said about Norwegians at the front. *Verdens Gang* reckons neo-Nazis were behind it. Do you really believe that?'

'*VG* might believe that. We don't believe anything and we don't rule out anything either. How's it going with the book?'

'It's going a bit slowly at this minute. But if I finish it, it will open a few people's eyes. That's what I tell myself, anyway, to get myself motivated on days like today.'

Fauke put the coffee on the table between them and sank back into the armchair. He had tied a cold cloth round the pot – an old trick he had learned at the front, he explained with a knowing smile. He was obviously hoping Harry would ask him how the trick worked, but Harry didn't have the time.

'Even Juul's wife has disappeared,' he said.

'Jesus. Run off?'

'Don't think so. Do you know her?'

'I've never met her, but I know a lot about the controversy when Juul was about to get married. She was a nurse at the front and so on. What happened?'

Harry told him about the telephone call and her disappearance.

'We don't know any more than that. I was hoping that you knew her and could give me a lead.'

'Sorry, but . . .' Fauke stopped to take a sip from his cup of coffee. He seemed to be thinking about something. 'What did you say was written on the mirror?'

' "God is my judge",' Harry said.

'Hm.'

'What are you thinking about?'

'To be frank, I'm not sure myself,' Fauke said, rubbing his unshaven chin.

'Come on, say it.'

'You said that he might want to explain himself, to be understood.'

'Yes?'

Fauke walked over to the bookcase, pulled out a thick book and began to leaf through.

'Exactly,' he said. 'Just what I thought.'

He passed the book to Harry. It was a Bible dictionary.

'Look under Daniel.'

Harry's eyes ran down the page until he found the name. '"Daniel. Hebrew. God (El) is my judge".'

He looked up at Fauke, who had lifted the pot to pour coffee.

'You're looking for a ghost, Inspector Hole.'

80

Parkveien, Uranienborg. 11 May 2000.

JOHAN KROHN RECEIVED HARRY IN HIS OFFICE.
The book shelves behind him were crammed with volumes
of legal publications, bound in brown leather. They contrasted
oddly with the lawyer's childlike face.

'We meet again,' Krohn said, motioning Harry to take a
seat.

'You have a good memory,' Harry said.

'There's nothing wrong with my memory. Sverre Olsen.
You had a strong case there. Shame the court didn't manage
to keep to the rule book.'

'That's not why I've come,' Harry said. 'I've got a favour
to ask.'

'Asking costs nothing,' Krohn said, pressing the tips of his
fingers together. He reminded Harry of a child actor playing
an adult.

'I'm looking for a weapon which was imported illegally
and I have reason to believe that Sverre Olsen might have been
involved in some capacity or other. As your client is dead you
are no longer prevented by client confidentiality from provid-
ing us with information. It may help us to clear up the murder

of Bernt Brandhaug, whom we are fairly positive was shot with precisely this weapon.'

Krohn gave a sour smile.

'I would rather you let me decide the boundaries of client confidentiality, officer. There is no automatic assumption that it ceases upon death. And you clearly have not considered the fact that I may regard your coming here to ask for information as somewhat brazen, bearing in mind that the police shot my client?'

'I'm trying to forget emotions and behave professionally,' Harry said.

'Then try a little harder, officer!' Krohn's voice merely became even squeakier when he raised it. 'This is not very professional. In the same way as killing a man in his own home was not very professional.'

'That was self defence,' Harry said.

'A technicality,' Krohn said. 'He is an experienced policeman. He should have known that Olsen was unstable and he should not have burst in as he did. The policeman should obviously have been prosecuted.'

Harry couldn't let that go.

'I agree with you that it's always sad when a criminal goes free on account of a technicality.'

Krohn blinked twice before he realised what Harry meant.

'Legal technicalities are a different kettle of fish, officer,' he said. 'Taking an oath in court may seem to be a detail, but without legal safeguards —'

'My rank is inspector.'

Harry concentrated on speaking softly and slowly:

'The legal safeguard you're talking about cost my colleague her life. Ellen Gjelten. Tell that to that memory you're so damn proud of. Ellen Gjelten. Twenty-eight years old. The best investigative talent in the Oslo police force. A smashed skull. A very bloody death.'

Harry stood up and leaned across Krohn's desk, all one

metre ninety of him. He could see the Adam's apple in Krohn's scrawny vulture neck bobbing up and down, and for two long seconds Harry allowed himself the luxury of relishing the fear in the young lawyer's eyes. Then Harry dropped his business card on the desk.

'Ring me when you've decided the extent of your client confidentiality,' he said.

Harry was half out of the door when Krohn's voice brought him to a halt.

'He called me just before he died.'

Harry turned. Krohn sighed.

'He was terrified of someone. Sverre Olsen was always frightened. Lonely and very frightened.'

'Who isn't?' Harry mumbled. Then, 'Did he say who he was frightened of?'

'The Prince. That was what he called him. The Prince.'

'Did Olsen say why he was frightened?'

'No, he just said that this Prince was a kind of superior and had ordered him to commit a crime. So he wanted to know how far following orders was a punishable offence. Poor idiot.'

'What kind of orders?'

'He didn't say.'

'Did he say anything else?'

Krohn shook his head.

'Ring me any time at all if you think of anything else.'

'And one more thing, Inspector. If you believe that I will lose any sleep over having the man who killed your colleague acquitted, you are mistaken.'

But Harry had already left.

81

Herbert's Pizza. 11 May 2000.

HARRY RANG HALVORSEN AND ASKED HIM TO GO to Herbert's. They had the place almost to themselves and chose a table by the window. Right in the corner there was a man dressed in a long trench coat, with a moustache that went out of fashion with Adolf Hitler and two booted legs resting on a chair seat. He looked as if he was trying to set a new world record in being bored.

Halvorsen had caught up with Edvard Mosken, but not in Drammen.

'He didn't answer when I tried him at home, so I got hold of his mobile phone number through directory enquiries. It turned out he was in Oslo. He has a flat in Tromsøgata in Rodeløkka where he stays when he's at Bjerke.'

'Bjerke?'

'The racetrack. He must be there every Friday and Saturday. Places a few bets and has a bit of fun, he said. And he owns a quarter of a horse. I met him in the stables behind the track.'

'What else did he say?'

'He occasionally pops into Schrøder's in the morning when he's in Oslo. He has no idea who Bernt Brandhaug is and he has definitely never phoned his house. He knew who Signe Juul was – he remembered her from the Eastern Front.'

'What about his alibi?'

Halvorsen ordered a Hawaiian Tropic with pepperoni and pineapple.

'Mosken has been alone in his flat in Tromsøgata all week, apart from trips up to Bjerke, he said. He was there the morning Brandhaug was killed too. And this morning.'

'Right. How do you think he answered your questions?'

'What do you mean?'

'Did you believe him when you were with him?'

'Yes, no; well, believe, hm . . .'

'Go with your gut instinct, Halvorsen, don't be worried. And then say what you feel. I won't use it against you.'

Halvorsen looked down at the table and fidgeted with the menu.

'If Mosken is lying, then he's definitely a pretty cold fish. That much I can say.'

Harry sighed.

'Will you see to it that we put a tag on Mosken? I want two men outside his flat day and night.'

Halvorsen nodded and rang a number on his mobile phone. Harry could hear the sound of Møller's voice as he stole a glance at the neo-Nazi in the corner. Or whatever they called themselves. National Socialists. National Democrats. He had just been sent a copy of a sociology dissertation from the university which concluded that there were fifty-seven neo-Nazis in Norway.

The pizza arrived and Halvorsen sent Harry an enquiring look.

'Go ahead,' Harry said. 'Pizzas aren't my thing.'

The trench coat in the corner had been joined by a short, green combat jacket. They stuck their heads together and looked across at the two policemen.

'One more thing,' Harry said. 'Linda in POT told me that there was an SS archive in Cologne, partly destroyed by fire

in the seventies, but some information had been picked up
there about Norwegians fighting with the Germans. Commands, military awards, ranks, that kind of thing. I want you
to ring them and see if you can find out anything about Daniel
Gudeson. And Gudbrand Johansen.'

'Yessir,' Halvorsen said with his mouth full of pizza.
'When I've finished my pizza.'

'I'll have a chat with our young friends in the meantime,'
Harry said, getting up.

In a work context, Harry had always taken pains not to use
his size to gain a psychological advantage. Yet even though
Hitlermoustache stretched his neck to peer up at Harry, Harry
knew that the cold stare concealed the same fear that he had
witnessed with Krohn. Only this guy had had more training
in disguising it. Harry snatched the chair Hitlermoustache
was resting his boots on and his legs clattered on to the floor
before he had a chance to react.

'Sorry,' Harry said. 'I thought this chair was free.'

'It's the fucking filth,' Hitlermoustache said. The shaven
skull sticking out of the combat jacket swivelled round.

'Right,' Harry said. 'Or the fuzz. Or the pigs. Uncle Nabs.
No, that's a bit too cosy perhaps. What about *les flics?* Is that
international enough?'

'Are we bothering you or what?' the coat asked.

'Yes, you're bothering me,' Harry said. 'You've been both-
ering me for a long time. Say hello to the Prince and tell him
Harry Hole is going to bother him back. From Hole to the
Prince. Did you get that?'

The combat jacket blinked and stared open-mouthed.
Then the coat opened a mouth with teeth splayed out in all
directions and laughed until the saliva ran.

'Are you talking about HRH Haakon Magnus?' he asked,
and when the combat jacket finally got the joke he laughed
along with him.

'Well,' Harry said. 'If you're just the footsloggers, of
course, you won't know who the Prince is. So you'll have to

pass the message on to your next-in-line. Enjoy the pizzas, boys.'

He walked back to Halvorsen and could feel their eyes on his back.

'Eat up,' Harry said to Halvorsen, who was busy with an enormous piece of pizza stretching halfway round his face. 'We have to get out before I get more shit on my record.'

82

Holmenkollen. 11 May 2000.

IT WAS THE WARMEST SPRING EVENING SO FAR.
Harry was driving with the car window open and the gentle
breeze caressed his face and hair. From the top of Holmenkollen he could see Oslo fjord and the islands strewn around
like greenish brown shells, and the first white sails of the
new season were making their way towards land for the evening. A couple of red-capped school-leavers stood urinating
at the edge of the road, beside a red bus with loudspeakers
mounted on the roof. The music was booming out: *Won't –
you – be my lover* . . .

An elderly lady wearing hiking breeches, and with an
anorak tied around her waist and a tired but beatific expression on her face, was ambling down the road.

Harry parked down from the house. He didn't want to go
all the way up the drive, he didn't quite know why – perhaps
because he thought it would seem less invasive to park at the
bottom. Ridiculous, of course, since his visit had been unan-
nounced and uninvited.

He was halfway up the drive when his mobile phone
bleeped. It was Halvorsen ringing from the Traitors' Archive.

'Nothing,' he said. 'If Daniel Gudeson really is alive, he certainly wasn't convicted after the war.'

'And Signe Juul?'

'She was sentenced to one year.'

'But never went to prison. Anything else of interest?'

'Zilch. And now they're getting ready to chuck me out and close up.'

'Go home and sleep – perhaps we'll come up with something tomorrow.'

Harry had arrived at the foot of the steps and was going to take them in one jump when the door opened. He stood still. Rakel was wearing a woollen jumper and blue jeans; her hair was untidy and her face paler than usual. He searched her eyes for any indication that she was happy to see him again, but found none. But nor was there the neutral courtesy he had dreaded most. Her eyes expressed nothing, whatever that meant.

'I heard someone talking outside,' she said. 'Come in.'

Oleg was in the sitting room, watching TV in his pyjamas.

'Hi loser,' Harry said. 'Shouldn't you be practising Tetris?'

Oleg snorted without taking his eyes off the TV.

'I always forget that children don't understand irony,' Harry said to Rakel.

'Where have you been?' Oleg asked.

'Been?' Harry was a little baffled by Oleg's accusatory expression. 'What do you mean?'

Oleg rolled his shoulders.

'Coffee?' Rakel asked. Harry nodded. Oleg and Harry sat in silence watching the gnu's incredible migration through the Kalahari Desert while Rakel clattered around in the kitchen. It took time, the coffee and the migration.

'Fifty-six thousand,' Oleg said finally.

'That's not true,' Harry said.

'I top the all-time-high list!'

'Go and get it.'

Oleg was on to his feet and out of the sitting room as

Rakel brought in the coffee. She sat facing Harry. He found the remote control and turned down the sound of thundering hooves. It was Rakel who broke the silence in the end.

'So what are you going to do on 17 May this year?'

'Work. But if you're suggesting an invitation to something, I'll move heaven and earth . . .'

She laughed and dismissed the idea with a wave.

'Sorry, I was just making conversation. Let's talk about something else.'

'You've been ill, haven't you?' Harry asked.

'That's a long story.'

'You have a number of them.'

'Why are you back from Sweden?' she asked.

'Brandhaug. With whom, strangely enough, I was sitting right here.'

'Yes, life throws up bizarre coincidences,' Rakel said.

'So bizarre that you would never get away with it in fiction, anyway.'

'You don't know the half of it, Harry.'

'What do you mean?'

She sighed and stirred her tea.

'What is this?' Harry asked. 'Is the whole family communicating in coded messages this evening?'

She attempted a laugh, but it ended up in a sniffle. *Spring cold*, Harry thought.

'I . . . it . . .'

She tried to start the sentence a couple more times, but nothing coherent emerged. The teaspoon in her cup went round in circles. Over her shoulder Harry glimpsed a gnu being slowly and pitilessly dragged into the river by a crocodile.

'I've had a terrible time,' she said. 'And I've been pining for you.'

She turned to Harry, and it was only now that he saw she was crying. The tears rolled down her cheeks and collected under her chin. She made no attempt to stop them.

'Well . . .' Harry began, and that was all he managed to

say before they were in each other's arms. They clung to each other as to a lifebuoy. Harry was shaking. *Just this*, Harry thought. *Just this is enough. Just holding her like this.*

'Mummy!' The shout came from the first floor. 'Where's the GameBoy?'

'In one of the drawers in the dressing-table,' Rakel shouted in a quivering voice. 'Start at the top.'

'Kiss me,' she whispered to Harry.

'But Oleg might —'

'It's not in the dressing-table.'

When Oleg came downstairs with the GameBoy, which he finally found in the toy box, he didn't notice the atmosphere in the sitting room at first and laughed at Harry, who was hm-hming with concern at seeing the new score. But as soon as Harry set off to beat the new record, he heard Oleg say, 'What's up with your faces?'

Harry looked at Rakel, who was only just capable of keeping a straight face.

'It's because we like each other so much,' Harry said, replacing three lines with one long line out on the right. 'And your record is on the ropes now, loser.'

Oleg laughed and slapped Harry on the shoulder.

'No chance. You're the loser.'

83

Harry's Flat. 11 May 2000.

HARRY DIDN'T FEEL LIKE A LOSER WHEN, SHORTLY before midnight, he unlocked the door to his flat and saw the red eye on the answerphone blinking. He had carried Oleg to bed and drunk tea, and Rakel had said that one day she would tell him a long story. When she wasn't so exhausted. Harry had answered that she needed a holiday, and she agreed.

'We could go together, all three of us,' he had said, 'when this business is over.'

She had stroked his hair.

'This is not the sort of thing to be flippant about, Harry Hole.'

'Who's being flippant?'

'I can't talk about this now. Go on home, Harry Hole.'

They had kissed a little more in the hallway, and Harry still had the taste of her on his lips.

Without turning on the light, he crept into the sitting room in stockinged feet and pressed the PLAY button of the answerphone. Sindre Fauke's voice filled the darkness:

'Fauke here. I've been thinking. If Daniel Gudeson is more than a ghost, there's only one person on this earth who

can solve this riddle. And that's the man who was on watch
that New Year's Eve when Daniel Gudeson was apparently
shot dead: Gudbrand Johansen. You have to find Gudbrand
Johansen, Inspector Hole.'

Then there was the sound of the receiver being replaced,
a bleep, and where Harry expected the click, a new message
instead.

'Halvorsen here. It's 11.30. I've just received a call from
one of the officers outside Mosken's flat. They've been waiting and waiting, but he hasn't returned home. So they tried
to ring the number in Drammen, just to see if he would answer the phone. But he didn't answer. One of the men drove
to Bjerken, but everything was locked up and the lights were
off. I asked them to stick it out for a while yet and put out a
call for Mosken's car on police radio. Just so you know. See
you tomorrow.'

New bleep. New message. New record on Harry's answerphone.

'Halvorsen again. I'm going senile. I completely forgot to
mention the other thing. Looks as if we've finally had a bit
of luck. The SS archive in Cologne didn't have any personal
details about Gudeson or Johansen. They told me to ring the
central Wehrmacht archive in Berlin. There I talked to a
nice old grump who said that very few Norwegians had been
in the regular German army. But when I explained the matter to him, he said he would check anyway. After a while he
rang back and said that, as expected, he hadn't found anything about Daniel Gudeson. However, he had found copies
of some papers concerning one Gudbrand Johansen, also a
Norwegian. It appeared from the papers that he had been
transferred from the Waffen SS to the Wehrmacht in 1944.
A note was made on the copies that the original papers were
sent to Oslo in the summer of 1944, which, according to our
man in Berlin, could only mean that Johansen had been sent
there. He also found some correspondence with a doctor who
had signed Johansen's medical certificates. In Vienna.'

Harry sat down on the only chair in the room.

'The doctor's name was Christopher Brockhard, at the Rudolf II Hospital. I checked with the Viennese police and it turns out the hospital is still fully functional. They even gave me the name and telephone number of twenty-odd people who worked there during the war and are still alive.'

The Teutons know how to archive, Harry thought.

'So I began ringing round. I'm really crap at speaking German!'

Halvorsen's laughter crackled in the loudspeaker.

'I rang eight of them before I found a nurse who could remember Gudbrand Johansen. She was an old lady of seventy-five. Remembered him very well, she said. You'll have the number and her address tomorrow morning. By the way, her name is Mayer. Helena Mayer.'

A crackly silence was followed by a bleep and the click of the tape recorder stopping.

Harry dreamed about Rakel, about her face burrowing into his neck, about her strong hands, and Tetris blocks falling and falling. But it was Sindre Fauke's voice that woke him in the middle of the night and made him stare at the contours of a figure in the dark.

'You have to find Gudbrand Johansen.'

84

Akershus Fortress. 12 May 2000.

IT WAS 2.30 IN THE MORNING AND THE OLD MAN
had parked his car beside a low warehouse in a street called
Akershusstranda. Years ago the street had been a main thor-
oughfare in Oslo, but after the Fjellinje tunnel had been
opened Akershusstranda had been closed off at one end and
was only used during the day by those working in the docks.
And prostitutes' clients who wanted a relatively undisturbed
place for the 'walk'. Between the road and the water there
were several warehouses and on the other side was the western side of Akershus Fortress. Naturally, if anyone had taken
up a position in Aker Brygge with a quality riflescope they
would certainly have been able to see the same as the old
man did: the back of a grey coat which jerked every time the
man inside it thrust his hips forward, and the face of a very
made-up and very drunken woman who was being banged
against the west wall of the fortress, right under the cannons.
On each side of the mating couple was a floodlight projector
lighting up the rock face and the wall above them.

Akershus, the WWII Wehrmacht prison. The internal
section of the fortress area was closed for the night, and even
though he could probably find his way in, the risk of being

discovered in the actual place of execution was too great. No one really knew how many were shot there during the war, but there was a memorial plaque for fallen Norwegian Resistance men. The old man knew that at least one of them was a common criminal who had deserved his punishment whichever way you looked at it. And it was there they had shot Vidkun Quisling and the others who had been tried for war crimes and sentenced to death. Quisling had been imprisoned in the Powder Tower. The old man had often wondered if the Powder Tower had inspired Jens Bjørneboe's book, in which he described, in great detail, various methods of execution over the centuries. Was his description of execution by firing squad actually a portrait of the execution of Vidkun Quisling that October day in 1945 when they led the traitor out to the square to drill his body with bullets? Had they, as the author wrote, placed a hood over his head and fastened a white square of cloth over his heart as a marker? Had they given the command to shoot four times before the shots rang out? And had the trained marksmen shot so badly that the doctor with the stethoscope had been forced to say that the condemned man would have to be executed again – until they had done it four or five times and death occurred through loss of blood from the many surface wounds?

The old man had cut out the description from the book.

The grey coat had finished his business and was on his way down the slope to his car. The woman still stood by the wall; she had pulled her skirt back into place and lit a cigarette which glowed in the dark when she inhaled. The old man waited. Then she crushed the cigarette under her heel and began to walk down the muddy path round the fortress and back to her 'office' in the streets around Norges Bank.

The old man turned towards the back seat where the gagged woman stared at him with the same petrified eyes he had seen when she became conscious after being given diethyl ether. He could see her mouth moving behind the gag.

'Don't be frightened, Signe,' he said, leaning over and

fastening something on to her coat. She tried to bend her head to see what it was, but he forced her head up.

'Let's go for a walk,' he said. 'As we used to.'

He got out of the car, opened the rear door, pulled her out and shoved her in front of him. She stumbled and fell on the gravel in the grass beside the path, but he caught hold of the rope which bound her hands behind her back and pulled her to her feet. He positioned her directly in front of one of the floodlight projectors, with the light in her eyes.

'Stand still. I forgot the wine,' he said. 'Red Ribeiros. You can remember it, can't you? Quite still, otherwise I . . .'

She was blinded by the light and he had to put the knife right in front of her face for her to see it. Despite the piercing light, the pupils were so large that her eyes seemed almost completely black. He went down to the car and scouted around. No one in sight. He listened and all he heard was the usual drone of the town. Then he opened the boot. He shoved the black rubbish bag to the side and could feel that the body of the dog inside had already begun to go stiff. The steel of the Märklin rifle twinkled darkly. He took it out and sat in the front seat. He rolled the window half-down and rested the gun on it. When he looked up he could see her gigantic shadow dancing on the yellowish brown sixteenth-century wall. The shadow had to be visible all the way across the bay from Nesodden. Beautiful.

He started up the car with his right hand and revved the engine. He took a last look around before peering through the sights. The distance was barely fifty metres and her coat filled the whole of the circle in the sight lens. He shifted his aim marginally to the right and the black cross-hair found what he was searching for – the white piece of paper. He released the air from his lungs and crooked his finger around the trigger.

'Welcome back,' he whispered.

Part Eight

THE REVELATION

85

Vienna. 14 May 2000.

HARRY TREATED HIMSELF TO THREE SECONDS OF relishing the sensation of cool leather against the back of his neck and forearms on the seats of Tyrolean Air. Then he went back to his reflections.

Beneath them the countryside lay like an unbroken patchwork of green and yellow, with the Danube glittering in the sun like a weeping brown wound. The air stewardess had just informed them that they were about to land in Schwechat, and Harry prepared himself.

He had never been ecstatic about flying, but in recent years he had begun to be downright frightened. Ellen had once asked him what he was frightened of. 'Crashing and dying, what the fuck else?' he had answered. She had told him that the odds of dying in a plane on the occasional trip were thirty million to one against. He had thanked her for the information and said he wasn't frightened any longer.

Harry breathed in deep and then out as he listened to the changing sounds of the engine. Why did the fear of death get worse as you got older? Shouldn't it be the other way around? Signe Juul was seventy-nine years old. Presumably she had been scared out of her wits. One of the guards at

Akershus Fortress had found her. They had received a telephone call during their watch from a sleepless millionaire
celebrity at Aker Brygge, informing them that one of the
projectors on the southern wall had gone out, and the duty
officer had sent one of the young guards out. Harry had
questioned him two hours later, and he had told Harry that
as he approached the projector he had seen a lifeless woman
slumped across it, obstructing the light. At first he had thought
she was a junkie, but as he moved closer and saw the grey
hair and old-fashioned clothes, he realised she was an elderly
woman. His next thought was that she had been taken ill, but
then he discovered her hands were tied behind her back. It
was only when he was right up close that he saw the gaping
hole in her coat.

'I could see that her spine had been smashed,' he had told
Harry. 'Shit, I could *see* her spine.'

Then he had told him how he had propped himself against
the rock-face as he threw up, and it was only later when the
police had come to take away the body and the light shone
on the wall again that he realised what the sticky stuff on his
hand was. He had shown Harry his hand, as if it were important.

The Crime Scene Unit had arrived and Weber had walked
across to Harry while studying Signe Juul through sleepy
eyes. He said God wasn't the bloody judge, it was the bloke
down below.

The only witness was a night-watchman who kept an
eye on the warehouses. He had met a car going down Akershusstranda on its way east at 2.45, but because the driver's
lights had been on full beam he had been dazzled and hadn't
been able to see the make of the car or the colour.

It felt as if the pilot was accelerating. Harry imagined they
were trying to gain height because the captain had suddenly
seen the Alps right in front of the cockpit. Then it felt as if
the air beneath the wings of the Tyrolean Air plane had vanished and Harry felt his stomach shoot up under his ears. He

groaned out loud when the next moment they bounced up again like a rubber ball. The captain came on to the intercom and said something in German and English about turbulence.

Aune had pointed out that if someone didn't have the capacity to feel fear, they would not survive a single day. Harry squeezed the arm of the chair and tried to find comfort in that thought.

In fact it had been Aune who had supplied the impetus for Harry taking the first available plane to Vienna. Once he'd had the facts laid on the table, he had immediately said that time was of the utmost importance.

'If we're dealing with a serial killer, he's on the point of losing control,' Aune had said. 'Not like the classical serial killer who looks for sexual release, but is then disappointed every time and increases the frequency of the killings out of sheer frustration. This murderer clearly isn't sexually motivated. He has some sick plan or other which has to be completed, and up until now he has been cautious and has behaved rationally. The fact that the murders are close to each other and that he has gone to great lengths to emphasise the symbolism of his actions – as with this execution at Akershus Fortress – suggests that he either feels invincible or he's losing his grip, maybe developing a psychosis.'

'Or perhaps he's still totally in control,' Halvorsen had said. 'He hasn't slipped up yet. We still don't have any clues.'

And he was absolutely bloody right, Halvorsen was. There were no clues.

Mosken had been able to account for his movements. He had picked up the telephone in Drammen when Halvorsen rang in the morning to check, since the surveillance boys hadn't caught a sniff of him in Oslo. Of course they couldn't know if what he said was true: that he had driven to Drammen after Bjerke Stadium closed at half past ten and had arrived at half past eleven. Or if he had arrived at half past two in the morning and had thus been in a position to shoot Signe Juul.

Harry, without much hope, had asked Halvorsen to ring the neighbours and ask if they had heard or seen Mosken arrive. And he had asked Møller to talk to the Public Prosecutor to see if they could get a search warrant for both of Mosken's flats. Harry knew that their arguments were weak and, quite rightly, the Public Prosecutor had answered that he at least wanted to see something that resembled circumstantial evidence before he would give the go-ahead.

No clues. It was time to start panicking.

Harry closed his eyes. Even Juul's face was still imprinted on his retina. Grey, closed. He had sat slumped in the armchair in Irisveien with the dog lead in his hand.

Then the wheels touched down, and Harry could confirm that he was among the thirty million fortunate ones.

The policeman whom the police boss in Vienna had kindly placed at his disposal as driver, guide and interpreter was standing in the arrivals hall with dark suit, sunglasses, bull-like neck and an A4 piece of paper with MR HOLE written on it in felt-pen.

The bull-neck introduced himself as Fritz (*Someone has to be called Fritz*, Harry thought) and led Harry to a navy-blue BMW which a moment later was whizzing north west on the motorway towards the city, past the factory chimneys spewing out white smoke and past well-behaved motorists who tucked into the right as Fritz accelerated.

'You'll be staying at the spy hotel,' Fritz said.

'The spy hotel?'

'The venerable old Imperial. That's where the Russian and the Western agents defected during the cold war. Your boss must be floating in funds.'

They arrived at the Kärntner Ring and Fritz pointed.

'That's the spire of Stephansdom you can see across the rooftops to the right,' he said. 'Beautiful, isn't it? Here's the hotel. I'll wait while you check in.'

The receptionist at the Imperial smiled when he saw Harry eyeing the reception area with admiration.

'We've renovated it at a cost of forty million schillings so that it's exactly as it was before the war. It was almost completely destroyed by bombing in 1944 and it was fairly run down a few years ago.'

When Harry left the lift on the second floor it was like walking on springy peat, the carpets were so thick and soft. The room was not particularly big, but there was a broad four-poster bed that looked as if it was at least a hundred years old. On opening the window he could smell the bakery of the cake shop across the street.

'Helena Mayer lives in Lazarettegasse,' Fritz informed him when Harry was back in the car again. He hooted at a car switching lanes without signalling.

'She's a widow and has two grown-up children. She worked as a teacher after the war until she retired.'

'Have you spoken to her?'

'No, but I've read her file.'

The address in Lazarettegasse was a property that must have been elegant at one time. But now the paint was peeling from the walls in the spacious stairwell, and the echoes of their shuffling steps mingled with the sound of dripping water.

Helena Mayer stood smiling by the entrance to her flat on the third floor. She had lively brown eyes and apologised for the stairs.

The flat was slightly over-furnished and full of all the knick-knacks people collect over the course of their lives.

'Please sit down,' she said. 'I only speak German, but you may talk to me in English. I can understand well enough,' she said, turning to Harry.

She brought in a tray with coffee and cakes. 'Strudel,' she explained, pointing to the cake dish.

'Yum,' Fritz said and helped himself.

'So you knew Gudbrand Johansen,' Harry said.

'Yes, I did. That is, we called him Uriah. He insisted on that. At first we thought he wasn't all there. Because of his injuries.'

'What sort of injuries?'

'Head injuries. And his leg, of course. Dr Brockhard was on the point of amputating it.'

'But he recovered and was sent to Oslo in the summer of 1944, wasn't he?'

'Yes, that was the idea.'

'What do you mean by that?'

'Well, he disappeared, didn't he? And I don't suppose he turned up in Oslo, did he?'

'Not as far as I know, no. Tell me, how well did you know Gudbrand Johansen?'

'Very well. He was extrovert and a good storyteller. I think all the nurses, one after the other, fell in love with him.'

'You too?'

She laughed a bright, trill laugh. 'Me too. But he didn't want me.'

'No?'

'Oh, I was good-looking, I can tell you – it wasn't that. Uriah wanted someone else.'

'Really?'

'Yes, her name was Helena too.'

'Which Helena is that?'

The old lady furrowed her brow.

'Helena Lang, it must have been. Their love for each other was what caused the tragedy.'

'What tragedy?'

She stared at Harry and Fritz in surprise and then looked back at Harry again.

'Isn't that why you're here?' she said. 'Because of the murder?'

86

Palace Gardens. 14 May 2000.

IT WAS SUNDAY. PEOPLE WERE WALKING MORE slowly than usual and the old man kept up with them as he walked through the Palace Gardens. He stopped by the guardhouse. The trees were light green, the colour he liked best of all. All except for one tree, that is. The tall oak tree in the middle of the gardens would never be any greener than it was now. You could already see the difference. After the tree had awoken from its winter slumber, the life-giving sap had begun to circulate and spread the poison around the network of veins. Now it had reached every single leaf and promoted a luxuriant growth, which in a week or two would cause the leaves to wither, go brown and fall, and finally the tree would die.

But they didn't know that yet. They obviously didn't know anything. Bernt Brandhaug had not been part of the original plan, and the old man realised that the killing had confused the police. Brandhaug's comments in *Dagbladet* were just one of those weird coincidences and he had laughed out loud when he read them. My God, he had even agreed with Brand-haug. The defeated should swing, that is the law of war.

But what about all the other clues he had given them?

They hadn't even managed to connect the great betrayal with the execution at Akershus Fortress. Perhaps it would dawn on them the next time the cannons were fired on the ramparts.

He looked around for a bench. The pains were coming closer and closer together now. He didn't need to go to Buer to find out that the cancer was spreading through his whole body; he knew that himself. It wouldn't be long now.

He leaned against a tree. A royal birch, the symbol of occupation. Government and King flee to England. *German bombers are overhead*, a line from a poem written by Nordahl Grieg, made him feel nauseous. It presented the King's betrayal as an honourable retreat, as if leaving his people in their hour of need were a moral act. And in the safety of London the King had just been yet another of these exiled majesties who held moving speeches for sympathetic upperclass women over entertaining dinners as they clung to the hope that their little kingdom would one day want them back. And when the whole thing was over, there was the reception as the boat carrying the Crown Prince moored on the quayside and all those who had turned out screamed themselves hoarse to drown out the shame, both their own and the King's. The old man turned towards the sun and closed his eyes.

Shouted commands, boots and AG3 guns smacked into the gravel. Handover. Changing of the guard.

87

Vienna. 14 May 2000.

'So you didn't know?' Helena Mayer said.

She shook her head and Fritz was already on the phone to get someone to search through old filed murder cases.

'I'm sure we'll find it,' he whispered. Of that Harry had no doubt.

'So the police were positive that Gudbrand Johansen killed his own doctor?' Harry asked, turning to the old lady.

'Yes, indeed. Christopher Brockhard lived alone in one of the flats at the hospital. The police said that Johansen smashed the glass in the outside door and killed him as he was sleeping in his own bed.'

'How . . . ?'

Frau Mayer flashed a dramatic finger across her throat.

'I saw him myself afterwards,' she said. 'You could almost have believed the doctor had done it himself, the cut was so neat.'

'Hm. And why were the police so sure it was Johansen?'

She laughed.

'Yes, I can tell you that – because Johansen had asked the guard which flat Brockhard lived in and the guard had seen him park outside and go in through the main entrance.

Afterwards he had come running out, started his car and driven off at full speed towards Vienna. The next day he was gone and no one knew where, only that according to his orders he was supposed to be in Oslo three days later. The Norwegian police waited for him but he never turned up.'

'Apart from the guard's testimony, can you remember if the police had any other evidence?'

'If I can remember? We talked about that murder for years! The blood on the glass door matched his blood type. And the police found the same fingerprints in Brockhard's bedroom as on Uriah's bedside table and bed in the hospital. Furthermore, he had the motive . . .'

'Really?'

'Yes, they loved each other, Gudbrand and Helena. But she was to be Christopher's.'

'They were engaged?'

'No, no. But Christopher was crazy about Helena. Everyone knew that. Helena was from a rich family that had been ruined after her father had ended up in prison, and a marriage into the Brockhard family was her and her mother's way of getting back on their feet. And you know how it is – a young woman has certain obligations to her family. At least, she did, at that time.'

'Do you know where Helena Lang is today?'

'But you haven't touched the strudel, my dear,' the widow exclaimed.

Harry took a big bite, chewed and nodded in approval to Frau Mayer.

'No,' she said. 'That I don't know. When it became known that she had been with Johansen on the night of the murder, she was investigated, but they didn't find anything. She stopped working at the Rudolf II Hospital and moved to Vienna. She started up her own sewing business. Yes, she was a strong, enterprising woman. I occasionally saw her walking in the streets here. But in the mid-fifties she sold up and after that I didn't hear any more. Someone said she had gone abroad. But I know who you can ask – if she's alive, mind you. Beatrice Hoffmann, she worked as the house help for the Lang family. After the murder the family could no longer afford her and she worked for a time at the Rudolf II.'

Fritz was already on the telephone again.

A fly buzzed desperately around the window. It was following its own microscopic logic and kept banging into the glass without understanding quite why. Harry stood up.

'Strudel . . . ?'

'Next time, Frau Mayer. Right now we don't have the time.'

'Why's that?' she asked. 'This happened more than half a century ago. It isn't going anywhere.'

'Well . . .' Harry said, watching the black fly under the lace curtains in the sun.

Fritz received a call on his mobile on the way to the police station and did a highly improper U-turn which made the motorists behind them jump on their horns.

'Beatrice Hoffmann is alive,' he said accelerating through the lights. 'She's at an old people's home in Mauerbachstraße. That's up in the Vienna Woods.'

The BMW turbo squealed with glee. The blocks of flats gave way to half-timbered houses, vineyards and finally the green deciduous forest, with the afternoon sun playing on the leaves and creating a magical atmosphere as they sped along avenues lined with beech and chestnut trees.

A nurse led them out into the large garden.

Beatrice was sitting on a bench in the shade of an enormous, gnarled oak tree. A straw hat dominated the tiny, wrinkled face. Fritz spoke with her in German and explained why they had come. The old woman inclined her head with a smile.

'I'm ninety years old,' she said in a shaky voice. 'And tears still come to my eyes when I think about Fräulein Helena.'

'Is she still alive?' Harry asked in his schoolboy German. 'Do you know where she is?'

'What's that he says?' she asked with her hand behind
her ear. Fritz explained.

'Yes,' she said. 'Yes, I know where Helena is. She's sitting up there.'

She pointed up into the treetops.

There you go, Harry thought. *Senile.* But the old lady
hadn't finished speaking.

'With St Peter. Good Catholics, the Langs, but Helena
was the angel in the family. As I said, it always brings tears
to my eyes thinking about it.'

'Do you remember Gudbrand Johansen?' Harry asked.

'Uriah,' Beatrice said. 'I only met him once. A handsome,
charming young man, but sick unfortunately. Who would
have believed that such a nice, polite boy would have been
able to kill? Their emotions ran away with them, yes, with
Helena too. She never got over him, the poor thing. The police never found him and although Helena was never accused
of anything, André Brockhard saw to it that she was thrown
out of the hospital. She moved into town and did voluntary
work for the Archbishop until the family was in such dire financial straits that she was forced to find paid work. So she
started a sewing business. Within two years she had fourteen
women sewing for her full-time. Her father was released but
couldn't find work after the Jewish banker scandal. Frau
Lang took the family's fall from grace worst. She died after
a long illness in 1953 and Herr Lang the same autumn in a
car accident. Helena sold the business in 1955 and left the
country without any explanation to anyone. I can remember
the day. It was 15 May, Austria's liberation day.'

Fritz saw Harry's curious expression and explained.

'Austria is a little unusual. Here we don't celebrate the day
Hitler capitulated, but the day the Allies left the country.'

Beatrice spoke about how she had received news of
Helena's death.

'We hadn't heard from her for more than twenty years
when one day I received a letter postmarked Paris. She was

there on holiday with her husband and daughter, she wrote. It was a kind of final journey, I realised. She didn't say where she had settled down, whom she had married or what illness she had. Only that she hadn't long to live and she wanted me to light a candle for her in Stephansdom. She was an unusual person, Helena was. She was seven years old when she came to me in the kitchen and turned these grave eyes on me. "Humans were created by God to love," she said.'

A tear ran down the old lady's lined cheek.

'I'll never forget it. Seven years old. I think she decided then and there how she was going to live her life. And even though it definitely wasn't as she had imagined and her trials were many and sore, I'm convinced she believed it to the bottom of her heart all her life – that humans were created by God to love. That's how she was.'

'Do you still have the letter?' Harry asked.

She wiped away her tears and nodded.

'I have it in my room. Let me sit here and reminisce a little. We can go there afterwards. By the way, this will be the first hot night of the year.'

They sat in silence, listening to the rustle of the branches and the small birds singing as the sun went down behind Sophienalpe, as each of them thought of those gone before. Insects jumped and danced in the pillars of light under the trees. Harry thought about Ellen. He spotted a bird he could have sworn was the flycatcher he had seen pictures of in the bird book.

'Let's go,' said Beatrice.

Her room was small and plain, but light and snug. A bed stood against the back wall, which was covered with pictures of all sizes. Beatrice rummaged through some papers in a large dressing-table drawer.

'I have a system, so I'll find it,' she said. *Naturally*, Harry thought.

At that moment his eyes fell on a photograph in a silver frame.

'Here's the letter,' Beatrice said.

Harry didn't answer. He stared at the photograph and didn't react until he heard her voice right behind him.

'That photograph was taken while Helena was working at the hospital. She was beautiful, wasn't she?'

'Yes, she was,' Harry said. 'There's something oddly familiar about her.'

'Nothing odd about her,' Beatrice said. 'They've been painting her on icons for almost two thousand years.'

It *was* a hot night. Hot and sultry. Harry tossed and turned in the four-poster, threw the blanket on the floor and pulled the sheet off the bed as he tried to shut out all his thoughts and sleep. For a moment he had considered the minibar, but then he remembered he had taken the minibar key off the ring and handed it in to reception. He heard voices in the corridor outside. Someone grabbed the handle of his door and he shot up in bed, but no one came in. Then the voices were inside, their breath hot against his skin, the ripping sound of clothes being shredded, but when he opened his eyes he saw flashes of light and he knew it was lightning.

A rumble of thunder, sounding like distant explosions, came first from one part of town, then another. He went to sleep again and kissed her, took off her white nightdress. Her skin was white and cold and uneven from sweating, from the terror; he held her for a long, long time until she was warm, until she came back to life in his arms, like a flower filmed over a whole spring and then played back at breakneck speed.

He continued to kiss her, on the neck, on the inside of her arms, on the stomach, not with insistence, not even teasingly, but half to comfort her, half comatose, as if he could vanish at any moment. And when she followed, waveringly, because she thought it was safe where they were going, he continued to lead her until they arrived in a landscape not even he recognised, and when he turned it was too late and she threw herself into his embrace, cursing him, begging him and tearing at him with her strong hands until his skin bled.

He was awoken by his own panting and had to turn over in bed to make sure he was still alone. Afterwards, everything merged in a maelstrom of thunder, sleep and dreams. He awoke in the middle of the night to the sound of beating rain; he went over to the window and stared down at the street where water was streaming over the edges of the pavement and an ownerless hat drifted along with it.

When Harry was awoken by his early-morning alarm call it was light outside and the streets were dry.

He looked at his watch on the bedside table. His flight to Oslo left in two hours.

88

Thereses Gate. 15 May 2000.

STÅLE AUNE'S OFFICE WAS YELLOW AND THE walls were covered with shelves crammed with specialist books and drawings of Kjell Aukrust's cartoon characters.

'Take a seat, Harry,' Doctor Aune said. 'Chair or divan?'

That was his standard opener, and Harry responded by raising the left-hand corner of his mouth in his standard that's-funny-but-we've-heard-it-before smile. When Harry had rung from Gardemoen Airport, Aune had said Harry could come, but that he didn't have a lot of time as he had to go to a seminar in Hamar at which he was to give the opening speech.

'It's entitled "Problems Related to the Diagnosis of Alcoholism",' Aune said. 'You won't be mentioned by name.'

'Is that why you're all dressed up?' Harry asked.

'Clothes are one of the strongest signals we transmit,' Aune said, running a hand along a lapel. 'Tweed signals masculinity and confidence.'

'And the bow-tie?' Harry asked, taking out his notebook and pen.

'Intellectual frivolity and arrogance. Gravity with a touch

of self-irony, if you like. More than enough to impress second-rate colleagues, it seems.'

Aune leaned back, pleased with himself, his hands folded over his bulging stomach.

'Tell me about split personalities,' Harry said. 'Or schizo-phrenia.'

'In five minutes?' Aune groaned.

'Give me a summary then.'

'First of all, you mention split personalities and schizo-phrenia in the same breath, and that is one of these misunderstandings that for some reason has caught the public's imagination. Schizophrenia is a term for a whole group of widely differing mental disorders and has nothing at all to do with split personalities. It's true *schizo* is Greek for split, but what Doctor Eugen Bleuler meant was that psychological functions in a schizophrenic's brain are split. And if . . .'

Harry pointed to his watch.

'Right,' Aune said. 'The personality split you talked about is called an MPD, a multiple personality disorder, defined as the existence of two or more personalities in an individual which take turns in being the dominant partner. As with Dr Jekyll and Mr Hyde.'

'So, it exists?'

'Oh, yes. But it's rare, a lot rarer than some Hollywood films would have us believe. In my twenty-five years as a psychologist I've never been lucky enough to observe a single instance of an MPD. But I do know something about it all the same.'

'For example?'

'For example, it is almost always connected with a loss of memory. In other words, an MPD sufferer could wake up with a hangover without realising that it is because their other personality is a drinker. Well, in fact, one personality can be an alcoholic and the other a teetotaller.'

'Not literally, I take it?'

'Certainly.'

'But alcoholism is a physical ailment too.'

'Yes, and that's what makes MPDs so fascinating. I have a report of an MPD case where one of the personalities was a big smoker while the other never touched cigarettes. And when you measured the blood pressure of the smoker it was 20 per cent higher. Women with an MPD have reported that they menstruate several times a month because every personality has its own cycle.'

'So these people can change their own physical nature?'

'To a certain degree, yes. The story about Dr Jekyll and Mr Hyde is in fact not so far from the truth as one might think. In one well-known case described by Dr Osherson, one of the personalities was heterosexual while the other was homosexual.'

'Can the personalities have different voices?'

'Yes. Actually the voice is one of the easiest ways to observe the shift between personalities.'

'So different that even someone who knows this person extremely well would not recognise one of these other voices. On the phone, for example?'

'If the individual concerned knew nothing about the other personality, yes. With people who have only a superficial knowledge of the MPD patient, the change in gestures and body language can be enough for them to sit in the same room and not recognise the person.'

'Could someone with an MPD keep it hidden from those closest to them?'

'It's feasible, yes. How frequently the other personalities appear is an individual matter and patients can to some degree control the changes themselves, too.'

'But then the personalities would have to know about each other?'

'Yes, indeed, but that's not unusual either. And, just as in the novel about Dr Jekyll and Mr Hyde, there can be bitter clashes between the personalities because they have different goals, perceptions of morality, sympathies and antipathies with respect to the people around them and so on.'

'What about handwriting? Can they mess around with that too?'

'This is not messing around, Harry. You aren't the same person all the time, either. When you get home from work a whole load of imperceptible changes take place in you too: your voice, body language and so on. It's odd that you should mention handwriting because somewhere here I've got a book with a picture of a letter written by an MPD patient with seventeen totally different and totally consistent handwriting styles. I'll see if I can find it one day when I have more time.'

Harry noted down a few reminders on his pad.

'Different menstrual cycles, different handwriting; it's just absolutely insane,' he mumbled.

'Your words, Harry. I hope that helped because I've got to run.'

Aune ordered a taxi and they went out on to the street together. As they stood on the pavement Aune asked Harry if he had any plans for Independence Day on 17 May. 'Wife and I are going to have a few friends round for a meal. You're very welcome.'

'Kind of you, but the neo-Nazis are planning to "take" the Muslims who celebrate Eid on the seventeenth and I've been instructed to coordinate surveillance round the mosque in Grønland,' Harry said, both happy and embarrassed at the surprise invitation. 'They always ask us singles to work on such family celebration days, you know.'

'Couldn't you just drop in for a while? Most of the people who come have something of their own to go to later on in the day.'

'Thanks. Let's see what happens and I'll give you a ring. What are your friends like anyway?'

Aune checked his bow-tie to make sure it was straight.

'They're like you,' he said. 'But my wife knows a few respectable people.'

At that moment the taxi pulled into the kerb. Harry held the door open while Aune scrambled in, but as he was about to shut it he suddenly remembered something.

'What are MPDs caused by?'

Aune bent over in his seat and looked up at Harry.

'What's this actually about, Harry?'

'I'm not quite sure, but it might be important.'

'Alright. MPD cases have often been subject to abuse in their childhood. But a disorder could also be caused by extremely traumatic experiences later in life. Another personality is created to flee from problems.'

'What sort of traumatic problems might that be if we're talking about an adult male?'

'You just have to use your imagination. He might have experienced a natural disaster, lost someone he loved, been a victim of violence or lived in fear for a protracted period of time.'

'Like being a soldier at war, for example.'

'War could certainly be a trigger, yes.'

'Or guerrilla warfare.'

Harry said the latter to himself, as the taxi taking Aune was already on its way down Thereses gate.

'Scotsman,' Halvorsen said.

'You're going to spend 17 May in the Scotsman pub?' Harry grimaced, putting his bag behind the hatstand.

Halvorsen shrugged his shoulders. 'Any better suggestions?'

'If it has to be a pub, at least find one with a bit more style than the Scotsman. Or better still, relieve one of the fathers here and do one of the watches during the children's parade. Double pay and zero hangover.'

'I'll think about it.'

Harry slumped down into the chair.

'Aren't you going to get it fixed soon? It sounds decidedly out of sorts.'

'It can't be fixed,' Harry said sulkily.

'Sorry. Did you find anything in Vienna?'

'I'm coming to that. You first.'

'I tried to check Even Juul's alibis for the time his wife went missing. He claimed he was walking round the city centre, popped into the Kaffebrenneri in Ullevålsveien, but he didn't meet anyone there who could corroborate his story. The staff working in the Kaffebrenneri say they're too busy to be able to prove or disprove anything.'

'The Kaffebrenneri is right across the street from Schrøder's,' Harry said.

'So?'

'I'm just stating a fact. What did Weber say?'

'They haven't found anything. Weber said that if Signe Juul had been taken to the fortress in the car the night-watchman saw, they would have found something on her clothes, fibres from the back seat, soil or oil from the boot, something.'

'He'd spread out bin liners in the car,' Harry said.

'That's what Weber said too.'

'Did you check the dry hay they found on her coat?'

'Yep. It *could* be from Mosken's stable. Plus a million other places.'

'Hay. Not straw.'

'There's nothing special about the hay, Harry, it's just . . . hay.'

'Damn.' Harry looked around him grumpily.

'What about Vienna?'

'More hay. Do you know anything about coffee, Halvorsen?'

'Eh?'

'Ellen used to make decent coffee. She bought it in some shop here in Grønland. Maybe . . .'

'No!' Halvorsen said. 'I'm not making you coffee.'

'Promise me you'll try,' Harry said, getting up again. 'I'll
be out for a couple of hours.'

'Was that all you had to say about Vienna? Hay? Not
even a straw in the wind?'

Harry shook his head. 'Sorry. That was a dead end too.
You'll get used to it.'

Something had happened. Harry walked up along Grønlandsleiret as he tried to put his finger on what it was. There
was something about the people in the streets, something
had happened to them while he was in Vienna. He was a
long way up Karl Johans gate before he realised what it was.
Summer had arrived. For the first time in years Harry was
aware of the smell of tarmac, of the people passing him, of
the flower shop in Grensen. As he walked through the Palace Gardens the smell of freshly mown grass was so intense
that he had to smile. A man and a woman wearing Palace
overalls stood looking up at the top of a tree, discussing and
shaking their heads. The woman had unbuttoned the top of
her overall and tied it around her waist. Harry noticed that
when she looked up at the tree and pointed, her colleague
was stealing furtive glances at her tight T-shirt instead.

In Hedgehaugsveien the hip and the not quite so hip fashion boutiques were going through their final paces to dress
people up for the Independence Day celebrations. The kiosks
were selling ribbons and flags, and in the distance he could
hear the echo of a band putting its final touches to the traditional marching tune. Showers were forecast, but it would be
warm.

Harry was sweating when he rang the doorbell at Sindre
Fauke's.

Fauke was not particularly looking forward to the national holiday.

'Too much fuss. And too many flags. No wonder Hitler

felt close to the Norwegians. Norwegians are hugely nation-alistic. We just dare not admit it.'

He poured the coffee.

'Gudbrand Johansen ended up at the military hospital in Vienna,' Harry said. 'The night before he was supposed to leave for Norway he killed a doctor. Since then no one has seen him.'

'Well, I never,' Fauke said, loudly slurping the scalding hot coffee. 'I knew there was something wrong with that boy.'

'What can you tell me about Even Juul?'

'A lot. If I have to.'

'Well, you have to.'

Fauke raised a bushy eyebrow.

'Are you sure you're not barking up the wrong tree now, Hole?'

'I'm not sure of anything at all.'

Fauke blew at his coffee thoughtfully.

'OK. If it's absolutely necessary. Juul and I had a rela-tionship which was like Gudbrand Johansen and Daniel Gudeson's in many ways. I was a surrogate father for Even. It probably has something to do with the fact that he had no parents.'

Harry's coffee cup stopped in mid-air on the way to his mouth.

'Not many people knew that because Even used to make things up as he went along. His invented childhood consisted of more people, details, places and dates than most people would remember from their childhood. The official version was that he had grown up with the Juul family on a farm in Grini, but the truth is that he grew up with various foster par-ents and in various institutions around Norway before finally landing in the childless Juul family as a twelve-year-old.'

'How do you know he lied about it?'

'It is rather a strange story, but one night Even and I were on watch outside the camp we had set up in the forest, north

of Harestua, when something strange happened to him.
Even and I were not particularly close at that point and I was
extremely surprised when he began to tell me about how he
had been abused as a child and how nobody had ever wanted
him. He told me some extremely intimate details of his life,
and some of it was painful listening. Some of the adults he
had been placed with ought to have been . . .' Fauke shuddered.

'Let's go for a walk,' he said. 'Rumour has it the weather's
nice outside.'

They walked up Vibes gate to Stenspark, where the first
bikinis were on display and a glue-sniffer had strayed from
his shelter at the top of the hill looking as if he had just discovered planet Earth.

'I don't know what brought it on, but it was as if he became another person that night,' Fauke said. 'Very odd, but
the strangest thing was that the next day he behaved as if he
had forgotten the conversation we had had.'

'You said that you weren't very close, but you told him
about some of your experiences on the Eastern Front?'

'Yes, of course. Not a lot else was happening in the forest.
For the most part we were moving around and keeping an
eye on the Germans. And there were quite a few long stories
while we were waiting.'

'Did you talk much about Daniel Gudeson?'

Fauke stared at Harry.

'So, you've found out that Even Juul is obsessed by Daniel Gudeson?'

'I'm just guessing for the time being,' Harry said.

'Yes, I talked about Daniel a lot,' Fauke said. 'He was like
a legend, Daniel Gudeson was. It's rare to meet such a free,
strong and happy spirit as him. And Even was fascinated by
the stories. I had to tell them again and again, especially the
one about the Russian he went into no man's land to bury.'

'Did he know that Daniel had been to Sennheim during
the war?'

'Of course. Even remembered all the details about
Daniel I was beginning to forget and he reminded me. For
some reason, he seemed to have totally identified with Daniel, although I can hardly imagine two more different people.
Once when Even was drunk he suggested I start to call him
Uriah, just as Daniel had done. And if you ask me, it was no
coincidence that he only had eyes for young Signe Alsaker
at the end of the war.'

'Oh?'

'When he found out that Daniel Gudeson's fiancée's case
was due to come up, he went to the courtroom and sat there
all day just looking at her. It was as if he had decided in advance that he was going to have her.'

'Because she had been Daniel's girl?'

'Are you sure this is important?' Fauke asked, walking
up the path towards the hill so quickly that Harry had to
walk faster to keep up with him.

'Absolutely.'

'I'm not sure if I should say this but, personally, I believe
Even Juul loved the myth of Daniel Gudeson more than he
ever loved Signe Juul. I'm sure that his admiration for Gudeson was a strong contributory factor in his not resuming
medical studies after the war, but studying history instead.
Naturally enough, he specialised in the history of the Norwegian Occupation and the Norwegian soldiers at the Eastern
Front.'

They had arrived at the top and Harry wiped away his
sweat. Fauke was hardly out of breath.

'One of the reasons that Even Juul established himself so
quickly as a historian was that as a former Resistance man
he was a perfect instrument for writing the history that the
authorities felt postwar Norway deserved. By keeping quiet
about the widespread collaboration with the Germans and
focusing on the little resistance there was. For instance, Juul
devotes five pages to the sinking of the *Blücher* on the night
leading to 9 April in his history book, but he quietly ignores

the fact that prosecutions against almost 100,000 Norwegians were being considered at the trials. And it worked. The myths of a Norwegian population fighting shoulder to shoulder *against* Nazism live on today.'

'Is that what your book will be about, herr Fauke?'

'I'm only trying to tell the truth. Even knew that what he was writing was, if not lies, then a distortion of the truth. We talked about it once. He defended himself by saying that it served the purpose of bringing the people together. The only thing he couldn't bring himself to put in the desired heroic light was the King's escape to freedom. He wasn't the only Resistance man who felt deserted in 1940, but I've never met anyone so one-sidedly condemnatory as Even, not even among soldiers on the front. Remember that all his life he had been abandoned by people he loved and trusted. I think he hated every single one of them who left for London with the whole of his heart. Really.'

They sat down on a bench and looked down over Fagerborg church, the roofs in Pilestredet which led down towards the town and the blue Oslo fjord twinkling far away.

'It's beautiful,' Fauke said. 'So beautiful that it can sometimes seem worth dying for.'

Harry tried to take it all in, to make it fit. But there was one minor detail missing.

'Even began to study medicine in Germany before the war. Do you know where in Germany?'

'No,' Fauke said.

'Do you know if he had any specialisation in mind?'

'Yes, he told me that he dreamed of following in the footsteps of his famous foster father and his father.'

'And they were?'

'You don't know about the Juul consultants? They were surgeons.'

89

Grønlandsleiret. 16 May 2000.

BJARNE MØLLER, HALVORSEN AND HARRY WERE walking side by side down Motzfeldts gate. They were in deepest Little Karachi and the smells, the clothes and the people around them reminded them as little of Norway as the kebabs they were chewing on reminded them of Norwegian grilled sausages. A boy, dressed up for the festivities in a Pakistani style, but with a 17 May ribbon on his gilt jacket lapels, came slapping down the pavement towards them. He had a strange, snubbed nose and was holding a Norwegian flag in his hand. Harry had read in the papers that Muslim parents were arranging a 17 May party for children today so that they could concentrate on Eid tomorrow.

'Hurrah!'

The boy flashed them a white smile as he sped past.

'Even Juul is not just anyone,' Møller was saying. 'He's perhaps our greatest authority on war history. If this is right, there'll be a hell of a fuss in the newspapers. It doesn't bear thinking about, if we're mistaken. If *you* are mistaken, Harry.'

'All I'm asking for is permission to bring him in for questioning, with a psychologist present. And a search warrant for his house.'

'And all I'm asking for is at least one piece of evidence or a witness,' Møller said, gesticulating. 'Juul is well-known, and no one has seen him anywhere near the crime scenes. Not once. What about the telephone call Brandhaug's wife received from your local hostelry, for example?'

'I showed the photo of Even Juul to the woman working at Schrøder's,' Halvorsen said.

'Maja,' Harry prompted.

'She couldn't remember seeing him,' Halvorsen said.

'That's exactly what I'm saying,' Møller groaned, wiping the sauce from his mouth.

'Yes, but I showed the photo to a couple of them sitting there,' Halvorsen said, casting a quick glance at Harry. 'There was an old guy in a coat who nodded and said we should arrest that one.'

'Coat,' Harry repeated. 'That's the Mohican, Konrad Åsnes, wartime seaman. He's quite a character, but not a reliable witness any more, I'm afraid. Anyway, Juul has told us that he was at the Kaffebrenneri across the road. There are no pay phones over there. So if he was going to ring it would be natural to go over to Schrøder's.'

Møller pulled a face and looked sceptically at his kebab. He had only tagged along, somewhat unwillingly, to try the burek kebab which Harry had talked up as 'Turkey meets Bosnia meets Pakistan meets Grønlandsleiret'.

'And do you really believe all that split-personality stuff, Harry?'

'I think it sounds just as incredible as you do, boss, but Aune reckons it's a possibility. And he's willing to help us.'

'And so you think Aune can hypnotise Juul and can coax out this Daniel Gudeson inside him and get a confession?'

'It's not definite that Even Juul has any idea what Daniel Gudeson has done, so it's absolutely essential that we speak to him,' Harry said. 'According to Aune, people suffering from MPDs are very susceptible to hypnosis, since that's what they're doing to themselves all the time – self-hypnosis.'

'Great,' said Møller, rolling his eyes. 'So what's the idea with the search warrant?'

'As you've said yourself, we have no evidence, no witnesses and we know you can never rely on the court buying all the psycho-stuff, but if we find the Märklin rifle, we're home and dry. We don't need any of the rest.'

'Hm.' Møller came to a halt on the pavement. 'Motive?'

Harry probed Møller's face.

'My experience is that even confused people usually have a motive in their madness. And I can't see Juul's.'

'Not Juul's, boss,' Harry said. 'Daniel Gudeson's. Signe Juul's sort of going over to the enemy might have given Gudeson the motive for revenge. What he wrote on the mirror – *God is my judge* – may suggest that he views the murders as a one-man crusade, that his is a just cause, despite the condemnation of others.'

'What about the other murders? Bernt Brandhaug and – if you're right that it is the same murderer – Hallgrim Dale?'

'I have no idea what the motives are, but we know that Brandhaug was shot with the Märklin rifle and Dale knew Daniel Gudeson. And according to the autopsy report Dale was cut up as if a surgeon had done the job. OK, Juul was beginning to study medicine and dreamed of becoming a surgeon. Perhaps Dale had to die because he had discovered that Juul was acting like Daniel Gudeson.'

Halvorsen cleared his throat.

'What?' Harry asked sourly. He had known Halvorsen long enough to anticipate that an objection was on its way. And very probably a well-founded one.

'From what you've told us about MPDs, it must have been Even Juul who killed Hallgrim Dale. Daniel Gudeson wasn't a surgeon.'

Harry swallowed the last bite of kebab, wiped his face with the serviette and looked around for a litter bin.

'OK,' he said. 'I could have said that we should wait until we have the answers to all our questions before we do anything. And I am aware that the Public Prosecutor will consider the evidence pretty thin. But none of us can ignore the fact that we have a suspect who might kill again. You're frightened of the media circus, boss, if we charge Even Juul, but imagine the row that would break out if he committed any more murders. And then it came out that we had suspected him all along without doing anything to stop him . . .'

'Yes, yes, yes, I know all that,' Møller said. 'So you think he'll kill again?'

'There are a lot of things in this case I'm unsure about,' Harry said. 'But if there's one thing I'm absolutely certain of it's that he hasn't completed his project yet.'

'And what makes you so sure about that?'

Harry tapped his stomach and pulled a sardonic grin.

'There's someone in here, morsing it up to me, boss. There's a reason why he bought the most expensive and best assassination rifle in the world. One of the reasons Daniel Gudeson became a legend was that he was a fantastic marksman. And something down here is telling me that he's decided to take this crusade to its logical conclusion. It's going to be the crowning glory, something to immortalise the legend of Daniel Gudeson.'

The summer heat vanished for a second as a last wintry gust swept up Moztfeldtsgate, swirling the dust and the litter. Møller closed his eyes, pulled his coat tighter around himself and shuddered. *Bergen*, he thought. *Bergen*.

'I'll see what I can manage,' he said. 'Make sure you're ready.'

90

Police HQ. 16 May 2000.

HARRY AND HALVORSEN WERE READY. SO READY that when Hole's telephone rang, they both jumped up. Harry seized the receiver: 'Hole speaking!'

'You don't need to shout,' Rakel said. 'That's why the phone was invented. What was it you said about the seventeenth the other day?'

'What?' It took Harry a few seconds to connect. 'That I'm on duty?'

'The other thing,' Rakel said. 'That you would move heaven and earth . . .'

'Do you mean that?' Harry felt a strange, warm feeling in his stomach. 'You would like to be with me if I get someone to do my shift?'

Rakel laughed.

'Now you sound nice. I should point out that you weren't my first choice, but since father has decided that he wants to be on his own this year, the answer is yes, we would like to be with you.'

'What does Oleg say to that?'

'It was his suggestion.'

'Yes? He's a clever lad, that Oleg.'

Harry was happy. So happy that it was difficult to speak with his normal voice. And he didn't give a damn that Halvorsen was sitting across the desk from him with a grin spread from ear to ear.

'Have we got a deal?' Rakel's voice tickled his ear.

'If I can make it, yes. I'll ring you later.'

'OK, or you could come over for something to eat this evening. If you had the time, that is. Or the inclination.'

The words came across as so exaggeratedly offhand that Harry knew she had been practising them before she rang. His laughter was bubbling inside him, his head as light as if he had taken a narcotic substance, and he was about to say yes when he remembered something she had said in the res-taurant: *I know it won't stop with the one time.* It wasn't some-thing to eat she was offering him.

If you had the time, that is. Or the inclination.

If he was going to panic, now was the time.

His thoughts were interrupted by the telephone flashing.

'I've got a call on the other line which I have to take. Rakel, can you hang on for a second.'

'Of course.'

Harry pressed the square key. It was Møller.

'The arrest warrant is ready. The search warrant's on its way. Tom Waaler is all set with two cars and four armed men. I hope to Christ that the morse-code guy in your guts has a steady hand, Harry.'

'He fucks up the odd letter, but never a whole message,' Harry said, signalling to Halvorsen that he should put on his jacket. 'See you.' Harry slammed down the phone.

They were standing in the lift on their way down when it occurred to Harry that Rakel was still on the other line, wait-ing for an answer. He didn't have the mental energy to work out what that meant.

91

Irisveien, Oslo. 16 May 2000.

THE FIRST SUMMER'S DAY OF THE YEAR HAD BE-
gun to cool as the police car rolled into the quiet residential
area of detached houses. Harry was ill at ease. Not only because he was sweating under the bulletproof vest, but because
it was *too* quiet. He stared at the curtains behind the meticu-
lously trimmed hedges, but nothing stirred. It felt like a
Western and he was riding into an ambush.

At first, Harry had refused to put on a bulletproof vest, but
Tom Waaler, who was in charge of the operation, had given
him a simple ultimatum: either put on the vest or stay at
home. The argument that a bullet from a Märklin rifle would
cut through the vest like the proverbial knife through butter
had occasioned only a bored shrug with Waaler.

They went in two police cars. The second, in which
Waaler sat, had gone up Sognsveien, into Ullevål Hageby, to
enter Irisveien from the opposite direction, from the west.
He could hear Waaler's voice crackle over the walkie-talkie.
Calm and confident. Asked for position, went through the
procedure again and the emergency procedure, asked every
single officer to repeat their assignment.

'If he's a pro, he might have connected an alarm to the gate, so we'll go *over* not *through*.'

He was efficient, even Harry had to concede that, and it was clear that the others in the car respected Waaler.

Harry pointed to the red timber house.

'There it is.'

'Alpha,' the policewoman in the front seat said into the walkie-talkie. 'We can't see you.'

Waaler: 'We're right round the corner. Keep out of sight from the house until you can see us. Over.'

'Too late. We're there now. Over.'

'OK, but stay in the car until we come to you. Over and out.'

The next moment they saw the nose of the second police car coming round the bend. They drove the last fifty metres to the house and parked the car to block the exit from the garage. The second car stopped in front of the garden gate.

As they got out of the cars, Harry heard the dull echo of a tennis ball being struck by a not too tautly strung tennis racquet. The sun was moving towards Ullernåsen and he caught the smell of frying pork chops coming from one window.

Then the show was on. Two police officers jumped over the fence with MP-5 machine guns at the ready and sprinted round the outside of the house, one to the right and one to the left.

The policewoman in Harry's car stayed where she was; her job was to maintain radio contact with the central switchboard and to keep potential spectators away. Waaler and the last officer waited until the other two were in position, secured their walkie-talkies in their breast pockets and jumped over the gate with service pistols raised. Harry and Halvorsen stood behind the police car, watching the whole show.

'Cigarette?' Harry asked the policewoman.

'No thanks,' she smiled.

'I was wondering if you had any.'

She stopped smiling. *Typical non-smoker*, Harry thought.

Waaler and the officer were standing on the step, having taken up positions on either side of the door, when Harry's mobile phone rang.

Harry saw the police officer's eyes roll. *Typical amateur*, she was probably thinking.

Harry was about to switch off his mobile – he just checked it wasn't Rakel's number on the display first. The number was familiar, but it wasn't Rakel's. Waaler had already raised his hand to give the signal when Harry realised who was ringing. He took the walkie-talkie from the open-mouthed police officer.

'Alpha! Stop. The suspect is ringing me right now. Can you hear me?'

Harry looked over to the step where Waaler was nodding his head. Harry pressed the button on his mobile and pressed it to his ear.

'Hole speaking.'

'Hello.' To Harry's surprise, it wasn't Even Juul. 'This is Sindre Fauke. My apologies for disturbing you, but I am standing in Even Juul's house and I think you should come here.'

'Why? And what are you doing there?'

'I think I might have done something stupid. He rang me an hour ago and told me to come over immediately, his life was in danger. I drove up and found the door open, but no Even. And now I'm afraid he's locked himself in his bedroom.'

'Why do you think that?'

'The bedroom door is locked and when I tried to peep through the keyhole, the key was on the inside.'

'OK,' Harry said, walking round the car and through the gate. 'Listen carefully. Stay exactly where you are. If you are holding anything in your hands put it down and keep your hands where we can see them. We'll be there in two seconds.'

Harry walked towards the doorstep, with Waaler and the other policeman following his movements with amazement. He pressed down the door handle and went in.

Fauke was standing in the hall with the telephone receiver in his hand, gaping at them in amazement.

'My God,' was all he could say when he spotted Waaler with the revolver in his hand. 'That was quick . . .'

'Where's the bedroom?' Harry asked.

Fauke pointed mutely towards the stairs.

'Show us,' Harry said.

Fauke led the way for the three officers.

'Here.'

Harry felt the door; quite right, it was locked. There was a key in the lock which he tried to turn, but it wouldn't move.

'I didn't manage to tell you. I was trying to open the door with one of the keys from the other bedroom,' Fauke said. 'Sometimes they fit.'

Harry took out the key and put his eye to the keyhole. Inside he could see a bed and a bedside table. There was what seemed to be a lightshade lying on the bed. Waaler was talking in a low voice on the walkie-talkie. Harry could feel the sweat beginning to filter down the inside of his vest again. He didn't like the look of the lightshade.

'I thought you said there was a key on the inside too?'

'There was,' Fauke said. 'Until I knocked it out trying to get the other key in.'

'So how will we get in?' Harry asked.

'It's on the way,' Waaler said, and at that moment they heard heavy boots running up the stairs. It was one of the officers who had taken up a position behind the house and he was carrying a red crowbar.

'This way,' Waaler said, pointing.

Splinters flew. The door sprang open.

Harry strode in and heard Waaler telling Fauke to wait outside.

The first thing Harry noticed was the dog lead. Even Juul had hung himself with it. He had died wearing a white shirt, open at the neck, black trousers and checked socks. A toppled chair lay behind him in front of the wardrobe. His shoes were neatly placed under the chair. Harry looked up at the ceiling. The lead had been tied to a ceiling hook. Harry tried to refrain, but couldn't stop himself from examining Even Juul's face. One eye stared out into the room while the other was fixed on Harry. Independently. Like a two-headed troll with an eye in each head, Harry thought. He walked over to the window facing east and watched the children cycling along Irisveien, drawn by the rumours of police cars which always spread with inexplicable speed in areas like this.

Harry closed his eyes and reflected. *The first impression is important. The first thought that came into your mind at the scene is often the most accurate.* Ellen had taught him that. His own trainee had taught him to concentrate on the first thing he felt when he came to the scene of the crime. That was why Harry didn't need to turn to know that the key was on the floor behind him. He knew they wouldn't find any fingerprints in the room and that no one had broken into the house. Quite simply because both the murderer and the victim were hanging from the ceiling. The two-headed troll had split.

'Call Weber,' Harry said to Halvorsen, who had joined them and was standing in the doorway, staring at the hanging body.

'He may have planned a different start to tomorrow's festivities, but console him with the fact that this one is cut and dried. Even Juul discovered the murderer and had to pay for it with his life.'

'And who is it?' Waaler asked.

'Was. He's dead too. He called himself Daniel Gudeson and lived in Juul's head.'

On the way out, Harry told Halvorsen Weber should call him if he found the Märklin.

Harry stood on the doorstep outside and surveyed the area. It was striking how many neighbours suddenly had jobs to do in their gardens and were standing on the tips of their toes to see over the hedges. Waaler came out too and stood beside Harry.

'I didn't quite understand what you said in there,' Waaler said. 'Do you mean the guy committed suicide out of guilt?'

Harry shook his head.

'No, I meant what I said. They killed each other. Even killed Daniel to stop him. And Daniel killed Even so that he wouldn't be unmasked. For once their interests coincided.'

Waaler nodded, but didn't seem to be any the wiser.

'There's something familiar about the old guy,' he said. 'The living one, I mean.'

'Right. It's Rakel Fauke's father, if you —'

'Of course, the totty up at POT. That's the one.'

'Have you got a smoke?' Harry asked.

'No can do,' Waaler said. 'The rest of what happens here is your responsibility, Hole. I'm thinking of leaving, so if you need any help, tell me now.'

Harry shook his head, and Waaler walked towards the gate.

'Oh, by the way,' Harry said. 'If you're not doing anything special tomorrow, I need an experienced officer to take my shift.'

Waaler laughed and kept walking.

'You just have to organise surveillance during the service at the mosque in Grønland,' Harry shouted. 'I can see you're pretty good at that sort of thing. We just have to make sure the skinheads don't beat up the Muslims for celebrating Eid.'

Waaler had reached the gate and suddenly stopped.

'And you're in charge of that?' he asked over his shoulder.

'It's no big deal,' Harry said. 'Two cars, four men.'

'How long?'

'Eight till three.'

Waaler turned round with a broad smile.

'Do you know what?' he said. 'Now that I think about it, I owe you a favour. That's great. I'll do your shift.'

Waaler saluted, got into the car, started it up and was off.

Owes me a favour for what? Harry mused, and listened to the lazy thwacks of the ball coming from the tennis court. But the next moment he had forgotten because his mobile rang again, and this time the number on the display *was* Rakel's.

92

Holmenkollveien. 16 May 2000.

'ARE THOSE FOR ME?'

Rakel clapped her hands and took the bunch of daisies.

'I couldn't get to the florist, so these are from your own garden,' Harry said, stepping inside the door. 'Mm, that smells of coconut milk. Thai?'

'Yes, and congratulations on the new suit.'

'That obvious, is it?'

Rakel laughed and stroked the lapels.

'Good quality wool.'

'Super 110.'

Harry had no idea what Super 110 meant. In a moment of exuberance he had marched into one of the trendy shops in Hedgehaugsveien as they were closing and had managed to get the sales staff to find him the only suit into which they could fit his long body. Of course, seven thousand kroner was way over what he had intended to pay, but the alternative was to look like something out of a farce in the old suit, so he had closed his eyes, put his card in the machine and tried to forget.

They went into the dining room, where a table was set for two.

'Oleg is asleep,' she said before Harry could ask. There was a silence.

'I didn't mean . . .' she began.

'Didn't you?' Harry said with a smile. He hadn't seen her blush before. He pulled her into him, breathed in the aroma of freshly washed hair and felt her slight tremble.

'The food , , ,' she whispered.

He let her go and she disappeared into the kitchen. The window facing the garden was open and the white butterflies which had not been there yesterday fluttered like confetti in the sunset. Inside it smelled of green soap and damp wooden floors. Harry closed his eyes. He knew that he would need many days like this before the image of Even Juul hanging from the dog lead would completely go away, but it was fading. Weber and his boys hadn't found the Märklin, but they had found Burre, the dog. In a bin bag in the freezer with its throat cut. And in the toolbox they had found three knives, all bloodstained. Harry guessed that some of the blood was Hallgrim Dale's.

Rakel called him from the kitchen to help her to carry in a few things. It was already fading.

93

Holmenkollveien. 17 May 2000.

THE JANIZARY MUSIC CAME AND WENT WITH THE wind. Harry opened his eyes. Everything was white. White sunlight gleaming and flashing like morse code between the flapping white curtains, white walls, white ceiling and white bedding, soft and cool against hot skin. He turned. The pillow retained the mould of her head, but the bed was empty. He looked at his wristwatch. Five past eight. She and Oleg were on their way to Akershus Fortress parade ground where the children's parade was due to start. They had arranged to meet in front of the guardhouse by the Palace at eleven.

He closed his eyes and replayed the night one more time. Then he got up and shuffled into the bathroom. White there too: white tiles, white porcelain. He showered in freezing cold water and before he realised it he was singing an old song by The The.

'. . . a perfect day!'

Rakel had put out a towel for him, white, and he rubbed his skin with the thick woven cotton to get his circulation going as he studied his face in the mirror. He was happy now, wasn't he? Right now. He smiled at the face in front of him. It smiled back. Ekman and Friesen. *Smile at the world and the world . . .*

He laughed aloud, tied the towel around his waist and walked slowly on damp feet across the hall to the bedroom door. It took a second before he realised it was the wrong bedroom because everything was white again: walls, ceiling, a dressing-table with family photographs on and a neatly made double bed with an old-fashioned crocheted bedspread.

He turned, was about to leave and had reached the door when he suddenly went rigid. He froze, as if part of his brain was ordering him to keep going and forget while another part wanted him to go back and check whether what he had just seen was what he thought it was. Or, to be more precise, what he feared it was. Exactly what he feared and why, he didn't know. He only knew that when everything is perfect, it can't be better and you don't want to change a thing, not one single thing. But it was too late. Of course it was too late.

He breathed in, turned round and went back.

The black and white photograph was in a simple gold frame. The woman in the photograph had a narrow face, high, pronounced cheekbones and calm, smiling eyes, which were focused on something slightly above the camera, presumably the photographer. She looked strong. She was wearing a plain blouse, and over the blouse hung a silver cross.

They have been painting her on icons for almost two thousand years.

That wasn't why there had been something familiar about her the first time he had seen a photograph of her.

There was no doubt. It was the same woman he had seen in the photograph in Beatrice Hoffmann's room.

Part Nine

JUDGMENT DAY

94

Oslo. 17 May 2000.

I AM WRITING THIS SO THAT WHOEVER FINDS IT SHALL KNOW a little about why I have taken the decisions I have. The decisions in my life have often been between two or more evils, and I have to be judged on the basis of that. But I should also be judged on the fact that I have never run away from decisions; I have never evaded my moral obligations. I have risked taking the wrong decision rather than living like a coward as part of the silent majority, as someone seeking security in the crowd, someone who allows others to take decisions for them. I have taken this final decision so that I will be ready when I meet the Lord and my Helena.

'Fuck!'

Harry stamped on the brakes as the crowd of people wearing suits and national costumes streamed out on to the pedestrian area at the crossing in Majorstuen. The whole city seemed to be on the move already. And it felt as if the lights would never change to green again. Finally he could slip the clutch and accelerate. He double-parked in Vibes gate, located Fauke's doorbell and pressed. A toddler ran past on loud leather soles and the ear-piercing bray of his toy horn made Harry jump.

Fauke didn't answer. Harry went back to his car and collected the crowbar he always kept in the car rather than the boot because of the fickle boot lock. He returned and put both arms across the two rows of doorbells. After a few seconds there was a cacophony of animated voices, probably belonging to people rushing against the clock, with hot irons or shoe polish in their hands. He said he was from the police and someone must have believed him, because there was an angry buzz and he was able to push open the door. He sprinted up, four steps at a time. Then he was on the third floor, his heart now beating even faster than it had since he had seen the photograph a quarter of an hour earlier.

The task I have set myself has already cost several innocent human lives, and of course there is the risk it may cost more. It will always be that way with war. So judge me as a soldier who wasn't given many options. That is my wish. But if you should judge me harshly, know that you too are only fallible, and it will always be thus, for both you and me. In the end there is only one judge: God. These are my memoirs.

Harry hit Fauke's door twice with his fist and shouted his name. On hearing nothing, he jammed the crowbar in beneath the lock and launched himself at it. At the third attempt the door gave with a loud bang. He stepped across the threshold. It was dark and quiet in the flat and in a strange way it reminded him of the bedroom he had just left. There was something vacant and utterly abandoned about it. He understood why when he went into the sitting room. It *was* abandoned. The papers that had been strewn over the floor, the books on the slanting book shelves and the half-full coffee cups were gone. The furniture had been shoved into a corner and draped with white sheets. A stripe of sunlight through the window fell on a pile of papers bound together

with string, lying in the middle of the cleared sitting-room
floor.

*When you read this, I hope I will be dead. I hope we will all be
dead.*

Harry crouched down beside the pile of papers.

On the top sheet was typed *The Great Betrayal: A Soldier's Memoirs.*

Harry untied the string.

Next page: *I am writing this so that whoever finds it shall
know a little about why I have taken the decisions I have.*
Harry leafed through the pile. There must have been several
hundred densely written pages. He glanced at his watch: 8.30.
He found Fritz's number in his notebook, pulled out his mobile
phone and caught the Austrian on his way home after night
duty. After talking to Fritz for a minute, Harry rang directory
enquiries, who found the number and put him through.

'Weber.'

'Hole. Happy Independence Day. Isn't that what we're
supposed to say?'

'To hell with that. What do you want?'

'Well, you probably have plans for today . . .'

'Yes, I was planning to keep the door locked and the windows closed and read the papers. Spit it out.'

'I need to have some fingerprints taken.'

'Great. When?'

'Right now. You'll have to bring your case with you, so we
can send them from here. And I'll need a Smith & Wesson.'

Harry gave him the address. Then he took the pile of
papers with him to one of the shrouded chairs, sat down and
began to read.

95

Oslo. 17 May 2000.

Leningrad. 12 December 1942.

The flares light up the grey night sky, making it resemble a filthy top canvas drawn over the drab, bare landscape surrounding us on all sides. Perhaps the Russians have launched an offensive, perhaps it is a feint, we never know until afterwards. Daniel has proved himself as a fantastic marksman again. If he was not a legend before, he assured himself immortality today. He hit and killed a Russian from a range of half a kilometre. Then he went into no man's land alone and gave the dead man a Christian burial. I have never heard of anyone doing anything like that before. He brought the Russian's cap back with him as a trophy. Afterwards he was in his usual high spirits and sang and entertained everyone (apart from a few envious killjoys). I am extremely proud to have such a resolute, courageous person as my friend. Even though some days it seems as if this war will never end and the sacrifices for our home country are great, a man like Daniel Gudeson gives us all hope that we will stop the Bolsheviks and return to a safe, free Norway.

Harry checked his watch and read on.

Leningrad. New Year's Eve 1942.

. . . when I saw the fear in Sindre Fauke's eyes I had to say a
few reassuring words to him to relax his vigilance. It was just
us two out there at the machine-gun post; the others had gone
to their bunks, and Daniel's body lay rigid on top of the ammunition boxes. Then I scratched more of Daniel's blood off
the cartridge belt. The moon was shining and it was snowing,
an extraordinary night, and I thought that now I would collect
the remains of Daniel and put him together again, make him
whole so that he could stand up and lead us. Sindre Fauke didn't
understand this. He was a hanger-on, an opportunist and an
informer who only followed those he thought would win. And
the day things looked darkest for me, for us, for Daniel, he
would also betray us. I took a swift pace back, so that I was
behind him, seized his forehead and swung the bayonet. You
have to be fairly deft to get a deep, clean cut. I let go as soon as
I had sliced him for I knew the job was done. He turned round
slowly and stared at me with those small piggy eyes of his; he
seemed to want to scream but the bayonet had severed his
windpipe and only a whistling sound came from the gaping
wound. And blood. He grabbed his throat with both hands to
prevent his life running out, but that only made the blood
squirt out in fine jets between his fingers. I fell and had to
scrabble backwards in the snow not to get it on my uniform.
Fresh bloodstains would not look good if they decided to investigate Sindre Fauke's 'desertion'.

When he no longer moved, I turned him on his back and
dragged him over to the ammunition boxes on which Daniel
was lying. Fortunately, they had a similar build. I found Sindre
Fauke's ID papers. (We always keep them on us, day and night,
because if we are stopped and have no papers on us saying
who we are and what our orders are (infantry, Northern Front,
date, stamp and so on) we risk being shot on the spot as deserters.) I rolled up Sindre's papers and stuffed them into the canteen attached to my cartridge belt. Then I took the sack off

Daniel's head and wrapped it round Sindre's. Next I put Daniel on my back and carried him out into no man's land. And there I buried him in the snow, as Daniel had buried Uriah, the Russian. I kept Daniel's Russian cap. Sang a psalm. 'A mighty fortress is our God'. And 'Join the circle of men round the fire'.

Leningrad. 3 January 1943.

A mild winter. Everything has gone according to plan. Early in the morning of 1 January the corpse-bearers came and took away the body from the ammunition boxes as they had been instructed. Naturally, they believed it to be Daniel Gudeson they were dragging on the sledge to the Northern Sector. I still have to laugh whenever I think about it. I don't know if they took the sacking off the head before dumping him into the mass pit; it would not have bothered me anyway as the corpse-bearers knew neither Daniel nor Sindre Fauke.

The only thing that bothers me is that Edvard Mosken seems to suspect Fauke did not desert and that I killed him. There is not a great deal he can do. Sindre Fauke's body is lying with hundreds of others, burned (may his soul burn for ever) and unrecognisable.

But last night when I was on watch I had to undertake the boldest operation so far. Gradually I had come to realise that I couldn't leave Daniel's body buried in the snow. With the mild winter there was a good chance the body could become exposed at any moment and reveal the switch. And when I began to dream at night about what foxes and polecats would do with Daniel's body as the snow melted in spring, I decided to dig up the body and have it put in the mass grave – after all, that was consecrated ground.

Of course, I was more frightened by our own sentry posts than by the Russians, but fortunately it was Hallgrim Dale, Fauke's slow-witted comrade, sitting in the machine-gun nest. On top of that, it was a cloudy night and, even more important,

I felt that Daniel was with me, yes, that he was in me. And when I had finally manoeuvred the corpse on to the ammunition boxes and was about to tie the sack around his head, he smiled. I know that lack of sleep and hunger can play tricks with your mind, but I did see his rigid death-mask change in front of my very eyes. The extraordinary thing was that instead of frightening me, it made me feel secure and happy. Then I sneaked back into the bunker, where I fell asleep like a child.

When Edvard Mosken woke me up an hour later, it was as if I had been dreaming the whole thing, and I think I managed to appear genuinely surprised to see that Daniel's body had turned up again. But this was not enough to convince Edvard Mosken. He was sure it was Fauke's body, sure I had killed him and had put his body there in the hope that the corpse-bearers would think they had forgotten to collect him the first time and take him along. Dale removed the sacking and Mosken saw that it was Daniel. They both gaped, open-mouthed, and I had to fight to restrain the laughter inside me from bursting out and giving us – Daniel and me – away.

Field Hospital, Northern Sector, Leningrad.
17 January 1944.

The hand-grenade that was thrown from the Russian plane hit Dale on the helmet and spun around on the ice as we tried to move away. I was closest and was sure all three of us would die: Mosken, Dale and me. It is strange, but my last thought was what an irony of fate it was that I had just saved Edvard Mosken from being shot by Dale, the poor man, and my sole achievement was to extend the life of our section leader by exactly two minutes. Fortunately, however, the Russians make terrible hand-grenades and we all survived with our lives intact. As for me, I had an injured foot and shrapnel had sliced through my helmet into my forehead.

By a remarkable coincidence I ended up in Daniel's fiancée's ward, with Sister Signe Alsaker. At first she didn't recognise me, but in the afternoon she came over and spoke to me in Norwegian. She is very beautiful and I know only too well why I wanted to be engaged to her.

Olaf Lindvig is also in this ward. That white leather tunic of his hangs on a hook by his bed. I don't know why – perhaps so that he can walk right out and back to the duties awaiting him as soon as his injuries have healed. Men of his calibre are needed now; I can hear the Russian artillery fire closing in. One night he was having nightmares, I think, because he screamed, and Sister Signe came in. She gave him an injection of something, morphine perhaps. When he went to sleep again, I saw her stroke his hair. She was so beautiful that I felt like calling her over to my bed and telling her who I was, but I didn't want to frighten her.

Today they said I was to be sent to the west because medicines were not getting through. No one said anything, but my foot is painful, the Russians are coming closer and I know this is my only hope for survival.

Vienna Woods. 29 May 1944

The most beautiful and the most intelligent woman I have ever met in my life. Can you love two women at once? Yes, you certainly can.

Gudbrand has changed. That is why I have taken Daniel's nickname – Uriah. Helena preferred it. Gudbrand was an odd name, she thought.

I write poems when the others have gone to sleep, but I'm not much of a poet. My heart beats wildly when she appears in the doorway, but Daniel says you have to stay calm, well, almost cold, if you want to win a woman's heart. It is like catching flies: you have to sit quite still, preferably looking in another direction. And then, when the fly has begun to trust you – when it lands on the table in front of you, goes closer and finally almost

begs you to try and catch it – then you strike as quick as light-
ning, firm and sure in your convictions. The latter is the most
important. It is not speed but conviction that catches flies. You
have one chance – and you must be ready for it, Daniel says.

Vienna. 29 June 1944.

. . . freeing myself from my beloved Helena's arms. Outside the
air raid had been over for a long time, but it was the middle of
the night and the streets were still deserted. I found the car
where we had left it, beside the restaurant Zu den drei Husaren.
The rear window was smashed and a brick had made a huge
dent in the roof, but otherwise, fortunately, it was unscathed. I
drove as fast as I dared back to the hospital.

I knew it was too late to do anything for Helena and me. We
were simply two people caught in a maelstrom of events over
which we had no power. Her fears for her parents doomed her
to marrying this doctor, Christopher Brockhard, this corrupt
person who in his boundless selfishness (which he called love!)
was an affront to the innermost essence of love. Couldn't he
see the love that drove him was the absolute antithesis of the
love that drove her? Now I had to sacrifice my dream of shar-
ing a life with Helena to give her a life, if not one of happiness,
then at least of decency, free of the degradation that Brock-
hard would force her into.

The thoughts raced through my mind as I sped along roads
which were as tortuous as life itself. But Daniel was in com-
mand of my hands and feet.

. . . discovered I was sitting on the edge of his bed and gave me
a look of disbelief.

'What are you doing here?' he asked.

'Christopher Brockhard, you are a traitor,' I whispered. 'And
I sentence you to death. Are you ready?'

I don't think he was ready. People are never ready to die;

*they think they will live for ever. I hope he got to see the fountain
of blood stretching up towards the ceiling, I hope he got to hear
the splash on the bedding as it came down again, but above all I
hope he realised he was dying.*

*In the wardrobe I found a suit, a pair of shoes and a shirt
which I hurriedly rolled up and carried out under my arm.
Then I ran out to the car, started it . . .*

*. . . still asleep. I was soaked and cold from the sudden down-
pour and crept under the sheets towards her. She was as warm
as an oven and groaned in her sleep as I pressed myself up
against her. I tried to cover every centimetre of her skin with
mine, tried to delude myself into thinking it was for ever, tried
to avoid looking at the clock. There were just two hours until
my train left. And just two hours until I would be a hunted
murderer over all of Austria. They didn't know when I would
leave or which route I would take, but they knew where I
would go – and they would be ready for me when I arrived in
Oslo. I tried to hold her tight enough to last me a lifetime.*

Harry heard the bell. Had it rung before? He found the intercom and buzzed Weber in.

'Right after sport on TV, this is what I hate most,' Weber
said as he stamped in fuming, and slammed a flightcase the
size of a suitcase down on the ground. 'Independence Day,
the whole country off their heads with national fervour, roads
closed so you have to drive all the way round the centre to get
anywhere. Holy Jesus! Where shall I begin?'

'There are bound to be some good prints on the coffee
pot in the kitchen,' Harry said. 'I've been talking to a colleague in Vienna who is busy looking for a set of prints from
1944. You brought a scanner and a computer, did you?'

Weber patted the flightcase.

'Great. When you've finished scanning in the prints, you
can connect my mobile to the computer and send them to the
email address listed under "Fritz, Vienna". He is sitting ready

to compare them with his set of prints and let us know immediately. That's basically it. I just have to read through a few papers in the sitting room.'

'What's the . . . ?'

'POT stuff,' Harry said. 'Need-to-know basis only.'

'Is that so?' Weber bit his lip and gave Harry a searching stare. Harry looked him in the eye and waited.

'Do you know what, Hole?' he said finally. 'It's good that someone in this country still behaves like a professional.'

96

Oslo. 17 May 2000.

Hamburg. 30 June 1944.

After writing the letter to Helena, I opened my canteen, shook out Sindre Fauke's rolled-up ID papers and replaced them with the letter. Then I carved her name and address on it with the bayonet and went out into the night. As soon as I was outside the door I could feel the heat. The wind tore at my uniform, the sky above me was a dirty yellow vault and the only thing to be heard above the distant roar of flames was cracking glass and the screams of those who no longer had anywhere to flee. It was more or less how I imagined hell to be. The bombs had stopped falling. I went along a street that was a street no more, just a strip of tarmac running through an open area with heaps of ruins. The only thing left standing in the 'street' was a blackened tree pointing up at the sky with witches' fingers. And a house in flames. That was where the screams were coming from. When I was so close that my lungs were scorched by every breath, I turned and began to walk towards the harbour. That was where she was, the little girl with the terror-stricken black eyes. She pulled at my jacket, screaming her heart out as I passed.

'Meine Mutter! Meine Mutter!'

I continued on my way, there was nothing else I could do. I had already seen a human skeleton standing in the bright flames on the top floor, trapped with one leg on either side of the window ledge. But the girl continued to follow me, screaming her desperate pleas for me to help her mother. I tried to walk faster, but her small child's arms held me, would not let go and I dragged her with me towards the great sea of flames below us. We went on, a strange procession, two people shackled together on our way to extinction.

I wept, yes, I wept, but the tears evaporated as soon as they had come. I don't know which of us it was who stopped but I lifted her up, and I turned, carried her up to the dormitory and wrapped my blanket round her. Then I took the mattresses from the other beds and lay down beside her on the floor.

I never found out her name, or what happened to her, because she disappeared during the night. But I know she saved my life. I took the decision to hope.

I awoke to a dying city. Several of the fires were still ablaze, the harbour buildings were razed to the ground and the boats which had come with provisions or to evacuate the wounded stayed out in the Außenalster, unable to dock.

It was evening before the crew had cleared a place where they could load and unload, and I hurried over. I went from boat to boat until I found what I was looking for – passage to Norway. The ship was called Anna *and was taking cement to Trondheim. The destination suited me well since I didn't imagine that the search papers would have been sent there. Chaos had taken over from the usual German order, and the lines of command were, to put it mildly, confused. The SS on my collar seemed to create a certain impression, and I had no problem getting on board and persuading the captain that the orders I showed him implied that I had to find my way to Oslo via the most direct route possible. Under the prevailing circumstances, that meant on* Anna *to Trondheim and from there by train to Oslo.*

The journey took three days. I walked off the boat, showed

*my papers and was waved on. Then I boarded a train for Oslo.
The whole trip took four days. Before getting off the train I went
to the toilet and put on the clothes I had taken from Christopher
Brockhard. Then I was ready for the first test. I walked up Karl
Johans gate. It was warm and drizzling. Two girls came towards
me, arm in arm, and giggled loudly as I passed them. The in-
ferno in Hamburg seemed light-years away. My heart rejoiced. I
was back in my beloved country and I was reborn for a second
time.*

*The receptionist in the Continental Hotel scrutinised my ID
papers before looking at me over his glasses.*

'Welcome to the Continental Hotel, herr Fauke.'

*And as I lay on my back in bed in the yellow hotel room,
staring at the ceiling and listening to the sounds of the city outside, I tried out our new name on my tongue, Sindre Fauke. It
was unfamiliar, but I realised that it might, it could, work.*

Nordmarka. 12 July 1944.

*. . . a man called Even Juul. He seems to have swallowed my
story whole, like the other Home Front men. And why shouldn't
they, anyway? The truth – that I fought at the Eastern Front
and am wanted for murder – would be even harder to swallow
than my deserting and returning to Norway via Sweden. They
have checked their information with their sources and have
received confirmation that a person by the name of Sindre
Fauke was reported missing, probably a defection to the Russians. The Germans have order in their systems!*

*I speak fairly standard Norwegian, a result of my having
grown up in the USA, I imagine, and no one notices that as
Sindre Fauke I have quickly got rid of my Gudbrandsdal dialect. I come from a tiny place in Norway, but even if someone I
met in my youth (Youth! My God, it was only three years ago
and yet a whole lifetime away) were to turn up I am positive
they would not recognise me. I feel so totally different.*

What I am much more frightened of is that someone should turn up who knows the real Sindre Fauke. Fortunately, he comes from an even more isolated place than I, if that is possible, but of course he has relatives who could identify him.

I walk around chewing on these things, and my surprise was therefore immense when today they gave me orders to liquidate one of my own (Fauke's) Nasjonal Samling brothers. It is supposed to test whether I have really changed sides or whether I'm an infiltrator. Daniel and I almost burst out laughing – it is as if we had discovered the idea ourselves. They actually asked me to get rid of the people who could blow the whistle on me! I'm well aware the leaders of these pretend-soldiers thought that fratricide was going a bit far, unaccustomed as they are here in these safe forests to the brutality of war. But I have decided to take them at their word before they change their minds. As soon as it is dark I will go down to the town and pick up my gun, which is hidden with my uniform in the left-luggage locker at the station, and take the same night train as I arrived on. I know the name of the closest village to the Faukes' farm, so I have only to ask . . .

Oslo. 13 May 1945.

Another strange day. The country is still high on liberation fever, and today Crown Prince Olav arrived in Oslo with a government delegation. I could not be bothered to go to the harbour to see, but I heard that 'half' Oslo was gathered there. I walked up Karl Johans gate in civilian clothes today even though my 'soldier friends' cannot understand why I do not want to strut around in the Resistance uniform and be given the hero's welcome. It's supposed to be a huge turn-on for young women at the moment. Women and uniforms – if I'm not mistaken they used to love running after the green uniforms in 1940 just the same.

I went up to the Palace to see if the Crown Prince would show himself on the balcony and say a few words. Many more had gathered there too. The guards were changing when I appeared. A pathetic display by German standards, but people were cheering.

I have hopes that the Crown Prince will pour cold water on these so-called good Norwegians who have been sitting like passive spectators for five years without lifting a finger for either side and are now screaming for revenge on the traitors. In fact, I think Crown Prince Olav can understand us as, if the rumours are true, he was the only one out of the King and government who, by offering to remain with Norwegians and share their fate, showed a bit of spine during the capitulation. But the government advised against it. They knew very well that it would put them and the King in a very peculiar light, leaving him in Norway while they themselves made a run for it.

Yes, I have hopes that the young Crown Prince (who unlike the 'latter-day saints' knows how to wear a uniform) can explain to the nation what the soldiers on the Eastern Front achieved, especially since he has seen for himself the danger the Bolsheviks in the east posed (and still do) for our nation. Back in early 1942, as we were preparing to be posted to the Eastern Front, the Crown Prince is said to have had talks with President Roosevelt and expressed concern about the Russians' plans for Norway.

There was some flag-waving, a few songs, and I have never seen the trees greener. But the Crown Prince did not come out on the balcony today. So I will just have to arm myself with patience.

'They've just rung from Vienna. The prints are identical.'

Weber stood in the doorway to the sitting room.

'Fine,' Harry said with an absent nod, immersed in his reading.

'Someone has thrown up in the bin,' Weber said. 'Someone who is very sick. There's more blood than vomit.'

Harry licked his thumb and turned over the next page. 'Right.'

Silence.

'If there's anything else I can help with . . .'

'Thanks very much, Weber, but that was it.'

Weber inclined his head, but didn't move.

'Shouldn't you radio an alert?' he asked finally.

Harry raised his head and gave Weber an absent-minded look.

'Why?'

'Damned if I know,' Weber said. 'On a don't-need-to-know basis.'

Harry smiled, perhaps because of the older policeman's comment. 'No. That's precisely why.'

Weber waited for more, but it didn't come.

'As you wish, Hole. I brought a Smith & Wesson with me. It's loaded and there's an extra clip there. Catch!'

Harry looked up just in time to catch the black holster Weber had thrown to him. He took out the revolver. It was oiled and there was a matt shine on the newly polished steel. Of course. It was Weber's own gun.

'Thanks for your help, Weber,' Harry said.

'Take care.'

'I'll try. Have a good . . . day.'

Weber snorted at the reminder. As he trudged out of the flat Harry was already deeply engrossed in the papers again.

Oslo. 27 August 1945.

Betrayal – betrayal – betrayal! Stunned, I sat there, well concealed in the last row as my woman was led in and sat down in the dock. She gave him, Even Juul, this fleeting but unambiguous smile. And this tiny smile was enough to tell me everything, but I sat there, nailed to the bench, incapable of doing anything except listening and watching. And suffering. The hypocritical liar! Even Juul knows very well who Signe Alsaker is. I was the one who told him about her. He can hardly be blamed. He thinks Daniel Gudeson is dead, but she, she swore fidelity unto death. Yes, I'll say it again: betrayal! And the Crown Prince has not uttered a word. At Akershus Fortress they are shooting men who risked their lives for Norway. The echoes of the shots hang in the air over the city for a second, then they are gone and everything is quieter than before. As if nothing had happened.

Last week I was told that my case was dismissed; my heroic acts outweighed the crimes I had committed. I laughed until the tears flowed as I read the letter. So they think the execution of four defenceless farmers in Gudbrandsdalen is a heroic act, one which outweighs my criminal defence of the home country in Leningrad! I threw a chair at the wall and the landlady came up and I had to apologise. It's enough to drive you insane.

At night I dream of Helena. Only of Helena. I have to try to forget. And the Crown Prince did not say one word. It's unbearable. I think . . .

97

Oslo. 17 May 2000.

HARRY CHECKED HIS WATCH AGAIN. HE FLICKED through a few more sheets until his eyes fell on a familiar name.

Schrøder's. 23 September 1948.

. . . a business with good prospects. But today what I had long feared happened.

I was reading the newspaper when I noticed someone standing at my table observing me. I looked up and the blood in my veins froze to ice! He was somewhat run-down, I could see. His clothes were quite worn. He no longer had the erect, rigid bearing I remember. Something about him had gone. But I immediately recognised our old section leader, the man with the cyclops eye.

'Gudbrand Johansen,' said Edvard Mosken. 'You're supposed to have died. In Hamburg, rumour has it.'

I didn't know what to say or do. I only knew that the man who sat down in front of me could have me sentenced for treason, or even murder.

My mouth was completely dry when I was finally able to talk. I said yes, I certainly was alive, and to gain time I told him I had ended up in the military hospital in Vienna with head injuries and a bad foot. What had happened to him? He said he had been repatriated and ended up in the hospital in Sinsen, funnily enough the same one I would have been sent to. Like most of the others he had been given a three-year sentence, and had been let out after serving two and a half.

We talked a bit about this and that, and after a while I began to relax. I ordered him a beer and talked about the building-supplies business I ran. I told him my opinion: it was best for people like us to start up something on our own since most companies refused to employ ex-Eastern Front men (especially the companies who had co-operated with the Germans during the war).

'What about you?' he asked.

I had explained that joining the 'right side' had not helped me much. I had still worn a German uniform.

Mosken sat there the whole time with this half-smile playing on his lips, and in the end he could not hold it back any longer. He told me he had been trying to trace me for a long time, but all the tracks ended in Hamburg. He had almost given up when one day he spotted the name Sindre Fauke in a newspaper article about Resistance men. That had rekindled his interest; he had found out where Fauke worked and rang. Someone had tipped him off that I was probably at Schrøder's.

I tensed up and thought, here it comes. But what he said was utterly different from what I had imagined.

'I never thanked you properly for stopping Hallgrim Dale from shooting me that time. You saved my life, Johansen.'

I played this down with a shrug and an open-mouthed stare. It was the best I could do.

Mosken said I had shown myself to be a man of morals when I saved his life because I'd had good reason to wish him dead. If Sindre Fauke's body had been found, Mosken could have testified that I was probably the murderer. I simply nod-

ded. Then he looked at me and asked if I was frightened of him. I realised that I had nothing to lose by telling him the whole story exactly as it had happened.

Mosken listened, focused his cyclops eye on me a couple of times to check if I was lying, and occasionally shook his head, but he knew well enough that most was true.

When I had finished, I ordered two more beers and he told me about himself. His wife had found another man to look after her and the boy while he was in prison. He understood. Perhaps it was best for Edvard Junior too, not to grow up with a traitor as a father. Mosken seemed resigned. He said he wanted to work in transport, but hadn't got any of the driving jobs he had applied for.

'Buy your own truck,' I said. 'You should start up on your own, too.'

'I haven't got enough money to do that,' he said, with a quick glance in my direction. I had a vague idea where the conversation was leading. 'And the banks are not that keen on ex-Eastern Front men. They think we're all crooks.'

'I've saved up some money,' I said. 'You can borrow some from me.'

He refused, but I said the matter was closed.

'I'll add interest, of course. That goes without saying,' I said, and then he brightened up. But he was soon serious again and said it could be an expensive time until he really got going. So I assured him the rate of interest wouldn't be very high, it would be more symbolic. Then I ordered another round of beer and when we had drunk up and were on our way out we shook hands. We had a deal.

Oslo. 3 August 1950.

. . . a letter postmarked Vienna in the letterbox. I placed it on the kitchen table in front of me and stared at it. Her name and address were written on the back of the envelope. I had sent a

letter to the Rudolf II Hospital in May in the hope that someone might know where Helena was in the world and send it on.
In case prying eyes should happen to open the letter I hadn't
written anything that could be dangerous for either of us and,
of course, I hadn't written my real name. And I definitely hadn't
dared hope for an answer. Well, I don't even know if, deep down,
I wanted an answer, not if the answer was the one you might
expect. Married and mother of a child. No, I didn't want that.
Even though that was what I had wished her, what I had given
my consent to.

My God, we had been so young. She had only been nineteen.
And now, as I held her letter in my hand, it was all suddenly so
unreal, as if the neat handwriting on the envelope couldn't have
anything to do with the Helena I had been dreaming of for six
years. I opened the letter with trembling fingers, forcing myself
to expect the worst. It was a long letter and it is only a few hours
now since I read it for the first time, but already I know it by
heart.

Dear Uriah,

I love you. It is easy to know that I will love you for
the rest of my life, but the strange thing is it feels as if
I have already loved you for all of my life too. When I
received your letter I wept with happiness. It . . .

Harry went to the kitchen with the manuscript in his hands,
found the coffee in the cupboard over the sink and put on the
coffee pot while continuing to read. About the happy, though
also difficult and painful, reunion at a hotel in Paris. They
get engaged the next day.

From here on, Gudbrand writes less and less about Daniel, and finally it seems as if he has completely disappeared.

Instead he writes about a couple very much in love who,
because of the murder of Christopher Brockhard, still feel
their pursuers' breath down their necks. They have secret

trysts in Copenhagen, Amsterdam and Hamburg. Helena knows Gudbrand's new identity, but does she know the whole truth about the murder at the Eastern Front, about the executions at the Fauke farm? It didn't seem so.

They get engaged after the Allies have left Austria and in 1955 she leaves the country she is sure will be taken over again by 'war criminals, anti-Semites and fanaticists who haven't learned from their mistakes'. They settle in Oslo, where Gudbrand, still using Sindre Fauke's name, continues to run his small business. The same year they are married by a Catholic priest at a private ceremony in the garden in Holmenkollveien where they have just bought a large, detached house with the money Helena received from selling her sewing business in Vienna. They are happy, Gudbrand writes.

Harry heard a hiss and to his surprise saw that the pot had boiled over.

98

Oslo. 17 May 2000.

Rikshospital. 1956.

*Helena lost so much blood that her life was in the balance for
a while, but fortunately they acted promptly. We lost the child.
Naturally, Helena was inconsolable even though I kept repeat-
ing that she was young and we would have many more oppor-
tunities. The doctor was not so optimistic, however. He said
the uterus . . .*

Rikshospital. 12 March 1967.

*A daughter. She is going to be called Rakel. I cried and cried,
and Helena stroked my cheek and said God's ways were . . .*

Harry was back in the sitting room. He placed his hand over
his eyes. Why hadn't he made the connection as soon as he
saw the picture of Helena in Beatrice's room? Mother and
daughter. His mind must have been elsewhere. Probably that
was exactly it – his mind was elsewhere. He saw Rakel everywhere: on the street in passing women's faces, on ten TV

channels when he was zapping around, behind the counter in a café. So why would he pay any particular attention to seeing her face in a photograph of a beautiful woman on a wall?

Should he ring Mosken for confirmation of what Gudbrand Johansen, alias Sindre Fauke, had written? Did he need to? Not now.

He flicked through the manuscript until he arrived at the entry for 5 October 1999. There were only a few pages left. Harry could feel his palms were sweaty. He felt a trace of the same thing that Rakel's father had described when he received Helena's letter – a reluctance to be confronted finally with the inevitable.

Oslo. 5 October 1999.

I'm going to die. After all the things I have been through it was curious to find out I was to be given the coup de grâce, *as most people are, by a common illness. How will I tell Rakel and Oleg? I walked up Karl Johans gate and felt how dear this life, which I have experienced as worthless ever since Helena's death, had suddenly become to me. Not because I don't yearn to be with you again, Helena, but because I have neglected my purpose on earth for so long and now there isn't much time left. I walked up the same gravel path I did on 13 May 1945. The Crown Prince still hasn't come out on the balcony to say he understands. He just understands all the others in need. I don't think he will come. I think he has betrayed us.*

Afterwards I fell asleep against a tree and dreamed a long, strange dream, like a revelation. And when I awoke, my old companion was awake too. Daniel is back. And I know what he wants to do.

The Ford Escort groaned as Harry brutally forced the gearstick into reverse, first and second gears in succession. And it roared like a wounded beast when he pressed the accelerator pedal to the floor and held it there. A man wearing a festive Østerdal outfit, on his way over the zebra crossing at the inter-section between Vibes gate and Bogstadveien, jumped and thus narrowly avoided an almost perfectly treadless rubber-tyre mark on his stockinged leg. In Hedgehaugsveien there was a queue of traffic for the city centre, so Harry drove down the left-hand side of the road with his hand on the horn, hop-ing oncoming cars would have the sense to swerve out of the way. He had just manoeuvred his way around the verge out-side Lorry Kafé when a wall of light blue suddenly filled his entire field of vision. The tram!

It was too late to stop, so Harry jerked the steering wheel round hard, gave the brake pedal a little squeeze to straighten the back up and bumped across the cobblestones until he crashed into the tram, left side on left side. There was a sharp bang when the wing mirror disappeared, but the sound of the door handle being dragged along the side of the tram was long and piercing.

'Fuck. Fuck!'

Then he was freed and the wheels spun themselves out of the tram rails and found a grip on the tarmac, propelling him towards the next traffic lights.

Green, green, amber.

He drove off at full throttle, still with one hand pressed against the centre of the steering wheel in a vain hope that one paltry car horn would be able to attract attention at 10.15 on 17 May in the centre of Oslo. Then he shrieked, jumped on the brakes and, as the Escort desperately tried to cling to mother earth, empty cassette cases, packets of cigarettes and Harry Hole flew forwards. He hit his head on the windscreen as the car came to rest. A cheering crowd of children waving flags had streamed out onto the zebra crossing in front of him. Harry rubbed his forehead. The Palace Gardens were right in front of him and the path up to the Palace was black with people. From the open cabriolet in the queue next to him he heard the radio and the familiar live broadcast which was the same every year.

'And now the royal family is waving from the balcony to the procession of children and the crowds which have gathered here in the Palace Square. People are cheering, especially for the popular Crown Prince, who has returned home from the USA. He is of course . . .'

Harry let the clutch out, accelerated and headed for the kerb in front of the gravel path.

99

Oslo. 16 October 1999.

I HAVE STARTED LAUGHING AGAIN. IT IS DANIEL LAUGHING, of course. I didn't say that one of the first things he did when he woke up was to call Signe. We used the pay phone at Schrøder's. And it was so heart-rendingly funny that the tears flowed.

More planning tonight. The problem is still how to get hold of the weapon I need.

100

Oslo. 15 November 1999.

. . . THE PROBLEM FINALLY SEEMED TO BE SOLVED. HE TURNED up: Hallgrim Dale. Not surprisingly, he had gone to the dogs. I hoped at least he wouldn't recognise me. He had obviously heard the rumours that I had been killed during the bombing of Hamburg because he thought I was a ghost. He suspected some jiggery-pokery and wanted money to keep his mouth shut. But the Dale I know wouldn't have been able to keep a secret for all the money in the world. So I saw to it that I was the last person he would talk to. It gave me no pleasure, but I have to confess I felt a certain satisfaction at observing that my old skills were not quite forgotten.

101

Oslo. 17 May 2000.

Oslo. 8 February 2000.

For more than fifty years Edvard and I have been meeting six times a year at Schrøder's. The first Tuesday of every second month, in the morning. We still call it the staff meeting, as we used to do when Schrøder's was in Youngstorget. I have often wondered what it was that bound Edvard and me together, being as different as we are. Perhaps it is simply a shared fate. We are marked by the same events. We were both at the Eastern Front, we have both lost our wives and our children are grown. I don't know. The most important thing for me is that I have Edvard's total loyalty. Naturally, he never forgets that I helped him after the war, but I have also given him a helping hand in later years. Such as at the end of the 1960s, when his drinking and betting on horses got out of control, and when he would have almost lost his entire truck business, had I not paid off his gambling debts.

No, there is not a lot left of the fine soldier I remember from Leningrad, but in recent years Edvard has at least come to terms with the fact that life is not quite as he had imagined, and he is trying to make the best of it. He concentrates on his

*horse, and he no longer drinks or smokes; he contents himself
with passing on racing tips to me.*

*And, speaking of tips, it was him who tipped me off about
Even Juul asking whether Daniel could still be alive. The same
evening I rang Even and asked him if he had gone senile. But
Even told me that a few days ago he had lifted the receiver of
an extra telephone they kept in the bedroom and had over-
heard a man claiming to be Daniel scaring the wits out of his
wife. The man on the telephone had said she would hear from
him on one of the following Tuesdays. Even had recognised the
sounds of a café, and now he had decided to trawl the cafés in
Oslo every Tuesday until he found the telephone pest. He knew
the police wouldn't be bothered with such a trivial matter, and
he had not said anything to Signe in case she tried to stop him.
I had to bite the back of my hand to stop myself from laughing
out loud and wished him luck, the old idiot.*

*After moving into the flat in Majorstuen I haven't seen much
of Rakel, but we have talked on the telephone. We both seem to
have tired of waging war now. I have given up explaining to her
what she did to me and her mother when she married that Russian from the old family of Bolsheviks.*

*'I know you think it was betrayal,' she says. 'But it's a long
time ago now. Let's not talk about it any more.'*

It is not a long time ago. Nothing is a long time ago any more.

*Oleg has asked after me. He is a fine boy, Oleg. I only hope
he doesn't become obstinate and wilful like his mother. She
has that from Helena. They are so similar that tears have come
into my eyes as I'm writing this.*

*I have borrowed Edvard's chalet for next week. I'll test out
the rifle then. Daniel will be happy.*

Harry hit the kerb with the front wheels and the impact recoiled through the car. The Escort leaped inelegantly through
the air and suddenly it was on the grass. There were too many
people on the path, so Harry drove over the lawn. He lurched
between the lake and four young people who had decided to

have their breakfast on a blanket in the park. In the mirror he saw the blue flashing light. The crowds were already packed around the guardhouse, so Harry stopped, jumped out of the car and ran towards the barriers around the Palace Square.

'Police!' Harry shouted as he ploughed his way through the crowds. Those at the front had got up at the crack of dawn to ensure they had a good view of the band and were reluctant to move. As he jumped over the barrier a guardsman tried to stop him, but Harry put his hand to his side, flashed his ID card and staggered on to the open square. The gravel under his feet crunched. He turned his back on the children's procession, Slemdal kindergarten and Vålerenga youth band, which was at that moment filing under the Palace balcony, with the royal family waving above them, to a terribly out of tune rendition of 'I'm Just a Gigolo'. He stared at a wall of shiny, smiling faces and red, white and blue flags. His eyes scanned the lines of people: pensioners, photo-snapping uncles, fathers with toddlers on their shoulders, but no Sindre Fauke. No Gudbrand Johansen. No Daniel Gudeson.

'Fuck! Fuck!'

He shouted more in panic than anything else.

But there, in front of the barriers, he at least saw a face he knew. Working in civilian clothes, with a walkie-talkie and reflector sunglasses. So he had followed Harry's advice about giving the Scotsman a miss and supporting the fathers in the police force.

'Halvorsen!'

102

Oslo. 16 May 2000.

Oslo. 16 May 2000.

Signe is dead. She was executed as a traitor three days ago, with a bullet through her false heart. Having been with him for such a long time, I wavered when Daniel left me after firing the shot. He left me in lonely confusion. I allowed doubts to creep in and had a terrible night. The illness didn't help. I took three of the pills Dr Buer said I should take one of, but still the pain was unbearable. I managed to sleep in the end and the following day Daniel was back with renewed vigour. That was the penultimate stage and now we are boldly pressing on.

Join the circle of men round the fire,
gaze at torches so golden and bright,
urging soldiers to aim even higher,
pledge their beings to stand up and fight.

It is approaching, the day when the Great Betrayal shall be avenged. I am undaunted.
The crucial thing is that the Betrayal will be made public. If these memoirs are found by the wrong people, there is a chance

*they will be destroyed or kept secret out of concern for public
reactions. For safety's sake, I have also given the necessary
clues to a young policeman in POT. It remains to be seen how
intelligent he is, but my gut instinct is that he is at least a person with integrity.*

The last days have been dramatic.

*It began on the day I determined I would settle accounts
with Signe. I had just phoned to say I was coming for her and as
I walked out of Schrøder's I saw Even Juul's face through the
glass front of the coffee bar on the other side of the street. I pretended I hadn't seen him and walked on, but I knew he would put
two and two together once he had thought things through.*

*Yesterday the policeman called on me. I didn't think the
clues I had given him were so obvious that he would understand how they fitted together until the mission was complete.
However, it turned out he had followed the trail of Gudbrand
Johansen to Vienna. I knew I had to gain time, at least forty-
eight hours, so I told him a story about Even Juul which I had
dreamed up in case precisely such a situation should arise. I
told him Even was a poor damaged soul and that Daniel had
taken up residence in him. Firstly, the story would make it
seem as if Juul was behind everything, Signe's killing too. Secondly, it would make the suicide I had meanwhile planned for
Juul more credible.*

*When the policeman left, I set to work immediately. Even
Juul didn't seem unduly surprised when he opened the door
today and saw me on the step outside. I don't know whether he
had worked it out or was simply no longer capable of surprise.
He already looked dead. I held a knife to his throat and assured him that if he made one false move I could slice him up
just as easily as I had done his dog. To make sure he understood what I meant, I opened the bin bag I had with me and
showed him the animal. We went upstairs to his bedroom where
he readily allowed me to place him on the chair. He tied the
dog lead to the ceiling hook.*

'I don't want the police·to have any more clues until this is

*over, so we have to make this look like suicide,' I said. But he
didn't react, he seemed indifferent. Who knows, perhaps I was
doing him a favour?*

*Afterwards, I wiped off my fingerprints and put the bin bag
containing the dog in the freezer and the knives in the cellar.
Everything was in place and I was just giving the bedroom a last
check when I heard the crunch of gravel and saw a police car
in the road. It was parked, as if it was waiting for something. I
knew I was in a tight corner. Gudbrand panicked of course, but
fortunately Daniel acted swiftly.*

*I grabbed the keys from the other two bedrooms, and one of
them fitted the room where Even was hanging. I put it on the
floor inside the door, took out the original key from the lock and
used it to lock the door from the outside. Then I switched it with
the key that didn't fit and left that one in the lock. Finally, I put
the original key in the other bedroom door. It was done in a few
seconds. Then I calmly walked down to the ground floor and
called Harry Hole's mobile.*

And the very next moment he strolled in.

*Although I could feel the laughter bubbling up inside me, I
think I managed to put on a look of surprise, probably because
I was a little surprised. In fact, I had seen one of the policemen
before. That night in the Palace Gardens. But I don't think he
recognised me. Perhaps it was Daniel he saw today. And, YES,
I remembered to wipe the fingerprints off the keys.*

'Harry! What are you doing here? Is something up?'
    'Listen, get through on your walkie-talkie to . . .'
    'Hey?'
    Bolteløkka School drum band was marching past.
    'I said to . . .' Harry shouted.
    'What?' shouted Halvorsen.
    Harry snatched the walkie-talkie out of his hand.
    'Listen carefully, everyone out there. Keep your eyes peeled
for a man, seventy years old, one metre seventy-five, blue
eyes, white hair. He's probably armed, repeat armed, and

extremely dangerous. There is reason to suspect an assassination attempt, so check open windows and roofs in the area. I repeat . . .'

Harry repeated the message while Halvorsen stared at him with his mouth hanging open. When Harry had finished he threw the walkie-talkie back to him.

'Now it's your job to get 17 May cancelled, Halvorsen.'

'What did you say?'

'You're on duty. I look like someone . . . who's been on the piss. They won't listen to me.'

Halvorsen's stare focused on Harry's unshaven chin, the badly buttoned, creased shirt and the sockless feet in shoes.

'Who's they?'

'Have you still not understood what I'm talking about yet?' Harry roared, pointing upwards with a quivering finger.

103

Oslo. 17 May 2000.

THIS MORNING. A RANGE OF FOUR-HUNDRED METRES. I HAVE managed that before. The gardens will be fresh and green, so full of life, so devoid of death. But I have cleared the way for the bullet. A dead tree without foliage. The bullet will come from the sky, like God's finger it will point out the offspring of the traitor, and everyone will see what He does to those who are not pure of heart. The traitor said he loved his country, but he left it, he left us to save it from the intruders from the east and then branded us traitors afterwards.

Halvorsen ran towards the Palace entrance while Harry remained in the open square, walking round in circles like a drunk. It would take a few minutes to clear the royal balcony. Important men would have to make decisions first which they would have to answer for. You didn't cancel 17 May simply because a policeman from the sticks had been chatting to a dubious colleague. His gaze swept the crowd, up and down, without quite knowing what he was looking for.

It would come from the sky.

He looked up. The green trees. So devoid of death. They were so tall and the foliage was so dense that even with good

rifle sights it would be impossible to shoot from neighbouring houses.

Harry closed his eyes. His lips moved. *Help me now,*
Ellen.

I have cleared the way.

Why had they been so surprised, the two Palace gardeners,
when he was walking by yesterday? The tree. It didn't have
any leaves. He opened his eyes again, looked across the
treetops and there it was: the dead brown oak. Harry felt
his heart begin to thump. He turned, almost knocked over a
drum major and ran up towards the Palace. When he reached
the direct line between the balcony and the tree, he stopped.
His eyes followed the line to the tree. Behind the naked
branches towered a frozen blue giant made of glass. The SAS
Hotel. Of course. So easy. One bullet. No one would notice
a single gunshot on 17 May. Then he strolls calmly into a
busy reception area and out into the crowded streets where
he will vanish. And then? What happens after that?

Couldn't think about that now; had to act. Had to act. But
he was so tired. Instead of excitement Harry felt a sudden
urge to get away, to go home, to lie down and sleep and wake
up to a new day in which all of this was a dream. He was
roused by the sirens from a passing ambulance in Dram-
mensveien. The sound cut right through the blanket of brass-
band music.

'Fuck. Fuck!'

He broke into a run.

104

Radisson SAS. 17 May 2000.

THE OLD MAN WAS LEANING AGAINST THE WIN-
dow with his legs drawn up beneath him, holding the gun
with both hands and listening to the ambulance siren slowly
fading away into the distance. *It's too late*, he thought. *Everyone dies.*

He had been sick again. Mostly blood. The pain had almost
deprived him of consciousness and afterwards he lay bent
double on the floor, waiting for the pills to take effect. Four of
them. The pain had subsided, with one last stab to remind him
that it would soon come back, and the bathroom had assumed
normal proportions again. One of the two bathrooms. With a
jacuzzi. Or was it a sauna? There was a TV anyway, and he
had turned it on. There were patriotic songs, the national an-
them, festively dressed journalists reporting on the children's
parade on all the channels.

Now he was sitting in the living room, and the sun hung
in the sky like a huge flare, lighting up everything. He knew
he shouldn't look straight at the flare, because you would become night-blind and you wouldn't be able to see the Russian
snipers wriggling through the snow in no man's land.

I can see him, Daniel whispered. *One o'clock, on the balcony right behind the dead tree.*

Trees? There were no trees here in the crater landscape.

The Crown Prince has walked out on to the balcony, but he doesn't say anything.

'He'll get away!' a voice sounding like Gudbrand's shouted. *No, he won't*, Daniel said. *No bloody Bolshevik gets away.*

'He knows we've seen him, he's crawling into the hollow.' *No, he isn't.*

The old man rested the gun against the edge of the window. He had used a screwdriver to open it further than the permitted crack. What was it that the girl in reception had told him that time? It was to prevent guests from 'getting silly ideas'. He looked through the rifle sights. People were so small down there. He set the range. Four-hundred metres. Shooting from above and down, you have to take into account the fact that gravity affects the bullet differently; it is a different trajectory from shooting on the level. But Daniel knew that, Daniel knew everything.

The old man looked at his watch: 10.45. Time to let it happen. He rested his cheek against the cold, heavy rifle butt, placed his left hand on the barrel slightly further down. Contorted his left eye. The railing on the balcony filled the sights. Then black coats and top hats. He found the face he was searching for. There was certainly a strong resemblance. It was the same young face as in 1945.

Daniel had gone even quieter and took aim. There was almost no frost smoke coming out of his mouth any more.

In front of the balcony, out of focus, the dead oak pointed its black witches' fingers to the sky. A bird sat on one of the branches. Right in the firing line. The old man shifted nervously. It hadn't been there before. It would soon fly away again. He put down the gun and drew fresh air into his aching lungs.

* * *

Click – click.

Harry slapped the steering wheel and twisted the ignition key one more time.

Click – click.

'Start, you bastard! Or else it's off to the scrap heap tomorrow.'

The Escort started with a roar and the car shot off, spitting grass and earth. He took a sharp right by the lake. The young people stretched out on the blanket raised their bottles of beer and cheered Harry on as he lurched towards the SAS Hotel. With the engine screaming in first gear and his hand on the horn he effectively cleared a way down through the crowded gravel path, but by the kindergarten at the bottom a pram suddenly appeared from behind a tree, and he flung the car to the left, wrenched the wheel to the right, went into a skid and only just avoided the fence in front of the greenhouses. The car slid sideways into Wergelandsveien, in front of a taxi with Norwegian flags and a birch twig festooning the radiator grille. The taxi driver jumped on his brakes, but Harry accelerated and threaded his way through oncoming traffic and into Holbergs gate.

He braked in front of the hotel's swing doors and leaped out. When he sprinted into the packed reception area there was an immediate moment of silence, with everyone wondering if they were going to witness a unique experience. But it was just a very drunken man on 17 May. They had seen that before and the volume was turned up again. Harry raced across to one of the absurd 'islands'.

'Good morning,' a voice said. A pair of raised eyebrows under curly blonde hair resembling a wig sized him up from top to toe. Harry spotted her name badge.

'Betty Andresen, what I'm going to tell you now is not a joke in poor taste, so listen carefully. I'm a policeman and you have an assassin in the hotel.'

Betty Andresen contemplated the tall, half-dressed man with the bloodshot eyes whom she had, quite understandably,

judged to be either drunk or crazy, or both. She studied
the ID card he held up for her. She scrutinised him again.
At length.

'Name,' she said.

'His name's Sindre Fauke.'

Her fingers danced across the keyboard.

'Sorry, there's no one here by that name.'

'Fuck! Try Gudbrand Johansen.'

'No Gudbrand Johansen either, Inspector Hole. Wrong
hotel perhaps?'

'No! He's here, he's in his room right now.'

'So you've spoken to him, have you?'

'No. No, I . . . it'll take too long to explain.'

Harry ran his hand across his face.

'Let's see. I have to think. He must be high up. How many
floors are there here?'

'Twenty one.'

'And how many of them have not handed in room keys
yet?'

'Quite a few, I'm afraid.'

Harry threw both hands into the air and stared at her.

'Of course,' he whispered. 'This is a Daniel job.'

'I beg your pardon?'

'Please check for Daniel Gudeson.'

What would happen afterwards? The old man didn't know.
There was nothing afterwards. At least, there hadn't been so
far. He had put four bullets on the window-sill. The yellowish-
brown matt metal of the housing reflected the rays of the sun.

He peered through the rifle sights again. The bird was still
there. He recognised it. They had the same name. He pointed
the sights at the crowds. Scanned the lines of people at the
barriers. Stopped when he saw something familiar. Could it
really be . . . ? He focused the sights. Yes, no doubt about it,
it was Rakel. What was she doing in the Palace Square? And

there was Oleg too. He seemed to be running over from the children's parade. Rakel lifted him over the barrier with outstretched arms. She was strong. Strong hands. Like her mother. Now they were walking up towards the guardhouse. Rakel looked at her watch. She seemed to be waiting for someone. Oleg was wearing the jacket he had given him for Christmas. Rakel said Oleg called it Grandpa's jacket. It seemed to be a little on the small side already.

The old man chuckled. He would have to buy him a new one for autumn.

The pains came without warning this time and he gasped helplessly for air.

The flare was sinking and their stooped shadows scrambled towards him along the walls of the trench.

Everything went dark, but just as he felt himself slipping into the blackness, the pains released their hold again. The gun had slid on to the floor, and the sweat made his shirt stick to his body.

He straightened up, put the gun back on the window ledge. The bird had flown away. He had a clear line of fire.

The youthful face filled the telescopic sights again. The Prince had studied. And so should Oleg. That was the last thing he had said to Rakel. That was the last thing he said to himself before he shot Brandhaug. Rakel had not been at home the day he had dropped into Holmenkollveien to pick up a couple of books, so he had let himself in and he happened to see the envelope lying on the desk and the Russian embassy on the letterhead. He had read it, put it down and stared through the window at the garden, at the snowflakes lying there after the shower, the last throes of winter. Afterwards he had sifted through the other drawers in the desk until he found the other letters, the ones with the Norwegian embassy on the letterhead, and also those without letterheads, written on serviettes and sheets torn out of notepads, signed by Bernt Brandhaug. And he had thought about Christopher Brockhard.

No Russian arsehole will be able to shoot at our watch tonight.

The old man released the safety catch. He felt a strange calm. He had just remembered how easy it had been to cut Brockhard's throat. And to shoot Bernt Brandhaug. Grandpa's jacket, a new Grandpa's jacket. He emptied the air out of his lungs and crooked his finger around the trigger.

With a key card to all the rooms in his hand, Harry did a sliding tackle into the lift and got one foot between the closing doors. They slid open again. Amazed faces met him as he stood up.

'Police!' Harry shouted. 'Everyone out!'

It was as if the school bell had rung for lunchbreak, but a man in his fifties with a black goatee, a blue striped suit, a thick 17 May ribbon on his chest and a thin layer of dandruff on his shoulders remained where he was.

'We are Norwegian citizens, my good man, and this is not a police state!'

Harry walked round the man into the lift and pressed 21. But the goatee had not finished.

'Tell me one good reason why I as a taxpayer should put up with . . .'

Harry took out Weber's Smith & Wesson from his shoulder holster.

'I have six good reasons here, taxpayer. Out!'

Time passes quickly, and soon it is another day. In the morning light we'll see him better, see whether he is friend or foe.

Foe, foe. Too soon or not, I'll get him anyway.

Grandpa's jacket.

Shit, there is nothing afterwards.

The face in the sights looks serious. Smile, boy.

Betrayal, betrayal, betrayal.

The trigger has been pulled back so far now there is no longer any resistance, the threshold lies somewhere in a no man's land. Don't think about the noise and the recoil, just press, let it come when it comes.

The bang took him completely by surprise. For a fraction of a second it was totally quiet. Then the echo reverberated and the wave of sound settled over the city and the sudden silence of thousands of sounds that died away at this instant.

Harry was sprinting through the corridors on the twenty-first floor when he heard the bang.

'Fuck!' he wheezed.

The walls coming towards him and passing him on both sides gave him the feeling he was moving inside a funnel. Doors. Pictures, motifs of blue cubes. His strides were almost inaudible on the thick carpet. Great. Good hotels think about reducing noise. And good policemen think about what they have to do. Fuck, fuck, lactic acid on the brain. An ice machine. Room 2154, room 2156. Another bang. The Palace Suite.

His heartbeat drum rolls against his ribs. Harry stood beside the door and pushed his key card into the lock. There was a dull buzz. Then a smooth click and the light on the lock went green. Harry gingerly pressed down the handle.

The police had fixed procedures for situations like this. Harry had been on the course and learned them. He had no intention of following a single one of them now.

He tore open the door, rushed in with his gun held in front of him with both hands and threw himself into a kneeling position in the doorway to the living room. The light flooded into the room, dazzled him and stung his eyes. An open window. The sun behind the glass was like a halo over the head of the white-haired man who slowly turned round.

'Police! Drop the gun,' Harry shouted.

Harry's pupils shrank and out of the light crept the silhouette of the rifle pointing at him.

'Drop the gun,' he repeated. 'You've done what you came to do, Fauke. Mission accomplished. It's over now.'

It was peculiar but the brass bands were still playing outside as if nothing had happened. The old man raised the rifle and rested the butt against his cheek. Harry's eyes had got used to the light and he stared down the barrel of this weapon he had hitherto only ever seen in pictures.

Fauke mumbled something, but it was drowned out by a new bang, this time sharper and clearer.

'Well I'm . . .' Harry whispered.

Outside, behind Fauke, he saw a puff of smoke rise into the air like a white speech bubble from the cannon on the ramparts of Akershus Fortress. The 17 May salutes. What he'd heard was the 17 May gun salutes! Harry heard the cheering. He breathed in through his nostrils. The room didn't smell of burned powder. He realised that Fauke had not fired the gun. Not yet. He gripped the butt of his revolver tightly as he watched the wrinkled face staring blankly back at him over the sights. It wasn't just a matter of his own and of the old man's life. The instructions were clear.

'I've come from Vibes gate. I've read your diary,' Harry said. 'Gudbrand Johansen. Or is it Daniel I'm talking to now?'

Harry clenched his teeth and crooked his trigger finger.

The old man mumbled again.

'What was that?'

'*Passwort*,' the old man said. His voice was hoarse and totally unrecognisable from the one he had heard before.

'Don't do it,' Harry said. 'Don't force me.'

A drop of sweat ran down Harry's forehead, down to the bridge of his nose until it hung off the tip, where it seemed unable to make up its mind. Harry shifted his grip on the gun.

'*Passwort*,' the old man repeated.

Harry could see the old man's finger tighten round the trigger. He could feel the fear of death squeezing his heart.

'No,' Harry said. 'It's not too late.'

But he knew it wasn't true. It was too late. The old man was beyond reasoning, beyond this world and this life.

'*Passwort.*'

Soon it would be over for them both. There was only some slow time left, the time on Christmas Eve before . . .

'Oleg,' Harry said.

The gun was pointing directly at his head. A car horn sounded in the distance. A spasm flitted across the old man's face.

'The password is Oleg,' Harry said.

The finger on the trigger paused.

The old man opened his mouth to say something.

Harry held his breath.

'Oleg,' the old man said. It sounded like a wisp of wind from his lips.

Harry was never quite able to explain it afterwards, but he saw it: the old man was dying at that very moment. And then it was a child's face looking at Harry from behind the wrinkles. The gun was no longer pointed at him and he lowered his revolver. Then he stretched out a hand and put it on the old man's shoulder.

'Do you promise me?' The old man's voice was barely audible. 'That they won't . . .'

'I promise,' Harry said. 'I shall personally see to it that no names will appear publicly. Oleg and Rakel will not suffer in any way . . .'

The old man rested his eyes on Harry for a long time. The rifle hit the floor with a thud and then he collapsed.

Harry took the magazine out of the rifle and put it on the sofa before dialling reception and asking Betty to call an ambulance. Then he rang Halvorsen's mobile and said the danger was over. Afterwards he pulled the old man on to the sofa and sat down in a chair to wait.

'I got him in the end,' the old man whispered. 'He was about to slip away, you know. In the mud.'

'Who did you get? Harry asked, pulling hard on his cigarette.

'Daniel, of course. I got him in the end. Helena was right. I was always stronger.'

Harry stubbed out his cigarette and stood by the window.

'I'm dying,' the old man whispered.

'I know.'

'It's on my chest. Can you see it?'

'See what?'

'The polecat.'

But Harry couldn't see a polecat. He saw a white cloud scud across the sky like a passing doubt. In the sunshine, he saw the Norwegian flags wafting on all the flagpoles of the city and he saw a grey bird flap past the window. But no polecats.

Part Ten

THE RESURRECTION

105

Ullevål Hospital. 19 May 2000.

BJARNE MØLLER FOUND HARRY IN THE WAITING room of the oncological department. The head of Crime Squad took a seat beside Harry and winked at a small young girl, who frowned and turned away.

'I heard it's all over,' he said.

Harry nodded. 'Four o'clock this morning. Rakel has been here the whole time. Oleg's in there now. What are you doing here?'

'Just wanted a little chat with you.'

'I could do with a smoke,' Harry said. 'Let's go outside.'

They found a bench under a tree. Wispy clouds hurried past in the sky above them. All the signs were that it would be another warm day.

'So Rakel doesn't know anything?' Møller asked.

'Nothing.'

'The people in the know are me, Meirik, the Chief Constable, the Minister of Justice and the Prime Minister. And you, of course.'

'You know better than I do who knows what, boss.'

'Yes. Naturally. I'm merely thinking aloud.'

'So what was it you wanted to say to me?'

'Do you know what, Harry? Some days I wish I worked somewhere else. Some place where there is less politics and more police work. In Bergen, for example. But then you get up on days like today, stand by your bedroom window looking at the fjord, the islands in it, and listen to the birds singing and . . . do you understand? . . . Then you don't want to go anywhere.'

Møller watched a ladybird crawling up his thigh.

'What I wanted to say is that we would like to keep things as they are, Harry.'

'And what *things* are we talking about?'

'Did you know that no American president in the last twenty years has lasted the full term without at least ten attempts on his life being uncovered? And that all the perpetrators without exception were arrested without anything coming to the ears of the media? No one profits from plans to assassinate a head of state becoming public knowledge, Harry. Especially not ones which could have succeeded, theoretically speaking.'

'*Theoretically*, boss?'

'Not my words. But the conclusion is, nevertheless, that we keep a lid on this. We don't want to sow instability. Or reveal weaknesses in the security system. Those aren't my words, either. Assassinations are contagious, just like . . .'

'I know what you mean,' Harry said, expelling smoke through his nose. 'Primarily we're doing this for those sitting in positions of power, aren't we? People who could have and should have sounded the alarm before.'

'As I said,' Møller replied. 'On some days Bergen seems like a handsome alternative.'

Neither of them said anything for a few minutes. A bird strutted in front of them, wagged its tail, pecked at the grass and kept a watchful eye open.

'Wagtail,' Harry said. '*Motacilla alba*. Cautious chap.'

'What?'

'*Our Small Birds*. What shall we do about the murders Gudbrand Johansen committed?'

'We cleared up all the early murders to our satisfaction, didn't we?'

'What do you mean?'

Møller squirmed.

'The only thing we'll achieve by stirring up things now is ripping open old wounds for the next of kin, and there's a risk someone will poke around and dig up the whole story. The cases were closed.'

'Right. Even Juul. And Sverre Olsen. What about the murder of Hallgrim Dale?'

'No one will kick up a fuss about him. After all, Dale was a . . . er . . .'

'Just an old piss artist no one would give a toss about?'

'Please, Harry, don't make this more difficult than it already is. You know I'm not happy with this, either.'

Harry stubbed out his cigarette on the armrest of the bench and put the cigarette end back in the packet.

'I have to go in again, boss.'

'So we can count on you keeping this to yourself?'

Harry gave a laconic smile.

'Is it true what I've heard? About the person who wants to take over my job in POT?'

'Absolutely,' Møller said. 'Tom Waaler has said he'll apply. Meirik wants to make the whole neo-Nazi section part of the job description, so it'll become a kind of springboard for the top jobs. I'm going to recommend him, by the way. I suppose you're just happy he's going to disappear now you're back in Crime Squad? Now that his inspector post with us will become vacant.'

'So that's the reward for keeping my mouth shut?'

'What on earth makes you think that, Harry? It's because you're the best. You've proved it yet again, haven't you? I'm just wondering whether we can rely on you.'

'You know which job I want to work on?'

Møller rolled his shoulders.

'Ellen's murder has been cleared up, Harry.'

'Not quite,' he said. 'There are a couple of details we still don't know. Among other things, what happened to the 200,000 Norwegian kroner for the purchase of the rifle. Perhaps there were several middlemen.'

Møller nodded.

'OK. You and Halvorsen have two months. If you don't find anything, the case is closed.'

'Fair enough.'

Møller stood up to go.

'There's just one thing I've been wondering, Harry. How did you guess the password was "Oleg"?'

'Well, Ellen was always telling me that the first thing that came into her mind was almost invariably right.'

'Impressive.' Møller nodded his head in appreciation. 'And so the first thing that came into your mind was the name of his grandchild?'

'No.'

'No?'

'I'm not Ellen. I had to give it some thought.'

Møller sent him a sharp look.

'Are you teasing me now, Hole?'

Harry smiled. Then he gestured towards the wagtail.

'I read in the bird book I mentioned that no one knows why wagtails wag their tails when they stand still. It's a mystery. The only thing we know is that they can't stop . . .'

106

Police HQ. 19 May 2000.

HARRY HAD JUST PLACED HIS FEET ON THE DESK
and found the perfect sitting position when the telephone
rang. So as not to lose his position, he stretched forward while
using his backside muscles to balance on the new office chair
with the treacherous well-oiled wheels. He was able to reach
the phone with the tips of his fingers.

'Hole.'

'Harry? Isaiah Burne in Johannesburg speaking. How
are you?'

'Isaiah? This is a surprise.'

'Is it? I'm ringing to thank you, Harry.'

'Thank me for what?'

'For not starting anything?'

'Starting what?'

'You know what I mean, Harry. For not starting any diplomatic moves for a reprieve or anything like that.'

Harry didn't answer. He had been half expecting this call
for a while. The sitting position wasn't comfortable any longer.
Andreas Hochner's begging eyes were suddenly present. And
Constance Hochner's imploring voice: *Do you promise to do
what you can, Mr Hole?*

'Harry?'

'I'm still here.'

'The sentence was passed yesterday.'

Harry stared at the picture of Sis on the wall. It had been an unusually warm summer that year, hadn't it? They had gone swimming even when it was raining. He felt an inexpressible sadness wash over him.

'Death penalty?' he heard himself ask.

'With no right of appeal.'

107

Schrøder's. 2 June 2000.

'WHAT ARE YOU DOING THIS SUMMER, HARRY?'

Maja was counting up the change.

'I don't know. We've talked about hiring a chalet somewhere here in Norway. Teach the boy to swim and all that.'

'I didn't know you had any children.'

'No, well, it's a long story.'

'Really? Hope I get to hear it one day.'

'We'll see, Maja. Keep the change.'

Maja performed a deep curtsey and went off with a wry grin on her face. It was empty in the café for a Friday afternoon. The heat had probably sent most people up to the terrace restaurant in St Hanshaugen.

'Well?' Harry said.

The old man stared down into his glass without answering.

'He's dead. Aren't you happy, Åsnes?'

The Mohican raised his head and looked at Harry.

'Who's dead?' he said. 'No one's dead. Just me. I'm the last of the dead.'

Harry sighed, stuffed the newspaper under his arm and walked out into the shimmering afternoon heat.

Turn the page for a glimpse of

THE DEVIL'S STAR,

featuring Police Detective Harry Hole.

In the heat of a sweltering Oslo summer a young woman is found murdered in her flat—with one of her fingers cut off and a tiny, red, star-shaped diamond placed under her eyelid. An off-the-rails alcoholic barely holding on to his job, Detective Harry Hole is assigned the case with Tom Waaler, a hated colleague whom he believes is responsible for the murder of his partner. When another woman is reported missing five days later and her severed finger turns up adorned with a star-shaped, red diamond ring, Harry fears a serial killer is at work. But Hole's determination to capture a fiend and expose Waaler's crimes is leading him into shadowy places where both investigations merge in unexpected ways, forcing him to make difficult decisions about a future he may not live to see.

Friday. Egg.

THE HOUSE WAS BUILT IN 1898 ON A CLAY BASE that had since sunk a tiny bit on the west-facing side, causing water to cross the wooden threshold where the door was hung. It ran across the bedroom floor and left a wet streak over the oak parquet, moving west. The flow rested for a second in a dip before more water nudged it from behind and it scurried like a nervous rat towards the skirting board. There the water went in both directions; it searched and somehow sneaked under the skirting until it found a gap between the end of the wooden flooring and the wall. In the gap lay a five-kroner coin bearing a profile of King Olav's head and the date: 1987, the year before it had fallen out of the carpenter's pocket. But these were the boom years; a great many attic flats had needed to be built at the drop of a hat and the carpenter had not bothered to look for it.

It did not take the water much time to find a way through the floor under the parquet. Apart from when there was a leak in 1968 – the same year a new roof was built on the house – the wooden floorboards had lain there undisturbed, drying and contracting so that the crack between the two innermost pine floorboards was now almost half a centimetre. The water dripped onto the beam beneath the crack and continued westwards and into the exterior wall. There it seeped into the plaster and the mortar that had been mixed one hundred years before, also in midsummer, by Jacob Andersen, a master bricklayer and father of five. Andersen, like all bricklayers in Oslo at that time, mixed his own mortar and wall plaster. Not only did he have his own unique blend of lime, sand and water, he also had his own special ingredients: horsehair and pig's blood. Jacob Andersen was of the opinion that the hair and the blood held the plaster together and gave it extra strength. It was not his idea, he told his head-shaking colleagues at the time, his Scottish father and grandfather had used the same ingredients from sheep. Even though he had renounced his Scottish surname and taken on a trade name he saw no reason to turn his back on six hundred years of heritage. Some of the bricklayers considered it immoral, some thought he was in league with the Devil, but most just laughed at him. Perhaps it was one of the latter who spread the story that was to take hold in the burgeoning town of Kristania.

A coachman from Grünerløkka had married his cousin from Värmland and together they moved into a one-room flat plus kitchen in one of the apartment blocks in Seilduksgata that Andersen had helped to build. The couple's first child was unlucky enough to be born with dark, curly hair and brown eyes, and since the couple were blond with blue eyes – and the man was jealous by nature as well – late one night he tied his wife's hands behind her, took her down to the cellar and bricked her in. Her screams were effectively muffled by the thick walls where she stood bound and squeezed between the two brick surfaces. The husband had perhaps thought that she would suffocate from lack of oxygen, but bricklayers do allow for ventilation. In the end, the poor woman attacked the wall with her bare teeth. And that might well have worked because as the Scottish bricklayer used blood and hair, thinking that he could save on the expensive lime in the cement mix, the result was a porous wall that crumbled under the attack from strong Värmland teeth. However, her hunger for life sadly led to her taking excessively large mouthfuls of mortar and brick. Ultimately she was unable to chew, swallow or spit and the sand, pebbles and chunks of clay blocked her windpipe. Her face turned blue, her heart-beat slowed and then she stopped breathing.

She was what most people would call dead.

According to the myth, however, the taste of pig's blood had the effect of making the unfortunate woman believe she was still alive. And with that she immediately broke free of the ropes that bound her, passed through the wall and began to walk again. A few old people from Grünerløkka still re-member the story from their childhood, about the woman with the pig's head, walking around with a knife to cut off the heads of small children who were out late. She had to have the taste of blood in her mouth so that she didn't vanish into thin air. At the time very few people knew the name of the bricklayer and Andersen worked tirelessly at making his special blend of mortar. Three years later, while working on the building where the water was now leaking he fell from the scaffolding – leaving only two hundred kroner and a guitar – and so it was to be another hundred years before bricklayers began to use artificial hair-like fibres in their ce-ment mixes and before technicians at a laboratory in Milan discovered that the walls of Jericho had been strengthened with blood and camel hair.

Most of the water, however, did not run into the wall, but down it, because water, like cowardice and lust, always finds the lowest level. At first the water was absorbed by the lumpy, granular insulation between the joists, but more followed and soon the insulation was saturated. The water went right through it and soaked up a newspaper dated July 11, 1898, in which it said the building industry's boom time had probably reached its peak and the unscrupulous property speculators were sure to have harder times ahead. On page three it said that the police still had no leads regarding the murder of a young nurse who had been found dead from stab wounds in a bathroom the previous week. In May, a girl mutilated and killed in a similar way was found near the River Akerselva, but the police would not say whether the two cases could be connected.

The water ran off the newspaper, between the wooden boards underneath and along the inside of the painted ceiling fabric of the room below. Since this had been damaged during the repair of the leak in 1968, the water seeped through the holes, forming drops that hung on until they became heavy enough for gravity to defy the surface tension; they let go and fell three metres and eight centimetres. There the water landed and terminated its trajectory. Into water.

Vibeke Knutsen sucked hard on her cigarette and blew smoke out of the open window on the fourth floor of the apartment building. It was a warm afternoon and the air rose from the sun-baked asphalt in the back yard, taking the smoke up the light blue house front until it dispersed. On the other side of the roof you could hear the sound of a car in the usually busy Ullevålsveien. But now everyone was on holiday and the town was almost deserted. A fly lay on its back on the windowsill with its six feet in the air. It hadn't had the sense to get out of the heat. It was cooler at the other end of the flat facing Ullevålsveien, but Vibeke didn't like the view from there. Our Saviour's Cemetery. Crowded with famous people. Famous dead people. On the ground floor there was a shop selling 'monuments', as the sign said, in other words, headstones. What one might call 'staying close to the market'.

Vibeke rested her forehead against the cool glass of the window.

She had been happy when the warm weather came, but her happiness had soon worn off. Even now she was longing for cooler nights and people in the streets. Today there had been five customers in the gallery before lunch and three after. She had smoked one and a half packets of cigarettes out of sheer boredom. Her heart was pounding and she had a sore throat; in fact, she could hardly speak when the boss rang and asked

how things were going. All the same, no sooner had she arrived home and put the potatoes on than she felt the craving in
the pit of her stomach again.

Vibeke had stopped smoking when she met Anders
two years before. He hadn't asked her to. Quite the contrary.
When they met on Gran Canaria he had even bummed a cigarette off her. Just for a laugh. When they moved in together,
just one month after getting back to Oslo, one of the first
things he had said was that their relationship would probably
be able to stand a little passive smoking, and that cancer researchers were undoubtedly exaggerating. With a little time
he would probably get used to the smell of cigarettes on their
clothes. The next morning she made up her mind. When, some
days later, he mentioned over lunch that it was a long time
since he had seen her with a cigarette in her hand, she answered that she had never really been much of a smoker. Anders smiled, leaned over the table and stroked her cheek.

'Do you know what, Vibeke? That's what I always thought.'

She could hear the pan bubbling behind her and looked at
the cigarette. Three more drags. She took the first. It didn't
taste of anything.

She could barely remember when it was that she had
started smoking again. Perhaps it was last year, around the
time he had started staying away for long periods on business
trips. Or was it over New Year when she had begun working overtime almost every evening? Was that because she was
unhappy? Was she unhappy? They never rowed. They almost
never made love either, but that was because Anders worked
so hard, he had said, putting an end to any discussion. Not that
she missed it particularly. When, once in a blue moon, they
did make a half-hearted attempt at love-making it was as if he
wasn't really there. So she realised she didn't really need to be
there, either.

But they didn't actually row. Anders didn't like raised
voices.

Vibeke looked at the clock: 5.15. What had happened to

him? Generally he told her if he was going to be late. She stubbed out the cigarette, dropped it into the back yard and turned towards the stove to check the potatoes. She put a fork into the biggest one. Almost done. Some small black lumps bobbled up and down on the surface of the boiling water. Funny. Were they from the potatoes or the pan?

She was just trying to remember what she had last used the pan for when she heard the front door being opened. From the corridor she could hear someone gasping for breath and shoes being kicked off. Anders came into the kitchen and opened the fridge.

'Well?' he asked.

'Rissoles.'

'OK . . . ?' His intonation rose at the end and formed a question mark. She knew roughly what it meant. Meat again? Shouldn't we eat fish a little more often?

'Fine,' he said with flat intonation, leaning over the pan.

'What have you been doing? You're absolutely soaked with sweat.'

'I didn't do any training this evening, so I cycled up to Sognsvann and back again. What are the lumps in the water?'

'I don't know,' Vibeke said. 'I just noticed them.'

'You don't know? Didn't you work as a sort of cook once upon a time?'

In one deft movement he took one of the lumps between his index finger and his thumb and put it in his mouth. She stared at the back of his head. At his thin brown hair that she had once thought was so attractive. Well groomed and just the right length. With a side parting. He had looked so smart. Like a man with a future. Enough future for two.

'What does it taste of?' she asked.

'Nothing,' he said, still bent over the cooker. 'Egg.'

'Egg? But I washed the pan . . .'

She suddenly paused.

He turned round. 'What's the matter?'

'There's . . . a drip.' She pointed to his head.

He frowned and touched the back of his head. Then, in one movement, they both leaned backwards and stared up at the ceiling. There were two droplets hanging from the white ceiling fabric. Vibeke, who was a little short-sighted, wouldn't have seen the drops if they had glistened. But they did not.

'Looks like Camilla's got a flood,' Anders said. 'If you go up and ring her bell, I'll get hold of the caretaker.'

Vibeke peered up at the ceiling. And down at the lumps in the pan.

'My God,' she whispered and could feel her heart pounding again.

'What's the matter now?' Anders asked.

'Go and get the caretaker. Then go with him and ring Camilla's doorbell. I'll call the police.'

DARK AND GRIPPING
HARRY HOLE NOVELS FROM

JO
NESBØ

NEMESIS
978-0-06-165551-7

After a drunken evening with his former girlfriend, Anna Bethsen,
Police Detective Harry Hole wakes up at home with a headache,
no cell phone, and no memory of the past twelve hours. That
same day, Anna is found shot dead in her bedroom, making Hole
a prime suspect.

THE REDBREAST
978-0-06-206842-2

While monitoring neo-Nazi activities in Oslo, Detective Harry
Hole is inadvertently drawn into a mystery with deep roots in
Norway's dark past, when members of the government willingly
collaborated with Nazi Germany. More than sixty years later dis-
graced old soldiers who once survived a brutal Russian winter are
being murdered one by one.

THE DEVIL'S STAR
978-0-06-113397-8

In the heat of the sweltering Oslo summer, a young woman is
found murdered in her flat—with one of her fingers cut off and a
tiny red star-shaped diamond placed under her eyelid. Detective
Harry Hole is assigned to the case with Tom Waaler, a hated colleague who Harry blames for the murder of his partner.